The French Orphan

By Michael Stolle

First published 2012
Second edition 2013
Third edition 2013
Text copyright © Michael Stolle, 2012, 2013
All Rights Reserved

ISBN-13: 978-1478232278
ISBN-10: 1478232277

Dedication

To Polly – thanks for your support.

To Katharine – thanks for making it happen.

CONTENTS

PROLOGUE

The log burning in the imposing marble fireplace disintegrated and sent a shower of dancing red-gold sparks into the air. The sound of the small explosion echoed in the library of the new palatial building known to everybody in Paris simply as *le palais du cardinal*, the home of His Eminence, Cardinal Richelieu, the revered – as much as reviled – prime minister of France.

The library was not only lit by the blazing fire; numerous candles had been placed lavishly and regardless of expense on tables and shelves and on the carved oak desk that dominated a room of truly impressive proportions. The heavy desk was laden with parchment scrolls, scribbled notes, leather-bound books on different subjects, a random book of prayers and a jewel-studded bible – as was to be expected in the inner sanctum of France's most powerful minister and clergyman.

As usual Cardinal Richelieu was working late, seated like a scarlet spider in the centre of a web of power he had assiduously spun. Hard work, genius and a stroke of luck had catapulted him from the position of an unknown provincial bishop to become the second – some would even say the first – man of the realm.

His dark eyes looked alert, but heavy circles around his eyes showed fatigue. His gaunt face was dominated by his prominent Roman nose and his skin was of an unhealthy waxen complexion. The formerly elegant hands – once a source of pride – were transformed into bony claws by the rheumatism eating into his body.

The candlesticks on his desk were made from solid gold set with diamonds and rubies. Huge oil paintings of the King of France and various saints in their moment of martyrdom adorned those walls that were not covered by bookshelves. The suffering of the saints in the paintings looked depressingly realistic as they seemed to be moving in their pain, such was the effect of the flickering light and the shadows cast by the fire and the candlelight.

The fire was kept burning day and night on the orders of His Eminence. It was late evening and the nights in Paris tended to be quite chilly during early springtime. But the Cardinal needed warmth as his health was failing.

Richelieu sat behind his desk, still clad in the scarlet robes that he had worn when he had attended the King's private council earlier that day. He was reading the latest confidential messages that had arrived by special courier from Lisbon and all of a sudden a satisfied smile played on his thin lips; another fatal blow had been dealt to the Spanish enemy.

His dark eyes burned with delight while he watched the reflections of the candlelight flicker upon the candlesticks and his bible. The candlelight played with

1

the precious jewels, making the rubies and diamonds shoot fiery darts across the room. Richelieu loved gold, he worshipped power – and he adored success.

His secretary on duty entered almost noiselessly and announced that Brother Joseph from the order of the Dominicans would like to speak to him.

"Is it urgent?" the Cardinal asked, reluctant to leave the realms of triumph and return to the routine of daily business.

"I'm afraid, yes, Your Eminence, Brother Joseph would like to see you immediately but he has confided in me that he is the bearer of good news!"

Richelieu nodded his consent to admit the monk into the library and only seconds later a monk of middle age entered, kneeled and kissed the ring on the bony hand that was extended to him.

"You were successful!" the Cardinal stated, rather than asked.

"Yes, Your Eminence, I have discovered the hiding place of the person we've been looking for, and," he paused to draw breath, his face full of awe, "I examined with my own eyes documents that will be of the greatest importance."

"So the game can commence," the Cardinal said, his mind already weighing up the different options for his plan of action. He looked at Brother Joseph and added gravely, "And we shall make sure that there will be only one winner: our Holy Mother, the Church," and then silently to himself, careful not to upset Brother Joseph's faith in a good cause, he added, *and my own treasury, of course.*

Operating the biggest European network of spies and agents was a very costly enterprise and the Cardinal was in need of money – the one and only aspect of his life that never changed.

The hunt was on.

REIMS

The tall blond adolescent heard the steps coming closer and bent his head studiously over his slate where he was busy copying the words of the holy Augustine. At the same time he tensed the muscles in his back as he knew from previous painful experience that this would make it easier to bear the sting of the stick that usually came down on his back whenever Brother Hieronymus found fault in his copy of the scriptures. This was often enough the case, although Pierre was the best in his class at the famous monastery school in the city of Reims.

Today Brother Hieronymus seemed satisfied with Pierre's work. He moved on and his stick came down on a different victim, poor awkward Louis, who was standing at his desk close to the window which had been opened so as to let some rays of the spring sun stream into the dark room.

Pierre saw the stick bouncing off the boy's back as he tried to hide his expression of pain and stifle a moan – they all knew that any exclamation of pain would excite their teacher even more and prolong the dreaded act of punishment.

They were among the eldest of the finishing classes, almost all boys coming from noble or wealthy families in preparation for their own careers as high-ranking members of the clergy, ready to take their vows when the time was right.

The monastery school in Reims had a formidable reputation all over France. It was attached directly to the office of the Archbishop of Reims, the famous city where the kings of France were crowned, a position that made the school stand out from all other schools in the realm. Their teachers never ceased to repeat this and hammered into them the fact that they should praise the Lord that they were able to attend such a noble school, castigation being a necessary tool in the purification of their souls.

Pierre secretly tried to glance towards his friend Armand, who was standing close to the window. Communication between the boys during lessons was strictly forbidden, therefore he had to be careful or would end up being caned and banished to his cell without dinner.

Armand was smiling at Brother Hieronymus. His boyish charm was clearly working on the teacher who was correcting some words on Armand's slate with indulgence, where before he had deemed it necessary to punish Louis severely. Armand was strikingly handsome. He had a muscular body, brown eyes, brown hair that tended to fall into curls, and his smile was so contagious that nobody could resist him.

I wonder why Armand has chosen me, the only poor orphan in this class as his best friend, Pierre wondered.

Yet soon after they had met for the first time two years ago, a bond had formed and they had been close friends ever since. School would be ending soon for both of them as they approached the age to move on and become members of the clergy. Pierre had to fight a feeling of sadness when he thought that the time they shared in Reims was to end soon. Armand was the youngest son of an old and noble family in France and would rise fast through the ranks of the clergy. In fact he was predestined to become a bishop very soon, a position that the influence and protection of his family could easily buy – maybe he would even be appointed archbishop.

For Pierre, there was no career in sight; at best he could hope to stay in this monastery as a monk or teacher, or become a priest in a small village. He had no family, no money to buy an office.

When the bell of the chapel tolled to announce mass the boys walked into the courtyard that stretched between the school rooms and the chapel building to prepare for the boring routine of attending the religious service.

Pierre moved forward to join Armand and as soon as he had made sure that no teacher was around he punched Armand in the side, grinning at him. "You really had the slimy old toad eating out of your hand. I bet you hadn't even finished half of the text."

Armand returned the grin and replied, "He's got a crush on me, always suggesting private lessons after school. Until now I've kept him in good spirits." Then he suddenly looked more serious. "But he was nice to you too – too nice, if you get what I mean. Better take care, he likes teaching good-looking boys, and you've got no family to protect you…"

Pierre couldn't answer right away as they had reached the cold and dark chapel building with its stinging smell of smoky candles and stale incense. The central nave was dominated by a gilded triptych showing a beautiful painting of Our Lady of Reims, surrounded by a group of saints and angels rapt in adoration. This painting looked so alive that Pierre could never approach the inner sanctum of the chapel without a feeling of awe – it made his heart beat faster as if the smile of the holy Virgin held a special promise reserved only for him.

Armand's remark had made him uneasy – of course he had heard about Brother Hieronymus's private lessons from the other boys – and although he tried to concentrate on the mass and forget this remark, it kept nagging away at the back of his mind.

*****

The following weeks continued with their usual routine of praying, copying fragments of religious texts, learning and working hard until the day when Brother Hieronymus stopped during his usual round of inspection and put a soft and rather sweaty hand on Pierre's shoulder. Not only did he keep his hand there – making

4

Pierre feel extremely uncomfortable – but to Pierre's great surprise he started to praise his pupil's skills and mentioned good-humouredly, "My son, you just need some more *private* lessons to become an excellent scholar, you know that soon we'll have to choose a career for you, and as you are a mere orphan accepted only for reasons of Christian charity, you'll need a *special* recommendation to have any chance of joining our ranks!"

This remark made Pierre's flesh crawl but he managed to smile sweetly into Brother Hieronymus's face and thanked him for his kind concern for his well-being and his future career.

*****

On Sundays, immediately after morning mass, Pierre and Armand could escape into the monastery gardens where they had discovered a far-off group of trees that made excellent hiding places once they climbed up and hid in the thick green branches.

Spring was fast turning into summer and the monastery garden was glowing in the vivid colours of the numerous beautiful flowers planted and tended with meticulous care by the monks. Various shrubs and trees framed the garden, adding accents of delightful shades of green to the peaceful picture. The air was heavy with the scent of the medical garden that was the pride of the monastery hospital.

"I can't stand it," said Pierre, "I simply can't."

"I warned you, but it's a fact that most of us give in and just get on with it," Armand replied. "If you refuse to give in to Brother Hieronymus, he'll make your life here hell. I hate to be so crude, but being an orphan you have no option. You need the recommendation of the Abbot to land a good position or you'll end up as a priest in a small parish church with no income, depending on peasants and serfs who won't even have enough money to pay you for a decent funeral service."

Armand was biting into an apple while he was talking. He didn't seem to be too bothered about Pierre's worries. Pierre wondered where he had got fruit from at this time of year. Armand always had secret sources for everything – the apple harvest would not begin until the autumn so he must have sneaked this precious gift from the kitchen where they kept a secret store of rare delicacies.

Armand was a very practically minded person, so for him, why bother resisting if there was no alternative? Clearly in his mind the idea of becoming a poor parish priest was more appalling to him than accepting the overtures of their teacher.

"I know that you're right," sighed Pierre, "it's just so disgusting."

"Everything here is," said Armand. "Our teachers preach forgiveness and love for the poor souls but all they want is their money, they'll kill you for a sou – don't even mention real gold. We all know about this and yet we pay lip service to the

5

teachings of the Church. Nobody would dare mention the truth in this monastery or we'd be condemned as heretics or traitors."

He offered a large chunk of his apple to Pierre and then elegantly threw the remains at a bird that had been careless enough to have chosen a branch in their vicinity for a resting place.

Armand knew that Pierre struggled against his fate and cunningly he changed the subject to divert Pierre's mind.

*****

Discussing Parisian politics always fascinated Pierre. Rumour had it that the health of the Cardinal was becoming more and more delicate and consequently speculation and a sense of excitement were growing amongst the old nobility, to which Armand's family belonged. Such families hoped to seize the chance to regain their former strength and influence as soon as Richelieu loosened his grip.

It had been Richelieu who had not only mercilessly suppressed the resistance of the notoriously heretic Huguenots but had also brought down the old families of the Condé, Guise and Rohan, those famous families who had for so many generations considered France to be their natural playground.

Pierre loved these discussions as they brought him close to the pulse of what he thought was the essence of real life, precarious and exciting – a life so remote from his own dreary reality and even more boring future. This world was as exclusive as it was dangerous and enticing: its members seemed to be so closely related and yet ready to commit treason and murder at any minute if their power or interest was at stake.

But Pierre couldn't help but admire Cardinal Richelieu, who had probably saved France after the lavish spendings of Henry IV's widow, the terrible Queen Marie de' Medici, had nearly ruined the country.

Today France was a proud country, the strongest and richest kingdom on earth and nobody dared to challenge its power. Armand, of course, hated the Cardinal as he reckoned that his family should fill his position but they never seriously came to blows over this matter. Pierre was convinced that secretly Armand shared his assessment that the Cardinal Richelieu was in a class of his own – even if hated, he needed to be admired.

THE DECISION

Pierre had accepted the invitation to attend Brother Hieronymus's private lesson most reluctantly. Waiting for his teacher he leaned on the high desk. As dusk was falling the room was very quiet and looked even gloomier than usual. It was almost dark. The air of the room held the familiar smell of ink and vellum mingled with the damp smell of the garden emanating through the slightly open windows and the more unpleasant smell of his own wet clothes, as it was a rainy day, in fact, it had been pouring for hours.

Pierre must have dozed off while he was waiting as he was startled when he suddenly felt the light touch of a hand. He opened his eyes and found Brother Hieronymus standing facing him. His teacher carried an oil lamp and the flickering light showed that his lips had opened in a weird welcoming smile, exposing his gums and a row of decaying teeth. His open mouth exuded an odour of stale wine, garlic and even more disgusting ingredients that Pierre could not possibly begin to think of.

Bathing and cleaning was considered unchristian and unhealthy, hence not held in high regard, but Armand was notorious and even laughed at for being pedantic about washing regularly. Pierre had unconsciously started to follow his lead. Since then Pierre had cared about keeping himself clean and consequently he had started to loath the pervasive smell of unwashed bodies.

He tried not to inhale this toxic wave of bad breath and unwashed body odour that was closing on him and greeted Brother Hieronymus in the reverential ways that were expected when he met his teacher. He held his breath and looked down quickly to hide his disgusted face. This encounter was simply sickening!

Swiftly his teacher moved behind him and put his hand around Pierre's waist while he pretended to concentrate all of his attention on showing him a new decorative ornamentation. It was supposed to come at the start of the sheet of precious vellum Pierre was to copy onto and embellish for a prestigious book of prayers destined for the revered Archbishop of Reims.

Being allowed to handle virgin vellum and gold ink was a sign of the highest achievement and for a moment Pierre forgot the arm around his body and concentrated on the task of applying the precious ink in the correct way. He had to be very careful, as corrections could only be done by scraping away the ink from the vellum, thus spoiling the immensely precious fluid and making the vellum frail.

Slowly Pierre felt a second hand moving down his back and instantly he returned to reality. Pierre was mortified, despair seized him and his heart started to race. His first impulse was to hit and run – when suddenly an idea flashed through his mind. It was mad, of course, but what could he lose?

7

"Please don't touch my back, Brother Hieronymus!" Pierre whispered, and managed to look ashamed, flustered and shy, responding defiantly to the irate glance of Brother Hieronymus.

"Why, my child? It's a sign of special consideration that I even bother to teach you!"

Pierre pretended to be searching for words and whispered, "It's so shameful, I came here after seeing Brother Infirmarius from the hospital. I've been suffering from looseness of the bowels since this morning and was feeling so unwell, I even washed my robe before I came here, but – ," he faltered, and then continued, even more embarrassed, "it won't really stop."

Pierre turned to show Brother Hieronymus the big wet patch at the back of his robe.

He gave a small prayer of special gratitude that he had slipped backwards on the wet grass on his way to the classroom, straight into a puddle of dirty water.

Pierre continued in a whisper, "Brother Infirmarius gave me a potion and he's confident that it's not contagious." Pierre mustered a brave smile and, moving closer to Brother Hieronymus, continued, "But for nothing in the world did I want to miss this private lesson," and moving even more closer, turned big adoring blue eyes on his teacher.

Brother Hieronymus withdrew his hands immediately and hastily stepped back. He tried to put on a brave face and, whilst quickly moving away several yards, he replied, "It's very unwise of you, my child, to have come and not to have rested as Brother Infirmarius will have told you to. I suspend you from lessons for today and tomorrow. Pray to Our Virgin Mary that she may heal you!" and making the solemn sign of the cross he fled the room.

Pierre tried to stifle his laughter by pressing his fist into his mouth but tears of delight and relief were streaming down his cheeks. Armand would simply love this little story!

It would have been downright foolish for Pierre to revert to his normal routine. Therefore he quickly rushed to the hospital where he repeated his story of loose bowels and dutifully swallowed some herbal medicine. Brother Infirmarius gave him a long questioning look but as Pierre was not known to be a regular truant he gave him the benefit of the doubt and simply instructed him to drink a herbal infusion once again later in the day, to rest and come back if the symptoms continued.

To make his story more credible Pierre decided to skip dinner and went to the boys' dormitory where he settled on his straw mattress trying to work out a way to solve his dilemma. He was very much aware that he had only gained a week's respite at most, and wracked his brain to find a solution but Armand had been right, either he accepted the overtures of his teacher or he'd become an outcast – worse still, a beggar in the streets. He had no money, no family, and all he possessed were his two robes from the monastery.

Armand dropped by and asked what all of this was about but Pierre was in no mood to go into details and just told him that they should meet tomorrow at their usual place, as he was in a bit of a mess.

Later in the evening the dormitory filled up with the rest of the boys of the monastery school. Some older ones made rude remarks about a certain boy who'd been freed from his lessons because he kept shitting his breeches, so of course knowledge about his alleged state of health had spread quickly. But all of the boys kept a good distance from him – which made Pierre smile secretly to himself.

When night had fallen and the brother who was on duty had patrolled the beds and made sure that no one was missing and order was kept, Pierre still couldn't fall asleep. Brother Hieronymus's open mouth and decayed teeth moving in the light of the flame close to his face kept haunting him and the herbal drink had most definitely upset his stomach by now and nearly made him vomit. Now he truly felt sick.

He turned and tossed on his straw mattress and was painfully aware of the bedbugs that had decided to take their evening meal on his body. I need to get new straw, he thought wearily, but for the time being there was nothing he could do but endure the onslaught of the tiny beasts – and scratch.

Lying there on his back and staring into the darkness he heard the rustling of straw and blankets, the pattering of bare feet on the stone floor as some boys apparently left their beds. One of them made a lot of noise peeing into the chamber pot.

That's probably Jean, Pierre thought wearily – he always ate and drank like a pig. A while later he could discern again some moving silhouettes as the night was not entirely dark. Some of the boys were now joining others, and he heard again the rustling of the straw when they lay down, then shortly afterwards the moaning and other noises related to the sins of the flesh.

Pierre was neither surprised nor was he really bothered. Having lived in the monastery school all his life he knew the nightly routines and had put a lot of effort into fending off the overtures of some of the older boys who had tried to get into his bed until it was generally known that he wanted to be on his own.

Turning once again onto his left side he suddenly saw Armand getting up very cautiously and stuffing something underneath his blanket to make the bed look occupied. Armand then tiptoed with bare feet, boots in hand, to the door of the dormitory. The door opened noiselessly and wasn't bolted. Pierre concluded that someone must have oiled it recently – and greased the palm of the supervising monk.

9

Pierre sighed and gave him a jealous thought; Armand was known to be seeing girls regularly in the city at night, no need for him to get a boy into his bed. With his looks, no girl could resist, Pierre was sure of this.

For me it's only bedbugs and Hieronymus, he thought miserably and suddenly a feeling of rage and revulsion swept over him. *I won't do it, I'll leave!* he thought, and suddenly felt a lot better. *I'll go to sea or the army, whatever, but will not sell myself to get my place in the clergy*, and having made this decision, he suddenly felt as if a huge weight had been lifted off him.

Even better, he felt exhilarated; adventures and an exciting new life were finally waiting for him. He'd never seen the sea but he had always longed to see this immense lake without borders (at least, this is how he pictured it) and had always wanted to discover new countries, visit exotic places, maybe even go as far as Venice and the Orient. The monastery library had some beautifully painted maps of the world and whenever Pierre had found an opportunity, he had sneaked secretly into this section and looked at the wonderful pictures, following with his fingers the borders and rivers of the countries with names that had filled him with daydreams.

Pierre fell into a deep and peaceful sleep almost immediately after his decision. He must have been much more tired than he had realized. Once his eyes were closed he continued seeing all of those wonderful places and exciting foreign cities in his dreams and he slept with a smile on his face.

*****

The next day he made signs to Armand that he wanted to speak to him at their secret hiding place in the garden. The weather had changed, promising a beautiful and sunny weekend for Pentecost.

The grass of the lawn was still fresh, with some remaining raindrops scattered randomly, glistening like diamonds that had been strewn all over the garden. The birds had decided to put on their best performance and the stage was set for an idyllic afternoon until the next church service needed to be attended, but Pierre gave no real consideration to the splendours that were so lavishly displayed around him.

He climbed into the tree and waited impatiently for Armand to arrive. Finally he saw him approaching, casting careful glances around him to make sure that he was not being watched before joining him.

Armand took his time finding a comfortable position in the branches. Painstakingly he searched his pocket until he found a sugared plum, ignoring Pierre's wish to talk, until Pierre was almost ready to kill him, so impatient was he to share his decision with Armand.

10

"Come on, spill the beans. You look as if you're bursting with news!" Armand grinned at him, munching the plum and searching for the next one that he offered to Pierre, who refused as he couldn't possibly think about eating in such a situation.

"You're sick," Armand commented in a matter-of-fact way. "I never saw you refuse something sweet, it must be really serious, whatever it is you want to tell me!" In fact the end of the sentence was somewhat difficult to understand as Armand was happily munching on the second sugared plum and sighing with delight.

Pierre suppressed the urge to slap him as he sensed that Armand was making a show of it deliberately to mock him. They had known each other for so long that his friend simply must be aware that something extremely important and serious was up.

Pierre had been thinking for some time how to present the whole story eloquently to make sure that his friend would understand and support him – it never entered his mind that he might refuse.

His carefully studied approach somehow all went to pieces when he went back in his mind to the beginning of this encounter and he just stammered, "I have decided to leave, I simply can't take it," and to his great horror, unmanly tears started rolling down his cheeks, apparently ignored by Armand, for which Pierre was grateful.

Having seen Pierre sitting there, a bundle of nerves, Armand had known, even before Pierre had started telling him, what was coming. "I was afraid that you'd react like this. What happened?" and Pierre went rapidly through the story of Brother Hieronymus's 'private lesson'.

Pierre told the whole story in detail and Armand first listened seriously with an anxious face but when Pierre came to the climax and described his sudden attack of fictive diarrhoea, Armand nearly fell out of the tree with laughter, especially when Pierre – who by now had been able to relax a little – started to mimic Brother Hieronymus's unctuous voice turning slightly less unctuous and more and more shrill at the end of their encounter. Pierre described the details of his panicky face, sweat glistening on the fat monk's cheeks when he had backed away as if Pierre had turned into a poisonous snake. It was well known all over the monastery school that Brother Hieronymus was a classic hypochondriac, and was frequently seen interrogating Brother Infirmarius about matters concerning his personal well-being.

"That's wonderful! I love it!" his friend gasped between waves of laughter and it took them some time to stop giggling and become serious again.

"What do you want to do?" Armand finally asked, coming back to reality.

"To join the King's army or become a sailor!" Pierre answered proudly. "I'm nearly of age, most children start working much earlier, as you know," Pierre said. "I'll just leave and find my own way of living…"

But before he could go on, Armand retorted, "And be caught and be brought back in no time to the monastery – come on, wake up, this isn't a dream, you need a realistic plan!"

Pierre was amazed. Armand was right, as always. It had seemed so simple in his own mind. But he felt encouraged all the same; Armand had not told him to forget his plan right away.

They started pondering different options and strategies but nothing really seemed to work. Pierre had been living in the monastery orphanage since he could remember, meaning forever. He had to admit that he had no clue as to how to earn a living, ride a horse properly, had no money or worldly possessions of his own, he didn't even know the names of the cities on the way to the coast, consequently the more they discussed the details, the more depressing the situation started to look.

What had looked like an easy and exciting exit from misery and a great adventure had become a complicated riddle that was making Pierre's head spin.

Armand could feel and clearly see how his friend's eager expression had become downcast; the blue eyes that had been burning with excitement dimmed and his shoulders had sagged. Armand decided that it was time to lift his friend's spirits, having brought him back down to earth, and to start developing a realistic plan.

"Whatever you want to do, we must first find out your real identity," he said casually.

"I'm Pierre, stupid, who else?" Pierre said, and looked at Armand as if he were mad.

"Pierre *who*?" answered Armand. "Did you never ask yourself this question?"

Pierre hesitated and then said in low tone, "Whenever I come up with possible answers I don't like them: Son of a whore? An illegitimate child, left behind, unwanted? Of course I've asked myself this question again and again, but to be honest with you, I'm scared of finding out the truth, I'd rather not know."

"You're so naïve that it hurts." Armand seemed really upset. "This school is one of the best schools in France – we're under the direct patronage of the Archbishop of Reims, who has the sole right to anoint the kings of France. Do you really think our dear Christian brothers would have moved you from the monastery orphanage to this place if there hadn't been any money or influence involved, can you possibly have lived here for so many years and still believe that this Church would do anything without expecting a hefty, and preferably golden, compensation?"

Pierre looked at him, bewildered. He hated to admit it, but of course Armand was right, the monastery always expected something in return – even funerals weren't free. The poorest souls were denied the blessings of the sanctified earth of the cemeteries if their relatives had no money to spare.

"All right, you've got a point, but what does it change?" Pierre asked.

"Everything!" Armand answered. "If we know where you come from we can find relatives where you can go and hide until the monks give up the search. You're far too inexperienced to leave on your own without any money and without a place to hide."

Studiously he searched his pockets for another sugared plum, but to no avail. Making a face he continued. "We're lucky that we've got at least two weeks left to organize something. I propose that during the next two days you continue faking sickness. I happen to know that Brother Hieronymus is planning to visit one of the parishes outside Reims next week. Afterwards we'll celebrate Pentecost and all of us will be allowed to leave the monastery and attend service in the Cathedral."

During Armand's explanation they had been staring at the lawn where a lazy cat had appeared; stretching and yawning it was luxuriating in the rays of the sun. Suddenly the cat's demeanour changed, it became alert and twitched its tail.

"I bet she's spotted a mouse out there," Pierre mused. They knew the cat well – she was Brother Infirmarius's pet and appeared often in the monastery hospital, sometimes proudly presenting a dead mouse that she had brought as a special gift for her benefactor.

The cat pounced on an invisible target and vanished into the shrubs. Armand had watched the cat jump – and out of the blue he first looked startled and then he slapped his hand on Pierre's back. Excited and jubilant he exclaimed, "That's it! I have a brilliant plan, the cat will help us!"

Pierre was dying of curiosity but nothing could move Armand to explain his plan although Pierre pleaded, cajoled and finally even tried to bribe Armand by promising him part of his frugal dinner (a trick which normally always worked).

"You'll see, it'll be fun," was all Armand would say, keeping a straight face. "I can't really tell you now, you're far too straightforward and honest, it's better you don't know." Armand paused and added, "Surprise is the essence of warcraft, my father used to say, and I tend to agree with him!"

Time had moved fast and the sun had started to set. The light had become mellow and the shadows were growing longer. The last of the sun's rays were streaming through the dense foliage of the shrubs and trees, creating constantly moving patterns that danced on the ground. The bells started ringing for Compline, a summons they couldn't possibly ignore. Armand left for the chapel to attend the service and a very frustrated Pierre went back to the dormitory (after Armand had mischievously insisted that he should wet his back once more) to continue pretending to suffer another attack of his fictitious illness.

*****

Pierre had just about settled on his straw mattress when Brother Infirmarius appeared.

"Here's my young suffering patient," he remarked in his usual friendly and cheerful manner but his shrewd eyes were looking straight into the depths of Pierre's heart and soul. Armand had been right – Pierre was rubbish at hiding anything. Even he had to concede this.

In a confidential tone Brother Infirmarius continued, "What are you doing here? You're not really sick, are you?"

Pierre croaked, "I'm not feeling well," and tried to look convincingly sick. By now he was so scared that the truth might come out that he really did manage to look ill and extremely pale after all.

"You've never done this before," the brother said, looking suspiciously at him, and continued, "Strangely enough, you told Brother Hieronymus that you had been in my hospital *before* you came to see me – you must have had a very precise foreboding then…"

Pierre's blue pleading eyes were wide open and like a frightened animal he looked up at Brother Infirmarius who maintained a non-committal expression and paused at length.

Finally he smiled. In actual fact he genuinely liked Pierre, and said, "Don't worry too much, I must confess that I forgot to mention this strange coincidence to my dear Brother Hieronymus but I do suggest that you say three rosaries tomorrow in church and ask for forgiveness when you go to confession… and I hope to see you tomorrow morning joining the service in our chapel as usual!"

Pierre squeezed his hand thankfully as he couldn't speak but Brother Infirmarius had not expected any words and turned his eyes to the small empty bottle of medicine that lay next to mattress.

"Actually, you've had your punishment already," he smirked. "I'm sure my herbs made you feel pretty ill after all," and with a slight chuckle at his private joke he left the dormitory and a very much relieved Pierre behind him.

THE SURPRISE

Armand had remained silent and stubbornly refused to comment or let out any hint of his plan until Pierre was desperate for him to spill the beans. He just replied with a broad grin that did nothing to relieve Pierre's excitement and tension. He invited Pierre to stay close to him on Sunday when they were supposed to attend the church service in Reims cathedral before noon.

All monastery pupils loved this opportunity to leave the confinement of the monastery school. There was always something exciting to see in the streets, sometimes even special highlights like gruesome executions which would feed the classroom gossip and their imagination for weeks.

The boys were supposed to leave the cathedral after the service and go straight back to the monastery but as even their teachers loved to linger on the streets there was an understanding between the older boys and the majority of the teachers that as long as everybody was present by Compline, nobody would ask awkward questions about their previous whereabouts.

In essence it meant a rare free Sunday afternoon if they could manage to escape the direct control of the few diligent and nosy teachers who felt obliged to shepherd them back immediately after the church service to the monastery.

When they entered the huge gothic cathedral with its massive towers, Pierre couldn't suppress a shiver. He always found the cathedral overwhelming with its endless pillars, and vaulted roof, which to his mind must surely touch Heaven. Pierre could not imagine any bigger and more beautiful building in the world: this was the holy cathedral where sacred kings were crowned and anointed.

Reims cathedral was a symbol of the power and strength of the Catholic Church, towering above mankind; it proclaimed to every human being who ever came to see and pray in this edifice that the Church was God's sole representative on earth.

Pierre's gaze then moved to the beautiful windows that glittered in the sun like a collection of precious stones: shades of emerald, ruby, sapphire, amethyst and golden yellow made a breathtakingly beautiful kaleidoscope of shapes and colours – blending in with the gold that gleamed and glittered from all corners of the cathedral – from the different altars of the holy Saints to the chalices of gold that adorned the main altar and the gilded sculptures of the Virgin Mary and the Saints and the cross of Jesus.

The holy mass started with the chanting of the choir. Pierre loved the music and the feeling of elevation that invariably he had experienced when he used to sing in the choir or listened to it. He was now thankful, however, that he had been released from the choir when his voice had broken. Now he'd be able to sneak out prematurely from the service, as Armand had insisted that he should hang back innocently until his teachers had lost sight of him. He was to leave the cathedral a good quarter of an hour before the mass ended. Armand would do the same but would be using a different exit to make sure that nobody saw them leaving together.

Pierre felt terribly excited: Armand had been so secretive and he hoped to discover – finally, today – what this plan was about. But the service seemed to be stretching on endlessly this Sunday and when Pierre finally decided that it was the right time to leave the cathedral he was convinced that one more minute of waiting and the tension would make him explode.

In his nightmares he had imagined bumping directly into one of his teachers but nothing untoward happened as he ducked down and moved quickly through the packed crowd, hiding his face with the help of the hood on his Sunday robe, for once happy that all pupils wore the same, so it would be impossible to identify him.

However, he didn't notice Brother Hieronymus following him at a good distance; the teacher had detected Pierre's manoeuvre, having had his eyes on the beautiful boy during the service, picturing to himself their next private lesson…

Pierre came out of the darkness of the Cathedral and had to blink several times as the sun was shining brightly and his eyes hurt. Then he turned left as Armand had instructed him to do and quickly disappeared into one of the smaller streets, walking swiftly towards the church of St Rémy, where they were to meet, and which lay on the opposite side of the town, not far away from the city walls.

He hurried through the narrow streets of Reims avoiding collisions with the numerous peddlers, beggars and well-nourished townsmen and their wives who were crowding the streets, looking at the stalls displaying produce from the local farms or silks, wool, linen and all sorts of goods from foreign and exotic places such as neighbouring Flanders, Venice or even the Orient.

He reached St Rémy's out of breath and was disappointed to see that Armand had not yet arrived. He was starting to feel hungry as it was the habit in the school to have only a small breakfast, but as he had no money he decided that it would be better to ignore his stomach and try to concentrate on the question of what Armand might be planning to do.

Time passed. Pierre had chosen to hide behind a column at the entrance and stood there idly watching people passing the church of St Rémy when finally he spotted Armand approaching at a leisurely pace, his arm elegantly extended to a young lady.

No hurry there, Pierre thought grimly.

16

He was immediately impressed by the lavish elegance of her clothing, her precious scarf adorned with expensive lace, the proud way she held her head and the fact that she wore a veil to hide her face from the stares of the commoners – all of this told him, and the world, that she was a true lady from a noble family.

A maid followed at a short distance. *Maid or female dragon!* thought Pierre. Indeed the maid was impressive. She was quite tall and was as fat as the girl she was supposed to chaperon was thin. Her face displayed an air of displeasure; she clearly disliked the mission she was supposed to be performing.

Armand looked around, searching for his friend, and seeing him close to the entrance waved to him to come and meet them.

Pierre moved forward to meet the couple, finally taking down the hood of his robe, so as to greet the lady correctly, but nothing could have prepared him for the overwhelming effect of beautiful wide eyes, flecked with amber, and a face crowned by lustrous auburn-tinged hair.

Pierre froze in front of her and when the young lady recognized his confusion she lifted her veil, showing a lovely face that was smiling at him broadly, thus making things even worse, as Pierre had never in his life seen such a beautiful girl.

"This is Marie and her maid, Anne," Armand said helpfully. He had anticipated that Pierre would be stunned but the reality exceeded his expectations and he had to hide his delight at this surprise.

Pierre didn't move and didn't speak. Not that he didn't want to – he was turning scarlet and some magic spell must have tied his tongue in a knot as he couldn't manage to utter a single word. He must have looked and appeared a complete idiot.

Marie of course revelled in what she rightfully took as a display of admiration and started to giggle.

"Hmm," said Armand, "I tend to forget that our education in the monastery is somehow incomplete and that greeting beautiful ladies correctly is not part of the lessons we receive, so let me show you how it works!" and mockingly he bowed deeply in front of Marie, took three fingers of her slender hand and pretended to kiss them.

With a big grin he continued – mocking himself – "May I present myself, my lady? I am Armand de Saint Paul, sixth and youngest son of the Marquis de Saint Paul, therefore no hope of any money or titles, but entirely at your service!"

Marie followed his lead, sank to a deep curtsey and murmured, "I am obliged, my lord, I am Marie de Montjoie, the only but respectable daughter of the Baron de Montjoie, true subject of our great King Louis XIII, also at your service."

First Pierre had watched Armand, bewildered, but then started to laugh at their little performance.

He solemnly bowed as well and managed to say, "May I present myself? I am Pierre d'Orphanage sans Argent – no money, not even boots of my own, but surely, totally, and forever at your service!"

Now Armand and Marie burst out laughing and immediately they felt as if they had been friends forever.

Marie glanced at Pierre and liked what she saw. Pierre had grown to full height recently, with a slender but muscular body and a striking face; even with his shockingly short hair, the prescribed haircut for the monastery's pupils, he still looked extremely handsome with his blue eyes, slightly aquiline nose and white teeth that could show a dashing smile, such as he was displaying unconsciously right now.

It would be difficult to choose between them both, Marie mused. So different and both rather too handsome. Mother always warned me that handsome men make bad husbands, but this doesn't mean that I can't have a bit of fun now, she concluded and decided to thoroughly enjoy this little adventure.

She gave an apologetic glance to her maid and smiled sweetly at her. She knew that her maid had joined this excursion only after Marie had promised her she would behave, as the reputation of girls was quickly ruined in small cities like Reims and as her maid had also been her wet nurse, Marie knew that she loved her as her own child.

* * * * *

Brother Hieronymus watched the three youngsters and rubbed his hands with glee. Leaving the cathedral without authorization before the end of the service, wandering around the city without permission and, last but not least, meeting and conversing with a girl would carry severe punishments if he reported these misdeeds to the Abbot. Armand would of course just receive some light punishments as no abbot would dare to upset even the youngest son of a powerful Marquis but for Pierre, the full measure of the school's rules would be applied.

Already he pictured himself alone with a desperate Pierre in the monastery penance cell. He closed his eyes and let his fantasy run: he saw himself slowly approaching the boy who'd be sitting there, clad only in a loincloth and begging for his help, desperate to please him and to get some food, and return to his class and his friends.

He enjoyed this dream for a moment in exaltation but when he opened his eyes the three were gone.

18

He uttered a low curse, crossed himself automatically to beg forgiveness for cursing and then decided to move on, as he had been ordered to join his fellow brethren who worked on one of the numerous farms located outside the city walls belonging to the monastery. The Abbot had commissioned him to spend a week there and take inventory of the livestock and the wines that were maturing there from last year's harvest. The wine inventory would be the interesting part! Travelling outside the city walls was always risky – even for clergymen – and he wanted to arrive in daylight, and alive.

Brother Hieronymus would have been surprised to see that the three new friends went straight back to the monastery, followed by Marie's maid trailing behind. Pierre was still feeling as if he were walking on a cloud, very much afraid that he might wake up and find out that it had all been only a divine dream.

"Why are we walking straight back?" he asked Armand sulkily, as he hated the idea of having to say goodbye so soon to Marie.

"Marie's mother thinks that even a girl should have a good education. Actually she can even read and write, so I suggested that a visit to our school could be a nice accomplishment to her education," Armand said mockingly, while smiling broadly at Marie. Pierre couldn't see her reaction as she had fixed her veil again – but maybe by coincidence it no longer fully covered the bodice that made a lovely framework for her breasts.

"Why would you be interested in Marie's education?" he hissed to his friend suspiciously.

"Because she's one of my numerous cousins, of course," Armand answered evenly. "Her mother is one of my great-aunts, so I'm just doing my duty."

Pierre had the unmistakeable feeling that Armand was pulling his leg but as Marie was watching them he decided just to nudge Armand with his elbow instead of replying rudely.

Armand decided to stop on the way and buy some delicious hot pastries in one of the stalls and the four paused a while in the city square, munching their spicy meat pies and watching some jugglers displaying their tricks. Armand warned Marie in a low voice to pay attention when a young boy of six or seven, dressed in rags, approached them to ask deferentially for some coins after they had applauded the jugglers.

Armand jumped forward and quickly seized the boy's hand, forced it open and to her great surprise Marie's silken purse fell onto the street. The boy struggled free and ran away and a shocked Marie and her maid thanked Armand effusively.

"He looked so sweet, how could he steal my purse?" Marie wondered out loud.

"They choose them carefully. The sweet ones become the thieves, the maimed ones have to beg," Armand explained.

19

Pierre felt slightly annoyed. Armand always seemed to know everything – how Pierre would have loved to explain the world to Marie.

They were now approaching the cathedral and the monastery school and Pierre was disappointed that they had returned so fast. He had enjoyed every precious second of this afternoon. Fighting a feeling of sadness, he was preparing to take his leave and was busily trying to think about some especially witty or funny remark with which to impress Marie.

Consequently he didn't really notice that they had already entered the monastery's main building and was literally speechless when Armand requested the doorkeeper to ask Brother Archivarius for the honour of a meeting with the lady Marie de Montjoie and her chaperon.

The doorkeeper clearly disliked the idea of admitting a young lady but noticed that she was not only richly dressed but wore a veil and was chaperoned by an impressive-looking maid.

It was common knowledge that Armand's family belonged to the highest aristocracy in France and that his destiny was to become a bishop in one of the de Saint Paul sinecures as soon as he left the school. Therefore the doorkeeper made up his mind and decided that he did not want to risk any conflict with the Abbot or even higher authorities by upsetting a member of the Saint Paul family. He sighed deeply to convey his displeasure but he consented to present their request.

They had to wait a considerable time until Brother Archivarius turned up. When the doorkeeper had announced the request of such august visitors, Archivarius had thought that the doorkeeper was mistaken and they had requested the honour of paying a visit to the Abbot himself.

The doorkeeper had insisted that he had correctly understood the message and they had indeed asked for him. By nature Brother Archivarius was an orderly man of slow thoughts. He went to the Abbot's quarters to seek counsel but was informed that the Abbot had been summoned by the Archbishop and would probably stay in his chambers until dinner.

Reluctantly he returned and came to the conclusion that he would meet his visitors on his own. His instinct told him that upsetting a lady of rank and a son of the Marquis de Saint Paul would be a bad move.

He reached the door in a fluster, not really knowing what to say or do.

Armand bowed courteously and greeted Brother Archivarius formally.

"May I present a cousin of mine, the lady Elisabeth de Mezières and her chaperon?" Armand presented Marie and gave a quick kick of warning to Pierre to keep his mouth shut. Pierre's eyes were as big as saucers, he had no clue what was going on. Why had Armand presented Marie under a false name?

20

"We happened to be discussing in our family matters of administration and the young lady would not believe that you have developed a system of keeping the vast archives of this monastery in perfect order. Would you mind showing us your archives so as to convince the lovely lady that I spoke the truth? We understand that this would take a lot of your precious time, but we would really appreciate it if you would grant us this favour!"

Brother Archivarius was flattered. He had always shown modest pride that his archives were well kept but to imagine that he had become the topic of conversation in noble circles!

He started to turn crimson with embarrassment and uttered some incoherent phrases, among which could be discerned, "Not necessary... at your service... pleased to oblige..."

In his confusion the big key-ring that held all of his keys slipped out of his hand and landed with a loud clatter on the flagstones.

Marie was happy that she was still wearing her veil and could hide her amusement. She decided that it was about time to make the next move. She moved modestly forward, but made sure that poor Brother Archivarius would have an excellent view of her low neckline, which added considerably to his confusion.

"It must be such a *huge* responsibility to work in this place," Marie murmured, her pleasant voice full of admiration. "I would surely become lost here," she added, "but we poor women are not made for such tasks of high intelligence and organization."

Brother Archivarius started to take a fancy to the young lady. Nobody had ever explained so clearly the importance of the job that he was doing here; surprisingly it took a young lady to understand fully the quality and great responsibility of his work. Feeling on secure ground again he started to explain the different sections of his archives.

When Marie asked for his permission to remove her veil, explaining that she was feeling safe in the holy grounds of the Abbey and in his reassuring company, he could only agree and was even more taken in when he saw her beautiful face with adoring eyes fixed upon him, totally ignoring those worthless young boys who had brought her along.

"I imagine that you could easily retrieve documents for important or well known persons, such as His Eminence, the Abbot, or maybe even de Saint Paul," and she made a light gesture in the direction of Armand who had stayed a step behind the small group. "But I doubt that you could find immediately some record of something or someone less important..." She was hesitating and seemed to be pondering how to find an example and then fixing her gaze on Pierre, she said, "Like this boy, I must admit, I forgot his name..."

21

Pierre managed to keep a straight face but his heart sank – what game was she playing?

Brother Archivarius laughed and said, "That's Pierre, an orphan who has been around here for more than 10 years. This is an easy request. You see those chests? Those are reserved for the documents related to the monastery's pupils. Each chest contains the documents of the pupils who enter during a particular decade, so I would need to open the one starting 1620 and then all documents are filed in the boxes in alphabetical order. In his case, I would use his first name."

Marie's eyes were fixed on the archivist who seemed to grow under her adoration. "You could do this right now, without searching for hours in your big folios? I can't believe this," she said. "Oh, do please open this chest for me, I would so like to go home and tell our steward what he has to learn from you and that I saw it with my own eyes!"

Brother Archivarius moved forward like a puppet on a string, eager to show that he had spoken the truth. He opened the heavy chest with one of the keys from the huge bunch on his key-ring and after moving the heavy lid that creaked in protest, he pointed out the different wooden boxes inside, each of those boxes containing documents for each pupil. He didn't want to boast, but the idea of filing documents in separate boxes had been his alone.

As soon as he had pointed out the corner of the chest where Pierre's box should be found, a piercing sound suddenly shattered the silence of the archive room. Marie had started to scream hysterically, first grabbing the arm of the archivist and then hiding in the arms of her maid. "A mouse," she sobbed, "I saw a mouse!"

Brother Archivarius was alarmed. In his life he constantly faced two major enemies: the ignorance of his assistants who were lazy and would create havoc in his archive if he let them work without supervision, and all kinds of vermin that wanted to destroy his valuable papers and vellums.

"Where?" he cried, ready to strike. "Show me where!" and Marie pointed with a wavering finger into a corner where a door led into a different section containing precious books of prayer. Brother Archivarius grabbed a broom which was standing in a corner and ran with surprising agility to the door, opened it and disappeared.

Pierre had been watching, breathlessly trying to spot the mouse when he realized that his friend had quickly grabbed the box with his personal file from the chest, opened it and hidden all its contents under his lightly quilted waistcoat. In no time the box was closed and back in place and Armand stormed towards the door, shouting, "I saw the mouse, I'll kill it," banging with his sword on the stone floor and creating a dreadful noise.

Brother Archivarius came back just in time to see Armand smashing the remains of a mouse, hacking it to pieces.

The archivist thanked Armand profusely and Marie insisted that she would like to go back to her home; this adventure had been too much for the spirits of a young lady, she feebly led them to understand. Ignoring the boys once more she effusively thanked the archivist for his precious time and praised his excellent organizational skills.

They parted at the door in good spirits. The young lady and her maid would walk back to Marie's house and the two boys would stay in the monastery – as in fact they should have done the whole day.

Armand and Pierre ran to their preferred hiding place where Armand removed from his waistcoat the documents that he had just stolen from the archive. Pierre was dumbfounded. His friend had planned this little scene from the beginning: he could only admire his little ruse. And Marie, she too had known right from the start, what an incredible role she had played!

Armand was reading quickly through the documents and for the first time was happy that he had taken the pains to learn how to read and write. Pierre was suddenly paralysed with fear – would the documents confirm that he was a foundling or worse, the son of a prostitute or of convicts? He didn't dare to look into Armand's eyes, he didn't want to face the contempt that he would find there once Armand knew the truth.

Armand lowered the documents and looked at Pierre with wide bewildered eyes. Pierre started to panic – the truth must be worse than he could have imagined in his worst nightmares.

THE CARDINAL'S PALACE

The elegant carriage with the coat of arms of the Marquis de Beauvoir drove into the courtyard of the huge palace built by Cardinal Richelieu as testimony of his power. Rumour had it that even the King had experienced a fit of jealousy when he had set eyes for the first time on the lavish palace and could only be placated once the Cardinal had let it be known that he would bequeath the palace after his death to His Majesty.

The clattering of the iron-rimmed wheels of the carriage made a deafening noise on the cobblestones of the courtyard, drawing attention to the noble passenger who alighted. He was in his mid forties but his once beautiful face bore the traces of too much food and drink, and his thinning blond hair showed streaks of grey, hanging down to his shoulders in light curls as fashion dictated for members of the nobility.

He disregarded the helping hand of the footman and jumped impatiently out of the carriage, his face for an unguarded moment showing only contempt for his surroundings.

Louis Philippe de Beauvoir climbed the impressive staircase and was led through endless corridors adorned with antique sculptures. It was said that the Cardinal owned the biggest collection in France. Those walls that had not been decorated with statues displayed colossal paintings from the leading artists not only of France but from all over Europe. The stage was set to glorify the royal family, France, the Catholic Church and – of course – Richelieu himself.

Cream-coloured marble, gilded ornaments and crimson were the dominating colour scheme; the most expensive marbles of Italy had been brought to Paris, as only the best were good enough for the Cardinal. Genuine diamonds had been used to decorate his private chapel, the chalice, cross and chandeliers were of solid gold adorned with rubies and other precious stones. The Grand Palace had set a new standard of refinement and luxury in Europe.

Louis Philippe de Beauvoir controlled his face and made a show of stunned admiration, as was expected from any visitor coming to plead for favours from the Cardinal. It was common knowledge that every single person hired to serve the Cardinal was trained as a spy and would later report on every detail of the arrival.

Louis Philippe – like all members of the high aristocracy – secretly detested the Cardinal as a parvenu, a stranger who had sneaked his way up from the lowest ranks to the highest office in the government France had to offer, next to the King.

It was common knowledge that he had earned his first position as minister as a lover of the Medici Queen, a lady with unlimited lust for power but not blessed with a sharp brain, who only much too late had understood she had raised and nurtured a monster.

Richelieu knew of course about this animosity and had skilfully diminished step by step the power of the rival aristocracy since his ascent to power. He had played one great family against another and adroitly used the war against heresy to get rid of most of the protestant aristocrats – whose strongholds in fact had presented the biggest challenge to royal dominance.

The Cardinal had systematically strengthened his own position as prime minister; it was Richelieu alone who ran the government, but all the same he had been shaping a new position of absolute power for the King. His example of absolute monarchy would be copied all over Europe, but it would take a true master like Richelieu behind the scenes to make it work.

Louis Philippe arrived in the antechamber and was politely requested to accept a seat whilst he waited for the Cardinal. He accepted politely, keeping his face expressionless although he was fuming with rage. Making him wait here showed that he was regarded as just another petitioner, one in an endless chain of people asking favours from the Cardinal.

Well, he thought, *that's what I'm doing here, asking for a favour like a beggar, so I'd better go through with it in style.*

After half an hour of waiting he was admitted to the library. Although it was a hot day the Cardinal had had a fire lit and was sitting close to it. Everyone knew that his health had become poor, but he seemed to be one of those people who always complain about bad health and yet seemingly go on forever. It would be difficult to imagine France without him.

The Cardinal rose from his seat, slowly suppressing an exclamation of pain and tightly pressed his lips together. Louis Philippe de Beauvoir pretended not to have noticed the Cardinal's expression and approached him, bowed formally and kissed the Cardinal's ring of office on the ice-cold hand that was extended to him.

"Greetings, Your Eminence," Louis Philippe uttered. "I hope to find you in good health and supportive of my cause!"

"You are most welcome, my Son," Richelieu replied.

Louis Philippe's face, which had been flushed from the intense heat, suddenly went pale, leaving only two blotches of red burning on his cheeks, giving him a ghost-like appearance. Richelieu should have addressed him in return as 'My most honourable Marquis', if he had recognized his claim to the inherited title; once more, de Beauvoir's case didn't seem to be moving forward.

Richelieu, of course, had noticed his change of complexion and a faint derogatory smile was playing on his lips. Louis Philippe decided not to give in and

25

started praising the King and the Cardinal as was customary for audiences at court to do, but Richelieu just made a weary gesture with his hand and interrupted him.

"We have known each other for so many years, my Son," Richelieu continued, "and we know and trust our true values and ideas."

Richelieu paused at length and his shrewd eyes appraised Louis Philippe de Beauvoir who was trying to keep a straight face, although he had the impression that the Cardinal could not only look right through him but was mocking him.

"You have come to ask my help in order to be acknowledged by His Majesty, the King, as the sole and rightful heir of your brother, the late Marquis de Beauvoir."

The Cardinal's heavy scarlet robe rustled as he sat down on his chair and the diamonds on the golden cross that he wore on a long chain sparkled in the light. He made a slight gesture with his hand, inviting Louis Philippe to sit on one of the high and uncomfortable chairs that were reserved for his visitors of high rank.

"Let us get straight to the point, as I am expecting a summons to join His Majesty soon. He has bought a new stallion and as it is a decision of the highest importance, he wants my humble advice."

Louis Philippe wondered how the Cardinal managed to put so much sarcasm into only one sentence whilst speaking evenly and only slightly moving his eyebrows.

"Your chances are not favourable at all, according to our legal advisers. The present heir was born in wedlock and your request to invalidate the marriage based on the claim that his mother was a protestant is problematic, as she converted to the true faith before she died and, legally speaking, she was no heretic. These facts are well documented and changing the course of inheritance would mean to undermine the very foundations this kingdom and law and order are built on."

"But it's the truth," de Beauvoir exclaimed angrily. "Do I really have to accept that the title of one of the most noble families in France will go to a bastard, a foreigner?"

The Cardinal gestured him to calm down and continued. "There are still two possibilities that you might want to explore," and again he paused and saw that Louis Philippe quickly moistened his lips and looked at him in anticipation. *I have him hooked*, thought Richelieu, *he's getting greedy*.

The Cardinal continued in an even voice. "Our Holy Mother, the Catholic Church, of course would prefer to see a true son of her faith follow the steps of the late marquis. So if you would consider sending a petition to the Holy See I might add my humble support to your plea. If the Holy Father in His wisdom decides to invalidate the marriage on the grounds that the mother must be considered a heretic and most probably used witchcraft to make your brother marry her, the title would go to you. Once the marriage was officially invalidated, of course the law would foresee a new succession and the legal system would be entirely respected."

Louis Philippe looked at the Cardinal, moistened his lips and asked, "What would be the cost of this petition, Your Eminence, and what length of time would you estimate for its success?"

"You would need to invest around 150,000 livres in donations to my offices, the Holy Father and the cardinals in Rome who can enable us to open the proceedings. In case of success, of course the Church would expect at least the same amount once again to show your support of our cause and make sure that the decision of the Holy Father will be applied by Parliament, who will need to confirm your nomination."

Louis Philippe's face turned scarlet. The terrible heat in the room had its effect and this poisonous spider in the cardinal's robe sitting in front of him was daring to ask nothing else but half of his heritage to grant support for his case – without of course any guarantee of success.

"What would be the second option, Your Eminence?" His voice was hoarse, he felt as if he had no breath left.

"The second option would be logically to follow the natural course of a heritage. For a contribution to the funds of my charity I could propose to give you the opportunity to find your nephew who is considered as the rightful Marquis now and make sure that his health is not failing, as his sudden passing away would, of course, make you the next Marquis."

Louis Philippe blinked and suddenly understood why the Cardinal had changed the course of history – he had no inhibitions at all when his interests were served.

"What kind of contribution would be adequate in this case, Your Eminence?" Louis Philippe managed to ask.

Richelieu didn't hesitate for a second and replied smoothly, "Fifty thousand livres now and a further hundred thousand if ever an accident or any other kind of premature death should befall your nephew and you become installed as Marquis de Beauvoir with all rights." The Cardinal paused. "Payable in gold, of course," he added.

The golden ornaments in the stiflingly hot room started to spin in front of Louis Philippe's eyes. In essence, murder of his nephew was to be considered the cheaper option, as all the funds would go straight to the Cardinal's pockets, no need to share between him and Rome.

Before Louis Philippe had the time to digest and reply to this proposal, the Cardinal exclaimed, "Brother Joseph!" and out of the dim shadow in the corner a monk suddenly appeared clad in the habit of the Dominicans. Louis Philippe could not say if he had come through a secret door or if had been standing there during the whole of their conversation.

"In order to make sure that there will be no misunderstanding about our discussion – the content of course has to remain fully confidential – Brother Joseph will keep a record of all details and your signature will be required once you wish to go forward. Brother Joseph could also be of help in reuniting you with your young relative for whom you have been searching for so many years now. You will receive the information regarding where to locate your nephew in due course, once our little agreement has been signed."

Richelieu now looked fully into his eyes and Louis Philippe had the feeling that those dark eyes were fixed on him with all contempt.

"I assume this will be your preferred option?" Richelieu finished his speech and raised himself, once again not without pain and Louis Philippe hastened to do the same, preferring to ignore that contemptuous look.

He understood that this was his sign to take his leave. He bowed to the Cardinal and kissed once more the ring on his hand that was still ice-cold, gave a short nod to Brother Joseph and was led back to his carriage that miraculously was already waiting for him.

Traffic in Paris was always tricky as the streets were poorly maintained despite the splendour of the new palaces shooting up in the royal quarter and in Saint Germain. The city was still very much medieval in its layout, but today it was by far the biggest and fastest growing city in the world, home to more than half a million people.

Louis Philippe sat in his carriage, shaken by the rumbling on the potholed streets and normally would have used his whip for the coachman to go faster and be more careful at the same time but he was still in shock after his interview with the Cardinal. He had glimpsed the ruthless side of power today and he understood that the Cardinal had long been playing in a different league from all of those members of the old families who had thought themselves so superior. His mind was in turmoil, he needed to discuss things with his son, fast.

*****

Louis Philippe had settled in the library as he decided that he needed a confidential setting for a discussion with his son. He had changed his clothes as he had felt an urgent need to freshen up and change after the strange interview in that terribly hot room in the Cardinal's palace.

He was just about to empty his second glass of wine when his son entered the library, as Louis Philippe had given word to the butler that his son's immediate presence was desired.

28

Henri de Beauvoir was of more than average height, with a well-trained body of perfect proportions. He entered the library with the steps of a man who believes that the world is his.

His blond locks fell on his shoulders and the waistcoat made from expensive white silk with golden trimmings was tailored in the latest fashion. His face would have been the face of perfect beauty, had there not been a very visible scar above his left eye. But far from disfiguring him, the scar gave the young man a hint of danger that only added to his physical attraction.

Any father setting eyes on such a son who would easily outshine his noble companions at court should have been bursting with love and pride. But Louis Philippe saw Henri approaching with his usual confident stride and suppressed a slight shiver. He had not felt at ease in the presence of his son lately and looking into these big blue eyes, a de Beauvoir heritage, he saw no love, no filial reverence, just contempt – they were as cold as ice.

"What did our beloved Eminence tell you that could be so urgent as to summon me immediately?" Henri sneered. "I can see from your face that you've lost out again, you're quivering like a heap of jelly." He paused and gave his father a contemptuous look. "How fine it is to have someone as brave as you for a father," he added ironically, and settled in the chair in front of his father. He stretched out his long legs carelessly and reached for the wine decanter, pouring himself a glass without waiting for his father's invitation or approval.

"Would you mind showing a modicum of respect for your father," Louis Philippe protested, trying to show some authority.

"No, not really, why should I?" Henri shot him a cool glance. "I'd love to, you know, but you don't merit any respect, you're a disgrace to the de Beauvoir family – and you know it! You never succeeded at anything in your life." He paused, and added, "I wonder if you even succeeded in siring me, or if I should thank my mother that she asked someone else to give you a hand."

Louis Philippe jumped up in rage, wanting to slap his son, but the latter seized his arm with a steely grip and just murmured into his ear, "Don't, just don't even think about it or you'll regret it."

An uneasy silence settled between both of them but Henri continued as if nothing had happened. "Now, come and put me in the picture, what did His Eminence, the enlightened leader of our graciously stupid King, Louis XIII, tell you?"

Louis Philippe decided to press on with his story and ignore his son's insults; the truth was that he had grown used to them by now. He gave a short summary of the meeting in the Cardinal's palace and even before he had finished Henri had already jumped out of his seat, taking large strides across the room.

"This *espèce de cafard*," he groaned, "this scarlet-clad cockroach, he got hold of your balls and is squeezing them hard now. So he wants us to do the dirty work and get rid of my dear bastard cousin, he will just provide the intelligence as to how to find him, nothing else – and later," Henri was foaming by now, "this poisonous toad will continue to blackmail us all of our lives as everything has been recorded by that blasted monk."

Louis Philippe was nodding unhappily. In fact the latter implication was only becoming evident to him now as his son put it into clear words.

Henri continued to pace up and down the room, suddenly stopping in front of his father. "I'm broke," he said simply.

His father looked at him disbelievingly. "You must be joking. I gave you access to your mother's heritage last year and bailed you out the year before. You can't be serious!"

But looking into the eyes of his son he saw that he had spoken the truth and Henri continued, "You simply have no idea! Life at the royal court is expensive. I cannot accept that a de Beauvoir should live like a beggar. On top of this, I've also had a streak of bad luck with the cards recently." Henri shrugged. "After all, it's only money."

"You're insane," his father retorted. "I don't know where to raise any money any more, the estates have been mortgaged and I've no access to my brother's money whilst I don't carry his title."

"So there is only one solution left," Henri said and approached his father, looking with his cold eyes straight into the eyes of his father as they filled with fear. "We'll have to get rid of this bastard cousin of mine, there is no alternative," and raising his voice he added, "You'd better understand this and get moving, that is, if you're capable of doing anything at all."

His father looked like a trapped rabbit.

He'll ruin it, thought Henri dispassionately, *he's already wetting his breeches now. Let me arrange this and then, my dear father, let's look for a nice resting place for you too.*

Aloud he said, digging his hand like an iron claw into his father's back, "Stop crying and go to the Jews or the Italian bankers – do it today or tomorrow! They'll spit out the 50,000 immediately when they hear that the Cardinal is backing you and the heritage of my uncle is up for grabs."

"They'll kill us with the interest they'll be demanding," his father managed to say, trying to muster the remains of his courage but was cut off immediately by Henri, who just laughed.

"I'll be quick, I'll look after this matter, don't worry. Now, move, you've lost enough time!"

Louis Philippe looked into his son's eyes and although he had lost all illusions about him over the years, he was deeply shocked to see that these eyes of blue ice had started to glow with glee and excitement.

He is looking forward to murdering his cousin, Louis Philippe thought, and tried to suppress a feeling of panic. *My son is a natural killer.*

*****

Henri stormed out of the library as the presence of this whining bag of jelly who was supposed to be his father made him sick. In fact, he was quite delighted that finally he had managed to manoeuvre his father into a situation where he couldn't escape making decisions any more. Henri had been obsessed since his early youth with becoming Marquis de Beauvoir and this obsession had been growing like a cancer year after year. His cousin, the only obstacle in his way, needed to be removed – and he, Henri, would become Marquis or he'd rather die.

He hadn't expected though that the sheer anticipation of preparing the final demise of his bastard cousin would make the blood rush through his veins so fast, make him feel alive and vibrating with anticipation. The vision of hunting down his bastard cousin started to excite and arouse him.

He went up to his bedroom where his valet Jean was waiting already. He had chosen a good-looking and well-built mulatto who looked stunning in the de Beauvoir colours of gold and green. As had been his intention, he had become the creator of a new fashion in the noble circles of Paris where everybody now was trying desperately to find a coloured valet or chambermaid in order to compete in this mad race to be noticed and adhere to the latest whims of fashion.

Henri moved close to Jean and put his hand on his shoulder.

"Undress me and you!" Henri ordered his valet, who had tried to read the peculiar expression on Henri's face. "I want you now!"

Jean obliged the whims of his master without a change of countenance. He had learnt that any sign of displeasure would be punished severely and – even worse – he knew from past experience that Henri would often try to provoke him so he would have a pretence to punish him, as using the whip excited him even more.

Henri watched with satisfaction and mounting excitement the perfect body of his valet as he took off his shirt and breeches until he stood naked in front of him, like an antique statue of perfect proportions, and smooth skin the colour of bronze. When Jean approached the bed Henri spotted the tattoo of the lily of the convicts on his right shoulder. Henri loved this secret as it gave him absolute power over Jean: one word to the authorities and Jean would be deported back to the galleys. Jean was totally his, better than a mere valet, he was his slave forever.

31

Usually I tire of them after a short time, Henri thought, *but this one is different, he can still arouse me.*

His thoughts went back to the different valets who had been in his service during the past months and years. There had been one of them who had thought that the act of physical love would entitle him to become intimate and drop cheeky hints to the other servants. Well, he had surely regretted his insolence under Henri's whip before his half-dead body had been dispatched into the Seine. Henri still remembered how excited he had been when he had been handling the whip, and breathing hard, he reached his climax.

Jean saw that Henri had rolled over to sleep. Silently he took his clothes and dressed hurriedly. He sensed that Henri was in an explosive mood. He slipped out of the room as his master seemed to be asleep and went up the staircase to creep into the room he shared with the others in the servants' quarters. He felt the glances of the other footmen burning on his back. Of course they knew what had just happened and would make him suffer for it.

Jean reached the room and threw off his clothes. He felt an urgent need to wash. When he looked at the small metal plate that served as their mirror he stared into a handsome face with dark eyes where silent tears had started to run. "I hate him," he groaned, "I swear, I will kill this bastard one of these days."

Pierre had started to tremble and whispered, "Please don't look at me like this! I can live with the knowledge that my parents were outcasts but," and he looked with big pleading eyes at Armand, "please let's keep our friendship! It's all I have!"

Armand looked at him in a peculiar way. He carefully tucked the documents back into his waistcoat and grabbed Pierre's hands."You have to believe me, whatever I found in these documents wouldn't have changed our friendship. You have been my best friend since I arrived here and will remain my best friend regardless of the name you carry. Do you believe me?"

Pierre couldn't answer; the relief was simply too great. He just embraced Armand and after he had cleared his throat he was able to say more cheerfully, "All right, let's get on with it! I bet my father was the biggest gallows bird in Reims?"

"Not really," Armand retorted.

"Worse?" Pierre said. "The biggest in France, maybe?"

"Wrong again!" Armand said. "Did it never occur to you that your father could be an honourable person?"

"Sounds boring," Pierre retorted, but in reality he felt relieved, maybe the truth wasn't as bad as he had feared.

Armand's tone changed, he sounded very serious now. "Pierre, according to the documents I have in hand, your father was the Marquis Jean-Pierre de Beauvoir, Comte de Saumur, etc."

Pierre sat there and tried to understand. The echo of Armand's words was reaching his brain but inside he felt as if something was simply not connected. He heard the words but couldn't make any sense out of them. His father a Marquis? Impossible, he'd been a simple orphan at the monastery since he could remember: this was a dangerous and seductive dream but couldn't be the truth.

"Let me tell you what I can understand from the documents and try to explain to you the context," Armand continued. "It's extremely important that you understand all the details because, Pierre," he looked seriously into the blue eyes of Pierre, who was having difficulty in focusing on Armand's face, "I'm afraid you may be in danger."

"But why?" Pierre cried. "It's just not possible. I'm an orphan, my father couldn't have been a marquis, he would never have agreed to give me away to a monastery orphanage as if I were the child of a beggar. It's all wrong and doesn't make sense! Someone is joking there, it's not just that I'm not familiar with your aristocratic ways, but look at me," he continued and looked at himself in his drab orphanage tunic, "does this look noble in any way to you?"

He had worked himself into frenzy by now, his voice became shrill and Armand sensed that they would soon be discovered by the monks working in the garden close by if he didn't act quickly. He grabbed Pierre's arms, drew him close and put his hand over Pierre's mouth.

Pierre was still trying to struggle out of this iron grip, but Armand hissed into his ear, "Shut up, stupid. They'll find us here any minute; let me explain everything to you, *d'accord?*"

Pierre calmed down, nodded and Armand could finally remove his hand from his mouth to continue his explanation. "Your father, the Marquis de Beauvoir, was a very wealthy man owning big chunks of land in the Loire region. He had a younger brother, Louis Philippe de Beauvoir who has a son, your cousin Henri."

Pierre's head started to spin. He was catapulted from a situation where he had had no father or mother to a complete family with uncle and cousin in only two minutes. It was somehow unreal.

Armand continued looking around him to make sure that they weren't overheard. "Your father apparently fell in love with a foreign lady from England. Her name was Margaret de Neuville, a protestant," and involuntarily Armand made the sign of the cross to ward off evil.

"They married and you're the result. Luckily your mother confessed before her death and decided to join the true faith and become Catholic." Armand draw a deep breath and continued. "Your father, soon after your mother's death in childbed, also fell ill and knew that he was about to die. This part of the story I remember from the stories of my father: it was generally known that the brothers hated each other, all Paris was gossiping about their relationship at that time. Your father therefore suspected that your uncle would try everything to become the next Marquis, consequently your father was extremely worried about your safety. He wrote a letter to the Archbishop of Reims, the predecessor of our present one, as they had apparently been friends since their youth. A copy of this letter was stored in your archive box. He asked the archbishop to hide you in this orphanage under his authority and protect you until you became an adult and were ready to be acknowledged as his successor by the King."

Pierre felt a peculiar sensation of warmth and gratitude to this unknown mother who had given up her faith, probably to protect him, and to his father who had done everything he could to provide a safe haven for his son, knowing that his end was near. He looked into the sky – yes, they would be there, somewhere up in heaven and probably now eternally happy in the realm of God.

Armand was not letting him disappear off into a romantic daydream and continued in a matter-of-fact voice. "Then your father made a very dangerous decision, at least in my eyes. He made a last will confirming you as his sole heir – but," Armand's voice became sharp, "he added a paragraph, bequeathing to the Church and Crown most of the wealth that is not tied up in the fideicommissum in case you should die before you reach adulthood."

"What's a fideicom–" Pierre asked, having problems finishing the complicated word correctly.

"It's the part of your heritage that's tied to the title and cannot be given away, only the King could change these terms," Armand replied. He grinned. "That's the reason why in my case there is not a lot left for the youngest child, the majority of my father's heritage will go to my eldest brother."

"But that makes sense," Pierre protested hotly in defence of his father. "He wanted to protect me and make sure that the heritage will go to the church if my uncle tried to harm me!"

"As long as he could trust the Archbishop, yes," Armand retorted, "but now Cardinal Richelieu holds the reins in France and wherever he can see the smallest chance of making money for the government or the Church, he seizes every opportunity. If he knows about this will, we can order a tombstone for you already."

Pierre was shocked. "You're sure ?" he asked feebly. "We have to pray every Sunday for his health in church!"

"Well, better stop doing this," Armand said. "I could cite you at least a dozen cases where the Cardinal has his fingers in some pie or other. My father keeps track of this as he's convinced that even a great family like ours, the de Saint Pauls, must be careful nowadays. You cannot help but admire the Cardinal, he's simply brilliant but as dangerous as a poisonous snake!"

Pierre was trying to digest this overload of information but once more his brain seemed to have trouble processing all of these facts properly. He fully trusted Armand's knowledge of the world and politics. As he had stayed all his life in the monastery, he had no idea of real life in the world outside these walls – he'd never left Reims and visiting the cathedral and town on Sundays were considered to be the big events of his life so far – the only adventures he had ever experienced.

He understood instinctively that he needed to leave this confinement, this restricted world – not only because Armand was telling him that his life might be in danger, but also because he would need to grow up and learn, fast! If it was true that he was the heir and a Marquis in his own right, then better to be a good one and live up to it.

Armand couldn't read Pierre's thoughts but he found it amazing how his friend had taken the news and immediately he witnessed a change in Pierre. Pierre had never been just an average pupil in their school. He was very bright and had the looks and air of nobility about him – part of his charm had been that he had never been aware of this at all.

Now it seemed that the butterfly had left the cocoon. Pierre was radiating a new self-confidence, he seemed to have transformed from a pleasant boy to an aspiring man in a matter of minutes.

Heavens, thought Armand, *next time Marie sees him, he'd better watch it. She was already taken in by the humble boy, now she'll definitely fall for him.*

"So, you also think that I should leave fast, not only because of Brother Hieronymus," Pierre stated excitedly. "We'll need a plan then!"

"Better a good one," Armand answered, "as I'm pretty sure that you'll have your kind uncle, cousin and Richelieu's spies on your back in no time as soon you have finished school and can officially claim your inheritance. Just thinking about it is giving me goosebumps. You'll turn seventeen soon but you have no experience of how to travel, work, fight and earn your living. It's an impossible mission, actually!"

Pierre answered, putting on a brave face, "You're right, but maybe you don't need to rub it in all at once? Yes, I'm inexperienced, but you know, somehow I know that my parents will protect me from above. I know it sounds foolish but that's how I feel. Let's make a plan as to how I can get out of here fast and fool the monks for a day or two before they understand what's going on. It seems obvious that I have to get out of France fast and luckily the Spanish Netherlands are not too far away. As you said, my mother was English, let me try to go to England and try to get the support of my family there – doesn't this sound great, 'my family' – and maybe they're a less murderous bunch and may not try to kill me immediately?" Pierre looked at Armand and continued, "You know what upsets me most?"

"Not really," Armand replied.

"That I'll have to leave you! You're my only friend and just thinking that I have to leave you now, makes me really sad." Pierre's voice broke and he looked quickly aside, trying to hide his emotions.

"That's life." Armand looked at his friend with a smile full of affection. "Up to us to find a way to meet again."

They continued to discuss several ways of leaving the monastery. The school was not heavily guarded or supervised. As it was considered to be one of the most prestigious schools in France nobody had ever tried to escape before – it was difficult enough to be admitted. So no monk would really be concerned about a short absence if it happened once.

It did happen from time to time that a pupil would fall for the seduction of one of the sleazy and of course strictly forbidden taverns – the pupil would be punished and left in a cell for a week or so – but no one would become really very upset if the boy repented and kept to the rules afterwards.

Therefore Pierre and Armand concentrated more on the timing and how they could hide Pierre's absence for a day, at least in order to give him to time to reach the French border as fast as possible.

There was the question of money, finding his way to the Spanish Netherlands, which port to sail from for England, how to find and pay for a place on the boat, food that would be needed, and of course new clothes, as travelling in the monastery school robes would mean immediate detection. What identity should Pierre assume?

The bell for Compline started tolling all too soon and they rushed to the chapel, trying to look as normal as possible, although their heads were still spinning with thousands of questions and they had not really been able to come up with good answers.

*****

Pierre spent a horrid night on his straw mattress tossing and turning. He had put down some fresh straw recently and there were fewer creatures to torture him, but he tried to imagine what his father and mother could have looked like and then went through the endless list of questions he and Armand had discussed. As the hours moved on, he suddenly grew more and more afraid that he would wake up the next morning and find that it all had been just a mad dream, no heritage was waiting for him but that it was all an error and he, Pierre, would be the same orphan as before.

Pierre woke up the next morning at the bell for Matins and looked ghastly – some fleas must have found him after all, as his face was blotchy with flea bites. Nobody would have objected if he had gone straight to Brother Infirmarius. Pierre decided that it would be better though not to confront those alert eyes, so plunged his face into cold water and dragged himself to the chapel and continued the school routine. He saw Armand at breakfast and marvelled at how Armand could look his usual sunny self; no trace of any tortured conscience here, Pierre concluded with envy.

They were lucky, as Brother Hieronymus remained outside (probably extensively sampling the wines for his private inventory, Pierre thought) and therefore the lessons were given by an elderly clergyman named Raphael, who had a bald head, a prominent red nose and a large belly paying testimony to his love for food and wine. He was shortsighted to the extent that he couldn't see anything happening outside his immediate environs; his bewildered blue eyes kept blinking, giving him a somewhat unsure, baby-like appearance. Brother Raphael had no intention whatsoever of tiring himself by teaching what he considered to be

37

subjects unworthy of his academic attention and just let them copy some biblical phrases that came into his mind.

The pupils spent most of their time just pretending to scribble down something and generally a level of noise penetrated the school room that would have been unheard of and definitely not tolerated under the supervision of the stern Brother Hieronymus, but it didn't seem to bother Brother Raphael.

As they didn't want to draw any attention from their classmates to their discussion, Armand and Pierre came forward to Brother Raphael and volunteered to do some work in the hospital garden. Their teacher was inexperienced or indolent enough to accept this display of sudden diligence without suspicion and accepted their request, praising their commitment to a good cause. This provided of course a perfect opportunity to discuss their plans, undisturbed by their nosy classmates.

Saturday evening seemed to be the ideal timing for Pierre to escape, as on Sundays the tight routine and supervision of the school was interrupted by their Sunday rest and the usual excursion to the cathedral and it was only by Sunday evening that their dormitories would be checked and his absence noticed. They needed to find a way to cover his absence for Saturday evening and this could possibly be arranged if Pierre volunteered to stay for the vigil on Saturday night in the chapel after Compline, thus his absence in the dormitory would be accounted for.

They continued to discuss different options, working busily all the time, as Brother Infirmarius was watching with suspicion his two unexpected but welcome volunteers; being a man of science he didn't believe in easy miracles and this sudden show of diligence smelled fishy to him.

On Wednesday, school routine had not yet resumed. It was reported that Brother Hieronymus had fallen ill and would come back earliest Friday to teach his class. Pierre giggled as he could imagine the illness of Brother Hieronymus and pictured him lying snoring on a large but empty barrel of wine.

Thus they were still in their usual classroom, but once again under the supervision of baby-faced Brother Raphael when a young monk entered and requested the honourable Armand de Saint Paul to join him at the urgent request of the Abbot. Pierre looked surprised and tried to get some indication from his friend but Armand was already hurrying towards the door and didn't look back.

This would be the last he saw of his friend. Armand neither appeared for prayers in the chapel nor for meals. Pierre's mind was tortured by what could have happened to his friend and in his misery he went to see Brother Infirmarius, hoping that he could give him some news.

After some hesitation Brother Infirmarius melted under Pierre's pleading eyes and was willing to share his knowledge. Yes, indeed the brother had heard exciting news that a messenger, a maid of Armand's cousin, had called on the school and presented the Abbot with a letter bearing the seal of Armand's father, the Marquis de Saint Paul, practically ordering Armand's immediate return back home. The brother guessed that a close member of the family must have fallen seriously ill to justify such urgent and immediate summons but of course the Abbot had accepted immediately, as no one would dare to contradict the orders of the head of the influential de Saint Paul family. Armand had left accompanied by the maid, as she had informed the Abbot that a coach would already be waiting for him at his cousin's home.

Pierre thanked the brother and withdrew to the chapel, pretending to wish to pray for Armand. He was utterly shocked. He was on his own now and felt as if someone had cut off his right arm. He felt hurt to a point where there were no more tears that he could shed. Armand had given him precise instructions and been kind enough to insist that he should accept some money from him to be able to buy some food and shelter but this sudden departure made him feel utterly miserable. He had dreaded the moment of saying goodbye to Armand but his sudden disappearance without any opportunity to share some last words was just too painful.

Pierre dragged himself through the following days and as Friday approached they were back to the normal routine of the dreaded classes of Brother Hieronymus. Hieronymus of course had heard about Armand's departure and had relished the news. During class his stick came down several times on the back of Pierre, who looked exhausted and seemed incapable of concentrating on any task.

When class was finished and Pierre wanted to join his classmates to go to the refectory Hieronymus signalled him to sit down and wait. This was not a good sign; Pierre's heart sank.

When the classroom was empty Brother Hieronymus made him move closer and approaching his face he hissed, "I happened to leave Reims last Sunday and passed by the church of St Rémy. I couldn't believe my eyes when I saw you and your friend Armand in conversation with a young lady far away from the monastery to where you were supposed to have returned. You thus breached several rules of our monastery!"

He paused to see the effect of his speech before he continued. "Of course it was my Christian duty to report this misconduct to the Abbot."

Pierre couldn't tell if it was the content of this accusation or the horrible smell that emanated from the mouth close to him but he was starting to feel sick and had to fight hard not to vomit right there in front of the teacher.

Brother Hieronymus eyed him maliciously. He was happy at the effect his announcement was having on Pierre – the boy's resistance seemed to be melting and he could see Pierre's hands gripping the desk next to him with all his force, trying to steady himself.

I just need to push a bit further and he'll break, he'll be mine after all, Hieronymus thought, becoming excited.

Aloud he continued his speech, now assuming a pious pose. "Our beloved and wise Abbot has decided to be lenient as this is your first major failing. You may not have any lunch or dinner today in the refectory and I will accompany you to the penitence cell where you'll stay for a week in isolation with prayers and where you'll be expected to keep fast. This will give you the opportunity to purify your soul from the temptations of the devil."

He gave a long pause. "But you'll be spared whipping if you obey and show true remorse. The Abbot has decided that I shall be your spiritual guidance during this week to bring you back to the path of virtue of our Holy Church."

The trumpets shattering the walls of Jericho could not have had any different effect, Pierre thought. So this was it. No chance of escaping this Sunday as he would be sitting in a bolted cell at the mercy of Brother Hieronymus who'd be trying to put his sticky fingers all over him – sitting in the cell, probably, without a morsel of food until he gave in.

His first reaction was total panic and his eyes darted left and right to see if he had any opportunity to bolt and run. Then he felt a cold rage streaming through him with an intensity that he had never felt before. *If Armand is right, I'm the true Marquis de Beauvoir. I'll not show any fear or be intimidated by this piece of excrement. Before he gets me, I'll kill him to preserve the honour of my family*, and he clenched his fist until it hurt.

Brother Hieronymus had moved closer still and had lifted his hand to pat Pierre's shoulder. His smiling face turned down to look into Pierre's eyes but the smile froze on his face. He had expected eyes full of tears and fear, pleading for mercy but to his great annoyance those lovely blue eyes had turned into steely pools of ice and rage.

His hand recoiled quickly and his face became a stern noncommittal mask. "Let's go," he said. "And please remember that I will not tolerate any disobedience. You have just committed the sin of pride and believe me, my Son, our Church has plenty of means to break those who stray from the path of the true faith!"

Pierre didn't comment on this thinly veiled threat and just followed his teacher in a pretence of obedience to the cells that were reserved for the pupils or monks who had to serve their penance.

*****

Pierre sat down on the low bedstead that was covered with filthy blankets and looked around what would be his new home for the next week – or more. He noticed a desk and a worn prie-dieu, a small window with iron bars, and lime-plastered walls with a crucifix as sole decoration unless someone regarded the dirty chamber pot as such. The door squeaked in a melancholic manner when Brother Hieronymus closed and bolted it with probably more care and noise than would have been necessary, just to make sure that his rebellious pupil got the message that the key to becoming free or staying here was definitely in his hands.

Pierre looked around at the dim surroundings. He could see at first glance that the door and walls were well maintained and the bars of the small window were solid. There was no possibility of escaping from here unless a miracle happened.

Pierre had kept a brave face until now but here in the darkness the anger that had kept him strong was abating. He made a short but urgent prayer to his unknown parents to help him and then he gave himself over to a feeling of complete and utter misery.

It would have been difficult to measure time for any prisoner in the cell if it had not been for the regular tolling of the chapel bells that called the monks to the different services complying with the rigid routine of the monastery. When Pierre recognized the bells of Compline he banged at his door and finally he heard a shuffling noise of approaching feet.

An old monk appeared with a stern and disapproving face. "You're supposed to stay silent and repent," the monk said in an irritated voice. He knew these pupils were always a source of trouble. Pierre assumed a humble posture and in a low and modest tone he asked if the revered Brother would have the extraordinary kindness to bring him a prayer book and a candle as he would like to spend the night praying and repenting.

The monk was visibly moved by this unexpected request that showed the pupil's urge to repent and the earnest and eager face that looked at him with angelic blue eyes. After a short deliberation he could find no reason to object and even brought him some fresh water, together with an unexpected but very welcome piece of bread, for which Pierre thanked him profusely.

When the door was closed and the shuffling noise disappeared Pierre used the candle to inspect his bedstead with disgust, chewed the bread slowly and thankfully (at least one part of his prayer had been answered immediately, he chuckled) and then decided it would be better to read aloud some prayers so as to make his show of penitence credible.

He didn't know if it was the effect of the monotonous prayers or the general exhaustion of this crazy week that had turned his life upside down but he fell asleep almost immediately whilst he was still kneeling on the prie-dieu.

The old monk who looked later once more through the peephole in the door into the cell was moved when he saw this blond boy looking like an angel leaning at the desk in the cell and still holding the book of prayers firmly in his hand. Most pupils that were brought here had been drunk, protesting loudly or sulking. They'd stay most of their time sleeping in their bed, but this one was different and he decided to give a positive report to the Abbot and his teacher. Typical of Hieronymus to have a go at the wrong one, he thought.

Saturday morning came and when the screeching noises of the moving bolts and hinges announced the opening of the cell door, Brother Hieronymus appeared to visit Pierre. To his annoyance, he found Pierre in surprisingly good spirits, ignoring the stale bread that he had brought along and found it difficult to approach Pierre in the way he had planned. On the surface Pierre was an example of virtue and obedience but somehow Hieronymus sensed that his will was not yet broken and Pierre managed to keep him at a distance.

Pierre was repelled by everything Hieronymus represented for him. To make things worse, the nauseating smell of his bad breath blended in the confinement of the small cell with the strong body odour that was testimony to Brother Hieronymus's belief that personal hygiene was the work of the devil and should be avoided by any means. By the time Brother Hieronymus had left, Pierre was close to committing murder and clung to the bars of the window to inhale some fresh air, trying to come back to his senses.

The day passed without further surprises and Pierre slowly but surely started to despair. Today was the day that Armand had planned for his escape. He was stuck in this cell and he didn't know if he could manage another visit from Brother Hieronymus without becoming violent or hysterical. He didn't know what to do; he desperately missed Armand and his sound advice and common sense.

He could only hope to lull his guard into some false security and escape at the first chance, but when the door opened in the afternoon his heart sank, as his new prison warden was yet a different monk, whom he had only seen from afar before and who was much younger and seemed more alert. The new monk brought water and some mush; Pierre interpreted the mere fact that all of a sudden he was allowed to have food as a sign that his show of penitence had been successful and had been brought to the attention of the Abbot.

The monk hesitated for a moment and cleared his throat before he started to speak. "It has been brought to the attention of our gracious Father Abbot that you had already requested to keep a night vigil tonight, before your failings had been reported to him. It has also been brought to his attention that you have shown true penitence since yesterday and the Abbot has therefore decided to show clemency. As Saint Augustine said: 'Forgiveness is the remission of sins'. He thus grants you the favour to hold the vigil tonight so as to allow you to pray in the holy chapel and purify your soul. Brother Raphael will come tonight to fetch you and keep the night vigil with you."

Tears of relief sprang to Pierre's eyes and the monk was deeply moved by this display of true penitence.

Pierre couldn't believe it. No need to knock on the head of his new warden or slimy Brother Hieronymus, he would simply stand up and walk out of his prison!

Everybody in school knew Brother Raphael had a habit of drinking a good bottle of wine or two for dinner – with the exception of the Abbot apparently – and therefore at night not even an earthquake could wake him. Actually most of Pierre's classmates – and Armand of course – timed their nightly forays into the taverns of Reims precisely to coincide with the nights that Brother Raphael was on duty.

One problem to deal with would be the fact that his absence would be detected the next morning, but he'd have to cope with that. This was his one and only chance to escape before he was carried away by his hate and frustration and ended up being violent towards his teacher. Not that killing Brother Hieronymus would be a great loss to mankind, Pierre thought, grinning to himself, but it would be most inconvenient to end up in the hands of an executioner just for having killed vermin like Brother Hieronymus – and not a glorious end for someone who wanted to become a future Marquis.

The hours passed so slowly that Pierre longed to scream or bang on his desk to fight the frustration of waiting patiently. He tried to remember all the details of the instructions Armand had given to him before he had left so suddenly. Luckily he had kept Armand's money hidden in his garments and nobody had taken the trouble to search him. He would need to invent a good story as to why he was wearing a robe of the monastery school, inventing a dying relative maybe, but it would be safer to travel at night first, Pierre decided. With the optimism of youth he looked forward to having a great adventure and thought it petty-minded to worry about anything that could happen to him on his way to England. Seeing liberty approaching, he was ready to take on the whole world if necessary.

*****

Night had started to fall when finally, the door of his cell was opened by the monk serving as his warden, together with Brother Raphael who had come to fetch him. Pierre could smell with satisfaction that at least the first bottle of wine had been consumed already. Brother Raphael's eyes always looked unfocused because of his extreme short-sightedness but now they were definitely lost in space somewhere and the monk looked more than ever like a fat, grey mole – one with a very pink face.

They walked to the chapel together and as soon as they entered Pierre kneeled in front of one of the side altars close to the exit explaining to Raphael that he wanted to ask this saint for special help in his search for true penitence. Then their conversation ceased and they started the vigil prayers. Pierre was amazed to see that Brother Raphael did not go through the prayers mechanically as so many monks did just to follow the expected routine but he seemed to become deeply absorbed in a display of genuine faith.

Time moved on and slowly Pierre started to become impatient. By now his knees were hurting like hell (if such a comparison might be used in a chapel), his back was longing for a chair or a bed and his eyes starting to burn from fatigue and the smoke of the candles and the lingering fumes of incense.

Carefully he moved his head to see if the time was ripe, only to find that a second monk had come and was kneeling in front of the altar to the Virgin Mary. *Another complication,* Pierre thought wearily, *will this never end?*

He continued a while longer in his kneeling pose and then decided to throw himself flat on his belly so as to pretend to be in total dedication and prayer.

This feels so good, he thought, as the weight was lifted off his knees and his back could stretch. He heard the chapel door closing, so either the next monk had entered the chapel or the second monk had left.

He glanced carefully around him pretending to move back to his kneeling pose. To his great relief he saw that indeed the other monk had left. He got up and when he was standing he could hear Brother Raphael's voice: "Why are you standing, my Son?"

"I would like to pray to Saint Anne now, Father," Pierre answered. "I was feeling unwell recently and Brother Infirmarius told me I should pray to her in cases of pain in the stomach," and to himself he added, *and her altar is also closer to the door.*

The candles had continued burning down and sending their wisps of smoke into the chapel when Pierre heard a sound that was pure music to his ears. Brother Raphael had started to snore.

It's now or never, Pierre decided. He crawled slowly to the exit and inch by inch opened the chapel door, trying to make sure the squeaking noise of the hinges would not wake up the monk who lay sprawled over the bench, smiling innocently in his sleep.

"Hope to see all of you never again." Pierre spoke softly as he extricated himself slowly from the narrow doorway, afraid to open the door completely. He shut it with the same care. Then he drew a deep breath of the refreshing night air that carried all the wonderful fragrances of the approaching summer.

Pierre felt newly born, ready to embrace the whole world – freedom and adventure were waiting for him!

A bright moon was shining in the sky, which was something of a mixed blessing. The bright light made it much easier to find the route Armand had explained to him but there was a risk he would be detected much faster. Pierre moved cautiously, using the thick shrubs and bushes as cover down through the garden of the hospital. All schoolboys knew that the trees at the back would provide an easy climb over the walls of the cloister which were in urgent need of repair, as they had been neglected for many years.

Pierre quickly grabbed a branch and climbed up the apple tree the monks had lovingly planted and pruned in this part of the garden and jumped on top of the wall. Then he climbed down, thankful that plenty of stones in the wall had yielded and made it easy to find footholds in the gaps.

When he reached the street he tried to remember the directions that Armand had given to him. Reims was by no means as densely populated as a big city like Paris and it still contained many gardens inside its city walls. The city itself was surrounded by broad moats and connected to a river that made it impossible to leave without passing through the heavily guarded city gates.

Armand had instructed him to use the gardens as cover and then go straight to a city tavern that he frequented from time to time. The tavern was held by a couple, the wife looking after the tavern (and probably in her spare time after the well-being of some of her male guests…) and her husband trading wine with the surrounding vineyards of the Champagne region, famous for their fruity white wines the colour of straw.

Unusually, her husband would be leaving this Sunday with his wagon full of barrels of wine, as festivities in honour of one of the local saints would be held in a small village in the north and he was hopeful of doing some good business on this occasion.

Luckily Pierre knew Reims well from their visits on Sundays to the different churches and fairs in the past and was able to find the tavern easily. The streets were dark and empty and only the furious barking of some dogs interrupted the silence. The shutters of the windows were tightly closed to prevent entry of unwanted visitors. Pierre prayed that those stupid barking dogs would not arouse the city night watch and ducked even more into the darkness of the shadows of the houses that lined the narrow streets.

His luck held and he arrived at the tavern unharmed where he saw that some dim lights were still shining. Armand had instructed him not to go into the tavern but to enter the courtyard where the barn could be found, already equipped with a loaded wagon where he was to hide under the covers.

Armand had told him that he knew from the innkeeper's wife that her husband entertained excellent relations with the city guards who'd drop by regularly to get a free glass of wine – or preferably two. It was therefore quite safe to assume that any search of the innkeeper's wagon at the gate would be swift and superficial, no soldier would risk endangering his supply of free wine.

Pierre was happy that his journey until now had been smooth and gave a grateful thought to Armand who had hatched this plan. The strain of the last few days and his narrow escape were starting to take their toll and he was feeling dead-tired, longing desperately to lie down and get some sleep.

Cautiously he opened the door of the barn and slid into the dark interior. He hoped that his eyes would be able to make out some objects after having time to adapt, as he was afraid of bumping into some stray objects and making a noise that might betray him, or of hurting himself.

As he couldn't really see anything he extended his hands and tried to feel his way, slowly touching the objects in his path towards the large, dark shadow of a wagon in the back that he had seen when the door was still open.

He bumped his head against something that was probably a manger on the wall, and when he had rubbed his hurting head his fingers detected a new object. He touched it and it felt strangely warm and familiar, actually like something human, and before he could speculate any further, a hand reaching for him from the darkness pressed hard on his mouth and silenced his cry. A grip of iron held him as if in a vice, with absolutely no hope of escape. In his surprise and shock Pierre didn't even feel the heavy blow that sent him sprawling to the ground.

THE HUNT IS ON

Louis Philippe de Beauvoir sat in his carriage on his way back to the Palais de Beauvoir sweating profusely. It may well be said that men perspire and only horses sweat, but his lace collar was completely soaked and although he used a silk scarf to dab off the beads of perspiration that seemed to be forming ceaselessly on his head, small rivers of sweat were running down his back leaving dark stains on his overcoat and on the expensive green-gold velvet upholstery. He felt utterly miserable.

It was not only the heat of the first real sunny and hot day in Paris in late spring that was turning the inside of his carriage into a Turkish bath; Louis Philippe was a desperate man.

Knowing that Henri would not relent until his father obtained the money to strike a bargain with Cardinal Richelieu (and still shuddering when he thought about his murderous expression), Louis Philippe had decided to call for his coach and visit the Italian family bankers, a venerable institution that had been in charge of the de Beauvoir finances for generations.

He had been greeted with all the respect and protocol due to a member of one of the noble houses of France but when Louis Philippe had started to explain his request – in very diplomatic terms, as he thought – the elegant Italian banker sitting in front of him in a salon furnished expensively according to the latest fashion had shut up like an oyster.

"Oh, of course, I would *love* to serve the de Beauvoir family as we have done for generations. Service for our future Marquis is our true dedication," the elegant banker said with an exaggerated Italian accent although he was raised in Paris and probably spoke French better than most Parisians ever could. "But times are extremely difficult at the moment. The Cardinal Richelieu, God bless him of course, has levied so many new taxes on our trade with Italy lately that our humble bank could not raise 50,000 livres at the moment unless mortgages could be signed by the legal heir, not even a fraction of this, I'm afraid."

The banker's air had been one of distress, but Louis Philippe had understood the true message; the bank would not support any venture that was designed to undermine the situation of the legal heir, and they clearly felt committed to protect the family heritage.

Louis Philippe had managed to keep a straight face, deploring as well the bad times and wishing for better ones once they met again.

Back in his elegant townhouse he immediately stormed into the library and drained two glasses of the refreshing white wine from the famous family estates on the Loire River.

47

Then he sat down to think about a new plan to raise the money.

As all the Italian bankers would stick together he had no illusions at all that any other bank might accept his request. Word would be spreading fast that he was broke. So there was only one alternative left, he had to go to the Jews. Lending money was considered to be dirty business; no French citizen of acceptable reputation would lower himself to this kind of business – at least not officially.

The next day Louis Philippe dispatched a footman to a Jewish banker who had been recommended to him, to prepare the appointment and announce his coming. There were two sorts of Jewish lenders; the one he was going to see catered exclusively for the upper classes and was reputed to be as rich as Croesus.

Louis Philippe had arrived in front of the deceptively plain-looking house and was ushered in by a dark, serious-looking young lady into an office that was stuffed with all sorts of rolls of parchment, books and chests. The walls were painted in a Burgundy red. In the back of the stuffy room sat an old man clad in black silk with the dark eyes and the prominent nose typical of his people.

Louis Philippe had been educated with the conviction that Jews were part of the *canaille*, lower-class inferior beings, not worthy of the attention of the noble classes – they were people to be used and better quickly forgotten. Consequently he was expecting that the old Jew sitting in front of him should feel honoured merely by his presence and eager to do business with the noble house of de Beauvoir.

He brought his request forward with his usual arrogance but was startled by the response. The old man fixed him coldly with a self-assured and shrewd look. Louis Philippe had the uneasy feeling that his antagonist was not impressed at all by his noble airs.

He's the same type as the Cardinal, flashed through Louis Philippe's mind and he suddenly started to become nervous. *He'll not do anything just to please anybody; if he lends me any money it'll be to make more money, he doesn't care at all about my story or my title.*

The Jew didn't speak for some time and waited patiently until Louis Philippe was running out of words. When he started to reply, it was with a pleasant and educated voice; it would have been difficult to place his accent, as he could have come from the German empire, Spain, Antwerp or even Italy. Jewish money was international.

"You tell me that our famous Cardinal is supporting your quest if you pay 50,000 in advance?" The old man chuckled and continued. "Yes, this seems very much like him. He always needs money for his various… charities." He dwelt for longer on the word 'charities' than was necessary and again seemed to be highly amused at his private joke.

"We can of course provide you with the necessary means," he continued in a businesslike manner, "but there will be the question of securities that must be granted to ensure that repayment will be made."

When he started to list his terms, Louis Philippe felt an urgent need to strangle his host. The Jew had apparently prepared well for this meeting in advance and knew down to the tiniest detail all information about the de Beauvoir income, his personal debts and mortgages, probably also about his style of living. He also mentioned Henri's staggering debts – an amount that seemed much higher than anything Henri had ever deemed necessary to tell him. His host listed from memory the sole estates that had remained in Louis Philippe's full possession, those few precious estates that had been providing his daily income so far and had not yet been mortgaged. He claimed them all and on top asked for the personal guarantee of Louis Philippe and his son.

Interest would be 25 per cent per year with a 10 per cent fixed fee. The Jew's voice became cold and distant. The deal would have to be accepted thus or he would regrettably be unable to serve him.

Louis Philippe had never been good with numbers but even to his untrained mind this sounded outrageously expensive. He also was uncomfortably aware that the roles had been switched; the Jew had made it clear that his title and ancestry were worth nothing; only money ruled the world.

Louis Philippe tried to keep a straight face and answered haughtily that he would need to consider the deal and might consider whether or not to revert later. The old man didn't seem to mind this answer at all and bade him a polite farewell, mentioning that he'd be out of the city next week, so if there were any urgency, formalities would need to be concluded tomorrow, in fact.

As soon as Louis Philippe had left, the old Jew called his niece into the office. "Just as the Cardinal informed us, he's completely broke and needs the money fast. We will of course share the income, the Cardinal has always been fair with us and we'll pay him what's due."

His niece smiled and nodded; yes, this had been easy business for them.

Their business was booming: the Cardinal sent them the victims and most could be plucked easily. The Cardinal would have made a great Jew, the old man thought, and had to laugh at his own joke.

*****

A very depressed Louis Philippe had returned to his gilded carriage that had remained waiting for him in front of the house he just had left. Now he was sitting inside, sweating with heat and frustration. If he didn't accept the deal, he'd lose the heritage of his brother and his son would manage to ruin him in no time; if he did accept, and Henri didn't lay his hands fast on his nephew, the Jew would seize his last free estates and his life would be ended living in poverty somewhere in the provinces far from Paris.

He dragged himself into the study and rang for a footman to bring him refreshments; Louis Philippe craved wine, he felt completely parched and needed a drink to help digest this unpleasant experience. By the time Henri arrived, his father had already emptied two crystal decanters of wine and had reached a state of drunken self-pity.

Henri looked at his father and his handsome face froze into a mask of hateful contempt. He ordered Jean, who had entered the room behind him, to immediately bring a bucket of cold water.

Jean arrived quickly with the water, wondering what he was about to witness now. Before Jean had finished his train of thought, Henri had already seized the bucket and emptied it in one go above his father's head, regardless that he was about to ruin the expensive brocade upholstery and silk cushions of the armchair.

Louis Philippe started to wail hysterically but Henri slapped his face hard. His father sat frozen in stunned silence and when Henri turned to dismiss Jean he saw that his valet had taken the initiative and left the room already.

He's a really smart servant, Henri thought, *but hopefully not too smart.*

He turned back to look at his father who was watching him like a rabbit transfixed by a snake. Louis Philippe's hair was dripping and Henri saw with dismay that his father must had applied some make up as stains of red and black ran down his cheeks. He looked like a clown.

What a great Marquis you'll make! Henri thought scornfully, but as he could smell his father's panic Henri decided that he'd done enough today to show his father who was the real master in this house and changed his tactics.

"Now tell me in clear words, what happened to put you in such a state? Did you get the money finally?"

Louis Philippe managed to restore himself to some form of dignity and told Henri about the two encounters he had experienced, first with their Italian banker and then with the Jew. Henri sneered when he heard the story but he didn't seem to be shocked by the Jew's terms.

He looked at his father with contempt. "You're not only naïve, you're downright stupid," he said in an even voice, not even deeming his father worth his becoming angry any more. "We're all puppets on strings in a game directed by Richelieu. The great Cardinal thinks he can use us as he fancies. Richelieu will make vast sums of money in any case: if we sign the documents now he receives 50,000 upfront, and once we succeed he'll blackmail us for even more. I bet that he'll also bleed the Jew!"

50

His father looked at him with huge terror-stricken eyes – it seemed so obvious and he could see no way out. Henri only gave a short laugh and continued; fighting against the Cardinal only seemed to arouse him.

"But His Eminence does not understand that I can also play my cards – and play them well. If the Jew tries to seize our estates, his beautiful niece will suddenly disappear and if I feel kind enough, the Jew will even get back two of them: a niece with a child, maybe even a blonde child, definitely not a Jewish one."

His cold eyes were glowing now with anticipation. "And as for the Cardinal," he said softly, "he's known to be very sick and I know plenty of people who won't hesitate to make his passage to heaven as swift as possible."

During this discourse he had taken his sword unawares and caressed the blade lovingly. "I'm ready to fight," he continued. "Sign what must be signed in your own name and I'll sign in my name but get me the money fast, I'll prepare in the meantime a…" He paused. "Well, let's call it a nice little hunting holiday!"

Henri uttered a short laugh and strode out of the room, the enviable picture of a proud and beautiful gentleman. His father closed his eyes in pain. If the devil was beautiful, his son could impersonate him in every respect!

Louis Philippe had lost all illusions and wished he could turn back the wheel of time but now he himself had become a puppet on strings – torn between his son and the Cardinal.

*****

The following days were filled by all sorts of activities, shuttling back and forth from notary offices to his own palace and the Jew's house. After the requested documents had been signed the Jew handed him a letter of exchange – ironically drawn on the same Italian bank that had pretended not to be in possession of enough funds, but Louis Philippe decided to ignore this fact and suffer his humiliation in secret.

He immediately made an appointment with Brother Joseph in the Cardinal's palace as Richelieu had suggested during their last encounter. This time Louis Philippe was agreeably surprised by the efficiency of the Cardinal's household. No wonder he was a great administrator of the kingdom.

He didn't need to wait; his visit had been anticipated and the monk merely checked the authenticity of the banker's letter promising to pay 50,000 livres in gold to the bearer of the document and handed Louis Philippe in return a short document in an envelope.

Louis Philippe de Beauvoir took his leave and settled in his luxurious carriage. Because of the dust and dirt of Paris the windows remained closed but once again it became uncomfortably hot inside and he longed for some fresh air. How much time he had lately spent driving back and forth!

He leaned back in the cushions of the swaying carriage and opened carefully the envelope. It contained the full name of his nephew (Pierre, of course, like his grandfather) and the address of a monastery school in Reims. When Louis Philippe saw the documents he couldn't believe his eyes. He had just spent the rest of his fortune in acquiring an address that he could have guessed himself. Of course, it had to be Reims, his brother's best friend had become the Archbishop of Reims shortly before his nephew had been born.

The blood suddenly seemed to rush to his head, Louis Philippe's face turned crimson and he urgently needed air and some water. He moved forward to open the window as his breathing had become heavy but his body wouldn't follow. He sank bank into the cushions, still holding the envelope with an iron grip.

Henri had spent the last hours pacing up and down the library impatiently listening for the noise of an approaching carriage. He already wore his travelling boots and the wide trousers made fashionable by the king's Musketeers and just a lightly quilted waistcoat as he intended to ride on his own, only accompanied by his favourite valet in order to be able to progress fast. He had already loaded his pistols (a task he always undertook personally), and his dagger and sword were ready.

At last Henri heard the carriage grinding to a halt on the cobbled stones and he expected his father to come up the staircase any minute, wheezing and puffing as had become his habit during the last few days; he seemed to be aging quickly.

Instead Henri heard some commotion downstairs, light footsteps flying up the staircase and a young pageboy with wide frightened eyes rushed in pleading him to come down fast: "His lordship is very ill!"

Henri told him to be silent and shut his mouth and went swiftly down the long and elegant marble staircase that adorned the entrance hall. Through the open door he noticed three footmen who were trying to drag his father out of the carriage, a fourth coming forward to join them and carry his heavy father inside the house. Henri looked at the red disfigured face and ordered the young pageboy to go and fetch the doctor immediately.

His father was brought upstairs into his bedroom, undressed and refreshed, as from the babbling sounds that were coming out of his mouth his valet seemed to be able to discern the word "water".

Henri swiftly and efficiently took command of the situation. The household was in total uproar but was soon calmed down and went back to some sort of routine whilst waiting for the doctor to arrive.

It took a good hour before the doctor's carriage arrived in the driveway and the physician, who looked like a black crow, was ushered immediately into Louis Philippe's bedroom where he found his patient lying in splendour in a huge bedroom, the curtains drawn to shut out the harmful daylight.

The room was lit by candlelight, therefore the atmosphere and the smell resembled a church rather than a bedroom. The doctor was an adherent of the theory of bad humours being the source of all evil and decided to bleed Louis Philippe profusely to cleanse the blood. He left some dubious-looking medicines and recommended prayers to restore the health of his noble patient.

Henri followed the procedures patiently. He didn't believe for a minute that any of the doctor's actions would be helpful but he didn't care at all; it only seemed important that his servants saw with their own eyes and could testify that he had fulfilled all filial duties expected in such circumstances. He even offered to keep night watch in turn with his father's old valet who was moved to tears, seeing his master lying paralysed.

Thus it was around midnight that Henri took over his night watch and sat close to his father's face. Soon after Henri had installed himself close to his father's head, he heard his father sigh, then he opened his eyes with a visible effort and recognized his son. Henri saw his father's eyes filling with fear and tears. Henri loathed him more than ever.

"Do you want water?" he asked with false friendliness. Louis Philippe rolled his eyes and made a small movement of the head to show his consent.

Henri stood up, looked carefully around and checked that nobody could overhear or see them. When he was satisfied they were alone with no witnesses around, he walked back to the bed, lowered his head next to his father's ear and whispered softly, "I'll make sure that you won't ever feel thirsty again," and before Louis Philippe had understood the true meaning of his son's statement a cushion was pressed to his face, slowly suffocating him until his spasms ceased and he became limp.

Henri looked at the corpse of his father almost dispassionately; this sudden turn of events had been a gift from heaven for him. He had wanted to get rid of his father badly – especially now that he felt so close to gaining his heritage – and fate had handed him a unique opportunity on a golden platter. It had just needed the resolve to do it.

A pity that his departure would be delayed now; he would have to play the grieving and dutiful son for some days. Then he would withdraw in deepest sorrow and mourning from public view and be able to pursue the hunt for his bastard cousin. Henri had found the precious address on the slip of crumpled paper his father had held in an iron grip when he had been brought into the house by the footmen and Henri had tucked the paper carefully into his breeches.

He turned to arrange his father's body in a more natural position and decided to wait another hour or so before rousing the household to inform them that his dear and beloved father had passed away.

Jean had been watching him through the keyhole the whole time. He knew his master and had wondered why he was playing the dutiful son, staying awake to watch over him. Henri had always despised his father – the servants' quarters were brimming with gossip about their relationship.

Jean felt disgusted but not the least surprised. Henri was a beast. If only one day justice would prevail!

*****

Time passed quickly with the preparations for the funeral of Louis Philippe de Beauvoir, endless visits of relatives and friends to pay their condolences to his son, documents that needed to be signed regarding the heritage and a visit to the royal court in order to pay his respects to the King, the Queen, and of course, the Cardinal.

Generally, his portrayal of a deeply mourning son was impeccably played and passed off well, and only a few of his close friends allowed themselves a veiled allusion to the convenience of the timely passing away of the father he had always hated.

Henri was somewhat unsettled after his meeting with Cardinal Richelieu. The Cardinal didn't say anything concrete or humiliating but looked at him with his piercing dark eyes and let it clearly be understood that the timely parting of his father was probably very useful to Henri, wishing him good luck, ironically at least, in finding his cousin in good health. "We all know that fate can strike at any minute, don't we?" he added.

*****

A good week later, Henri started to pack for his expedition. He had decided first to ride north in the direction of Amiens, accompanied only by a groom. Henri had several good friends from his gaming and drinking forays up there and they would cover his traces if necessary in case he should have to go there and hide for some time once his mission was finished.

To his great relief and pleasant surprise Jean found himself left behind in Paris. Henri had decided secretly that Jean's dark skin made him too easily recognizable if ever he had to operate undercover. He also reckoned that he might have to kill his footman after his mission was concluded successfully to ensure full confidentiality and thought Jean still to be too valuable and exciting a toy to be sacrificed during this mission.

54

Henri's journey to Amiens and Reims went smoothly. The weather had remained pleasant and warm and the fields stretched like an endless emerald sea of grain and flowers already in full bloom. Blazing red poppies fought with the intense blue of cornflowers, while white daisies and the yellow dots of buttercups added their pleasant colours to the peaceful picture.

But the two horsemen had no eyes for the abundance of beauty Mother Nature was unfurling around them. They were riding fast, their watchful eyes continuously checking the roads and scanning their surroundings to make sure that no bandits could follow or prepare an ambush, as the two lone horsemen would present an ideal target.

They only stopped and rested when they felt that the horses needed a break or when night started to fall, asking for shelter in the nearest inn on the road. Riding through the northern provinces of France was actually quite pleasant and only short spells of rain troubled them from time to time.

Once they had left Amiens, they headed south-east to the city of Reims. Henri saw no need for any disguise at the moment. He had decided to present himself officially with the letter of recommendation signed by Cardinal Richelieu to the Abbot of the monastery school. Only then would he decide his course of action – once he had set eyes on his victim and once he'd been able to assess the surroundings.

He was sure that this boy would be no serious match for him; his major concern was to find an elegant way to get rid of his cousin, making sure that the boy's fatal accident couldn't be traced back to him. Being a natural gambler, Henri didn't worry at all – his luck would hold, he was sure.

Finally the skyline of Reims appeared, still far away but the towers of the cathedral and St Rémy's could be distinguished as soon as they came close. They slowed down once they reached the impressive fortifications of the city walls, surrounded by a broad moat, and entered the city through the western gates.

Brother Joseph had recommended a guesthouse of good quality with reasonable prices close to the cathedral and Henri decided to stop there to rest and refresh themselves, and then to seek audience with the Abbot the following day. From his experience it always paid to look well-groomed and every inch the gentleman when it came to dealings with high-ranking clergy.

It soon appeared that Brother Joseph had given them an excellent recommendation. The guest room was clean and the bedstead had been prepared with fresh straw. Henri had an excellent meal of different courses of pâté, rillettes, poultry and meat washed down with the typical fruity wine of this region, Champagne, to be finished with local cheese and fruit.

The meal was served by a young and attractive maid who cast inviting glances from her brown eyes under long lashes while she served Henri the different courses of his meal, brushing his knee from time to time with her skirt.

Henri decided that he had earned some fun and felt familiar waves of excitement pulse through his veins; the instinct of the hunter had been awoken. This girl looked enticing enough, if a bit plump for his taste. It was not long after he had entered his room and his groom turned valet had started to undress him when the maid entered the guestroom, pretending that she had heard him calling her. Henri stood there, his chest bare, and her appraising glance was only matched by the way she moistened her lips with her tiny pink tongue.

Henri dismissed his groom and immediately the maid took command and continued to undress him, her caressing fingers lingering on his chest and his loins until he became aroused and caught fire.

He spent an agreeable night with her, finding to his delight (but not to his great surprise) that she was well experienced and knew the tricks of her profession, making him climax several times.

She was absolutely delighted: making love to such a handsome young man was already a stroke of luck but on top of this he handed her a fat purse when she left in the morning. Hopefully she'd be able to serve him again tomorrow!

The next morning Henri had understood why this inn boasted moderate prices in a city where most inns would not refrain from skimming off foreign pilgrims. Although the food was excellent and the rooms were pleasant and clean it was impossible to get sufficient sleep with the cathedral bells such close neighbours! He stretched and yawned and decided that it was time to get up. His groom had already prepared hot water and his shaving kit and Henri had to admit that he had made remarkable progress during the past few days of their travel. It would be annoying to have to get rid of him later.

Henri slipped into a clean shirt, added a lace collar and saw to his satisfaction that his trousers and boots had been carefully cleaned. He grinned to himself with a conceited smile: apparently he had impressed the maid and this was her way of thanking him. Once his blond hair had been brushed and arranged into shimmering locks, he looked every inch the future Marquis.

They could have walked to the monastery but Henri had decided that owing to his high rank, arrival on horseback would be preferable and more impressive.

Therefore the doorkeeper at the monastery happened to witness the approach of two horses: the first ridden by a young man impeccably dressed and showing an air of contempt and self-conceited arrogance that made it easy to perceive that he was of high noble birth, the second by his groom.

56

The doorkeeper came forward eagerly to enquire as to the wishes of the noble visitor. He knew from experience this type of gentleman, waiting for the world to serve him immediately; if the doorkeeper dared to move too slowly or to ignore him, at best a complaint would be lodged with the Abbot straight away, and at worst, he'd make acquaintance with his whip. Eager to avoid either of these unpleasant scenarios he hustled outside the monastery to greet Henri with all the respect that was due.

Henri handed him the Cardinal's letter of recommendation and requested the honour of an immediate meeting with the Abbot. The doorkeeper couldn't read but understood from the heavy seal affixed to the document that someone of great importance and influence had recommended the young gentleman and therefore he ushered Henri with deep bows inside a waiting room; the groom remained outside to look after the horses.

A young intelligent-looking monk serving as secretary for the Abbot appeared and took the document that the doorkeeper handed over to him. He immediately spotted the seal of the mighty Cardinal Richelieu and told Henri that he would inform the Father Abbot at once of his request to meet him.

Henri had to remind himself that time most probably had a different notion for members of a monastery compared to the outside world and tried to hide his growing impatience. The waiting room was very sober, with only some pieces of plain furniture and a crucifix that adorned the whitewashed wall.

As there was nothing to divert his attention, Henri started to go through the next steps and actions that were to be undertaken. He was just about to plan the demise of his young cousin when the door opened and the Abbot appeared.

Henri saw immediately that this meeting might become more complicated than foreseen. He had expected a man of average intelligence, more interested in matters of religion than in the complications of life outside a monastery, easily impressed by his noble pedigree and easy to handle.

His counterpart did not live up at all to this simplistic image. He looked extremely sharp, had a noble head with grey hair escaping from under his cap and had alert grey eyes. The abbot seemed totally at ease as he extended his ring for Henri to kiss – reminding him by this gesture that he was the lord of this monastery and a high lord of the Church. Henri now remembered that most probably the Abbot himself was a descendant of one of the great families, as ascending to this high rank in the clergy of a major city like Reims needed family influence or deep pockets.

"What can I do for you, my Son?" the Abbot requested in a friendly tone, making a sign to Henri to sit down in front of him.

Henri bowed courteously as was due to the high rank of the Abbot and kissed his ring of office before he sat down on the simple chair that had been offered to him.

"Father Abbott, may I first present the warmest greeting from His Eminence, the Cardinal Richelieu who wishes you well. My name is Henri de Beauvoir, and I have sad news to deliver, as my beloved father has recently passed away." Henri tried hard to look convincingly sad. "And it is my dearest wish to pass on this sad news and meet the future Marquis de Beauvoir who is supposed to be living here in the shelter of the monastery school and see when he may come home to the fold of our family, as we urgently long for him to come and take up the succession of our family in Paris. His Eminence, the Cardinal Richelieu, was kind enough to establish this letter of recommendation so as to confirm my identity and to encourage the family reunion!"

The proud city of Reims might no longer have been a centre of any real power in the kingdom of France, but it was by far not so provincial as to prevent the Cardinal's reputation to be known by the majority of the leading people there.

This is strange, thought the Abbot, putting on a deceptively pious face. *I would wager neither this young man, nor the Cardinal, would lift a finger if some money or game of power weren't involved. Let's see what is behind all of this.* And in his pleasant deep voice he answered aloud, "I have the greatest respect for His Eminence, the protector of our Church, and of our well-being in France and we wish him well. It will be a pleasure for me to fulfil your request. I merely have to ask you to accept my presence during your reunion, as Pierre, that is the name of your young cousin, was brought up in the monastery's orphanage according to the request of the former Archbishop of Reims very strictly, as befits a monk, and he is not accustomed to visitors coming from outside."

You sly fox, Henri thought, *burning with curiosity – aren't you?*

Aloud he consented, heartily congratulating the Abbot for his true Christian spirit in caring for his pupil and so he invited the Abbot to stay.

The Abbot smiled and rang the bell on his desk and his secretary appeared almost immediately. "Please be so kind and ask Brother Hieronymus to appear with Pierre, and please tell him to hurry!"

He offered Henri a glass of wine and they started some small talk about Paris, the court, the health of the King. The Abbot seemed to be well informed. The conversation then reached the topic of the young heir to the throne, the Dauphin, who had been born only two years ago. The Queen had remained childless for twenty years and they agreed that his birth was to be qualified as a heavenly miracle.

Especially considering that our King also favours young men, Henri thought.

58

But he had to concede – as the Queen was supervised day and night by the Cardinal's spies – that the heir must have been conceived in wedlock. Some time ago Henri had toyed with the idea of winning the favours of the unhappy and unloved Queen in order to win influence at court, as the King already had his chosen favourites but he had dropped this idea as suicidal once he had understood how tightly the Cardinal controlled the royal court.

Henri and the Abbott continued to discuss the latest gossip from Paris and the marvels of the Cardinal's famous palace when the Abbot's secretary announced the entry of Brother Hieronymus.

Brother Hieronymus had never been particularly attractive but as he appeared now in front of his superior, flustered, with his crimson red face perspiring profusely and diffusing a smell of unwashed feet the lips of the Abbot were pressed tightly in disapproval.

Henri jumped from his chair and moved a step backward when the wave of body odour hit him. For the first time he could feel a form of pity for his unknown cousin, a feeling he dismissed immediately, however.

Brother Hieronymus tried to utter some coherent words but he must have run to get there and was panting heavily. "Not found..." he spluttered. "Night vigil..." gasping for more breath. "Searching and probably dying..." was all that could be distinguished from the babbling coming from his lips.

The Abbot sacrificed a glass of his excellent white wine and pressed Hieronymus to drink it first, sit down and start his story again.

Maybe it was the effect of the wine or that the Abbot had not immediately shouted at him; in any case, Brother Hieronymus started to relax and was able to tell the whole story.

They had only found out just about an hour before that Pierre was missing, as nobody had reported anything unusual. The cell was bolted from the outside and as Pierre was known to have passed the night vigil with Brother Raphael, his warden was convinced that he was sleeping inside.

It was only when he had opened the door to bring some fresh water and bread that the cell had been found empty and the warden had come to see him. As Pierre had been together with Brother Raphael they started the search for both of them, actually not being too much alarmed as they thought that both would be retained together somewhere.

But then this: they found Brother Raphael, alone – and now Brother Hieronymus looked helplessly towards the noble visitor, feeling terribly embarrassed.

"Go on, my Brother, he's a relative of Pierre, we have nothing to hide," the Abbot encouraged the monk, even if his voice had taken on a steely edge. Hieronymus swallowed deeply and continued his narrative.

Brother Raphael had been found in a bush close to the holes in the garden that served as latrines. He must have thought that Pierre had left the chapel to relieve himself in the garden. Brother Raphael's bad eyesight was well known, therefore Hieronymus guessed that he must have failed to spot the rake the gardeners had left next to the garden path and stepped on it in the dim light of the night. The rake had hit him hard and he had fallen down on the stone borders, unconscious.

Probably drunk again, the Abbot thought. *I shouldn't have let him supervise the boy.*

Hieronymus watched anxiously the stern face of the Abbot. As the latter didn't move, he dared to continue telling his story.

When they had found Brother Raphael he had already bled profusely during the night and Brother Infirmarius sadly was certain that our Lord would call him to Heaven, even today. Hieronymus made what he thought to be a pious pause and the sign of the cross; Henri made great pains not to jump on him and strangle this stinking idiot.

"When Brother Raphael regained his spirits for a short while we asked him, of course, about Pierre," Hieronymus continued. "But the poor soul couldn't remember anything," and in his eyes tears gathered and started running down his cheeks and he sobbed. "He even didn't remember who Pierre was."

"May I resume your story?" Henri interrupted him coldly. "You dare to tell me that my cousin is lost, you didn't notice his absence for a full day and didn't even start a search, you f– " Henri stopped his abusive speech at the last minute, remembering that he was visiting a monastery, and looked at Brother Hieronymus in blazing anger, ready to jump on him at any minute.

The monk was paralysed by this outbreak of vitriol and the Abbot decided that it was time to intervene. "May I remind you that you are a visitor on holy ground, my Son," he said with all of his authority and Henri stopped in his tracks.

"I will order immediately, of course, a search for the missing boy and we'll pray for him. In the meantime you are also welcome to support our search for your cousin and join our prayers. Pierre is easy enough to identify: he could be your twin brother from his looks, but," and the Abbot paused significantly, "his education seems to be more refined."

Before Henri could find a suitable answer to this provocation, he already found himself mechanically kissing the ring that the Abbot had extended towards him. He had been dismissed and the Abbot left the room completely self-assured, without bothering to cast a glance behind him.

60

Henri was boiling with rage.

*****

When Henri came back to the horses his groom could see that his spirits were in turmoil. This was bad news, his master had been so upbeat this morning, almost like a normal human being. A curious thought occurred to the groom: Henri had entered the monastery looking like an angel and come out looking like the devil!

Henri decided to search in the only hospital of the city, but to no avail, and once he came back to his inn, it took several glasses of brandy to get rid of the putrid stench of the sick and infirm that lingered in his nose.

His next move was to meet the captain of the musketeers who were supposed to supervise law and order in the city and who also were guarding the city gates. He bribed him with several tankards of ale to make him talk. No boy of almost adult age with blond hair and looks similar to his had been reported or seen; they knew the city inhabitants in and out, he couldn't have come out of the city alive, they were sure, they would have noticed and sent him back to the monastery school.

Henri came back to the inn and was ready to kill with frustration. When the maid came back to see him that night, he made love to her so violently that he hurt her. She wondered what had happened to change so profoundly the handsome and attractive lover she had adored yesterday and who had now turned into a devil. As soon as her ordeal was over, she crept back into her own bed, making sure to avoid Henri over the next few days.

Henri decided to stay for a good week, calling on the Abbot daily, just to hear the same answer: his cousin was still missing and they had no clue where he could be. He should pray for his well-being or his soul.

Consequently there was only one solution left: to go back to Paris and meet the great Cardinal himself. If someone in France knew what was going on, it could only be Richelieu. If Richelieu wanted to receive the rest of the money, up to him to deliver!

PIERRE DISCOVERS HEAVEN

Everything hurt: every single bone in his back hurt and even worse, someone had installed a blacksmith's shop inside his head, and was hammering away relentlessly. Pierre thought that his head must have reached the size of a water melon – the kind of gigantic fruit people sometimes brought from the South of France and that he had learnt to love once he had been given the rare opportunity to taste it, so unbelievably sweet and juicy.

Pierre opened his eyes and saw a lovely vision in front of him: the girl he had seen, what must have been ages ago with his friend Armand, whose lovely amber eyes he had wanted to sink into. Now she was sitting there with a sponge of cool water dabbing his head and her lovely long hair tickled his skin. If he was dead and this was heaven, it could have been worse, Pierre decided.

As his brain slowly came back to working order he reluctantly reached the conclusion that it was not logical that he should be dead and in heaven if his head and back were hurting like hell. He decided that this was the kind of riddle that was far too complicated to solve and fell back into a deep slumber.

"He's on the mend," Marie said with a relieved voice. She looked at Armand full of reproach. "Did you really need to hit him so hard?"

Armand looked rather guilty but defended himself hotly. "You know that the only chance of getting him out of Reims was to bind him in linen from head to toe and pretend he was dead. So he had to lie totally still like a corpse."

Armand paused to remember the scene that had nearly made his heart stop when the guards started searching their wagon.

"It was actually a brilliant idea of yours to smear some blood and pus on the bandages, the guards nearly panicked and waved us through in no time." Armand chuckled as he recalled this adventure. "And wearing the habit of one of our monks joining the alleged funeral I just let it drop that I *hoped* that the deceased had not succumbed to the plague, even if admittedly it looked a bit like something *very* serious, and they started bolting like rabbits, brilliant!" he gasped, with tears of laughter in his eyes.

They were sitting in a small room in the servants' attic in an estate located in the northern part of the Champagne region, a good day's riding distance from the city of Reims. It was a manor house that belonged to Marie's mother. Officially they were looking after Armand's valet who was ill, and had arrived together with Armand.

Armand and Marie had insisted on looking after the servant themselves as long as there was any possibility that his severe illness might possibly be contagious. If the servants wondered about so much commitment for a mere valet they knew that their masters often had peculiar fancies such as caring for one of their pet servants and were just happy that they didn't need to get involved.

Marie's mother had been downright suspicious when Marie had explained to her – just a bit too smoothly – that she wanted to spend two weeks in her remote manor house because the hot weather in the city had started to make her feel tired, especially when she suddenly came up with the idea of inviting Armand to accompany her.

Armand, being of the de Saint Paul family, was of course a potential target for a suitable husband and most mothers might have been delighted to create such an occasion for match-making, but as he was supposed to become a clergyman, probably even an archbishop, and Armand was a younger son only (regrettably with several older brothers who seemed to enjoy robust health) it would need more than one accident to get him to inherit the title and make Marie a marchioness. As Marie's mother was a sensible woman she had better plans for her daughter and Armand was judged as not being suitable.

She was a little less preoccupied once she had occasion to watch both of them when Armand had paid her a courtesy visit, and although they seemed genuinely to like each other, they behaved more like brother and sister than lovers.

As Marie was their only child, she tended to obtain from her father whatever she fancied. Her mother thus decided that it would be wise to avoid any family scenes and tantrums and she accepted the plea, only with the slightest hint of reluctance.

She secretly gave strict instructions to this soldier-like giant of a maid who had looked after Marie since her birth to watch her closely at all times. Finally – to alleviate any doubts she might still have – she had the devious idea of inviting a remote cousin of hers to stay with Marie during this time. Marie's mother smiled to herself. Yes, the dowager Countess of Chevreuil would suppress any unsuitable attempts at courting, she was sure: just one glance of her steely eyes would put Armand back in his place!

The arrival of the dowager Countess come to chaperon Marie was announced by the Countess's own majestic-looking manservant who commanded a fleet of carriages, filled with chests, linen and whatever she had judged as basic necessities for survival in a rural estate. The fleet ground to a halt in the driveway leading to the beautiful manor house built in the latest fashion from cream-coloured sandstone.

As if she intends to stay for the rest of her life, Marie thought, and her spirits plummeted as she and Armand watched this armada arriving.

A gilded carriage with the dowager's coat of arms was opened by the footmen, steps were lowered and the Countess de Chevreuil appeared, leaning heavily on the arm of her manservant; she was clad all in black lace like a crow and her grim face looked disapprovingly at Marie and then at Armand.

The countess hated travelling or discomfort of any kind; she had no illusions that looking after a young couple would disturb her tranquillity and be the kind of stress she would normally try to avoid, and had it not been that she owed a service to Marie's mother who happened to be one of her best friends...

Introductions were made stiffly according to protocol but soon after they had dined on their first evening together, Armand decided it was time to conquer the Countess. Using his considerable charms he started to entertain her with gossip from Paris and finally gained her respect by means of some secret recipes for herbal preparations to fight her gout and some infallible headache remedies he'd gleaned from Brother Infirmarius. The Countess started to thaw and was fast falling victim to Armand's good looks and easy charms.

During the course of their discussion she also discovered to her delight that there was a connection by marriage between the de Saint Pauls and her husband's clan somewhere in their intricate family tree and Armand could therefore be considered a remote nephew of hers – in fact she now viewed Armand as part of her family.

She loved listening to the gossip and stories he had heard from his brothers living in Paris, most of these slightly scandalous, of course, which made them even more appealing as Armand had the art of telling them in the most innocent manner. She was so spellbound that Marie's frequent periods of absence when she went to look after Pierre went unnoticed. The Countess decided that after this mission was finished she would go back to Paris for a season. Armand's stories had shown her how much she had actually been missing Paris during her prolonged period of mourning.

*****

The next time Pierre woke up was because his nostrils had detected the lovely smell of hot chicken broth. It must be Sunday, Pierre automatically thought, never in the school refectory would they serve anything delicious like this on an ordinary day.

He opened his eyes and found himself propped up in an unknown bed with cushions and blankets of a superior quality he had never seen or touched before. The sun was shining through the tiny window panes, its rays playing with Marie's auburn hair, creating red-gold reflections that Pierre found breathtakingly beautiful.

He opened his eyes and smiled at Marie. The same rays of sun that were playing with Marie's hair were dancing now on Pierre's eyes and it was for Marie now to hold her breath, looking into those lovely blue eyes directed at her in full adoration.

64

This is becoming dangerous, Marie, she chided herself but couldn't move away or take her eyes off Pierre. They were still sitting there – frozen in an embarrassing silence – when they heard someone clearing his throat behind them in a very pronounced manner.

Pierre jerked as it he had been pricked by a needle.

"Armand!" he yelled and tears of joy formed in his eyes. "It's a miracle!" and then an endless stream of questions came from Pierre's lips: "Where have you been, I thought I'd never see you again in all my life, I was feeling so miserable, what was going on, did you save me, what happened these last few days, do you know who ambushed me?"

Armand decided that it was about time to come clean and tell the full story, so he cleared his throat again and replied, "Calm down, Pierre, but let's start with the last question. I have to admit, yes, it was me who ambushed you and hit you from behind."

It was hilarious to watch Pierre's eyes changing from pure delight to disbelief and hurt indignation. Before he could comment on this confession though, Armand intervened quickly and said, "Have your chicken broth now, it's getting cold and I'll tell you what went on and why I had to hurt you. Believe me, it was one of the hardest things I ever had to do in my life."

Pierre decided that this proposal held a lot of common sense and followed Armand's sound advice as by now he was really hungry, so he started to eat and listened.

Armand gave a short recap of the last days in the monastery, and their discovery of Pierre's documents with Marie's help. Actually he was very proud of his little idea involving the mouse. Pierre and Marie did the right thing: they praised him abundantly and Armand beamed with delight.

Armand was still convinced that Pierre was in immediate danger and that he needed to leave fast – but he was scared to death of his friend getting caught as he knew that the Abbot and probably his relatives would launch an intensive search immediately after his disappearance. It was also common custom to put a tempting reward on the head of escaped monastery pupils.

Armand was in possession of an earlier letter from his father summoning him to come back to Paris after the school term as he had reached a secret agreement with Cardinal Richelieu to appoint him as bishop of one of the family's parishes in the south of France, meaning that he'd be ordained almost immediately, certainly before the end of the summer term.

Armand hadn't told Pierre anything about this letter because he hated the thought of losing Pierre as much as he hated the thought of becoming a bishop.

"You know," Armand said, full of mischief, munching on a piece of bread he had pinched from Pierre's tablet and dipping it into his soup, "I have got an older brother who's so convinced that he's a gift to mankind, let him also become a gift for heaven and become bishop instead of me!"

Armand had thus decided that Pierre's idea to escape from the monastery was to become their joint adventure and his long-sought opportunity to break away from the career path he had always hated.

Thinking logically, he had needed outside help to bring the slightly manipulated summons of his father to explain his immediate departure and Marie, being a remote cousin, had offered to send her maid as a credible messenger. Armand was evidently quite proud that he had tampered with his father's letter so successfully that even the Abbot hadn't seen that he had cut part of the letter and reattached the seal in a different place. "That's the advantage of being a Marquis de Saint Paul, most people will buy anything you try to sell," he said, grinning broadly.

He had then hidden in the stables of Marie's house and kept close watch on the monastery.

Now Pierre started to remember his own adventures, starting from the moment when he had thought that Armand had gone forever. He told his part of the story and when he described the night vigil and how he had deceived his teachers with his show of penitence, imitating at the end the snores of poor Brother Raphael, Armand was nearly rolling on the floor with delight. Panting with laughter, he said, "Oh Pierre, I always thought you were brilliant, but this is just fantastic, together we can take on the whole world!"

Marie watched them, sharing their joy but feeling strangely rebellious at the same time. This was really exciting! Why should it be her destiny to go back to her drab daily routine in Reims, just sitting there and waiting until her parents picked a suitable husband for her? Marie hadn't seen one single candidate that she could genuinely find attractive. She'd miss Pierre and Armand desperately.

Being a girl of some resolve, she decided that she wouldn't give in; she needed to sit down and make a plan. No, she wouldn't be sitting there like a flower waiting to be plucked when these boys had lots of fun and excitement waiting for them!

Armand continued his narrative until the moment when Pierre had entered the dark barn as planned and where Armand had tackled the difficult job of knocking him out, as he saw no other possibility of smuggling him out of the city walls. The ruse had worked beautifully and with Marie's help he had passed the city gates disguised as one of the many monks, he had even cut his hair shorter, allowing Marie's maid to cut his long locks so as to be convincing. Pierre giggled, as he knew how vain his friend was in reality and if he needed any proof that Armand was willing to make a sacrifice for him – here it was!

Once the city gates had been passed the false monk and his false corpse had reached Marie's manor house, thanks to Marie's excellent organization. She had provided a wagon, horse and a trusted servant who knew the way to the manor that was located just 20 miles north of Reims. It had been convenient to reach their hiding place so fast, but its proximity to Reims meant that they couldn't stay there forever without running the risk of being detected. Armand insisted that they'd need to leave France as fast as possible and stay there until they had been able to work out a realistic plan for how to reinstate Pierre to his rightful heritage.

All of this was so confusing that Pierre was starting to look pale and exhausted and reluctantly Marie and Armand left him to get some rest.

Although Pierre thought that he could never sleep again after the excitement of his escape and the wonderful surprise of finding Armand here – ready to share his adventure – he lapsed back into a deep slumber as soon as Marie and Armand had closed the door.

They had an understanding that officially they would meet only from time to time during the day so as not to arouse the suspicions of the Countess, who still kept a watchful – even if by now a more benevolent – eye on them.

*****

As soon as Pierre could get up and was fit to move he resumed his position as Armand's groom after the latter had given him a crash course on his duties and started secretly to teach him to ride. They had decided to do this in the small forest that lay close to the estate as it would have been a strange thing indeed to see a master teaching his groom to ride a horse. In front of the others Armand took great pleasure in playing the difficult master, sending Pierre to fetch things he didn't really need and complaining loudly that Pierre was a lazy scoundrel.

Pierre ground his teeth as he thought that Armand was overdoing the show somewhat, but he was so happy to have his friend back that he didn't really mind this little comedy and was soon playing the groom to perfection, also adopting the local patois that the servants spoke. He knew that he had succeeded in convincing the other servants he was one of them when one of the kitchen maids started making overtures to him, and he was even happier to see that Marie didn't like this at all, as soon as she got word from Armand of what was going on in the servants' quarters.

*****

Marie had made up her mind and decided that she would make sure she remained part of this adventure – and once she had put something in her pretty head she usually stuck to it. She didn't even contemplate failure.

After a short spell of cool weather, the days turned warm again and they had agreed to meet close to a small forest to discuss their next moves in private. Marie would arrive on foot with her maid and Armand by horse – accompanied by his favourite groom.

Armand and Pierre had already decided that they'd go further north to enter the Spanish Netherlands as fast as possible and escape the influence of Richelieu or Pierre's greedy relatives. Armand remembered that one of his numerous close relatives lived in a castle near the Spanish citadel of Mons where they could probably stay and rest before they would have to find a ship and go by sea to England, most likely via the port of Antwerp.

But now they were stuck and racking their brains in vain: Where to find enough money to pay for the channel crossing and travel on to London? Neither Armand nor Pierre had ever been in a port or seen a big ship at close quarters – even if they loved picturing this adventure, they had no clue as to how to make it become reality.

Marie was sitting in the shade of a tree on a blanket that her maid had provided, looking exceedingly pretty in a new dress that would probably be ruined by the damp ground, but she had insisted that Anne was to dress her with special care today.

Her maid was looking sulky as usual. Knowing Marie inside out she sensed that Marie was up to something, but as long as Marie let her look after her, her maid was prepared to close her eyes and ears and follow her.

They had brought along a surprise basket filled with wild strawberries freshly picked that morning and the boys dipped their fingers into the basket, savouring the rare fruit.

Satisfied that she had put them in a good mood, Marie said, "I have a proposal to make."

Two pairs of astonished eyes, one brown, one blue, were watching her attentively, strawberries forgotten for the moment.

"My parents want me to marry a man of excellent reputation, good family and," she added mockingly, "with a huge fortune, of course."

Marie noticed with great pleasure and satisfaction that Pierre's eyes had opened wide in panic, and she nearly purred like a cat as she went on. "As I'm being a good and obedient daughter, I need to meet suitable candidates, as maybe one day I'll find my Prince Charming."

Armand grinned as he knew Marie's character only too well. He was sure that she wouldn't think for a minute about gratifying any wish of her parents, unless it suited her own ideas. She would choose her prince and make sure she'd have him, and Armand had some notion of who the chosen one was going to be.

Pierre only blinked. Until now he had had no experience with the female sex and took Marie's introduction as the literal truth, thus shattering his secret dream.

Marie continued unperturbed. "The last candidates I met were either boring, fat or horribly arrogant. I'm therefore considering that I should at last accept my great-uncle's invitation to come and live with him for a time... especially as it is reported that he has a very promising son and heir who would certainly appeal to my mother." During her speech she had lowered her eyes, which enabled poor, suffering Pierre to see her long, seductive eyelashes.

"How does this relate to our plans?" Armand asked. "And, by the way, I can only pity the husband who falls into your trap," he continued. "He won't have a minute's peace!"

Marie giggled. She knew that her speech and portrayal of the model daughter would not deceive Armand for a minute, but she had seen the devastating effect of her announcement on Pierre and was very satisfied with this part of her work.

"Armand, I shouldn't speak with you any more," Marie pouted, "but I'm in the mood to be kind and forgiving today. By the way, did I mention that my uncle is the ambassador of the Duchy of Savoy?" and meeting their blank looks she paused before adding, "at the royal court of Whitehall."

Armand whistled, but Pierre just looked bewildered. What was she talking about?

Armand saw his friend's confusion and concluded that it was about time to explain. "Marie is telling us – of course, not in a straightforward manner, as a man would have done – that she'll ask her mother to allow her to sail to England under the pretext of wanting to get to know a potential suitable bridegroom. Whitehall is the name of the royal palace used by the kings of England. Knowing Marie a little, she already has a plan in her pretty head as to how we can cross the Channel together with her, right? And knowing her even better, she probably doesn't care at all for this candidate and is just looking for a way to share our adventure!"

Armand took Marie's hand and pretended to plant a kiss on it. This action was commented on immediately by her maid by a loud clearing of her throat and a very disapproving glance. Armand didn't care and blew a kiss in Anne's direction as well.

"Is this true?" Pierre asked her with big pleading eyes – unconsciously adopting the look of an adorable puppy that has just been rescued from disaster. Marie found it difficult not to melt there and then but common sense told her that a bit of ambiguity would keep the passion fresh; consequently, she just smiled sweetly at Pierre but didn't answer.

Looking at Armand she said, "It seems quite straightforward actually. I'll leave in two or three weeks' time. My mother has been repeating again and again that I should go, not only because of my cousin, who in her mind is a most eligible candidate for marriage, but mainly because she thinks that it's a unique opportunity for me to be introduced to the court of King Charles. She's very ambitious, and from time to time has complained to me in secret that she's been wasting her life here in the provinces."

Marie put on a funny face. "In essence, she wants me to become nothing less than a duchess, so as soon as you mention the word 'royal' she'll do anything to make it happen. My father, of course, will give in but will insist that I travel with a small army of maids, footmen and servants to make sure I arrive safely. It should be fairly easy to bribe two of the footmen to drop out in Calais and go back home and you'll have to be there to replace them before we sail. Anne will be in charge of finding new servants and she'll find and recommend you."

Armand and Pierre sat there totally stunned. The plan was simple, brilliant and the answer to their prayers. All they had to do was make sure they reached Calais on time and not be caught by Richelieu's spies.

Marie was satisfied with the impression she had left. Men always thought that they were superior beings. In reality it took a woman to make a good plan. She made a sign to Anne and miraculously from their carriage there appeared a bottle of wine, and more delicious fruit and cakes.

"I thought we should celebrate today," Marie said. "Let's drink to our adventure!"

"Yes," Pierre cried, "here's to Marie and to being friends forever!"

ON THEIR WAY

The time had come to say goodbye. Even though they knew that they had agreed to meet again some weeks later, it was hard to part. They had cherished these weeks together and their friendship had grown stronger every day.

For Pierre, a door to a new world had been opened, every experience was new and exciting; his life – so long regulated by the monotony of the monastery – suddenly had become colourful, filled with adventure and a wonderful new friendship. He decided never again to open a vellum scroll or prayer book if he could possibly help it!

Marie had given them two fine horses as a present – a proposal they had first categorically refused, as both of them felt embarrassed at being even more indebted to her. Marie told them curtly not to be so stupid. It was in their common interest that they should arrive in Calais on time and had they imagined arriving there on foot?

Of course the horses would not be regarded as a plain gift, she'd gladly agree to be paid for them once Pierre was in possession of his inheritance – if the great Marquis de Beauvoir would then still remember poor Marie from the provinces, she added with a broken voice and a doleful glance.

Armand just hugged her briefly; he felt immensely relieved, because he had already realized that they would need to steal horses from somewhere. Even if he didn't doubt that they would find a way to organize horses themselves, stealing horses would have put even more irate people on their trail and he was glad to avoid any unnecessary attention.

Pierre blew her a kiss and smiled, even he didn't fall for this show of false modesty. Nobody could imagine Marie withering away in the provinces, she with all the energy of a firecracker.

They decided to keep their true plans hidden and made sure that the servants would overhear them preparing to return to Reims, and then west to Paris where Armand would meet his father who had summoned him to return urgently.

Armand left a letter for his father with Marie, who promised to send it immediately she arrived back in Reims. He had toiled nearly a whole day to compose this message and asked Pierre to provide him with some ingenious ideas to explain their plan. Just imagining meeting his father afterwards and defending his actions made him extremely nervous.

Pierre saw him scratching his forehead nervously and commented, "Don't wet yourself, you look scared stiff!"

Armand shot him a murderous glance and having thrown away several elaborate letters he settled finally for a short letter, explaining to his father that he had been called away on a mission to save his best friend who was in danger. Pierre read the meagre result of Armand's prolonged labours and recommended that he add at least some lines expressing his filial love and devotion.

Armand accepted this excellent suggestion to add a sweetener to the message which he knew would cause a terrible storm at home – especially as the Marquis de Saint Paul was neither used to nor prepared to accept any act of disobedience from the members of the great family he ruled with a rod of iron.

"What can he do?" Pierre enquired anxiously.

"Kill me, torture me, disinherit me – nothing serious, in any case," Armand jested. As Armand was optimistic by nature he decided that it was useless to continue tormenting himself and decided to leave these worries for the future. First an exciting adventure was looming; confronting his irate father would come later.

Thinking about the great adventures that lay ahead of them did a lot to cheer him up and when they left very early the next morning on the road to Reims both of them felt in high spirits – probably as Alexander the Great must have felt when he had left the tiny kingdom of Macedonia with his best friend to conquer the boundless empire of Persia.

*****

Armand had decided that they must avoid the main roads in France and would travel very early or when darkness started to fall, as long as day or moonlight permitted them to move on. During the days they would hide in the vineyards or forests. As they had plenty of time, Armand decided that it was an ideal time to start Pierre's education and teach him the essentials of what a gentleman needed to know.

Forget about prayers, Latin or matters of religion. What really counted was how to greet a fellow nobleman, how to fight, how to pay a compliment to a lady, how to identify friend and foe – those were the real topics, if Pierre wanted to survive at court and later claim his heritage.

Pierre had spent all his life in the monastery and he understood quickly that he needed to learn a lot about this new world of the aristocracy into which he had been catapulted, totally unprepared – but he had no clue as to how much he'd have to learn.

He was very thankful that Armand had already given him some riding lessons when they had stayed with Marie but riding continuously for hours was a totally different – and very painful – experience.

When he alighted from his horse for a break, during the first days he could barely move, everything hurt. Pierre didn't complain as he didn't want Armand to pity or scorn him and take him for a weakling. He bit his lips and pretended that he had had a great time. Of course Armand knew that he hadn't.

Whenever they took a break, Armand became Pierre's teacher: he'd explain in great detail the family trees of the important noble families of France and the ruling families of Europe. Pierre discovered that although all of them were related at some level or another, the notion of love or compassion didn't exist between them. They were ready to cheat, kill or betray each other ruthlessly at any moment if they saw a chance to increase their territories, make a favourable marriage – or if their fortune or family interest was at stake.

France had become the undisputed powerhouse of Europe and Armand depicted Richelieu sitting like a poisonous spider in the centre of an intricate web of power, corruption and espionage that he had skilfully woven. It was Richelieu who would choose the King's favourites to keep him happy and who held poor Queen Anne like a hostage in her golden cage.

Armand despised the Cardinal as he had systematically reduced the power and privileges of the great noble families but reluctantly, Armand had to admit that he was a great man and that their hatred shouldn't make them blind to the fact that he was outstanding and therefore a very dangerous enemy to have.

Then followed the most important lessons if Pierre wanted to survive. Pierre had never in his life used a weapon, not even a dagger. Armand showed him how to hold a rapier; with Marie's consent he had appropriated some from her household and luckily he had found swords that were nicely balanced with good quality blades of excellent workmanship.

Armand tried to remember his own lessons and showed Pierre how to move his feet, and hold the rapier. Pierre had to do exercises daily until Armand found that he was ready to take part in simulated fighting against each other, which was dangerous, as they didn't have any protective clothing to hand.

As they wanted to avoid contact with the population while aiming for the northern border close to the city of Cambrai, they had taken enough bread, preserves and other foodstuffs to keep in hiding until they reached the border.

But Armand had planned to hunt some rabbits and small deer to improve their diet and to profit from the hunting by making Pierre practise with different weapons. Whereas Pierre had started to use the bow and arrows with reasonable skill, Armand felt that Pierre was still very reluctant to handle a dagger or a sword. Therefore he decided that Pierre needed a crash course in losing his inhibitions or he wouldn't stand a chance of surviving in a real fight.

The next day he shot a fawn, making sure that the poor animal was not dead, but badly hurt and suffering, desperately trying to escape.

73

"Finish him," Armand said to Pierre.

Pierre gulped. "I can't!"

"If you don't kill it, the poor animal will suffer for hours and there will be no dinner tonight, it's your decision," Armand replied coldly.

Pierre noticed the contempt in his eyes and saw with horror the helpless kicking of the animal. Gathering all his courage, he took his dagger and plunged it into the throat of the fawn as Armand had told him to do.

It was a horrifying feeling, but he clenched his teeth and went on with it. When the animal had stopped moving, Armand touched his shoulder reassuringly. He knew that this exercise must have been a terrible ordeal for Pierre.

Then he showed Pierre how to cut the animal to pieces and by the time they had finished their work Pierre had learnt to cut through skin and handle the dagger swiftly and had lost his initial revulsion.

They lit a fire and roasted some of the fresh meat; the meal wouldn't have been fit for a king but after several days of stale bread and dried fruit it was a welcome change and Pierre was proud that he had succeeded in using the dagger and becoming what he viewed as a real man.

Armand congratulated Pierre once more and told him that their provisions had began to run low, and consequently they would need to do regular hunting now or starve.

Armand reckoned that they were close now to the French border; only a few more miles and they'd have made it, they'd enter the Spanish Netherlands. The landscape had already changed some days ago. The picturesque vineyards of Reims and Champagne had disappeared and now they were travelling mostly across hilly pastures or crossing deep and untouched forests. They were congratulating themselves that this part of France was so sparsely populated that they had managed to avoid contact with the local population with the exception of the odd forlorn peasant. Pierre loved the freedom of their new life and secretly hoped that it would never end. He became quite a shot with his bow and on the day he managed to beat Armand, he truly felt like a king.

In the afternoon they reached an isolated part of a small river and Armand decided that it was definitely time to have a bath; they were both stinking and disgusting, he concluded, looking especially critically at Pierre.

As a result of their hunting exercises a lot of animal blood had spilled onto Pierre's clothes. Armand claimed that Pierre smelled like a butcher and furthermore he had started to attract a swarm of flies in the warm and humid weather, which plagued Pierre and drew sardonic comments from his friend.

They attached the horses to a bush close to the bank at a bend in the river. The slope was covered with grass and fragrant wild flowers – an idyllic spot for bathing, with the water glittering invitingly in the sunshine.

While the horses started to graze and enjoy the fresh grass and herbs, Armand cheered and ran to the water, dropping his clothes behind him in a trail and finally standing stark naked in the sun, feet in the water, like a Greek statue in the centre of a stage.

Pierre was genuinely embarrassed. In school it was forbidden to undress, he had been raised in the belief that the human body was born from sin and made for sin.

His cheeks flushed, he tried to find some excuse for not joining this sinful enterprise but Armand called him impatiently. "Come on, what are you waiting for? The water is just fantastic! You're not scared to dip your noble foot into a bit of cool water, are you?"

Pierre looked at Armand standing there in his naked splendour. No wonder the girls in Reims had been queuing up to meet him.

Cautiously he moved closer to the river and tried to hide his embarrassment as he undressed clumsily. Not that he had anything to hide. The sun was playing on the golden hair of his head and the fine hair that had started to cover his legs and his chest. He was well built for his age with long, muscular legs and soon would need to shave regularly. Pierre rushed into the water and once he was inside he loved it. To feel the pure and cool water streaming around his body was such a wonderful sensation! Armand showed him that he could even float on the water and after he had learnt this trick he revelled in this new feeling.

Afterwards they washed their clothes in the water and left them to dry on the bank whilst they too lay down to dry, Armand in the full sun as he tanned easily. He explained to Pierre that he thought it would be helpful to look tanned like a commoner and not to display the pale skin of a gentleman during their flight. Pierre had to move into the shade after a short while as his skin started to turn pink, and he knew from his experience of working in the monastery garden that he became sunburned much too fast for his liking.

Neither Pierre nor Armand noticed that the bushes on the opposite side of the water had been moving slightly although there was no wind. Just then their horses snorted nervously, as they had detected a human scent unknown to them.

As soon as their clothes were dry enough to be put on again the pair were ready to continue their journey. They followed a path through the forest that kept to the banks of the small river and later wound through the forest, until they reached another loop of the same river and the forest yielded to open fields. A primitive wooden bridge crossed the narrow river and they decided to follow the road along the fields of millet and barley.

Evening was approaching and both felt relieved to discover a small hamlet consisting of three isolated farms lying peacefully in the proximity of the river. Armand decided that it was time to try to get a decent meal and buy some new food to fill their empty bags. Pierre added that sleeping on some decent fresh straw in a barn or stable would make a nice change after several nights in the woods or fields spent in makeshift beds.

Their arrival was discovered by a group of filthy children as soon as they approached the first building. The children gathered round the strangers, viewing the arrival of the two young men as a major event in their lives, not to be missed for anything.

Armand knocked on the door of the farm that looked the cleanest of the three. An unfriendly woman of indefinite age appeared. She had a big broom in her hand, like a weapon, ready to strike.

She looks like a witch, Pierre thought, and secretly made a sign behind his back to ward off witchcraft, as Brother Hieronymus had instructed them to do when he had prepared his pupils for an encounter with evil.

The unfriendly witch looked at them full of suspicion and was just about to slam the door shut when the shimmering of silver coins appearing miraculously in Armand's hand had a remarkable effect on her. She didn't exactly become friendly but kept the door open and agreed to listen to their request.

"I'm on my way to Antwerp with my groom to meet my father who's a fabric merchant," Armand explained fluently. "We're honourable people but we have lost our way and are extremely hungry and tired. We'd like to buy a meal and would also need to buy some more food for the continuation of our journey, and if we could ask you to grant us your hospitality and allow us to spend the night in your stable, we would be indebted to you and would appreciate your extraordinary kindness."

He paused, trying to judge the effect of his flowery speech on the witch and then continued. "Of course, we will pay for this in good French silver coins and promise to be no trouble to you."

The witch was not falling for his charms and kept an almost hostile expression on her face but clearly the money was tempting her. Her hand shot forward and grabbed the first coins and she nodded curtly to show that she'd accept – uttering some short phrases in a northern dialect they could barely understand.

She made it clear to them though, that if they caused any trouble she'd set the dogs on them. Just to underline the words of his mistress, an enormous crossbreed like a gigantic sheepdog waved his tail and displayed an impressive array of healthy teeth.

76

Pierre and Armand hastened to explain that they meant no trouble, and the witch told them curtly to sit down. They had just started their meal when a girl of their age entered the room. She kept her eyes down and wore hideous clothes but all of this couldn't conceal her outstanding beauty and lovely hair, so that any observer could not help but desire to discover whether the body beneath the ugly outfit matched up to this glimpse of loveliness.

The witch watched the two young men suspiciously in front of her and was satisfied when she saw that they were apparently concentrating fully on their dinner, instead of trying to attract the attention of the young beauty who had just entered the room.

The girl silently slapped two tankards of ale on the table without looking around her. She seemed to completely ignore the presence of the two attractive visitors.

When she turned in order to leave the kitchen she slipped and lost her balance and nearly fell on Pierre. Leaning heavily on him she righted herself quickly, apologized in a low voice, more to the witch than to the two visitors, and left the room in a hurry but without any apparent confusion.

Pierre sat in stunned silence. The girl had murmured into his ear, "Don't drink too much ale... dangerous," and he wondered if this was real and if he was really sitting there, or was he stuck in a strange nightmare.

Armand shot him a surprised glance, as Pierre's flow of conversation – already not impressive and consisting merely of "yes", and "no, master" – had trickled away to total silence as he saw his friend pondering some problem unknown to him. As Armand was pragmatic and could see that something strange was going on, he kept his questions for later and decided to finish the frugal meal first and attack the block of cheese that looked almost edible. It would go nicely with the fresh ale – making a welcome change after all the water they had been drinking during their journey.

The witch had stayed in the kitchen together with them where she had served the dinner but the girl called her from outside and after a short hesitation the old woman left them – but they were still under the supervision of her impressive dog that lay in a corner and seemingly ignored them, as long as they didn't move.

Armand saw her leaving and said in a low tone, "What a charming hostess, she reminds me of those strange ladies in the fairytales my nurse used to tell me about, they just had an unfortunate habit of turning nice boys like us into toads," and raised the tankard to take a deep gulp of ale in order to wash down his first piece of cheese.

Pierre grabbed his hand, made him put down the ale again on the table and at the same time he made a sign to Armand to keep his mouth shut. He was just about to tell Armand what the girl had murmured in his ear when they heard the steps of

77

the returning witch. Armand obeyed but sent an enquiring and very curious glance to Pierre.

The witch entered the kitchen and enquired in an almost friendly manner if they had liked the ale.

"Oh yes," Pierre replied, rediscovering his speech, "it's delicious!" He took a sip and smacked his lips to show his appreciation.

"May we ask you if we can take the tankards with us to the barn, my master would love to have the ale before he goes to sleep – we'd rather have some water now."

"Oh, you can have more later," the witch replied. "Forget about water, be my guest and drink it now, you must be thirsty!"

Pierre looked at her and suddenly seemed to remember something important.

"Oh heavens, we forgot to pray before dinner!" he exclaimed and slapped his forehead. "We should pray now, as we forgot to do so before the meal. May God forgive us!" Pierre made the solemn sign of the cross inviting the others with a gesture to join in.

The witch was visibly confused, especially when Pierre started to imitate the chant of prayers that they had used during chapel service. Using Latin, he hoped that Armand would understand his hint as he prayed loudly and fervently: "Let us give thanks to the Lord who sent the beautiful virgin to warn us that the toxic liquid in front of us could harm our body more than our souls."

Armand's Latin was poor, despite two years of school in Reims, but he grasped the meaning immediately and answered in Latin, "Yes, thank the Lord!"

The witch seemed deeply impressed by this show and accepted their claim to be dead tired, but she insisted on handing them another pitcher of her ale for the night, suddenly playing the considerate hostess.

Pierre and Armand pretended not to notice this sudden and surprising change of attitude and thanked her profusely for her hospitality, and excellent food and drink.

Still guarded by the witch and her gigantic dog the small group went to fetch the boys' horses that had been waiting patiently in the courtyard and marched into a small stable, home to a scrawny and melancholic cow, some goats (their smell creating a sudden reminder of Brother Hieronymus), some rabbits and an errant chicken that fled outside protesting loudly and excitedly when they entered.

Their hostess – still strangely anxious for their well-being – seemed satisfied that they had settled in comfort and prepared to leave but ordered the dog to lie down near the entrance. "He'll protect you well," she said with a strange smile, but

Armand was somehow convinced that he had detected a note of irony in this statement.

The door was closed and they heard the noise of sliding bolts locking the door from outside.

Armand looked at Pierre when the door had closed. "I don't like that at all – tell me, what's this all about?"

Pierre repeated the girl's message and Armand whistled through his teeth – and to their great discomfort the huge dog started moving as if he understood this as an invitation to come closer. He fixed his large dark eyes expectantly on them and his breathing was uncomfortably close to their heads.

"Have a drink!" Pierre said flippantly and put the pitcher under the nose of the dog. To their great surprise the dog started to lap the liquid faster and faster and didn't object when they emptied the content of their tankards into the pitcher.

When the pitcher was finally empty and no refills were waiting for him, the dog made a satisfied belching sound and walked back to the door, slightly swaying, as Pierre noted.

"You're telling me that we've walked right into a trap," Armand stated, but not seemingly particularly bothered or alarmed.

"Let's see how the ale works on our doggy friend and wait until it's dark and the hamlet's asleep to see how to escape. There must be a way! Something really fishy is going on here. I really wonder what this girl is up to, a stunning beauty, did you notice? Funny that such an ugly broomstick like this witch should have such a lovely daughter in this lost part of the world. What a waste!"

Of course Pierre had noticed the girl, but the effect had been to make him feel ill at ease. He had been convinced that his love for Marie would make him blind to any other girl, and he was shocked to discover that he did feel attracted – actually very much attracted – to this strange girl with the beautiful face. He didn't want to discuss this issue with Armand though, as courting plenty of girls came naturally to him and he just would have laughed at Pierre – but Pierre felt almost guilty and his conscience was pricking him.

The light inside the stable was disappearing quickly now. The stable was made from wooden planks but in many places splits and cracks left enough space for the light to enter from outside. As the sun was setting the dim light inside became darker and darker and they sat in an uneasy silence, interrupted only by the mooing of the cow, the noises of the goats and the panting and munching of their horses and other more subtle noises that Pierre attributed uneasily to the scurrying feet of mice or rats – he hoped it was mice.

The dog lay in front of the door and started to snore deeply – proof that the ale had been drugged. This was excellent news, as it allowed them to take the weapons that they had hidden in their luggage that was still bound to the horses without having to face the all-impressive fangs of their canine guardian.

It was very dark now, and in safe possession of their weapons Armand said that it was about time to do something and see how to escape this trap. Carefully he moved along the walls, pressing on the wooden planks in the hope of finding some weak spots. He was still busy with his exploration when Pierre, who was on watch at the door, whistled softly as a sign that he had heard something.

They took their weapons and positioned themselves on both sides of the door, ready to strike first. The door swung cautiously open and when they were just about to jump they realized that it was the girl who had saved them who had appeared. She looked once more behind her and quickly closed the door.

"Where are you?" she cried softly.

Armand suddenly appeared behind her, holding her in his strong arms.

"Here we are, my beauty, now please explain what's going on!"

His surprise was complete when she didn't speak but answered his embrace with a long kiss. "I like this sort of trap," he mused, delighted.

"My aunt is sleeping deeply, I put some of her favourite sleeping draught into her soup tonight," she giggled. "This means I have some time to explain. But tell me first, what happened to the dog?"

"Our doggy friend likes ale," Armand replied. "I'm sure he'll have a severe headache tomorrow!"

The girl giggled again and, snuggling herself even more into Armand's arms, she started her narrative.

She had seen them approaching the river and then watched them secretly as they had been bathing. Luckily it was dark, as Pierre was blushing bright red. She must have seen him naked! The girl confessed she had liked very much what she had seen. Another giggle followed.

Then she became serious again and explained that a messenger had arrived two days ago to their hamlet promising a reward for any information about a blond boy, nearly an adult, who had escaped from the monastery of Reims – probably accompanied by another boy or young man with dark hair. Both of them were of more than average height, dress unknown, etc, etc.

Having seen them and knowing that strangers never really came into this region unless they were heading for the frontier located behind the river, she had concluded that they were the two individuals the constables were looking for.

When she had noticed them approaching her aunt's house she had sensed danger immediately, as her aunt would sell her own children to the devil if it was for money.

Therefore she had decided to warn one of them and by chance it had been Pierre. She gave a dramatic pause before she finished, "And here I am to set you free!"

"Who signed the search warrant?" Armand asked. "Did they say this?"

"It was published in the name of the King and his lawful representative, the Governor and the Archbishop of Reims."

"Hmm, I wonder how they found out about our escape so fast," Armand said to himself, "I'd bet that the Cardinal has his fingers in this pie as well, I'm astonished that he seems convinced that I might be involved too…"

"Why would you do this for us?" Pierre asked incredulously, interrupting Armand's thoughts.

"You're right to ask, everything in life comes at a price," the girl answered, smiling at them.

"There is one condition. Next week I am to marry a boring, elderly husband. I accepted his proposal because I want to be rid of my aunt and leave. He's not rich but I'll be comfortable. I want to spend this night with you before I become his faithful wife."

Pierre couldn't believe his own ears. Armand just laughed and answered, "That sounds like the best deal that was ever made to me. At your service, my beautiful lady!" and he planted a kiss on her cheeks.

Embarrassed, Pierre got up to leave them alone when she spoke softly, "I said, I want to spend the night with both of you! A deal is a deal!"

Pierre's jaw dropped, a sensation of panic flooded through his body. He went hot and cold at the same time, his brain seemed to be screaming just one command: run! He had never slept with a girl and doing it right here and now and in the presence of his best friend was just too much, they couldn't be serious!

"But I can't!" he squeaked, and even to his own ears this sounded unmanly – even childish. Armand and the girl laughed softly.

"You have to forgive him, he's still a virgin," Armand explained, "but I guess he'll learn quickly. As you saw him naked today, you can judge for yourself if he's mature enough…" Armand's words sounded very crude in Pierre's ears.

"Let's find somewhere comfortable," Armand continued in good spirits and he went to fetch a blanket from their baggage. Pierre sat there, still panic stricken as

81

he watched his friend preparing a bed for them. He felt like a prisoner watching his own gallows being erected.

Armand took off his shirt and the girl loosened her beautiful hair. The dim night swallowed most of the colours and shapes but just watching her silhouette with her long hair started to have an effect on Pierre. His pulse started to race.

Armand gently undressed the girl and then loosened his breeches – making signs for Pierre to do the same. Awkwardly Pierre started to undress when he felt that her soft hands were taking over and soon he let himself be guided by the girl, forgetting reality and gliding fully into this exciting dream – to his own surprise he fully enjoyed their joint act of lovemaking.

He gave himself over to waves of excitement; he had never even imagined before that a feeling of such intensity could exist.

He listened to Armand's moaning and the girl's answering and it didn't disturb him any more – on the contrary he became more and more excited and when he exploded in his joy once the girl had turned to him he only regretted that it came so fast.

"I told you that he'd be a good pupil," Armand said laughingly. "He pretends to be shy but I always suspected that there's a sensual devil behind this mask of innocence! Still waters run deep – you've just had proof of this!"

The girl gave both of them a quick kiss. "I'd love a repeat," she sighed, "but it's high time for you to leave – the border is not far away and if you start now, you'll make it by morning before my aunt wakes up and raises the village."

Pierre felt wonderful but was totally exhausted and extremely tired. All he wanted to do was to sink into a deep sleep and snuggle into the blanket in the soft straw. He closed his eyes for what he thought would be a second and was asleep in no time. Armand finished the packing, dragged the blanket away from Pierre and kicked him several times with his foot – no reaction.

There seemed only one remedy left. Armand moved carefully in the dark towards the cow as he remembered having seen a bucket of water there before. It was still half full and he gave a satisfied grin, mockingly saluted the sad cow and tiptoed back to his friend.

For Pierre it seemed that only seconds had passed since he closed his eyes when a torrent of cold water hit him and woke him up brutally. He made to protest wildly but Armand's hand closed over his mouth.

"No time to sleep, my friend," he said. " Our – or should I call her our *joint* – girlfriend explained to me the shortest way to the border and we have to leave right now or you'll soon be back in the arms of Brother Hieronymus – you choose. I guess Hieronymus would have loved to watch your performance, by the way."

Pierre shot him an angry look but saw the logic behind his friend's words although he still felt tired. The cold water had done its magic though, and cautiously they led the horses out of the stable as silently as possible. Pierre was relieved that the hysterical chicken was gone and couldn't raise the alarm.

Luckily they had found some old bags to wrap around the horses' hooves. The girl had left them while Pierre had fallen asleep so there was no occasion for a last kiss or a sentimental goodbye. As a finishing touch they bolted the door from the outside. "Just imagine the stupid face our dear hostess will make when she finds a sleeping dog and her valuable hostages vanished into thin air," Armand whispered, and they both had to try really hard not to laugh out loud.

*****

For generations to come the inhabitants of this region would tell their children and grandchildren the dark tale of two young men, one blond with the looks of an angel, one black like the devil, that had come to a remote village, but had disappeared overnight without a trace. These visitors had put a spell on the fierce dog that had been left to guard them, a clear sign that one of them must have been the devil himself!

Eight months after his marriage the elderly husband of the beautiful girl would announce proudly the birth of twins, one blond, one brown-haired – another miracle, of course.

*****

The two friends followed the river until they came to the shallow crossing that their girlfriend had described. The locals kept this place secret as it allowed them to trade all sorts of goods without attracting the undue attention of the authorities as people here really didn't care if their king was French, Spanish, Dutch or German as long as they could farm their fields peacefully and have a little income that went unnoticed by their greedy masters.

The following days passed in a rhythm of riding, hunting or trying to obtain some food and night shelter if some farmers accepted their request. Often enough they were chased away and had to escape with angry dogs or pitchforks close on their heels.

The first two days it was a relief to get back to normality as the adventure with the witch had rattled them more than they'd admitted to each other but finally they found it pretty boring and missed the tension of adventure.

Pierre was still secretly dreaming about his first experience with a girl. He was convinced that he was hiding his feelings extremely well until Armand commented, "She was lovely. What a pity that we had to leave her!"

"How did you know that I was thinking about her?" Pierre protested.

"You haven't done a lot else since we left France!" Armand laughed at him. "You'll never learn to deceive me – and to be honest, I've been thinking about her as well!"

Armand continued his lessons with Pierre to make sure he'd be able to stand his ground in a fight. When the basics had been taught and rehearsed again and again, he thought it was about time to show him some of the more refined tricks with the rapier and he was proud to see that Pierre learnt quickly and eagerly.

If Pierre had been reluctant to use or touch any weapon after he had escaped the monastery, he now started to love the feel of the sword in his hand and was trying to become one with it. Armand had told him that a good fighter didn't use a weapon – the weapon had to become a part of him.

Armand had decided that it was safe to travel now by daylight as they had escaped France and they could use major roads from time to time in order to get to Calais faster, as they didn't know exactly when Marie would arrive there and they must not miss this unique opportunity to cross the Channel with her.

During the past two days they had been fantasizing about the comfort of sleeping in a real bed, so it was easy to make up their minds when they spotted the inviting sign of an inn in the late afternoon. They decided to invest their meagre funds into having a decent meal and bed for once.

But maybe this wasn't such good idea after all.

BACK TO PARIS

Henri rode back to Paris in a frenzy. His groom followed silently, knowing that a wrong word or mistake could be lethal. Something terrible must have happened in Reims and he was sure that it was related to their frequent visits to the monastery. The groom decided to disappear in Paris as soon as possible, but he couldn't risk escaping right now. Paris with its underground world of thousands of migrant workers from the rest of France and other parts of Europe would provide easy shelter for him. Therefore he followed his master dutifully on his return to Paris, riding at breakneck speed until the horses were literally ruined, changing them at the next station for new ones – just to ruin the next pair until finally the city walls of Paris came into sight.

Henri needed this riding exertion, taking his body to its physical limits until he finally felt that the exhaustion was starting to help him to cope with his frustration and rage.

Success and the immediate acquisition of what he regarded to be his rightful heritage had been stolen from right under his nose. Henri felt better when his hot rage started to turn into cold anger. He could handle this more easily – cold anger and hate would motivate him into continuing to play this game.

He was a gambler, and wasn't it the essence of gambling that you lost as well as won? He convinced himself that this single failure didn't really matter – he had only lost one part of the game and it was time now for him to plan the next move and get back to his winning streak.

When his valet Jean saw him coming back to the Palais de Beauvoir with a face like a thunderstorm he was prepared for the worst, but luckily Henri just went straight to bed and fell into a deep sleep that lasted nearly a full day.

During the next day, stretching well into the night, Henri stayed in the library, drinking heavily and conversing with himself when he thought that nobody was around to listen.

Sitting in the same brocade-covered armchair that his father had favoured, Henri looked at the paintings showing his impressive line of ancestors. The lineage went far back in time, his family had held castles and important offices even before the Valois kings had reigned over France, without even mentioning the present upstart Bourbons with their ancestor Henry IV, a foreigner come right from the stables of a meaningless kingdom to ascend to the holy throne of France.

Henri snorted. His eyes wandered to the portrait of his uncle, the last Marquis de Beauvoir. He'd been a handsome man – a pity that he had thrown himself into the arms of this English slut. Well, not a pity really, it gave him, Henri de

Beauvoir, the possibility of becoming the next Marquis – if he now made the right moves.

Pondering his situation for hours, Henri finally came to the conclusion that the key to his heritage lay in the hands of the Cardinal. The King wouldn't bother to interfere if Richelieu had taken a decision, he was weak and the Cardinal, newly promoted to Duke and a peer of France, would know how to present his case with the brilliant logic that never failed to impress his majesty.

But Richelieu had received 50,000 livres from his father already – so would he bother to invest time or effort to get the rest? Henri's mind was racing. Richelieu could milk his cousin in full legality at a later stage – but maybe not as much as he could milk him? He rose from his armchair, picked up another glass of wine and started wandering around his library. The crystal candelabras made a tinkling noise when he passed close to them – they were made of the most expensive glass from Murano. Henri loved this room, as the tapestries, furniture and painting were all testimony to the fabulous wealth of the Marquis de Beauvoir.

Could he afford to sit here and wait?

Henri started to perspire at the thought of his cousin turning up in front of the King before he could interfere, young, probably handsome, pleading for the help of the King. The King would probably be moved and graciously confirm his position as Marquis de Beauvoir, and Henri would become a nobody – an insignificant cousin of a new star that had been born, left with a heritage that had shrunk to a mere pittance by now.

Already rumour had started to spread that his father had needed to borrow money from the Jews. These things always leaked out. If he didn't act fast, he'd become an outcast with no money left, no heritage to claim.

Automatically he took another glass of wine and it disappeared as fast as the previous ones. He resumed his train of thought. It was becoming crystal clear to him that he needed to speed up the course of events. Richelieu had time, he didn't... but how to put pressure on the powerful prime minister, the master of the game who had them all dancing like puppets on a string? Henri's head was spinning, as the next glass of the precious wine was gulped down like water.

The Cardinal was the key... Hadn't he recently launched a new favourite of the King? Having suddenly produced two heirs, the King was convinced that he had done his duty to France as regards procreation and was reverting to his preference for young and good-looking companions.

The cunning Cardinal – knowing the King's penchant for dashing young men – had introduced the handsome young Cinq-Mars into the King's close environment. Cinq-Mars had been an immediate success; it was generally known that the King was falling fast for him. All the salons of Paris were humming with this news. As long as the King was happy with his new toy and took greater interest in his hunting parties than in ruling France he wouldn't interfere with Richelieu's decisions… what a sly old fox Richelieu was! Once more the Cardinal had shown how brilliantly he could manipulate his sovereign – maybe he, Henri, should show the great Cardinal that he could be cunning as well? If he managed to attract the King's attention, Richelieu's plan to distract the King with a man of his own choice would be in danger.

If Henri succeeded in disturbing Richelieu's master plan, the latter would need to react – and Henri could bargain from a position of strength to withdraw from court against Richelieu's commitment to support his claim to the heritage.

Henri knew that he was handsome; men and women would vie to gain his favour, and he could be deadly attractive to both sexes if he chose.

Actually he loved to make them hot, give them hope, sometimes even make love to them – and then drop them, as he found relationships boring. Until today, he had never fallen in love. Rumour had it that at least one unhappy Countess had preferred to leave this world and drink poison than to face a life without him – yes, how very entertaining this dramatic scene had been! And the young man who had shot himself leaving an idiotic letter, how melodramatic!

He smirked; yes, he'd start to tackle the job of attracting the King's attention – and then take on Richelieu's wrath… That sounded like a plan!

Dangerous, subtle, it held everything that Henri de Beauvoir found appealing and exciting. In a sudden and complete change of mood he paused in front of a mirror and saluted his reflected image with a glass of wine.

Even a Cardinal had balls, and he would squeeze them! He started to laugh. "I'll squeeze them hard!" he roared aloud.

Jean, who had secretly been listening and watching through the keyhole as Henri paced the room and saluted himself, thought that his master had definitely become insane.

But Henri sat down, now calm and composed and methodically he started to go through his options. He knew that wooing attention at court would be costly beyond his actual means. His father had told him that their Italian bankers had gone cold, these bastards were of course playing a safe hand. He would show them later how a de Beauvoir would take such an insult.

But for now he needed fresh money fast, and lots of it! Go to the Jew again? Kidnap his niece? He raced through the options but considered the risks too high. He preferred not to show his face in the Jewish quarter for the time being. So where to get the money?

Suddenly the solution flashed through his mind: it seemed so easy! Yes, he knew exactly what to do now.

Over the next days Henri started a chain of activities to put his plans into reality. He started to court the dowager Duchess de Limoges, a lady of fabulous wealth who had dropped some hints that she was open for an adventure before he had left Paris. At the time he had rebuked her arrogantly – but now things had changed!

Henri decided that it was time to pay her a visit and refresh their acquaintance.

The Duchess was torn between the wish to tell her valet to deny him access (she was still very much upset at Henri's rebuff) and her burning curiosity to meet Henri and see firsthand why suddenly he had changed his mind and taken the trouble to pay her a visit.

Being a true woman, curiosity won and she told her valet to let him into her salon where she let him wait for a good hour as a punishment – and of course to change her attire. Finally she arrived, carefully dressed and made up to look her best and her youngest.

Henri had some experience with moody lovers and had anticipated being kept waiting. In fact he was secretly relieved that she hadn't completely shut her door to him.

The Duchess was surprised to find a good humoured and absolutely charming guest paying her plenty of compliments for her beauty and the wonderful gown she was wearing. It was an extremely expensive creation made of a shimmering dark pink silk with appliquéd golden threads and rubies – an outfit more suited for court but her maid had sworn that it made her look at least ten years younger.

Henri calculated in his head that this gown alone must have cost the equivalent of his entire yearly income and congratulated himself on his decision to come here – the late Duke had indeed catered extremely well for his widow.

Their conversation was stiff and formal at the start but Henri cleverly managed to thaw the frozen atmosphere by telling some juicy and deprecating anecdotes about one of her greatest enemies, a current lady-in-waiting of the Queen who had been surprised with her lover – what a scandal – in the Queen's own bedroom!

Soon the Duchess found herself drawn closer and closer to her charming, witty and extremely handsome visitor and when he murmured into her – admittedly somewhat wrinkled – bosom that he would need to leave Paris soon if his luck in cards didn't turn immediately – she understood the message. She offered a discreet and very generous arrangement to allow Henri to stay close to her, making him understand that it depended though on further regular visits to pay back her investment.

Henri protested dutifully that he couldn't accept such generosity, but of course would be pleased to see her soon again – he was astute enough to keep up appearances at least for his first visit.

When they met the next time in her ducal palace he found himself ushered into her lavish bedroom. The Duchess was officially suffering from a migraine, which hadn't stopped her from wearing skilfully applied make-up and a nearly transparent nightshirt. Henri made sure that she forgot her migraine and found her investment worthwhile. When he had accomplished his mission – actually giving her more than she could have hoped for – he considered that it was the right time for a subtle hint that he desperately needed a new hunting horse.

Two days later a beautiful black stallion was his. Henri showed the Duchess in her immense bed what a true stallion could do and the Duchess melted in his arms, ready and willing to accept further requests and ready for new generosities that might be asked of her.

One of Henri's next suggestions really pleased her. Henri proposed to fund a ball in his own palace, but a ball where she should act as his guest of honour, actually more as a hostess, close to his side.

What a surprisingly thoughtful lover, she thought, lying next to him in pleasant exhaustion. *Never would I have expected him to be so considerate and make me his guest of honour*, and once more she accepted with pleasure, opening the strings of her purse, seeing herself dancing with Henri under crystal chandeliers fitted with hundreds of candles. She'd wear of course her famous family jewels, sparkling in all colours of the rainbow, and she'd be followed by the envious glances of the less fortunate ladies – all vying to have a chance to dance with her handsome cavalier.

She knew of course that she was paying in hard currency for her pleasure but until now she felt that she had got a good bargain and moving closer to Henri in her large bed she whispered to him, "Henri, show me once more how the black stallion makes love!" and soon she was crying out with pleasure. Henri hadn't forgotten the tricks he had learnt from the maid in Reims.

*****

Henri was really pleased with his progress. He had filed a request for an interview with the Cardinal and wasn't surprised at all when his secretary, Brother Joseph, came back with the message that the Cardinal apologized, but wouldn't be available before the end of the month as urgent affairs of state had retained his attention.

Brother Joseph knew Henri's reputation for being choleric and was most surprised when Henri accepted his message in an almost humble way.

"I appreciate that His Eminence is continuously working for the glory of the King and France," Henri said smoothly. "Please let him know that I do pay my greatest compliments to His Eminence and look forward to the pleasure of our meeting as soon as he deems it convenient."

Brother Joseph, who had expected tantrums and drama, felt uneasy. *He's up to something*, he thought. *His Eminence should watch him!*

Henri returned at a leisurely pace in the luxurious carriage that his late father used to take and as he thought it important to show the luxurious pomp expected of a future marquis he had ordered several footmen to accompany him.

He was quite pleased with his progress. Tonight the Palais de Beauvoir would look its best. Thousands of candles would be lighted, the best wines of France would flow and music and food would be of exquisite quality. These festivities would beautifully serve several aims at the same time.

The Duchess would be pleased with him and be eating out of his hand even more; he would make sure that she danced several times with him and she would be his envied guest of honour.

He knew that rumours regarding his financial situation were about. This display of wealth and abundance would silence them for the next weeks – and a bit of time was all he needed.

Tables for guests wanting to play cards had been installed and he would make sure to play with large amounts – thanks to the Duchess he could afford to lose. Those not yet convinced by the show he put on for the festivities would be silenced if it was generally known that he still had enough money to play for high stakes.

Last but not least he had succeeded in making sure that Cinq-Mars and his group of young nobles would attend. This clique of the young and beautiful was setting the fashion at court and he needed to become part of them to have easy access to the King and pursue his plan to become noticed.

He needed to befriend Cinq-Mars this night. The latter was a good-looking man, vain but not very bright (a fitting companion for our dowdy King, thought Henri sardonically). He guessed that paying him some fat compliments and telling some saucy jokes and society secrets would probably do the job.

Henri leaned back in the carriage, relaxed, with a wicked smile on his face. He had the feeling that the Cardinal would want to receive him much earlier than he had imagined...

Night fell, and as expected, *tout Paris* had come to meet Henri. The courtyard was overflowing with sedans and expensive coaches, footmen fighting to gain a path for their noble masters. The general knowledge that Henri's father had failed to acquire the title of Marquis de Beauvoir and probably ruined himself shortly before his death (rumour had it that his death might have been a covered-up suicide) added exquisite spice to this story and so they all came, burning with curiosity and ready to snub what they viewed as a once great and powerful family now in full decline of power and wealth.

They were amazed to find a palais blazing with light, freshly decorated with golden tapestries and lined with footmen in the golden-green livery of the de Beauvoir family. They were greeted by a tremendous and very self-assured looking host, his golden locks shimmering like a halo in the light of the torches that lit the courtyard. Only Henri's scar detracted from this image of perfect beauty, but as most ladies or gentlemen such as the Comte de Roquemoulin would admit, the scar only added a seductive air of dangerous attraction.

Henri was at his most handsome and charming, and much as the society vultures sought to criticize and bring him down, all they perceived was quality, wealth and an abundance of food and drink everywhere.

Consequently, rumours about his precarious financial situation and his father's ruin must have been wrong. Soon a new rumour was circulating: the great Cardinal himself seemed to be supporting Henri's quest to become the next Marquis.

The general mood swayed and the former lame duck was becoming the new ascending and beautiful swan. In one night, Henri had succeeded in returning to the limelight.

Some guests raised their carefully made up eye-brows when it became apparent that Henri's guest of honour was the Duchess de Limoges, but as her family was above reproach and her wealth fabulous beyond imagination, they found it difficult to spurn Henri – maybe he'd even end up marrying the golden goose, in any case, he needed to be reckoned with.

Henri had managed to seat Cinq-Mars next to him at a gambling table later in the evening and found it easy to capture the young man's attention. Cinq-Mars was very much aware of his own good looks and bathed in the glory of his new position as the King's favourite, which put him at the centre of attention wherever he went.

He swallowed the compliments that Henri freely heaped on him and they quickly became excellent friends after Henri skilfully lost a considerable amount of money to him. Before the night was over Henri found himself invited to their next hunting party; Cinq-Mars told him that he was quite confident that the King would attend, as they'd be hunting in Versailles and the King loved to stay at his small château nearby.

Henri fell into his bed only when the first rays of the rising sun shone on the now deserted Palais de Beauvoir.

Jean had undressed him and now Henri lay in his big bed – physically exhausted – but so excited that he found it difficult to fall asleep. His master plan had worked beautifully until now! The next step would be to attract the attention of the King – and he didn't think for a second that he might fail. Cinq-Mars might be a good-looking fellow, but he was a simpleton and no match for Henri, this he was sure of.

*****

The formal invitation to join Cinq-Mars's hunting party came the next day as promised but after a brief feeling of exuberance Henri decided to keep his arrival low-key. He chose not to ride the spectacular stallion that the Duchess had offered him but to use a well-bred horse of lesser pedigree. He carefully chose riding attire of excellent quality but avoided putting on an impressive collar or a tightly fitting waistcoat that would highlight his splendid physique.

He intended to blend into the group, to make acquaintances and mix well. He didn't want to draw any special attention to himself; he'd watch how the King behaved, what he preferred, and would plan his next steps as soon as he felt that he could move safely.

The hunting party was a complete success. Knowing that the King would probably attend, the servants had taken the precaution of having enough game to flush in the direction of his bow and Henri saw in fascination, but not surprise, that the great King of France greedily swallowed all the false compliments paid to him for his skills in riding and hunting.

Henri also discovered that the King was surprisingly shy. He seemed to be attracted to Cinq-Mars, his eyes shining brightly when he commanded him to ride next to him but he didn't touch him and would probably not even command him to his bed at night, Henri mused. Louis XIII was behaving like boy in the flush of first love rather than an adult king, sure of his absolute command over his subjects.

Henri felt relieved; he didn't have a problem going to bed with a young and good-looking man but the vision of being ordered to bed by his elderly sovereign had revolted him.

The King had formed the habit on informal occasions, such as this hunting party, of withdrawing with a limited number of his nobles to his more intimate castles. The Queen would stay in Paris which served as a good excuse; no ladies were thus admitted. The King loved these days and evenings; he'd be surrounded by what he regarded as his circle of intimate friends, most of them dashing young men from the high aristocracy. The fact that he stuttered made him extremely shy and he was only too happy to avoid his official duties as often as possible.

Henri decided that he needed to become part of this intimate circle as soon as possible and before Cinq-Mars was aware how it had happened Henri was invited to join them next week once again.

A new life had started for Henri. He continued wooing the Duchess to keep the stream of gifts and income constant but as often as possible he joined the parties of Cinq-Mars.

After two weeks he decided that it was about time to accelerate the speed of events and become more visible to the King. He dressed with more care and luxury than before and decided to ride the spectacular stallion that the Duchess had offered to him and ask Jean to accompany him.

His arrival drew envious glances from the others. Seated upon his impressive stallion, Henri looked spectacularly handsome and his fair appearance was made even more evident by the bronze coloured skin and dark hair of his groom who looked most handsome in his exotic way.

Only Cinq-Mars didn't seem to notice that a rival had just been born. He greeted Henri in a friendly manner, slapping his shoulders and manoeuvred him next to the King who had set his admiring eyes on this young Apollo.

They started the hunt in the dense forest that surrounded the small château of Versailles, riding hard for hours. Discreetly hidden servants made sure that an endless stream of game was once again flushed in the King's direction.

Finally the grooms in the livery of the King gathered, the trumpets sounded in triumph and the dead game was lined up for the final display. The King looked flushed and extremely pleased; praise and compliments were showered on him from all in his entourage for his outstanding riding and hunting skills.

Henri managed to come close to the King who was radiant with joy from the successful hunt and when Louis's eyes fell on the horse he graciously congratulated Henri on his beautiful stallion.

Henri had hoped this occasion would arise and he had rehearsed beforehand how to answer. Swiftly and elegantly he descended from his horse, fell on his knee and beseeched the king to accept the horse as a gift from his humble servant.

Louis XIII looked into the beautiful and adoring blue eyes that were fixed on him, noticing a face of rare beauty to make his heart beat faster. He made a sign for Henri to stand up and graciously accepted this gift.

Henri thought that he had achieved more than enough for one day and dropped back in the group of cavaliers surrounding the King, modestly leaving to Cinq-Mars the place of honour next to the King, as he had felt his jealous eyes already burning into his back.

Keeping himself covered he noticed with amusement that the King's eyes kept searching for him from time to time and he wasn't astonished to receive the next day a royal messenger, presenting him with a gift. Curiously Henri opened the precious leather case. It contained a thick golden chain adorned with precious stones, bearing the King's coat of arms.

In the language of the court there could not exist any clearer sign that the King had invited him to become his friend and not only was he sure that the spies of the Cardinal had recorded this event but he knew that a reaction from the Cardinal was due to come soon!

I'm squeezing his balls already now, Henri said to himself and laughed.

*****

Paris was suffering under a spell of hot weather but inside the Cardinal's palace the temperature was pleasant and Brother Joseph appreciated that he could walk with his sandals on the cool white marble. He hurried as he knew that the report he had just received would be of great interest to the Cardinal.

He knocked softly on the beautifully carved door of the small study the Cardinal preferred to use when he was ill and not attending official audiences. A couch serving as a bed covered with purple blankets and cushions was placed discreetly in a corner and the Cardinal would lie down from time to time when his body was tortured by spasms of pain and he desperately needed a break. He was used to pain being his constant companion but during the last few months his health had deteriorated and he needed rest more and more frequently. It was important that he kept his failing health a secret as the vultures at court were only waiting for any sign of his infirmity before descending on him.

Inside the study it was stiflingly hot as Richelieu had ordered a fire to be lit. He needed to burn some secret papers and he found the heat soothing to his pain.

Brother Joseph entered the room and soon started to perspire; he was feeling extremely uncomfortable. He silently handed the Cardinal a short report hoping that Richelieu wouldn't notice his sweaty hands and the stains he had left on the parchment.

Richelieu opened it and read it with a speed that was testimony to his great practice of digesting thousands of documents in an age where most people had difficulty reading at all. His eyebrows rose during the reading and his thin lips displayed signs of displeasure.

"Our friend is trying to play smart," he said to Brother Joseph, contemplating carefully once more the content of the report. "Actually I appreciate having to deal with intelligent enemies, it's so much more entertaining, but I think our friend is trying to play above his league if he wants to interfere with our plans."

The monk didn't answer. He knew that the Cardinal was in deep thought and hadn't really meant to start a conversation.

The Cardinal sat in total silence, like a chess player pondering his next move, and finally continued in a hoarse voice, "Tell Henri de Beauvoir that I'll have the pleasure of meeting him tomorrow as there has been a sudden change of agenda and I feel indebted to the commitment that I gave to his father. You'll see, he'll be waiting for my message. Probably he'll play difficult to get so in case he needs a bait, you may tell him that news of his cousin has arrived today; I imagine that he's eager to discuss urgently with me how to be reconciled with his dearest lost cousin."

94

Richelieu made a disparaging noise in his throat and Brother Joseph understood that it was time to kiss the Cardinal's ring and take his leave.

Actually the monk was relieved that the interview had been short and he walked back into the cool antechamber where a helpful servant was already holding a fresh towel waiting for him; the Cardinal's servants had sympathy for those who had to endure the heat in his study.

Brother Joseph allowed himself a rare, but silent joke. *Some people who hate His Eminence say that he'll go to hell when he dies,* Joseph mused and chuckled. *Maybe he's already training for the heat down there...*

*****

Even though the Cardinal hadn't given a specific time, Brother Joseph had understood that immediate action was expected of him. He took a mule in order to attract the minimum of attention and dressed in the garb of one of the many friars that were seen in the crowds in the packed streets of Paris.

Joseph arrived at the Palais de Beauvoir asking humbly to meet the Count de Beauvoir, the future Marquis. He was met by a very arrogant looking manservant who asked him to present his credentials first. A quick presentation of Cardinal Richelieu's coat of arms brought a remarkable change and the manservant ushered him into the library asking in his most servile manner if he could bring him refreshments while he went and informed his lordship of his visitor's arrival.

Luckily it was still quite early in the evening and Henri had just been dressing for one of his night forays to the darker side of town.

The Duchess had become more and more demanding, pleading constantly for his companionship and he wanted to escape this night, visit one of the seedy taverns of the city, get totally drunk and have fun. He desperately needed some fresh flesh – he didn't care if it was a girl or a boy, maybe even both for a change?

He was surprised that the Cardinal's messenger had turned up so fast. This was an excellent sign! He had no illusions about the extensive network of spies that the Cardinal was operating – probably even in his own household at least one or two of his servants were reporting to him. All the same he was amazed at the speed. Thousands of reports must land on the desks of Richelieu's secretaries daily. If he had moved this fast, the King's lavish gift and invitation must be truly worrying the Cardinal.

Henri entered the room and Brother Joseph understood intuitively that this mixture of elegance, good breeding and handsome face would impress the King. Henri had already dressed to go out and although he had chosen a more comfortable than elegant apparel he still looked every inch the prince he wanted to become.

Henri came straight to the point and sneered, "How surprising and most edifying that the messenger of His Noble Eminence has found time to visit my humble home. I had thought that His Grace must have already forgotten that I existed?"

Brother Joseph pretended not to notice the irony of this statement and solemnly presented his greetings from the Cardinal.

Henri continued arrogantly, "What a pity that I don't have any time available – I was just about to leave to meet some important people, well, you probably know as well as I do whom I am friends with right now. His Eminence's quality of information is," he seemed to clear his throat, "let's say... it's legendary! Maybe we will have the opportunity to talk next time, it was a pleasure," and while he was finishing his sentence he turned abruptly and walked towards the door.

"I'm sorry," Joseph answered smoothly, " I certainly did not wish to interfere unduly, Monsieur, but his Eminence the Cardinal was under the impression that you seemed anxious to receive the latest news of your cousin, the present Marquis, so as to have the opportunity to arrange the family reunion that you were so much looking forward to!"

Henri turned around and looked sharply at the monk. "I'll grant you five minutes then."

The monk repeated the Cardinal's invitation to join him tomorrow as he would like to tell Henri personally the status of their research.

A cruel smile was playing on Henri's lips when he said, "Oh, yes! I nearly forgot my beloved cousin, I really did regret missing the opportunity of reuniting with him! Tell His Eminence I'll be present tomorrow but please let him know that unless he can give some concrete information and help in this matter, I'd rather take up a different invitation and join our gracious King!"

Henri had already turned his back while he was still talking and the closing door muffled the sound of his triumphant laughter.

Brother Joseph just shook his head in disbelief – did this arrogant youngster really believe he could outplay the Cardinal?

The next hours passed quickly. Henri was in high spirits and followed his initial plan to have a good time. Accompanied by Jean he visited the tavern of ill-repute that was the meeting point for the more adventurous of his friends. This establishment was known all over Paris for the special services of excellent quality provided by its female servants – performed in the guest rooms upstairs.

For those guests who preferred a bit of fighting and fresh blood, its famous cock fighting drew a large audience, gentlemen and commoners mingling in the crowded pub and placing their bets. As soon as they became drunk from the cheap wine and strong *eau de vie*, brawls would break out and daggers would be drawn easily, adding additional spice to the evening. Henri knew that he had to be in shape to face and fight with Richelieu's brilliant mind shortly, so he decided with great regret to stay sober – but all the same, he loved this place and the sight of the bloodied cocks always gave him a thrill.

*****

The next day Henri was informed by a footman dressed in the livery of His Eminence that he was invited to arrive during the late afternoon at the Cardinal's palace.

When he was led into the library, the Cardinal seemed to have shrunk in his big armchair. His dark eyes had sunk deeply into his face and his long, white fingers gave him a ghostly appearance.

When he looked at Henri it became immediately clear though that these eyes had lost nothing of their fire and power.

Good-looking, smart, arrogant, not a weakling like his stupid father, Richelieu thought, hiding his feelings behind a non-committal mask of politeness. *He's a danger indeed and I need to remove him fast from court.*

He nodded slightly and Henri kissed the ring as was demanded by protocol, but Richelieu lost no time and went straight to the point.

"I hope, my son, that you found time and prayers helpful in overcoming the sudden and unexpected passing of your father?" he said, staring at Henri who felt uncomfortable for a second – this man really had a way of letting him feel that he knew everything.

"I promised your father that I would help you to reunite with your dear young cousin. I feel bound by this promise. When the news arrived that your cousin had mysteriously disappeared from the monastery school of Reims I asked my secretary immediately to start a search and make sure that it would yield results… Well, I'm happy to tell you that it was reported that your cousin was seen close to Reims in the disguise of a groom on the way to our northern borders. Therefore, I guess, we're fairly safe in assuming that he's in the Spanish Netherlands right now and will probably move on to Antwerp and then to England in order to claim his mother's inheritance before he comes back to France. It may be of interest for you to know that he's in the company of a friend, another youngster called Armand de Saint Paul who also decided to leave this school presenting a… let's say… slightly modified version of his father's summons to join him and was released from school therefore without any difficulty. It seems too much of a coincidence that two boys should go missing together completely by chance."

Richelieu tapped on the desk with a quill he held in his hand. "I therefore recommend that you leave Paris and go to England immediately."

97

"Why should he or I go to England? His mother was a heretic slut – so what should he claim?" Henri retorted arrogantly. "And why should I waste my time there?"

"Heretic and protestant, she was indeed," the Cardinal answered sharply. "But you must learn not to let your emotions be a substitute for knowledge and reflection. His mother was the daughter of His Grace, the Duke of Hertford, head of one of the most powerful families in England. Her noble pedigree is beyond any doubt. Your cousin will therefore discover soon – if he succeeds in crossing the Channel – that he was born into a very powerful family in England. This family might be wooed by his youthful innocence and help him to support his claim here. His mother might even have left him a substantial legacy in her own right."

Henri paused to digest this news. His bastard cousin was no bastard but the son of a Marquis and the grandson of a Duke! He cleared his throat; he hated every aspect of this.

"How do I now come into this picture, Your Eminence? What do you propose, because it might be more interesting for me to stay here and cultivate my latest and very fruitful acquaintances."

Richelieu pretended not to have noticed this thinly veiled challenge and continued. "The deal was sealed between your father and me. We would help you to find your cousin and sort out your family matters. If your cousin by any chance of fate should become victim of any accident or serious illness, the next in line will inherit the full rights of the Marquis de Beauvoir and he will be liable to pay us the remaining 150,000 livres as soon as he ascends to the rank of Marquis."

The Cardinal paused and searched on his desk. His long fingers carefully chose an official looking vellum with a large red seal and he made a sign to Henri to come closer.

"Here is a document signed and sealed by myself acting as representative for our gracious King appointing you as special ambassador for a diplomatic mission to the Court of Whitehall if you confirm the deal I had with your father. You'll be in charge of confidential negotiations relating to the territorial conflicts we have in our colonies – of course to our greatest regret – with King Charles and his ministers. You'll be briefed by my secretaries about the situation – even if ..." he smiled dryly, "even if – of course – no solution is really expected to result from these talks. The status of special ambassador will provide safe sailing and immunity from prosecution if something... er... such as an accident should happen to your cousin."

Henri was impressed. He had come here expecting a showdown of wills, accusations, tantrums and threats – none of this had happened. He was pleasantly surprised how smooth it had all been. Too smooth, perhaps? It was obvious that Richelieu wanted him out of his way as fast as possible – but he delivered value for the money they had paid. He even offered protection to him. Remarkable, brilliant!

"How and when should I sail and where will I stay?" Henri asked.

"My secretary will arrange these matters," the Cardinal replied. "But don't worry. You'll receive exact information on how this mission has to be accomplished and I took the liberty of making sure that a suite will be at your disposal in the royal embassy of France when you arrive. You'll be introduced to court by our ambassador but as your mission is secret you are not supposed to present yourself as a special ambassador to third parties beyond the ministers who will be your partners during this discussion. Please keep the document secret and only use it in case of an emergency."

Henri thanked Richelieu and went through the motions of protocol, but his mind was already absent and triumphing! This was the opportunity of his life! Not only could he become the rightful Marquis – he might also catch the fat fish of an additional heritage in England. Between his dream and reality lay just the frail life of one person and he, Henri de Beauvoir, vowed that this would be terminated soon. As if in a trance he returned to his carriage.

Henri had left the library when the frail-looking Cardinal suddenly straightened himself and looked very animated.

His secretary cleared his throat. "Your Eminence, may I speak out?"

The Cardinal looked surprised and answered, "Of course, my Son, are you worried about anything?"

"I'm concerned that the document of appointment for your visitor is not correct and I wonder who has established it. The appointment of a royal Ambassador necessitates the signature of the King in order to be approved by the Court of Whitehall; de Beauvoir will risk not being treated as an official Ambassador nor granted immunity if the instrument of his appointment is not correct."

The secretary now looked truly worried. Richelieu looked at him and chuckled. "I know, my Son, of course, I know – but he doesn't," and the Cardinal started to laugh, to the great surprise of the young secretary who only now started to realize that the Cardinal had been playing – once again – one of his subtle games of power.

*****

As a result of his audience with the Cardinal, Henri was preparing once more for a journey – but this time in style, shutting down the household in Paris for an undetermined period of time. He paid a farewell visit to the Duchess de Limoges, secretly happy to get rid of her in an elegant way – leading a royal mission to London was of course above any reproach. The Duchess had already spotted his potential successor and was herself not too sad, as Henri's constant demands for

99

money or expensive gifts had started to eat even into her substantial means. She had already dreaded the day she would need to turn down a renewed request to open the strings of her purse.

They both shed some false tears and parted as excellent friends, but both extremely relieved.

Summer in all its splendour had arrived by the time Henri's entourage was ready to travel to Calais where the ever efficient office of the Cardinal Richelieu had booked a guesthouse of impeccable reputation and secured a passage on a comfortable ship that would sail to London.

A NEW EXPERIENCE

The inn was solidly built from sand-coloured quarried stone but looked rather shabby, worn out by time and a distinct lack of care. Its chairs and tables were in a pitiful state, worn out and repaired several times as they must have witnessed several violent brawls. The tavern at least did not look too uninviting – if one disregarded the stench of smoke, cheap wine and ale. Armand and Pierre were met by the bald, greasy-looking keeper of this proud establishment.

Their aspiring host was of medium size and emanated a strong smell of brandy when he came close. His shirt hung loosely as if it had given up fighting against the huge belly that swelled impressively out of the stained buckskin breeches. He let them in with an almost hostile look but once again the magical appearance of money in Armand's hand produced an almost comical change in his attitude.

Suddenly the innkeeper's personality transformed, he became deferent and zealous while he showed them a small room upstairs, moving up the decrepit staircase with puffing noises but impressive speed. With a proud gesture – lavishly praising the offered accommodation – he proposed an outrageous price and this entailed a procedure of almost endless bargaining until they reached an agreement, and yet Armand had the unpleasant impression that he had been shafted all the same.

Armand announced that his groom was to sleep on the floor of his room on a makeshift mattress and not in the stables as was customary. Immediately the eyebrows of their host went up and he leered at them. He didn't bother to hide his thoughts: they were apparently not the first young men to share a room and have fun together.

Pierre blushed crimson when he grasped their host's line of thought but when he opened his mouth to protest, Armand just kicked his foot and said haughtily to the innkeeper, "My groom is a bit too fast with the maids. I prefer to keep him under my control, I don't want any trouble with you later," and managed to throw an admonishing glance to Pierre who got the message and looked guiltily at the floor as if he was pouting sulkily.

The innkeeper laughed and said soothingly,"He is handsome enough to have an easy way with the maids, but you're right, I run a decent inn, either you pay or you keep your hands off." As with most of the people they had met recently he used a local dialect of French with a thick Dutch accent but the meaning of his words was clear and he left the room.

Armand's eyes swam with tears of suppressed amusement and he repeated, "A decent house, indeed this is!"

About an hour later they had refreshed themselves after a giggling maid, displaying her bust to her best advantage, had brought hot water upstairs. She sent inviting glances to Pierre who had already removed his shirt and was pressing it awkwardly to his chest when she had entered – his reputation had clearly spread.

The alluring smell of roasted meat made them realize how hungry they truly were. They went down to the tavern, choosing the table and chairs that looked most solid in this dilapidated collection of furniture, which showed even in the dim light signs of age and wear.

Once more there was a bargaining session with the innkeeper until they had fixed the price for a rich meal of roasted sucking pig, chicken and mutton with dark bread and a chicken broth with vegetables. The cheap wine burned their throats but after having been on the road for so many days, the meal and the wine simply tasted delicious.

They had nearly finished their meal, when a group of five men entered the room. It was quite late in the evening already.

Pierre eyed them up and down and it wasn't difficult to guess that their major source of income would sooner or later lead them to the gallows. But they were apparently regulars, speaking the local patois mix of French and Dutch and the maid immediately put tankards of ale in front of them and didn't object when one of the men fondled her back. As the innkeeper watched with a satisfied smile on his lips it was clear to the young men that these visitors provided regular and welcome additional income for the maid and the inn.

The men started to gamble and took out their dice. Soon they invited Armand and Pierre to join in throwing the dice and Armand accepted, as he wanted to avoid causing any offence or, more likely, ending in a row.

He explained that Pierre was his groom and had no money of his own, therefore Pierre was judged useless and to be discarded and would sit on the side and watch the group playing.

Armand quickly discovered that the dice were loaded but pretended to enjoy the game. He ordered free wine for all to show that he was their best friend. Suddenly he started to yawn profusely and after a last round of throwing dice – which not surprisingly he lost again – and heavy protest from the other gamblers, he retired with Pierre to his room.

As soon they had entered their small room, the expression on his face changed and he looked very serious. "No sleep for us tonight, I'm afraid," he said to Pierre. "They'll try to rob us and steal the horses. Let's get out of here as fast as possible. We know how to fight but one of the louts has a pistol and I guess the innkeeper will take their side. Riding now in the dark into the woods won't help us. I propose we prepare them a nice surprise down in the stables and let's hope that they'll be drunk enough so that we can finish them off easily."

Pierre was amazed and impressed to see that Armand didn't seem to be worried, he even seemed to be looking forward to a fight! Pierre regretted that he wasn't as cool as his friend. He felt a mix of elation and panic – this was going to be his first real fight! He had to show now if he was worthy of carrying the title of Marquis and his throat suddenly went dry. He swallowed hard but managed to send an encouraging and reassuring smile to his friend.

They decided to bolt their room from the inside and leave through the window. Luckily the thatched roof of the stables was just below their window which meant that climbing down was relatively easy and didn't make any noise to give them away.

The clamouring of the drunken louts was audible all over the courtyard. On entering the stable Pierre and Armand were greeted by their horses, who prodded the boys with their soft muzzles, hoping to find some treats.

After a short deliberation Pierre and Armand installed themselves in strategic positions close to the door of the stable. They left the door slightly ajar so as to let in the moonlight and make sure that they'd hear the enemy approaching as early as possible.

The noise from the tavern increased to drunken singing and a good hour later they could hear several men rumbling around upstairs and soon afterwards the noise of smashing wood and afterwards loud curses.

"They have discovered that the fat birdies are gone," Armand commented in a low tone and Pierre could almost imagine his broad smile although it was too dark to see his friend's face clearly.

The men clattered down the staircase again and almost immediately they heard a whole gang of people moving out of the tavern into the cobbled yard and heading towards the stables in search of some other booty and the precious horses.

Pierre and Armand had agreed not to attack until most of the villains had entered the dark stable. It seemed to be the right strategy: the drunken men stormed into the stable, with only one of them holding a flickering light in his hand. They were oblivious to any trap that might have been laid for them – who'd expect two green boys to pose a threat?

Four of the drunkards lurched noisily into the stable and loudly aired their satisfaction when they found the horses – they were at their ease, and one of them even dropped his breeches and started to pee into the hay.

But their luck wasn't to hold as Armand had just been waiting until he had them close enough and cold bloodedly he shot at the first ones with the two flintlock pistols he had carefully loaded beforehand. He was aware that his plan was not very fair, but this was a matter of life and death.

The man holding the light fell down right away on his face and the light went out, plunging the stable into almost complete darkness. The remaining two villains were still trying to work out what had happened when Armand drew his sword to finish them off. They were cursing in the darkness and slashing around violently with their weapons in the hope of striking down their assailants, attacking them viciously from the cover of darkness.

Pierre had received firm instructions from Armand not to get involved and to wait silently at the door until the last villains arrived to make sure that he could shoot them. Their plan seemed to be working beautifully as Armand was clearly able to cope with his four assailants on his own.

While Armand was still fighting with two of the villains, Pierre glimpsed the silhouette of what he supposed to be their leader. He took his pistol and let the hammer loose on the gunpowder as Armand had taught him to do.

Pierre heard the clicking sound of the pistol but nothing happened: the powder had probably become damp when they had been travelling.

Pierre was horrified and cursed to himself as he could see that the silhouette out there was now taking a flintlock out his pocket and calmly pointing it in the direction of Armand who was visible from the entrance fighting and trying to finish off his last opponent.

Without having any real time to plan properly or any opportunity to think, Pierre drew his sword and jumped directly in the direction of the villain. The surprise was such that the man dropped his pistol; Pierre heard the clattering noise of the metal on the cobbles.

The villain turned to the shadow that had leapt towards him, drew his sword and Pierre was engaged for the first time ever in a real fight – a fight for life or death!

Trying desperately to remember all the lessons that Armand had taught him, Pierre stormed forward. The enemy was an experienced fighter and as soon as he realized that his opponent was an inexperienced youngster he made a contemptuous noise and fought with all of his might to get the job finished fast, and attack the second boy inside the stable who seemed to be a more worthy target.

Things looked desperate for Pierre who was retreating under the impact of the relentless fighting until he suddenly remembered Armand's voice – *You must become one with your rapier!*

Pierre focused his mind on the one and only target: make sure that his weapon and his body were acting in unison and his moves became notably more and more fluid and elegant. All of a sudden his rapier made contact with his adversary's arm, injuring him. Pierre was jubilant and his mind seemed to transform and focus on

104

one task only: the inexperienced youngster turned into a swift and efficient fighting machine.

The villain didn't understand what was going on. What had seemed to be a quick and easy job – just finishing off an inexperienced youngster – suddenly turned into a desperate fight for his life. The boy fought like the devil and when Pierre's face was lit by the moonlight it showed his determination to win and kill – and that this young devil thoroughly seemed to be enjoying the fight.

Pierre's enemy changed his mind. He decided to flee when his saw this frightening and determined face in the pale moonlight, but he hesitated a second too long, and Pierre's sword went right into his belly and he collapsed.

Pierre drew his sword out of the crumpled body ready to kill the next opponent when he saw Armand leaning at the stable door raising his hands and crying, "Have mercy, great fighter, spare the innocent!"

It took Pierre some seconds to comprehend that his friend was joking and to come back to reality.

Armand came closer and embraced him. "You did a fantastic job, I'm afraid you've become a much better fighter than I'll ever be! You've a natural talent – who'd have believed it, seeing you in the monastery school concentrating on your vellum, scribbling down your prayers!"

Pierre told him to shut up, he had only finished off one adversary whereas Armand had coped with four of them. Suddenly Pierre noticed a sharp pain in his left arm and he saw that his shirt was dripping with blood. During the fighting he hadn't even noticed that he had been hurt.

"We have to wash out the wound and bandage it as Brother Infirmarius showed us in his hospital. Let's see if I can sneak inside and get hold of some clean linen," Armand said, using his common sense. A bit of blood wouldn't send him into a panic.

Carefully they walked towards the tavern, their swords drawn, ready to strike as they expected the innkeeper and servants to come out at any minute and search for their companions. Carefully Armand opened the door – but the inn lay still and deserted.

The tallow candles had almost burnt down and their smoke filled the air with acrid fumes and soot. They moved further, tiptoeing towards the kitchen, expecting an ambush at any minute.

Pierre had to hold his breath as his wound was starting to hurt more and more. Carefully they opened the door of the kitchen. The deserted kitchen was only lit by the flickering flames of the fire in the hearth and lay in total silence. At first glance it seemed to be empty but scanning the kitchen floor carefully Armand spotted a foot poking out from underneath the big kitchen table. He moved silently towards the table and, pointing his sword downwards, he shouted in a menacing tone, "Come out immediately – or I'll kill you!"

The table started to move and two trembling servants appeared: the young maid who had waited on them in the tavern during their dinner and another servant, probably the cook, as he wore a greasy and blood-stained apron. The cook was a tall man with a big belly, but was shaking like a leaf.

The maid fell to her knees, begging for their lives; apparently she liked a bit of drama. Armand told her to get up and calm herself, that she and the cook had nothing to fear. "Where's the keeper of the inn?" he enquired. The girl apparently felt reassured and answered surprisingly calmly, "He always goes down to the wine cellar at the end of the evening and checks his bottles of brandy. By this time he'll be sound asleep and totally drunk down there. Cook has to drag him to bed every night."

She looked at Pierre and saw his bloodied shirt. "What has happened? We heard the noises but we were so afraid that we decided to hide here; as our groom has taken a day off we're the only servants here today. Take your shirt off, we must bind your wound immediately," and resolutely she took command in no time.

Pierre was a little worried but he followed her orders and took his shirt off. The girl looked at his body with appreciative eyes. The past weeks of riding and exercise had made his body muscular; the skinny school boy was turning into an appealing young man.

Pierre could see that this was not the first time that she had treated an injury. He clenched his teeth when she washed the wound with brandy explaining that her mother had shown her this trick and it usually worked. She took some fresh linen from the cupboard, tore it to pieces and in no time Pierre had a bandage worthy of the hospital in Reims. She had sent the cook to search for a shirt from the innkeeper; even if it was far too large for his slender figure it felt good to have a fresh shirt, so he thanked the girl. She was of course very curious to know what had been going on in the stables so Pierre recounted to her the story of their fight.

"So you killed them all!" she said excitedly. "That's wonderful! I hated them, a filthy and bad lot but best friends with my master."

The cook nodded in agreement; apparently he wasn't a great one for talking and let the girl do it instead.

"Do you have any idea of how we can get rid of them?" Armand enquired with a frown. "If your master finds them tomorrow morning we'll have the constabulary immediately on our backs!"

Pierre had drunk the rest of the brandy that hadn't been used for his wound and was feeling slightly drunk and in high spirits. He could deal with hundreds of opponents, he was sure of that now.

106

"I think I know what to do," the girl answered after a short deliberation. "Cook and I will help you to clean the stables and we'll show you the way to a small lake nearby. People from this region avoid going there because they say that it's haunted, it's called *le lac des enfants noyés*, the lake of the drowned children. The water there is very dark and you can't see the bottom. It's full of tree trunks that fell into it and float at the surface. You'll have to drop the bodies there and they'll probably never be discovered. When our master questions us we'll tell him the following story: we heard a big row between the guests, went into hiding and have no idea where they went or if they found you."

Armand give her a big kiss to thank her and she insisted on receiving a second one from Pierre, sighing, "What a pity he's wounded and we have no time to spend… " Pierre just grinned – life had really changed for him, and for the better, he thought.

The dead bodies were loaded onto the horses and in a hurry they washed away the bloodstains on the cobbles to avoid suspicious questions from the innkeeper. Armand insisted on giving some coins to the girl and the cook for their help and they accepted readily. The cook was then ordered by the girl to accompany them for a short while to show them a shortcut to the haunted lake of the drowned children.

*****

Pierre would never forget this bizarre journey by night. The dead bodies swayed on the horses and the cold moonlight shone on their faces, frozen into bizarre grimaces in death. One of the bodies showed a distorted, almost cynical smile, as if the body was expecting to come back to life soon.

Pierre feared any minute that a demon or ghost would appear behind the dark trees that stretched their branches like menacing tentacles towards them. The elation that he had felt earlier this evening was replaced by total exhaustion. The lack of sleep and the loss of blood were starting to take their toll.

Armand could see that his friend was struggling more and more to keep pace but he was desperate to move forward and get rid of the corpses. He estimated that they were still a fortnight away from Calais and they would have to move on if they wanted to meet Marie – he had never harboured the slightest fear that Marie would not get her way and wait for them as promised.

Finally they arrived at the sombre lake, their nerves shattered and their tired bodies crying for rest. The wailing cries of a little owl sitting in a tree above them sent shivers up and down their spines. The first corpse was dispatched into the sinister lake and the splashing sound of the water sent a hollow echo that made them shudder even more. Of course they put on a brave face – for nothing in the world would they admit to being in the grip of fear.

107

The lakeside atmosphere was truly eerie and the boys dumped the remaining corpses as fast as they could into their wet grave, mounted the horses in a frenzy and rode off back in the direction of the road in the hope of finding some place or shelter where they could hide and sleep – and forget this episode.

Heavy clouds had started to gather and gusts of wind were the harbingers of the rain that was to come soon. The moonlight now filtered only rarely through the dense clouds. Riding on the uneven paths in the wood became impossible and they had to alight and lead the horses in the hope of staying on the right track that would lead them back to the main road. Pierre put one foot before the other mechanically. He had entered a state of mind and body where he didn't care anymore if he should live or die.

After some time it dawned on them that they must have lost the road in the darkness and had entered deeper and deeper into the wood. Armand secretly started to despair. The first drops of rain started falling and he was afraid that once the rain set in it wouldn't stop. He felt that Pierre was close to collapse – how long would they be able to keep going?

They were toiling on slowly when a small animal bolted across their path. Armand automatically looked to the left where it had disappeared into the undergrowth. There was no more trace of the animal but he noticed a strange silhouette against the bushes in a clearing and curiously moved closer to investigate it from nearby.

He carefully approached the silhouette and to Armand's immense joy and relief it appeared to be the abandoned hut of a charcoal burner. Slowly he pushed the makeshift door open. The door moved lopsidedly on decrepit leather hinges and gave access to a small hut with the almost intact remains of a makeshift stove and a chimney – apparently abandoned for several months, as nature had slowly started to take over and weeds were growing in abundance.

Rain had got in and was dripping through a gap in the roof but most of the interior of the hut was comfortably dry and Armand felt like a king when he discovered the inviting remains of a bedstead covered with dried moss. Armand led a totally exhausted Pierre into the dry corner and covered him with a blanket from his luggage. He wasn't even sure that Pierre was registering what was going on – Pierre followed him and moved like a puppet on strings. He drank greedily from the leather flask that the maid had filled before their departure from the inn with a mixture of wine and water and was dead asleep a minute later.

Armand would have loved to join Pierre as he too felt utterly exhausted but he anticipated the rain becoming stronger soon and wanted to close the gaping hole in the roof. Moving around the small hut he stumbled upon some old wooden boards on the floor and as the ceiling of the hut was quite low thought it should be fairly easy to use them to repair the leaking roof.

108

Early morning was already approaching and the pale twilight heralding the imminent sunrise helped him to find some branches and large leaves in the proximity of the hut. He placed them on top of the planks, hoping that his construction could avoid the worst. By the time he had finished, the clouds had become more and more menacing and a slight drizzle was transforming into a dense curtain of rain.

When Armand came back into the hut he noticed that Pierre was freezing now and so he lay down close to him, covering both of them with the last spare blanket, trying to warm the shivering Pierre. Armand now was exhausted and fell into a deep slumber – not even the trumpets of Jericho could have kept him from sleeping.

Armand woke up some hours later and it took him some minutes to remember where he was and what had happened. He still lay close to Pierre and realized that his friend was burning hot now, perspiring profusely. Armand started to panic; tears sprang into his eyes when he looked at his suffering friend as he awkwardly stroked his hot face.

*****

During the next two days Pierre was plagued by continuous high fever. Armand prayed fervently that the fever was only caused by the exhaustion of their night fighting, his loss of blood and their exhausting escape but in his nightmares he was tortured by the vision of finding his friend with a wound that had started to fester. There were only two known options for the treatment of festering wounds: cut off the infected limb or die.

While Pierre was burning with fever, Armand constantly tried to relieve his pains with fresh water, trying to cool his burning body – luckily he had found a stream with clean water not far from the hut.

To Armand's great relief the repaired roof proved to be a good shelter from the constant rain. Armand even succeeded in lighting a fire in the old stove; it seemed his prayers had been heard and Pierre's fever started to abate. When Pierre whispered for the first time that he was feeling hungry, Armand could have hugged the world, they had made it! But how frail his friend looked now, like a living skeleton.

It took them some more days before they felt confident enough to continue their journey to Calais. Armand had used the time waiting for Pierre to recover in exploring their neighbourhood and had found out that they had moved in a huge circle in the darkness. The hut was in fact located very close to the lake where they had dumped the corpses after midnight and this probably also explained the fact that it had been abandoned – even in daylight the atmosphere of the place was truly eerie.

He now also found his way back to the main road and staying hidden in the green leaves of the bushes he registered a regular traffic of locals but no unusual movement of officials or searching soldiers. He hoped that the innkeeper hadn't raised any alarm yet – maybe he'd keep his mouth shut: would he really be keen to acknowledge officially that he had been acquainted with those villains?

The sun was shining when they said farewell to the hut that had saved their lives and now their target was to reach Calais as fast as possible. They'd need to skip the planned trip to Armand's relative in Mons if they wanted to meet Marie on time. Pierre had spent the last days exercising with Armand with the sword to regain his strength, with the effect that he felt constantly hungry. It needed all of their hunting skills to fill his groaning belly, but he felt strong enough and ready to continue their adventure.

They had left the monastery only about three months before, but it seemed to Pierre that it must have been ages ago that he had been sitting in the stuffy schoolroom under the admonishing glances of Brother Hieronymus and it must have been an altogether different Pierre who had been sitting there, dutifully scribbling Latin phrases. A Pierre who was gone and wasn't missed – he liked the new Pierre much better!

As they rode side by side he tried to explain these feelings to Armand and told him that he didn't know how to thank him for what he had done for him.

"Utter nonsense," Armand answered curtly, although he felt secretly flattered by Pierre's little speech.

"You'd have done the same for me – and as for the 'new' Pierre, well in my eyes he was always there, just waiting for his chance to hatch out!"

They continued their journey to Calais, carefully avoiding coming too close to French territory for as long as possible, and decided to head to Dunkirk first before they descended to Calais. Summer was in full swing and travelling in the sun had given Armand a dark suntan. Armand had also stopped shaving as he wanted to change his appearance radically, confident that he would remain unnoticed with his new looks as soon as they entered France. Pierre did the same but his result was nowhere near as impressive. Armand with his dark locks, broad shoulders and fully grown beard looked like one of the fabulous and dangerously attractive corsairs from the Mediterranean – nobody would ever imagine that he had escaped from a tame institution like a boys' monastery school.

Their journey to the Channel continued smoothly – a little too smoothly, as Pierre found it somewhat boring after all the adventures of the past week. Nobody seemed to be bothered by the two young travelling youngsters, one dark, one blond.

The mud on the streets had dried and become as hard as rock. Riding became more and more exasperating as clouds of dust hung above the roads hampering their progress and irritating their eyes and lungs, making them cough even at night when they had stopped travelling.

It was another hot day when they finally caught sight of Dunkirk. Pierre had eyes as sharp as an eagle, and cheered loudly, as he was the first to spot the towers of the distant city. They spurred on their horses and did their best to reach Dunkirk as fast as possible. Neither of them had ever seen the sea and they were burning with curiosity to see with their own eyes what had been a distant dream and the stuff of fairy tales until today.

City and port were heavily fortified but the two friends were lucky to arrive in one of the rare intermittent periods of peace, and they were waved through the city gates without any profound scrutiny; the heat had paralysed even the most zealous of city guards. Dunkirk was famous for its fleet, heavily armed ships that had the infamous reputation of haunting the Dutch in the name of the King of Spain, seeking out precious booty like gold and spices. At this time Dunkirk belonged to the Spanish part of the Netherlands but the French, English, Dutch and of course the Spanish were locked in century-old disputes, vying to conquer or re-conquer a port of enormous strategic value, as Calais was now firmly in French hands.

On the outskirts they found a pleasant-looking guesthouse that was impeccably clean, kept by a widowed landlady. She had lost her son and her husband at sea and took immediately to the two young men, calling them 'my boys' and pampering them with everything she could find in her well-stocked kitchen.

One look at Pierre, who was still looking extremely haggard after his illness, and then into his big blue eyes had been sufficient to awake all of her dormant maternal feelings and she wouldn't listen to any protest that they didn't have enough money to pay for all the wonderful things she started to feed them on.

"Boys must eat," she said resolutely. "Don't bother about money, we'll look after that later, you can do some work for me," and consequently they were happy to do some repairs and garden work in exchange for wonderful food and beds that were so soft and comfortable that Pierre could have stayed inside the whole day.

Armand and Pierre happily tucked into what they considered to be gourmet meals of several courses with an amazing variety of meats, poultry and, of course, fresh fish, as the daily catch from the North Sea was landed every morning and sold immediately by the fishmongers, praising the quality of their fish in loud and shrill heavy patois.

The boys' hostess usually joined them for dinner and it was difficult to determine if she derived more satisfaction from eating her own meal or from watching Pierre and Armand relishing the dishes she had prepared for them.

They had started to explore the city and visited the market stalls as they desperately needed to buy new clothes. Their old ones were falling to pieces after three months of travelling and riding and Pierre's shirt, which had once belonged

111

to the inn keeper, looked even more ridiculous now that he had grown taller and yet was still so slender.

Of course they had already visited the harbour – easy to find as the smell of the sea, fish and coal tar guided them through the narrow streets. They marvelled at the huge sailing ships rocking gently at the quay. The largest one had apparently just arrived and they watched it being unloaded by a small army of sailors and footmen.

Pierre had neither seen the sea before in his life nor a big ship and was amazed: the reality of it easily surpassed his wildest imagination.

They decided to stay some more days and take their time to explore the coast in the direction of Calais to find the best way to enter France – without being noticed or caught immediately. Pierre took great enjoyment in riding along the long stretches of fine sandy beaches and the endless ocean on one side, with water that changed colour several times during the day, and huge cream-coloured dunes on the other.

Feeling the gusts of wind in his face he could even taste the sea, as the fresh air left a salty tang on his lips. He adored the rays of light that played on the water, turning it from a mysterious grey to an inviting blue as soon as the sun lifted its veil of clouds. Under the light of the sun the beach changed from a sombre cream to a dazzling white, framed by the green crowns of marram grass, eternally dancing in the wind that never stopped blowing in from the sea. Growing up in the Champagne region with its lovely rolling hillsides and carefully cultivated vineyards he had never imagined in his wildest dreams that such a vast and borderless landscape could exist.

Splashing into the water with their horses they galloped for hours along this beautiful flat coast, Pierre savouring a boundless freedom that he had never experienced before, a sensation that surpassed anything that he could have imagined.

He looked at Armand to see if he could understand and share these feelings and he was satisfied when an exuberant Armand turned towards him at the same moment crying, "Pierre, this feels so good, this day should never end!"

But as they were now approaching the end of August, the time had come for them to leave for Calais and meet Marie and continue their adventure. In the meantime their landlady had become a close friend and she invited them to call her by her first name, 'Madame Claire'.

One evening Pierre decided to come clean and tell her that they needed to go to Calais soon – and incognito. Their hostess didn't seem at all surprised as she had sensed all the time that these boys were not the simple merchants they had pretended to be.

Claire shed some secret tears when she realized that their time in Dunkirk was about to end soon but as she was a very practically minded person, she quickly sat down with them to plan their next moves. She discarded all of the wild plans the friends had made up and told them to rely on good old Claire to make it happen.

First she persuaded a good acquaintance of hers with the bribe of a fat pig to write a letter of recommendation to a friend of his, a ship owner in Calais, to receive two young and honest men of Savoyard origin eager to learn the trade of the seas.

Calais was much more heavily guarded than Dunkirk and there was no hope of entering the city unnoticed as they had done in Dunkirk, she explained. It was absolutely necessary that they should assume a new identity and stick to it whenever the gate keepers interrogated them. The Duchy of Savoy would be ideal, as many people there spoke French and the population was a mix of different origins – neither blond nor brown hair would arouse any undue suspicion. Furthermore France and Savoy were at peace at the moment. Pierre and Armand nodded – they were deeply impressed by this ingenious line of thought.

Then she recommended to them a small inn inside the city walls that was also kept by a widow, a relative from the family of her late husband. Not that this lady could maintain the same high standards as she did but she would provide good and not too expensive shelter for them if ever they had to stay there for a fortnight or longer.

At last – and much too soon – the dreaded day of saying farewell came and she wouldn't even hear of any payment. Claire fussed around them like a mother hen, making sure they'd have plenty of food for the journey, enough water and clean shirts with them.

But when Pierre and Armand hugged and kissed her, her carefully kept poise broke down and they left her sobbing, waving good-bye with a large white kitchen towel. After some minutes Pierre suddenly turned his horse, rode back and kissed her once more. Solemnly he promised to come back and visit her one day. She managed a brave smile under her tears and watched and waved until the two horses became smaller and smaller and disappeared over the horizon. She had thought that her heart couldn't break again after she had lost a husband and a son but now she knew how wrong she had been.

"Silly old sentimental cow," she scolded herself but it didn't help, her sorrow remained and kept hurting deeply in the days and weeks to come.

*****

As the two young men had explored the region before, they knew the way to Calais by now, but the usual joy of riding close to the sea wouldn't materialize.

Pierre was unusually silent and when Armand sent an enquiring glance towards his friend to check what was going on, he saw tears slowly rolling down Pierre's cheeks. His face was not moving, and Pierre remained silent, but the tears kept running down his cheeks.

"You really liked her very much," Armand said soothingly, "and I understand why."

Pierre cleared his throat and spoke with some difficulty. "When I was a small boy, I imagined how it would be if I had a mother. Claire was exactly how I had imagined my mother should be. If you never felt the love of a mother – you miss her vaguely but it doesn't really hurt as you don't really know what to miss. Now I have experienced her love and suddenly it hurts terribly to give it up so soon." His voice died and he tried to wipe away his tears. Armand could see that Pierre felt very embarrassed by this outburst of emotion.

"That's all right," Armand answered. "Don't be silly and don't look so embarrassed. I don't think you're weak. Maybe it's a strange consolation: I do have a mother but being born into a big noble family like mine or even yours under normal circumstances doesn't mean that you receive maternal love in abundance." He gave a short laugh. "In fact we boys sometimes thought that we were more a necessary evil to provide a reserve of heirs for the de Saint Paul name – but most of the genuine kisses I received were those from our nurse – and later from my girlfriends. Life is strange, we all have our ideals and dreams – but we have to carry on and cope with reality."

As usual Armand and his faultless common sense put Pierre's feet solidly back on the ground. Indeed he had built for himself the image of an ideal mother but now here he was with the best friend he could imagine, riding at his side – and heading to their next adventure. His mood cleared and when he challenged Armand to gallop faster Armand knew that the black clouds casting dark shadows on his friend's mind had vanished.

*****

Calais was an imposing sight: built in the salty marches of the sea it was surrounded by impressive and extremely high walls, towers and ramparts that zigzagged into the marches, encircled by moats and it was living testimony to the strength and power that the French Crown had gained after Cardinal Richelieu had ascended to the position of Prime Minister under King Louis XIII.

Slowly they approached the northern gate and, as Claire had predicted, they were scrutinized in detail by young and alert-looking guards on duty at the gate. Luckily they held a credible letter of recommendation and as there was a lot of traffic and commerce going on between Dunkirk and Calais the writer of the letter was well known and had a good reputation.

114

Their horses were searched but as the boys possessed nothing but a few spare clothes, their personal weapons and some provisions, the soldiers quickly understood that there was no bargain to be made and the two young men were admitted to the city without further formalities.

Claire had described the way from the city gate to the guesthouse of their new landlady and quickly they found themselves gazing at a small but neat house in a narrow street with a tavern that was invitingly open.

They were greeted by a young maid of their age dressed modestly with a clean apron and a bonnet but her spirited eyes belied the modesty of her appearance and the bonnet couldn't hide the beautiful black hair that it was supposed to hold back.

The maid led them to the owner of the guesthouse, a widowed lady of fairly advanced age. She was slight of build, rather skinny in fact, with greyish hair and her face bore a sour expression frozen in discontent.

Pierre thought that she reminded him of a mouse. When she opened her mouth two sharp front teeth glistened and when she spoke her eyes darted left and right – all it needed to make her a perfect rodent would have been a pair of whiskers, Pierre concluded secretly.

Her attitude changed only slightly when they presented the warmest regards from her cousin Claire in Dunkirk but she condescended finally to welcome them and to offer them lodgings. She made it immediately clear to them all the same that Armand should pay a full week in advance and they were soon to find out that their new hostess was addicted to the tinkling sound of coins falling into her purse. She charged for every meal, drink or whatever special request they had.

"Very different indeed from Claire," Armand sighed when they entered the tiny room that she had assigned to them.

Armand had started to become worried about their financial situation. He had decided that they'd need to share room and bed. "We won't have enough money to pay for two rooms," he had told Pierre when the latter had asked why he had only bargained for one room. "We can't afford to pay for two rooms if we risk staying here for several days – and please don't forget that later we'll need to keep enough money for our journey in England!"

"How I'd love to be back at Dunkirk in my own bed," Pierre grumbled but he saw the point and felt ashamed because his friend had to pay for everything out of his own pocket. They had sold their pistols in Dunkirk to raise some money and avoid curious questions from the gate keepers in Calais. Pierre looked sceptically at the narrow bed and sighed – he knew from past experience that Armand was a restless sleeper, and it was all very well to talk about sharing a bed, but he'd probably need to sleep on the hard floor just to get some rest.

"Well, Marie is probably already waiting for us in Calais and we won't need to stay for a long time in this place," said Armand, and changing the subject abruptly he remarked, "Did you notice the maid, she's really terrific! She really makes up for this skinny monster of a hostess."

"Let's go into the city and to the port to see if Marie has arrived already," Pierre suggested, not interested in beautiful maids at the moment when he hoped to see Marie again soon. He was still in a foul mood as he didn't really see how he would get any decent sleep over the next few days, and dragging Armand with him they went out of the door.

Downstairs they met their landlady who was serving some customers in the tavern and Armand – using his casual charm – started a conversation with her, ordering some ale. Skilfully – without arousing any suspicion – he got to know from her which guesthouses or post stations would be suitable for distinguished persons of wealth. She gave them three different names, making some acerbic comments on how easily some people could make money and get away with overcharging their customers, and described their whereabouts. Armand and Pierre took their leave and went into the city in the direction of the market square and further on to the port.

If Dunkirk had been impressive because of its ships and the ocean that they had seen for the first time, their general impression of Calais was that it should be named the city of scaffolds and dust.

Heavy construction work was going on everywhere on the fortifications and even inside the city, and the noise was deafening. They had to watch their feet and cover their heads as it seemed to them that everywhere they moved there were pits, stones and timber strewn across their way and mortar or other debris constantly falling down from the many scaffolds lining the buildings, so it was wise to stay as far away as they could manage.

Calais had only recently been re-conquered by the Duke of Guise for the French Crown after hundreds of years of English rule and it appeared that the King or his prime minister wanted to make a visible statement for the world to see that France would build up the city in splendour and keep hands on it forever. The fortifications were to become the most impressive in Europe, Richelieu had decided. Calais would never revert to England!

They easily found the first guesthouse named by their landlady, indeed, a newly constructed elegant and rather large house built from bright red bricks and trimmings of sandstone with an impressive court and lavish stables, ready to accommodate noble coaches and elegant horses.

They interrogated the grooms casually as to whether a lady of Marie's age had arrived recently but they received a negative reply – no nice young lady had been seen here, the only ladies that were living here at present were neither young nor nice, the groom had said, chuckling at his own joke.

116

The second guesthouse was a bit smaller and built in the traditional style with timbered frames painted in black, creating a contrast to the white plastered walls. It looked neat but still impressive enough. Here they went into the public tavern and interrogated the maid that was eager to chat with them – just to hear the same statement. The maid suggested, giggling, that two nice and handsome gentlemen shouldn't wait for a young lady to arrive if she was already here and could be of any service in the meantime! Armand gave her a dashing smile and winked at her. They parted on the best of terms.

The third guesthouse was probably the nicest of the three. Also a fairly modern building, but opening onto the seaside with a beautiful view of the port and the sailing boats and ships that lay moored in the port.

They entered the building with trepidation after having experienced two failures and to their great dismay once more the servants here denied having a guest who could match Marie's description, nor did they remember having seen such a guest lately.

"So we're the early birds," said Armand, a bit too cheerfully for Pierre's taste. "Let's have a good time then in Calais and wait until she arrives."

Thus they settled into a daily routine of visiting the different guesthouses and didn't even need to ask anymore. Each time they passed by, searching out their new acquaintances, the latter just shook their heads, shrugging their shoulders as if they wanted to apologize for the bad news.

As the futile game of waiting started to have an effect on their nerves they decided to enlarge their radius of activities. They started to check on less exclusive establishments as well – but again to no avail. When Pierre called Armand later in the week to come once more to do their usual round of guesthouses Armand grumbled that he didn't feel too well and therefore Pierre would have to go on his own.

Knowing his way by now through the relatively small inner city he had finished his frustrating quest quite early and was looking forward to inviting Armand for a ride along the marches; he felt that he needed to leave this noisy city with its peculiar smell of sea, fish and fresh mortar and get some fresh air.

Silently he went up the staircase and was about to open the door when he heard his friend moaning in agony. Pierre stopped short as he pushed down on the door handle and looked around him: something dreadful was happening to his friend! He realized immediately that he must help his friend but all their weapons were inside the room, stored and hidden safely underneath their bed! Silently he rushed down the staircase – he had seen a big stick, probably the remains of a broom, in the corner of the tap room – this would have to do. He didn't dare raise the alarm and anyway, the inn downstairs was deserted. He was on his own and had to deal with this, he must help his friend!

117

Armand had explained to him that surprise was often a good substitute if you didn't have a clear plan of action. Pierre held his stick tight with his right hand and pushed the handle down vigorously jumping forward into the bedroom ready to strike the down the aggressor.

Armand lay naked on the bed with his bare legs open and under direct assault – but not by a villain. The strikingly beautiful maid from downstairs was sitting astride him in naked splendour, her long black hair no longer held back by a modest bonnet.

Pierre felt as if was in a trance but still he could see every detail of her perfect body, the round hips and the small and firm breasts with their pink nipples. The maid was riding with all her might on Armand's body, tossing her shining hair like a victorious flag. Pierre stood there frozen, and Armand, who didn't know if he should laugh or be angry, just managed to stammer, close to ecstasy, "Either join us or leave!" The girl didn't stop her actions, she just shot an appraising look at Pierre, giving him a broad and very naughty smile.

Pierre fled in panic, feeling unbelievably stupid.

When Pierre and Armand were alone in their room that night, both of them lay naked on the narrow bed. They were suffering badly from an onslaught of mosquitoes and perspiring as the room was still stiflingly hot. An uneasy silence prevailed; Pierre hadn't spoken a word since they had met for dinner.

Armand decided that it was about time to apologize for lying to Pierre to get rid of him that afternoon.

"I'm sorry, Pierre, I was very stupid, I should I have told you that she has been pursuing me constantly since we arrived. I really don't know why I didn't tell you openly, please don't be upset."

Pierre couldn't resist the pleading tone of Armand's apology. He cleared his throat. "You made me look like an idiot," Pierre said, trying to be stern with his friend but apparently failing miserably as Armand snorted with laughter.

"You should have seen yourself with this stupid stick, ready to lash out. It was hilarious. Oh Pierre, you were wonderful in your rage, like David ready to take on Goliath!" and whatever else he had wanted to add was drowned in peals of laughter.

Pierre couldn't help but join in, and reviewing the scene he could see the funny side of it by now. But he still thought that his friend should be taken down a peg or two. "I don't know if she was really satisfied with you though, she looked quite a bit more experienced than you did," he said, challenging his friend, but this shot didn't find its target.

118

"Indeed, she was!" Armand answered very smugly. "But she said she had never met a young man who learned so fast and she'd be happy to teach me more. It's generally known that brown-haired men have more fire than blonds!"

Pierre gave it up, turned his back on Armand and tried finally to get some sleep.

*****

The next days passed uneventfully in the same rhythm and each of them started to become secretly very concerned but put on a brave face to the other and pretended to be confident. After a good fortnight Armand suggested to Pierre that he would do the usual round of visits on his own. When he reached one of the smaller but still very elegant guesthouses he went to the stables to meet one of the grooms with whom he had made friends. He found the stables in turmoil and his friend busily grooming some elegant horses that had freshly arrived.

"What's going on?" Armand enquired. "Has the King himself arrived, you seem so busy?"

"Not quite," grumbled his friend, short of breath from the exercise of diligently brushing the horse. "It's some of them high animals from Paris, a Duke or something and he's got a foul temper," and crossing himself he added, "Arrogant as the devil himself, he is."

Armand had become curious and walked to the guesthouse to find out more about the mysterious visitor. Sitting in a corner of the public room he waited patiently and after half an hour his perseverance paid off and the mysterious guest arrived.

He was a handsome man; quite tall, elegantly dressed in the latest fashion and wearing shoulder-length hair of shining blond. He was accompanied by a handsome dark-skinned valet wearing green-gold livery. Both were apparently dressed to pay an official visit and the proud owner of the establishment and his wife were following them, bowing and paying compliments in abundance.

Armand squeezed himself even more into his corner, congratulating himself that he had decided to radically change his appearance. This man was the spitting image of how Pierre would probably look in a few years' time. It had been a long time since Armand had met Henri de Beauvoir at home in his family's palais in Paris at the occasion of one of the many official receptions that his father was supposed to organize regularly, but there could be no mistake – this was de Beauvoir, and if he had arrived in Calais there was only one explanation possible: he was heading for England as well. Armand needed to digest this news first.

Henri ignored the honours showered upon him by the innkeeper and his wife and let his eyes roam around the public room. He had to admit that the guesthouse

119

had been a nice surprise, an excellent choice by the Cardinal's office. It breathed elegance and refinement and even if he'd never admit it, he felt flattered by the fact that the Cardinal had apparently given orders to treat him already like the Marquis he was going to be. The whole guesthouse had been reserved for him and his entourage alone. He detected a young man sitting in the corner; there wasn't a lot to see, too much beard and brown hair partially hidden by a cap, a commoner who must have strayed here in error. His gaze went back to the innkeeper who was eagerly expecting orders for his private dinner tonight, finishing every phrase with 'Your honour', but Henri gave Jean a short order to arrange the details. He couldn't be bothered with such trivial matters.

When Armand had seen the cold blue eyes turning towards him he had felt a moment of panic but he could see no recognition whatsoever in this cold and bored glance. That would be the biggest difference, he thought – even if Pierre might look more and more like his cousin in the future, his eyes were warm and full of kindness, whereas this man was cold as stone and would kill any opponent without remorse.

Armand hurried back to their lodgings as fast as possible. He cursed when he overlooked a pothole, struggled and fell on a woman loaded with fish coming home from the fish stalls in the port. She yelled as if she had been attacked and as she had dropped her bucket, the fish had spilled all around them. Normally he would have apologized and helped her to gather the fish as the first stray dogs were coming close, eager to profit from a free meal that had literally fallen from heaven.

But Armand was occupied with more important matters, and he just yelled back some saucy insults and raced on to their guesthouse. He had to discuss this with Pierre.

He signalled to Pierre that something important had happened and suggested taking their horses and going for a ride into the marches where they could talk in confidence without being overheard. Having galloped for some time to get rid of the tension, they sat down and Armand told him that they were in trouble: Pierre's cousin had arrived.

Pierre sat in the shelter of a dune in the shadow of some strangely shaped bushes. The relentless winds tormented the poor plants that tried to survive at the edges of the endless sea.

Armand told his story and they sat for a moment in total silence. Although it was still summer the clouds were hanging heavy and grey in the sky and a cold wind was howling across the dunes. Not a single ray of sun emerged to lift their spirits.

"Come on, don't sit there like a stuffed puppet, tell me what's on your mind!" Armand insisted.

"It's probably weird," Pierre said, pausing and trying to put his thoughts into the right words. "And you'll say that I'm mad, but until today I was living this adventure like a wonderful dream. I was just happy to have you at my side, to have fun, excitement and experience something new happening every day. But in reality I always had the feeling it was unreal and sooner or later someone would come and say, sorry, we put the wrong papers into the box, it's Pierre the poor orphan boy after all. You see, I was prepared in my mind to go back to Reims or become a mere nobody once more after we had arrived in England. But now that you told me that there's a real cousin in this city and that he does look exactly like me, suddenly I start to realize that it's not fun any longer, we're up to our necks in a real adventure – something that might become very dangerous, as you said yourself when we saw the documents for the first time. I now have to take the responsibility and let go the old Pierre and become a true Marquis in my mind and heart. It's still very strange. I liked the old Pierre, and I don't know if I'll ever be a true Marquis..."

Pierre paused and his bright blue eyes filled with tears. "I also have to ask you to leave me alone in Calais. We both know that my cousin is following me with the sole intention of getting rid of me – I stand in the way of his heritage and the title. I'm convinced of this now and I don't want you to share this risk. No more fun, it's dangerous now. Our joint adventure stops here and now!"

Armand looked at him, unsurprised. He knew Pierre in and out by now and loved him all the more for his concerns. "Would you stop playing the noble Marquis, you idiot," he answered. "Should I go back alone to face the wrath of my father? How do you think I should play it? 'Oh yes, dear father, I admit I forged your signature, escaped school, ducked my nomination as a bishop and by the way, I thought it convenient to drop my best friend when he needed me most. Yes, father, I'm a true gentleman. A true de Saint Paul, you can be very proud of your son!'"

Armand had played the little scene so well that Pierre burst into laughter and just retorted, "All right, I get the message, your prefer facing danger with me to the prospect of finding yourself packed off by your father to the next provincial parish that's willing to accept a fugitive from the monastery school. I don't know how you do it, but you always make me look stupid and get your way in the end!"

"That's because I'm a genius, my most noble Marquis," Armand replied.

He embraced his friend and they rode back in harmony. Perhaps Pierre's bearing was a little prouder than usual – he had changed, it was true – and now he could face adventure with his best friend with all confidence.

DEALING WITH PARENTS

After Armand and Pierre had left Marie's parents' estate, a boring tranquillity had settled upon the place. The tedious daily routine of listening to the never ending complaints of her aunt about reckless, lazy, stupid and outrageously expensive servants started to annoy Marie greatly. She had more important issues on her mind.

One day Marie was sitting in her bedroom after a listless breakfast taken in bed while her maid Anne brushed her hair in silence. Having known Marie for so many years she sensed that her charge was in deep thoughts and she could easily fathom the cause, after all, she wasn't blind.

In fact Marie was analysing the past weeks and she admitted to herself that she was in great danger of falling in love. *No*, she scolded herself, *be honest with yourself, you're in love already!*

Pierre's blue eyes and dazzling smile had followed her into her dreams and she was realistic enough to understand that this was bad, very bad, in fact very upsetting, as this was the first time something like this had ever happened to her.

She liked to be the one to play games with potential suitors. But it was becoming more and more obvious to her that she desperately wanted to see her two friends again. Spending more time with Pierre would be essential to find out if she was just smitten by a romantic feeling or if she had seriously fallen in love. If she then came to the conclusion that her feelings were serious she would move heaven and earth to get Pierre and she wouldn't care at all whether he succeeded in his quest to become the next Marquis de Beauvoir or not. It was Pierre she wanted, not the title. And if she felt that he was the right one, nobody would stop her, she vowed.

If I just go on sitting here, I'll go mad, she said to herself and decided that it was high time to take action.

First of all she informed her aunt, the Comtesse de Chevreuil, that she longed to go back to Reims and see her parents. The Comtesse did not delve into the reason for this sudden daughterly sense of duty. Calculating in her mind the savings she'd make by extending her stay on the estate, she didn't really mind staying on her own, as long as she could remain here. Marie had been on edge since the two boys had left, the Comtesse thought secretly, it would be a relief to see her return to her parents.

Orders were given to pack and a servant was sent to Reims to announce that Marie was about to arrive soon. As an answer her father sent a small army of footmen to make sure that the carriages would be well guarded and his only daughter safe from any possible danger of assault.

Marie looked out of the open window of her carriage, casting a last glance at the manor house that she was about to leave. The elegant building of creamy stone was framed by ivy, glistening in different shades of green in the early morning sun. The slate roof with its small turrets gave it a castle-like appearance, fit for a princess – and hopefully a prince – she mused.

The gravel crunched under the weight of the iron-rimmed wheels of her carriage and slowly the horses started to pull forward and gain speed. Marie was sitting in her plush upholstered seat, gently swaying as if on a ship and she lay back against the luxurious cushions. As usual her father had made sure that only the best would do for his daughter. Although she glanced from time to time out of the window at the beautiful landscape with its lush foliage and small woods, rich vineyards in a gently rolling landscape and well-kept hamlets she was deep in her thoughts and rehearsed in her mind the story that she was going to tell her mother. Getting her mother's support would be essential, and she was sure that her father wouldn't resist long if she and her mother both supported the plan to leave for England.

She must have fallen asleep in the carriage, as she woke up to find the carriage grinding to a halt and a soldier at the city gates of Reims prying into the carriage window. As Marie's family was well known all over the city he just greeted her courteously and let the carriage pass without further delay. Marie had therefore just enough time to arrange her hair and smooth her skirts when they entered the street leading to her parents' impressive town house.

The household had been waiting for her arrival and as soon as the sound of the carriage wheels was heard drawing into the courtyard the servants streamed out to greet the daughter of their master.

Marie was genuinely liked by the servants. Sometimes demanding and certainly having a strong mind, she was never moody. She detested physical punishments for the servants and the use of the whip was unheard of – a punishment which was a daily and dreaded routine for servants in other households.

Marie decided to change and freshen up before she greeted her parents, as she had decided that playing the dutiful and diligent daughter would probably be the best strategy for the moment to make them mellow and receptive to her plans.

When she entered the drawing room where her mother was already waiting for her, she found her hunched in an armchair, looking at her with bright eyes and flushed cheeks. Marie was alarmed and shocked. Her mother didn't look at all well, indeed she was in pain – and nobody had prepared Marie for this. She flew towards her mother, hugged her and tried her best to cheer her up and gave her mother the warmest regards from the Comtesse de Chevreuil. But reminding her of her cousin, regrettably did nothing to cheer Marie's mother up, as she retorted disdainfully, "I really do regret that I sent for this woman!" and pointed towards an envelope that lay half-torn on the side table.

"Your aunt has just written to me that she'll be forced to stay on in my house for at least another two months as her own house seems to be undergoing major repairs," she snorted with dismay. "All she wants is to continue living and eating for free, she's the thriftiest old goat you could imagine."

Marie uttered some soothing words. Actually she was very delighted that the Comtesse hadn't deemed it necessary to make any comment on the visit of Armand and Pierre; this would greatly facilitate her next steps.

Enquiring after her father she learnt that he was inspecting some vineyards and was only expected to be back by the weekend.

Marie understood that she'd need to be patient but she dropped some hints that she'd started to consider her mother's suggestions to go to England. To her great surprise her mother wasn't keen at all; owing to her failing health, she said that she couldn't imagine being without her beloved daughter, and her eyes became misty.

The next two days saw a rapid deterioration in her mother's health. She refused to move out of her bed and when Marie visited her in her bedroom she saw her mother lying frail in the huge bedstead with its carved wooden poles and crimson curtains.

Marie started to be extremely worried. The curtains of the windows were drawn to hinder the harmful air from outside from entering the room and candles with incense were burning to cleanse the room, creating a church-like, depressingly sombre atmosphere.

Physicians came and went looking like crows or messengers of death in their black robes with their bald pates covered by sombre black caps that were part of their official attire. They prescribed different infusions and bled her mother until she was so feeble that she could only whisper, her skin like vellum, her eyes burning in her flushed face. When the agony of pain mounted more and more they offered pills made from the exotic milk of poppies to alleviate the pain, each pill costing a true fortune. Marie, seeing her mother's suffering didn't hesitate, but opened her purse and paid in gold; she knew that her father wouldn't mind.

Marie watched this continue for another two days and was about to despair. When she went down to the servant's quarters she noticed that most of them had been crying. Death seemed unavoidable, they all had seen it strike so often in their own families before.

She had to fight the mounting feeling of panic, as she loved her mother dearly. Calais seemed to have become no more than an unreal and remote dream.

But Marie was a girl of resolve, therefore she decided that she had to do something or she would go mad. She took a shawl and left the house, asking the faithful Anne to accompany her. They hurried to the monastery where she requested to meet with Brother Infirmarius immediately. She was made to wait in the reception rooms but he came swiftly, surprised to be summoned by such a young lady.

Marie quickly explained the situation and pleaded with him to come immediately; she was convinced that the physicians treating her mother were about to kill her. She knew from Armand that Brother Infirmarius was regarded as being a bit eccentric – his obsession with cleanliness, for instance, drew many disparaging comments – but as he was the most successful physician they had ever seen in the monastery he was held in great esteem and generally his cures were tolerated and he was left in peace.

Marie didn't know if the pleas of a young girl or the offer of a generous donation for the monastery did the job to convince him but he consented to help immediately and just asked her to wait some minutes. Soon he came back with a large bag that would later reveal an array of mysterious concoctions and instruments.

Marie created a scandal at home. Not only did she arrive with an unknown monk to look after her mother, she also threw the remaining physicians out of the house when she discovered them sitting in the kitchen and being fed on the most expensive dishes by the cook and drinking the family's precious wines from Bordeaux.

The monk did something very peculiar. First he opened the curtains and windows and snuffed out the candles, the only exception being the candle burning in front of the painting of the Holy Virgin. Marie was flabbergasted as this was against all common practice but she immediately observed that her mother's breathing became easier when the fresh air entered the room.

When he examined Marie's mother he asked Marie to leave the room. Marie waited nervously outside. If the monk failed, she knew that her father would never forgive her for having expelled the other physicians and she was already regretting her hasty temper.

Suddenly she heard an exclamation of sharp pain and when she rushed into the room she saw the monk hovering over her mother.

"What are you doing?" she exclaimed angrily. The monk turned towards her, holding in his hand a pair of pincers dripping with blood. Marie screamed with horror when he moved closer. In his hands he held a piece of a freshly extracted but quite rotten tooth smeared with blood and pus.

The monk smiled. "With good fortune your mother will be better soon," he explained in a soothing voice. "In fact she had a truly rotten tooth but as she was probably scared to death she didn't dare to go to a barbers' shop and have it extracted. During the past few days the bad juices of the tooth must have started to poison her body. Now the tooth is removed I'm confident that she'll improve soon if you follow my instructions. She's very feeble and she must not be bled any more. You were right: my esteemed colleagues nearly killed her by bleeding her too much!"

Marie felt tears of relief filling her eyes. She couldn't speak, she just took the hand of the surprised monk and kissed it.

The monk now gave very precise instructions: he indicated the precise amount and timing of the medicine, foods and drinks that should be administered to her mother. He refused to take any money for himself, a donation for the monastery would do. Still in a rage Marie told him how much his colleagues had charged for their medicines and her mother's treatment. The monk shook his head in disbelief.

"Not only are they not worthy to be called physicians, they're genuine thieves! If your mother is not much better by tomorrow, please send me a messenger and I'll come back to see her immediately!" This earned him another kiss – and he didn't seem to mind.

Marie had taken the habit of sleeping in her mother's room in order to watch over her. Early next morning she woke up frightened by the unusual silence. Marie had spent an uneasy night in an armchair close to her mother's bed. Her body was stiff from the night and she rose awkwardly. Holding her breath she tiptoed to her mother's bed, fearing the worst.

Then she saw her mother lying in her bed, sleeping peacefully for the first time in a week. Marie was ready to embrace the world. Now it was clear: her mother would soon be well again!

But it took some time for Marie's mother to regain strength and she proved to be a very difficult and trying convalescent.

No, she wouldn't complain, but maybe her cushion was a *little hard*. How kind to have brought a new cushion but this one was just a *little too soft*. Yes, she'd love to have her embroidery, but maybe her eyes and arms were a *little too tired* for this exercise after all – and thus she drove Marie and the servants to distraction.

She couldn't bear the thought of Marie being far from her and soon Marie started to feel imprisoned and utterly worn out.

Her father had returned but Marie found him very moody, torn between feelings of total adulation for his daughter – after all, Marie had saved her mother's life – and wild criticism of her behaviour, panicking at the thought of the immense risks Marie had taken by throwing the most famous physicians of Reims out of their house and putting the fate of her mother into the hands of an unknown monk. Like most husbands he couldn't stand the sight of seeing his wife suffer – he didn't know what to do and how to react and he quickly became more of a nuisance than a help.

When Marie sat in her armchair in her mother's bedroom despair and fatigue started to overwhelm her. She felt trapped and had no clue as to how she could escape. Her eyes wandered around the room that had become so familiar to her after she had spent days and hours glued to her mother's bedside. Her glance glided mechanically across the tables of polished wood gleaming in the morning sun with their beautiful dark rich hazelnut colour, the high armchairs with their impressive but totally uncomfortable carved backs. Those were usually reserved for visitors paying formal visits. Then her gaze wandered on to the walls painted in a dark shade of red decorated with pictures of some of her mother's favourite saints. There was the Virgin Mary with her child – Marie always thought that this picture was not very flattering and she heartily disliked the conceited look the artist had given to the mother of Jesus. Then her gaze fell on the next painting showing Sainte Céline, a revered local saint. *Sainte Céline, please help me*, she prayed silently and suddenly exclaimed loudly, "Céline, that's it, you're my salvation!"

Jumping up from her armchair she immediately summoned her maid and dispatched her to visit Céline, a remote cousin who lived close by, only some streets away. She was an attractive lady in her mid-twenties, which meant that she was generally considered a hopeless spinster, as young ladies were supposed to be married before they reached the age of twenty. Céline was very tall – nearly six foot, with laughing brown eyes and curly brown hair and when it came to horse riding she'd beat most men.

She was generally referred to as 'our poor Céline' when the family was gossiping about her. As a person, she was held in high esteem, but her father had been a notorious gambler and womanizer, a good friend and drinking companion of the King's closest friends, spending most of his time in Paris at the royal court hoping to bask in the sun of royal favour some day. Before he had been decent enough to get himself killed in a hunting accident he had thus managed to squander the huge family fortune, leaving nothing but a mere pittance.

Céline was not astonished to find out soon after her father's death that he had been living far beyond his means and after a short shock she had resolutely sold horses, carriages, jewels and most family estates to pay off the endless army of merchants and creditors that beleaguered her, even during the official period of mourning.

She then settled in a small but respectable house in the city just guarded by a faithful maid and a dragon of a chaperon to avoid the wagging of tongues that a spinster living on her own would invariably set in motion.

Everybody had expected her to try and snag a husband as fast as possible but to the dismay of the rumourmongers of Reims, she didn't seem concerned by convention and preferred staying on her own. As Céline got on well with nearly everybody in Marie's family, she would be a gift sent from heaven to entertain her mother and alleviate Marie's duties.

Fortunately, Céline was at home when Marie's maid paid her a call. She listened to the maid's message and she understood immediately Marie's distress. In a matter of seconds she decided to come and help. She had in fact felt rather bored lately and this opportunity might even be a welcome change to her daily routine.

She knew Marie's mother and father very well and could imagine easily what had been going on in their household during the past few days.

Poor girl, she thought, her face just showing polite interest while the maid continued pouring her own sufferings into her sympathetic ears. *I must help her!*

Marie didn't know how it happened or what kind of magic spell Céline had cast, but soon after Céline joined the household and started looking after her mother the whole atmosphere at home underwent a notable and very agreeable change.

Marie saw her mother happily chatting with her cousin about the terrible character of some mutual acquaintances, sitting animated and erect in her bed and forgetting her previous show of fragile invalidity. When she noticed Marie standing in the room she said, "Oh my dear, you've been such an angel. But we'll be doing fine here, I'm sure that you have neglected some other duties, you don't need to be around me the whole day."

Thus Marie to her great joy and amazement saw herself dismissed from further duty and free to leave the house or spend time on her own for the first time since her return.

A few words of admiration from Céline to Marie's father telling him how impressed she was that Marie had managed to drag this monk, actually the most famous physician in northern France to her mother's bed, and Marie's father was eating out of his daughter's hand, forgetting his earlier concerns.

Even the servants, who had become somewhat lazy and complacent while Marie had been constantly worried and distracted by her mother, felt immediately that Céline was a lady used to running a household and to be reckoned with. They scurried back to work as a few polite but acerbic remarks made them remember their duties. This lady would see everything, so they had better get the job done – the lazy times were finished.

Céline's visits had become a daily and very much appreciated routine. One afternoon she entered the library where Marie had retired trying to look dutiful over a book of prayers. To her surprise she found Marie in tears. Céline came closer and remarked casually, "I know these prayers are particularly boring, but they shouldn't be boring you to tears, my dear!"

Marie tried to smile through her tears but when Céline opened her arms, the floodgates opened and she fell into her embrace. It needed only a few inviting words from Céline and she sobbed her heart out as Céline patiently listened.

Finally she ended with, "I must find a way to get to Calais fast. If not – I think I'll go mad."

Marie glanced at Céline, ready to fight for her cause, expecting to be admonished, as it was evident that she was not at all behaving like a girl of decent upbringing.

Maybe she'll send for my father immediately, Marie thought in panic, a detached part of her brain telling her that she was completely insane and her behaviour and her plan of action were totally unacceptable for a young lady and sole heiress of a good family.

But to her great surprise Céline laughed and answered without the slightest hesitation, "But of course you must. Especially if you're not yet really sure if he's the one, you must meet him again and find out. I was once in love with a young man and my father did everything to stop our relationship. He was only a baron from a small village, you know. I still wonder today if I should have eloped all the same and that makes me mad. I fully understand your point."

Looking at Marie with an eager face she continued, "Would you mind taking me with you? I always dreamed about having at least one adventure in my life – and here is my opportunity. I've been sitting in my house now for two years and I'm bored to tears waiting for a prince charming who never bothers to come," she chuckled, and went on, "All the men who were after me were either old, bald, fat or awfully boring – sometimes even a terrifying combination of all four!"

Marie jumped around the room and cried out with joy. "Of course! That would be wonderful – and would solve a huge problem – my father would never accept my leaving without a chaperon and now that my mother is still recovering from her illness, I couldn't see how to solve this problem. You really are my saviour!"

"I'll not come cheap though," Céline retorted. "The downside is that I don't have a lot of money left from my father. I have no option but to travel at your expense. I'm sorry to be so blunt – but I couldn't go on my own money any further than Paris."

Marie waved these concerns away with a light gesture of her hand. "Money, my God, my father has more than enough for the two of us! He's always complaining, but in truth he could have the armada rebuilt and fill it with his own men to send us to England without any problem!"

It was thus decided not to wait any longer and Marie cunningly convinced her father to arrange a festive dinner party with Céline to celebrate her mother's recovery.

Her father didn't hesitate for a second; he congratulated Marie on this excellent idea and rang the bell to inform his manservant at once and later even descended to chat with the cook until the latter was close to a nervous breakdown as his master was asking for the impossible, leaving him no time for proper preparation of the delicacies that he had listed.

The cook might have been close to a breakdown but the dinner he managed to prepare was truly stunning. The dinner table gleamed in the candlelight, loaded with all kinds of mouth-watering dishes, tarts, pies, a sucking pig, and birds, roasted and stuffed with expensive spices and decorated with genuine feathers. As her father knew that the ladies had a sweet tooth, the servants brought gold-plated dishes with fruits and exotic honeyed sweets. Among the sweets Marie immediately spotted one of her favourites: delicious marzipan with dried apricots and pistachios. The lavish dinner was fit for a king and didn't fail to impress Céline and Marie's mother, who resided like a queen on the chair of honour, beaming with delight.

When they had reached the point where not even a last sugared plum would fit in anywhere, and the famous wine of the Champagne region had created a mood of happy dizziness in the warm evening, Marie mentioned casually that she was considering accepting her aunt's and uncle's invitation to join them in London.

Before the full meaning of her words started to dawn on her father and mother, Céline already exclaimed, "But this is marvellous. Is this the secret gift that your parents have prepared for you to thank for all your loving care during these terrible days of your mother's illness?" She paused briefly, and continued with a deep sigh, "Oh, to be the daughter of such a generous and loving father, Marie, your father is unbelievable! Let us drink a toast to him and to your mother!"

The 'unbelievable' father looked deeply unhappy and lost for words. This attack had come totally unexpectedly. Marie's mother cried, "Oh, Marie, I always wanted you to visit your aunt in London, but so soon after my illness, are you really sure you want to leave your poor mother just now?"

Marie's father was still trying to find a suitable answer. Secretly proud that he had found an infallible argument he leaned forward and said, "Of course I'd love to see my only daughter being presented to his Majesty, the King of England, by her aunt, but as your mother's health is still fragile, we'll have to put this off until next year! It would not be fitting with your position to stay unguarded even in France, let alone a foreign country that definitely does not have our level of civilization," and wiping his forehead with his napkin he sank down back into his chair and emptied another glass of the white wine, satisfied at having solved this issue elegantly and diplomatically, or so he thought.

Marie looked very disappointed and just said meekly, "Of course, my dear father, you're right, it would not be fitting for me to leave without a proper chaperon to look after me."

130

She tried to put on a brave face, but two big tears rolled down her cheeks and her father felt suddenly very ill at ease. He loved his daughter very much and seeing her in distress made his heart ache.

She really is an excellent actress, Céline thought, secretly amused by this little scene played to perfection. Aloud, she said, after an uneasy silence had settled at table, "Perhaps I should offer to join Marie and chaperon her? I fully understand that she needs to be accompanied by a lady from her family and if I could replace Marie's mother, I'd be happy to help out!"

Céline had delivered this sentence with an innocent air but the effect was remarkable indeed. Marie's father's mouth fell open. He was stunned. Searching for a new line of defence he was utterly silent. Marie's mother was totally surprised and Marie jumped out of her chair.

Taking Céline's hand she cried, "I'll never forget what you've done for me. I know it's a sacrifice but my mother always insisted that I should leave Reims and as my father is still at odds with the prime minister about some stupid dispute, I can't be presented to the royal court in Paris as he wouldn't go there. I have no choice," she added dramatically. "Either I can go to England hoping to find a suitable husband or I'll be wasting my youth, sitting here in Reims."

Marie's father knew when it was time to admit defeat and after some unconvincing attempts to argue for delaying the departure and win time he had to accept that crossing the Channel in late autumn or winter might be dangerous and that Marie would do better to leave as early as possible.

A radiant Marie, purring with satisfaction, left the dinner table. All had worked out exactly as she had planned it. Even Céline felt elated; adventure had finally knocked at her door.

A busy time started for all of them. Once the painful decision had been taken Marie's father made it clear that his only daughter would travel in style. Dressmakers were summoned and precious outfits fit for a royal princess ordered. Marie's father hired a small army of soldiers and footmen and to Marie's great dismay he even decided to accompany them to Calais to make sure that she would be safe, the ship in good shape and no mishap could happen in France to her. Letters were sent by special courier to London and back and forth and finally – for some too late, for some far too early – the great day of departure approached. It was high summer now and Marie was becoming more and more anxious to leave. In her nightmares she saw herself arriving in Calais and no more friends waiting for her.

Céline calmed her down. She was cherishing the prospect of her unexpected adventure and being herself in high spirits, she still managed to sooth Marie's mother's hurt feelings when the latter was complaining bitterly that Marie seemed rather too keen to leave her old and ill mother.

131

Céline was sensing that danger was brewing and made Marie understand that an urgent display of filial love and duty was absolutely necessary. Marie paid heed and when the final day of parting came, she didn't really need to pretend to be sad. She rushed back to mother and both were bathed in tears when the carriages started to pull out of the courtyard.

Marie's father had preferred to ride as the weather was fine and long journeys in the swaying carriage made him sick. Thus only Marie, her maid Anne and Céline occupied the carriage and as Anne had the full confidence of Marie, they could discuss openly how best to find their friends in Calais and how to make sure that they could travel on the same ship.

Marie's father had planned the journey diligently; they travelled slowly and stopped frequently to ensure the journey was as comfortable as possible. Marie knew that she should be thankful but after a week of leisurely progress, lavish lunches and dinners she had difficulties keeping up appearances and putting on the face of a grateful daughter. She had to suppress the urgent desire to grab a horse and gallop to Calais. Luckily Céline was there to chat with her father, to explain how thankful his daughter was for this opportunity and that her bouts of silence were due to exhaustion and the pain of missing her mother. Céline made it clear that this was the first long journey of her life. All the same she managed to convince Marie's father to accelerate the speed of their journey, pointing out that September would be the last month of smooth sailing and that any late arrival in Calais might put Marie at risk of facing the first rough autumn weather. Her father saw the compelling logic of her arguments and, to Marie's great relief, their coaches finally started making headway.

When Marie espied the impressive fortifications of Calais appearing on the horizon she hugged herself in secret joy.

BACK IN PARIS

The musketeer from the personal guard of His Eminence, Cardinal Richelieu, arrived at the royal post station. The white and black painted timber structure was surrounded by low stables and cattle grazed lazily in the hot sun of a late August day, seeking shade under the majestic oak trees that must have been growing there for more than a hundred years. The weather had become extremely hot and a rise in humidity held a slight threat of thunderstorms.

Rosebushes blossomed in abundance in front of the entrance of the main building. The roses sprawled in a mixture of colours, a vivid purple red and a lovely white variety displaying hearts of pink and yellow at the centre of their blooms. Their lovely scent filled the air, inviting the passing traveller to break the journey and stay on.

The musketeer was tired and worn out, parched by the intense heat, but he knew that he'd better change his horse quickly and only rest a few hours in order to reach Paris in the next two days – if his journey continued smoothly.

Showing his special passport with the seal of Cardinal Richelieu propelled the phlegmatic grooms into action. Nobody in France would dare to delay a special messenger of His Eminence. In no time refreshing cider was brought by a young buxom maid and a new horse was ready for him to continue his mission.

The musketeer gave a last longing glance at the idyllic scene and the maid who offered everything he would have loved to sample at his leisure. Heaving a deep sigh he spurred his horse on towards Paris. Having a demanding master like Richelieu meant giving priority to duty.

His ride continued smoothly until his horse stumbled in the early evening and he had to dismount. The musketeer cursed when he detected the cause: a horseshoe was missing which meant that he'd need to find a blacksmith and would lose at least half a day or even more.

He soon realized that his assumption had been too optimistic. The first farm he discovered close to the road offered shelter for the night but the farmer told him that the closest blacksmith could only be found in a small village several miles away and it would be suicide to walk with the horse at night through the dense woods known to harbour wolves and – crossing himself – witches.

The musketeer had heard too many stories about witchcraft in his life to be really impressed but he did pay attention to the mention of wolves and decided to stay overnight.

The next day he found the blacksmith's shop and after a little bargaining over the price, he got the horseshoe fixed. It was now early evening and theoretically he was now ready to move on but the weather had changed dramatically and huge menacing clouds promising hail and thunderstorms were gathering. Not only did the weather make any continuation of his trip highly dangerous, but as the clouds would later obliterate the moonlight, any further progress at night was virtually impossible.

The musketeer decided therefore to stay in the village overnight. Not surprisingly, he was in a foul mood by now as not only was he running very late but he could imagine that riding over the next few days would become hazardous. The roads would quickly turn into puddles of mud, slippery and tedious to master and he'd have no possibility of riding fast.

The storm broke before sunset, although he couldn't tell the exact time. Enormous black clouds were hanging so low that they seemed not only to touch the tips of the trees but were about to devour them – swallowing the rest of the daylight and leaving the village in total darkness.

When the thunderstorm finally struck, everybody in the village held their breath. Fierce bolts of lightning, alternating with deafening thunder, paralysed the villagers hiding in their homes and in the church, in a complete state of panic. In no time the torrents of rain and hail had ruined the precious harvest that had not yet been brought in, and two houses struck by the lightning burned down before any help could be organized by the terror-stricken villagers.

Heaven had decided to punish them and soon the musketeer found himself in the midst of a crowd of people, everybody on their knees praying fervently to God, the saint of the parish and the Holy Virgin. They were pleading to spare their lives, their families, their houses and their livestock.

After two or three hours – the longest hours ever – the storm abated and those peasants who still had a roof over their heads tried to deal with the floods of water that seemed to have entered their houses from everywhere – through the thatched roofs, the doors and leather hides that replaced the window panes in poor regions. There was no possibility of finding any sleep until very late when most people simply dropped down in despair and exhaustion.

The next morning the sun rose in full and renewed splendour – and revealed a trail of devastation. Corpses, dead animals with bloated bodies, plants and fallen trees were floating in an immense lake that suddenly surrounded the village like a moat, as the nearby river had risen overnight and flooded the surrounding pastures. Houses had burned down and roofs had been ruined. It took three days for the flood to recede and allow the musketeer to continue his journey to Paris, a journey that was slow and difficult as the roads seemed to have disappeared with the storm and all he could trace were muddied trails during the next two days. His mood had changed though, and having seen so much death and destruction he was thankful that his life had been spared and decided to light a candle in a church as soon as he reached Paris.

He arrived at the Grand Palace totally exhausted, his uniform torn, as he hadn't changed clothes or washed for days. Thanks to the seal on his message he was allowed immediate access to the Cardinal's secretary, an alert monk of similar age to him. The secretary retreated behind his desk to keep some distance from this musketeer who stank like a boar.

"Please hand the message to me so that I can relay it to His Eminence," the secretary said, slightly wrinkling his nose in contempt of the unwashed musketeer.

The musketeer hesitated but shook his head. "I received strict orders from my commander that I am only to relay this message personally to His Eminence. I may not give it to anybody else!"

The secretary shook his head in disbelief. What could be happening in Calais that was so important as to be addressed only to His Eminence in person, he wondered. He tried once more but the musketeer wouldn't budge, his refusal was final.

"You'll have to come back then, His Eminence is retained on important business and may not be available until the end of the week," the secretary said arrogantly. The important business was a bilious attack, but this knowledge was a state secret and certainly of no concern for this stinking messenger!

The musketeer went straight to his commander in Paris but his superior just shrugged his shoulders and confirmed that the Cardinal was indeed not available. He'd need to wait until access was granted. From this day on, the musketeer tried daily to meet the great Cardinal Richelieu. Since he had washed and changed it became apparent that he was actually a very attractive young man. The attitude of the secretary changed notably and now it was the musketeer who made sure that there was enough distance between him and the monk as the latter devoured him with his eyes whenever he entered the study.

It was about a week later when the great Cardinal granted him an audience. Dressed in his best, the musketeer entered the room, kneeled and kissed the gleaming ring of office of the Cardinal.

Being invited to present his message, he produced the document that had been entrusted to him. The Cardinal sat down but didn't make any sign for him to do so as well and therefore he stood, erect and waiting in front of the huge desk that was littered with numerous and impressive looking documents and messages. Just the thought that someone would need to read all these papers made the brave musketeer shiver.

The Cardinal read the message at amazing speed; never had the musketeer seen anybody read so fast before in his life. Richelieu skimmed over the usual phrases of elaborate greetings and went straight to the essence of the message:

It is my pleasure to report to your Eminence that we have a young and diligent female servant employed in our services in a guesthouse in Calais. The aforesaid person succeeded in winning the intimate confidence of two young guests, one dark, one blond, both individuals being young men at the threshold of adulthood.

The Cardinal could imagine the way this young maid had succeeded in getting their 'intimate' confidence – he may have been a man of the Church but he had not yet lost contact with human nature.

Our informer discovered among the luggage of one of the gentlemen a ring with a coat of arms that I could identify positively as the coat of arms of the de Saint Paul family. It therefore seems most probable that both young men are indeed those who escaped in Reims and are covered by the search warrant that has been signed by Your Eminence.

Richelieu's eyes blinked with satisfaction; once more his dense network of informers had yielded satisfying results.

I await instructions from Your Eminence as to how to proceed. In view of the prominent position of one of the young men and the political consequences that any imprudent action could provoke, it is my wish that Your Eminence in person should order their arrest.

The rest of the letter was once more dedicated to the usual formalities of politeness. The Cardinal's glance went further and to his immense annoyance he saw that the letter had been signed nearly three weeks ago! With a look as hard as steel he hissed, "Why has it taken nearly three weeks for this message to be delivered?"

The musketeer felt hot and cold at the same time under the scrutiny of the irate Cardinal. He stood erect and answered with a crimson face, "My horse lost a shoe and when it was mended, I was stuck for nearly three full days close to Amiens because a thunderstorm caused a flood and made passage impossible for several days. I continued as soon as possible but no roads were left, I had to ride day and night through fields of mud." Gathering more confidence he continued, "I arrived here nearly a week ago but was denied access by your secretary who informed me that you couldn't be disturbed because you were on important business of his Majesty, the King."

"I understand that this delay then was a force majeure," Richelieu consented but he pressed his lips together tightly. It was clear that he didn't appreciate God meddling with his business.

"You return to Calais immediately. I will give no written instructions, you are to remember and repeat to your commander exactly what I tell you now! Both young men are to be arrested immediately. The blond one has to be brought as my personal prisoner to Paris, arrest to be made on the grounds of unlawful escape from the monastery school of Reims, and the dark one has to be given ample opportunity to escape – if he finds himself waking up on a ship sailing to England that would be a very elegant solution."

The Cardinal's glance had returned to the message. "And better be fast this time, I'll not tolerate another delay, act of God or not!"

The musketeer was dismissed and understood that he had to return immediately to Calais. This was his last chance to remain in the service of His Eminence.

The Cardinal rang for his secretary, interrogating him once more about the delay. The secretary had already checked the story and indeed a terrible thunderstorm had flooded the region of Amiens and annihilated the summer harvest. The musketeer had insisted on seeing His Eminence urgently but as His Eminence had lain in bed suffering, his doctors had not allowed any disturbance for a mere message coming from the northern provinces.

Richelieu was a demanding and difficult master but as he couldn't detect any failings on the part of his secretary or of the musketeer his ice-cold glance relaxed.

"Let's pray then that God will deliver the Marquis de Beauvoir into the hands of our Church," he said and was already opening the next report that was waiting for him. Relieved, the monk retreated into the study dedicated for the use of all the secretaries. He had been working for the Cardinal now for nearly a year and had rarely seen him so upset. Laying hands on the Marquis must be of the utmost importance for France, or for him…

HOW TO LEAVE CALAIS?

Marie's father had rented the most fashionable and luxurious guesthouse in Calais, overlooking the port and recently erected in the new style of Louis XIII with high ceilings and large windows allowing air and light to enter the elegantly appointed rooms. When the carriages ground to a halt, the passengers climbed out, feeling stiff and numb.

The owner of the establishment had already arrived and gave efficient instructions to the servants to deal with the luggage whilst he courteously greeted his guests with a welcome drink of local cider.

The marble staircase inside the house was impressive, and the rooms very large compared to the small and cramped inns they had visited and sometimes endured on their way. Marie was starting to feel more cheerful, and all of them were happy to escape the routine of the swaying carriage and stay for at least a week in the same lodgings on firm ground.

*****

Armand had taken over the usual round of interrogations as he judged it too dangerous for Pierre to show his face near the harbour as long as his cousin was in town. Pierre had given up his initial resistance, distracted agreeably from time to time by the same maid who had enjoyed Armand's amorous favours before – but then the maid had suddenly started to avoid their company. Being stuck in their small guesthouse for days and weeks to come was beginning to work on his nerves, and he became as moody and restless as a caged lion.

Armand felt a huge weight being lifted from him when he witnessed by chance the cavalcade of Marie's entourage entering the court of a most elegant guesthouse. He recognized her familiar face as she alighted from the coach and he had to restrain himself in order not to rush forward and greet her immediately in a warm embrace. Their ingenious plan had worked; now he was sure, they'd be in England soon!

Marie was accompanied by a tall woman whom he had never seen before, her father and a small army of footmen.

"Typical of Marie's father to bring his treasured daughter to Calais in person," Armand thought, somewhat irritated. They would need to find a way to get rid of him – hopefully he wasn't joining them on the trip to England!

Armand thought it wise to come back the following day and get a message to Marie in the meantime through the groom who worked in the stables. They'd become good friends over numerous glasses of *eau de vie* and cider over the previous weeks.

Pierre couldn't believe the news at first. He looked at his friend, his eyes wide open as if he was looking at a stranger. In truth he had already given up hope of meeting Marie once more, even if he would never have admitted the truth to his friend. The last days had been terrible, his mood had been foul, he had even started to quarrel with Armand.

When Pierre had finally digested the news, he wanted to leave for the guesthouse immediately and greet her, but Armand convinced him to wait until tomorrow – they'd need to approach her carefully as she was accompanied by her father and an unknown lady – probably her chaperon.

Reluctantly Pierre accepted the logic of this and agreed to Armand's suggestion to celebrate this auspicious event properly. As the celebrating was conducted with several bottles of wine, they slept like logs until noon the next day.

Armand awoke with a splitting headache but he remembered dimly that he needed to see Marie. He plunged his head into a basin of cold water and hoped that a combination of water and fresh air would be remedy enough for his headache. Pierre was eager to join but he had to relent – being so close to success, they couldn't run any risk of his being recognized.

Armand went downstairs to look for some bread and milk. The maid's behaviour had changed lately. She looked very smug and was wearing a new ring – probably she had found a new lover who could entertain her more lavishly than two young but essentially penniless visitors.

To Armand's surprise, not only did she bring his breakfast very quickly, she also settled next to him asking him when and how they were planning to leave. Feeling rather uneasy at this sudden and unexpected interest in his affairs, Armand preferred to remain cautious with his answers.

He quickly improvised a credible story: He told her that they were waiting for the arrival of their uncle who was in possession of their money and would probably already have booked a passage to the next ship to Antwerp. Armand concluded that this could take another fortnight until they left. Maybe he should see with the innkeeper if she had place for another visitor, he concluded, and was satisfied to see that the maid apparently had swallowed the bait as she was offering to arrange the reservation of the new room with the landlady and seemed content that they were staying on.

Why on earth does she want to know these details? he wondered, as soon as she had left. *She won't even look at us lately and she dumped Pierre. This sudden interest in our plans is rather strange and smells a bit fishy...*

*****

Marie was surprised when a groom from the stables approached her the next morning. She had come down to look after the horses when the groom suddenly offered to hold her arm so as not to slip and fall down in the dirty stables. She hadn't expected such chivalrous behaviour from a mere groom. She was even more surprised when she felt him slip a piece of paper into her hand, making a sign to keep her mouth shut.

At first she felt really upset, hot with rage – how dare a servant approach her like this! Immediately though she realized how stupid her thoughts had been – a groom wouldn't know how to read or write! She became very excited – maybe this was the message she had so been longing to receive from Armand and Pierre?

She went upstairs to her room making a sign to Céline to join her. Both heads hovered over the short message: *Meet me in the stables this afternoon before dinner – Armand.*

The ladies hugged each other with joy: their adventure would continue.

At noon their landlord had prepared a delicious lunch. Marie's father joined them, as he never missed a good lunch. Afterwards he belched in a satisfied manner; maybe he had eaten a bit too much, he admitted guiltily.

He then excused himself, but he would need to leave them on their own in the guesthouse for a short period. He wanted to go out and meet the owner of the ship where he had booked cabins for Marie, Céline and the maids and footmen that were to accompany them to London – at least twelve people in total – although Marie's uncle had promised to come down to Dover and take charge of her personally. Marie's father didn't think it appropriate for young ladies to walk in a city – Calais, being a city with an important port, equalled the sinful town of Gomorrah in his eyes. Only closed sedan chairs with curtains would be acceptable for ladies of good renown. But both ladies politely declined – they had had enough of swaying – and soon a ship and more reeling on the waves would be waiting for them.

For his return Marie had ordered some sweet wine and cakes. She wanted to thank her father for the excellent care and concern that he was taking for her and she knew that he had a weakness for sweet things.

But he soon came back from his venture, his face white with rage. It took many soothing words and some glasses of wine to calm him down and to enable him to explain what had happened.

"I had chartered the best ship available and all of the cabins, paying in advance in gold! When I arrived this afternoon this inflated, fat, treacherous scoundrel of a ship owner told me that he had received an order of sequestration from the prime minister for his ship to sail to Dover with a new special ambassador, a Henri de Beauvoir. The ship owner therefore said that he *regrets*" – Marie's father nearly spat out the word – "that he'll have to take his best cabins for the ambassador and his retinue and is flatly refusing to give me back one single penny as this should be considered a case of force majeure!"

140

Marie's father was breathing heavily, his face turning alarmingly from pale to a burning shade of crimson. Marie immediately handed him another glass of wine. For a moment she had panicked that the ship might have been rented out altogether but when she heard that Henri de Beauvoir would be on the ship together with her, her heart sank. The prospect of being cooped up in a cabin with Céline for a short trip didn't disturb her at all, but how would she hide Pierre and Armand?

But having a practical mind, she decided that calming her father down should be her first priority. Consequently she used all of her skills to sooth her irate father and suggested he let his lawyers deal with this thief of a ship owner – but preferably after they had reached Dover.

*****

Time is a curious animal; either it races ahead, or it's so lazy that it doesn't seem to move forward at all. Waiting impatiently to meet Armand the hours seemed to be passing far too slowly for Marie's taste. She listened again and again to the chiming of the many church bells, announcing diligently the hour and inviting the faithful to attend mass from all corners of the city. Finally, around six o'clock she decided that any additional minute spent waiting in her room would definitely make her go crazy. It was about time to go down and visit the stables! Luckily her father had retired to his bedroom; the agitation of this afternoon and the multiple glasses of soothing but strong sweet wine had finally taken their toll and he had felt the urgent need to recuperate by means of a prolonged siesta.

Marie arrived at the stable door and once more the same taciturn groom who had passed her the message that morning mysteriously appeared and made a sign to follow him. Marie hesitated; she felt uneasy following a stranger into the dark and shadowy stables.

But curiosity triumphed and she followed him inside where she could smell the pungent odour of the horses mixed with smells of leather, hay and perspiration.

The groom led her into one of the abandoned horse boxes and Marie's anxiety grew when a total stranger suddenly materialized in front of her, giving her quite a fright as he emerged out of the darkness with his burning eyes, sporting a dark tan and an unkempt beard. Marie was just about to cry out for help when the familiar voice of Armand spoke to her.

"Marie, shush, don't worry! I know that I look a bit strange, but I need to remain incognito, so I stopped shaving. I'm so happy to see you here, I can't tell you how much! I had almost given up hope, why did it take you so long?"

"Armand! Good grief, you really do look dreadful, but it's wonderful to see you again! How's Pierre?"

Armand smiled and, although his smile was partially obscured by his wild beard, he still radiated his usual charm when he answered.

"We're all right – I looked well after your treasure, it's a long story though. But now tell me first, what has been happening with you?"

Knowing that time was pressing, Marie suppressed her desire to tell Armand that Pierre was not 'her treasure', therefore she just ignored his remark and tried to give him a very concise version of her adventures. Armand was full of admiration at how she had managed to save her mother by calling on the physician from the monastery and had solved the problem of having a respectable companion.

"You truly are an extraordinary young lady!" he exclaimed, with enough admiration in his voice to please Marie enormously.

Then it was Marie's turn to ask what kind of adventures they had experienced but Armand dodged this question and just told her that they'd soon have a lot of time to tell their story – as soon as they were on the ship to England together.

"Listen, Marie: how can you get us on the ship?" he insisted. "We have an enormous problem, Pierre's cousin is here and he's apparently all set to leave for England as well – this can't be a coincidence. Pierre is in immediate danger!"

But before Armand could go on, Marie interjected, "I know – and the worst is to come: he's sailing on the same ship with us!"

This news came as a bombshell and Armand looked at her, totally perplexed.

Marie continued excitedly, "Cardinal Richelieu has apparently sequestered half of the ship for Henri and his retinue, he seems to have become a big cheese at court. My father is beside himself with rage, as he had paid for the journey in advance. But there's nothing we can do if we don't want to delay our departure – we'll have to find a way to hide you somehow!"

Armand sat down on a hay bale and tried to find some way out of this riddle. Had they struggled all the way from Reims to Calais just to fall into the hands of Henri de Beauvoir – or even worse, the Cardinal, who seemed to be involved rather too much for his liking?

"You don't need to bother about me," Armand said, "he'll never recognize me. I met Henri de Beauvoir several times – but it's been years ago and I've changed my looks completely – well, even you didn't recognize me. It's Pierre we need to worry about. He's the spitting image of his cousin and far too easy to recognize!"

Marie sat down next to him, hoping that the hay wouldn't stain the beautiful evening gown she had already put on for dinner. This did seem really rather difficult, unless...

"I know exactly what to do!" she exclaimed all of a sudden, and carefully looking around her she whispered her suggestion into Armand's ear.

Armand was stunned, and simply grinned. Her suggestion was so simple – and quite ingenious!

They agreed to meet again the next morning as the sailing date was imminent. The ship owner – having rented out his ship at fabulous prices to two illustrious passengers – didn't care to wait for any additional cargo and had told Marie's father that departure was scheduled for tomorrow evening. The weather seemed fine, and if they left promptly they'd have ideal weather for sailing.

Armand hurried back to meet Pierre who'd been staying in the guesthouse, counting the seconds. Pierre still couldn't believe that they'd shortly be reunited with Marie and even make it to England. Their adventure was about to continue and he tried to imagine what this strange country of his mother's would look like. Would his relatives be helpful – or would they treat him as an unwanted foreigner, a bastard intruder?

To the dismay of the maid, who had started her amorous overtures once more, he showed her the cold shoulder and was lost in thought, pretending not to notice when she brushed his arm with her sleeve. As soon as Armand entered the public room, Pierre jumped up eagerly.

"I have great news," Armand exclaimed loudly. "Our uncle is arriving soon. His ship is due to arrive this week!"

Turning to the maid, he asked, "Did you ask the landlady if she could reserve us a room – but a good one, not the kind of shabby small room where she tried to suffocate us, our uncle is a real gentleman, very demanding!"

The maid assured them that she had done everything, and guessing that information on a third suspicious person to arrive this week would probably yield a fat bonus she tried to devise a suitable excuse to leave the guesthouse tomorrow morning and report her findings. She couldn't think of anything convincing; it would have to be the usual excuse of looking after her sick aunt – yet again...

Dragging Pierre out of the guesthouse and away from the maid's attentive ears, they ended up two streets further on and entered a small chapel that lay deserted in the hot sun of the afternoon. The chapel must have been very old indeed with its ancient thick walls, uneven floor and old gothic paintings. It was surprisingly cool inside and Pierre shivered.

The rough wooden benches were shabby from the wear of so many hopeful, and sometimes desperate, pilgrims who had passed here for generations to pray beneath century-old wooden statues of venerated saints that had probably once been painted in bright colours. But now they looked worn, having been touched in worship by so many faithful believers and stained by the smoke of the stinking tallow candles that burned day and night.

143

"I thought you'd appreciate a monastic atmosphere for our discussion, I'm pretty sure that you've missed it desperately," Armand quipped and gave a quick resumé of the meeting with Marie.

"Marie confirmed that we'll be sailing tomorrow, or latest the day after tomorrow." Armand added a short version of Marie's adventures. Pierre listened, full of admiration but before he could express his admiration of Marie's accomplishments, Armand changed the subject.

"By the way, did you notice that the maid has started hanging around us once more? I find her behaviour strange and she's become extremely nosy. I guess we'd better be careful and make sure that she doesn't know our real plans. I've arranged for us to sleep tonight in the stables of Marie's fashionable hotel. Thus we're sure we won't miss their departure. Now, I have a little bonus for you." He grinned, full of mischief, and started to explain the plan that he had developed with Marie. Pierre first howled in protest, but it didn't help. Armand was adamant, he had no choice, the danger was too great to be ignored.

"Take it or leave it," Armand said very firmly; sensing defeat, Pierre accepted.

They decided to pay their weekly rent as normal but moved out secretly that evening. Luckily they did not have many belongings; they had already been forced to sell their horses to replenish their dwindling cash reserves, consequently moving out of the guesthouse was fairly easy.

As discussed, Armand paid the weekly rate and even offered a bit more to make the reservation of an additional room and their prolonged stay credible.

Their rodent-toothed landlady quickly dropped the shining coins into her seemingly bottomless purse and pressed it fervently to her meagre bosom. Making a huge effort she even managed a vinegary smile.

Afterwards the friends went up to their room. Armand decided to empty his secret cache behind the bed. When he opened it, he hesitated. He could have sworn that his ring had been wrapped differently in the piece of cloth when he had hidden it, rather less tidily in fact. He would have never folded it so neatly. He decided not to mention this discovery to Pierre, but if their identity had been discovered, they were in far worse danger than he had imagined so far.

In the meantime the maid had reached the impressive buildings that housed the office of the Bishop of Calais. It was late afternoon, as her landlady had insisted that she must finish several tasks in the kitchen before she was allowed to leave. Citing her password, she was admitted immediately to a monk with a bald head and an ascetic face. He listened attentively to the information.

"Thank you, my Daughter, if a third person is involved it will certainly be of interest for us. I'm regrettably still waiting for the instructions of His Eminence in Paris. Please keep an eye on the suspects and report any news immediately!"

The maid made a polite curtsey and moved out of the room. She was disappointed that she had been dismissed so fast and that the monk hadn't mentioned any additional reward. As she had invented an urgent visit to a sick aunt, she'd better stick to her story and stay away overnight and make the best of a free day.

On her way out she became witness to a commotion. A dust-covered musketeer had arrived and requested urgent access to the monk she had just left. The musketeer was accompanied by a second soldier, apparently his commander, as it was clear that he was used to giving orders. The maid, now burning with curiosity, wanted to linger to find out what was going on but was chased away roughly by another soldier who was on duty in the bishop's palace. She shrugged, made an obscene gesture to the stunned soldier and left.

In the meantime Armand had made a decision. "Let's get out now," he suggested. "I have started to hate this room."

Hiding their few belongings under their clothes they left the inn. The public room lay deserted and they strolled out of the guesthouse in a leisurely fashion like two young men who hadn't yet decided how to pass their time.

*****

The landlady had happened to notice that the two young guests were not back yet by the early evening. She wasn't particularly concerned – they often came back late, having dinner elsewhere, and as she had received her money she didn't mind. In fact she had more than enough work as that lazy slut of a maid had once more demanded a day off to visit her sick aunt outside the city walls.

"Sick aunt," she snorted. "An aunt who probably wears a moustache and pays handily for her caring services. I'll fire her the next time she comes around with a story like this."

Her face looked as sour as usual and she concentrated on the task of kicking her indolent groom into some action. He was supposed to help out in the inn's public room full of guests waiting to be served and who promised to further swell her beloved purse, safely stored underneath her mattress.

She was still serving her customers when the door of the public room opened with a bang and a group of musketeers led by their officer marched into her inn. All conversation stopped at once. A pompous officer leading four fully armed musketeers requested in an official tone to speak to the owner. Looking more than ever like a mouse the landlady scurried forward and presented herself.

The officer produced a sealed document and informed her haughtily that she was under suspicion of having rented a room to two young delinquents who had escaped from their monastery school and were to be arrested in the name of His Majesty, the King. Any hindrance of the execution of the law would be severely

145

punished. The officer paused dramatically before continuing that in the name of the gracious King Louis XIII she was requested to deliver all information and remit her guests into the hands of justice immediately.

The landlady shook, and trying to defend herself started a complicated and long-winded statement that she would of course do her duty... she didn't know... she wouldn't have thought... She pleaded innocence and cursed those naughty boys for ever having entered her respectable house, and eventually stopped, as she had lost the trail of what she really wanted to say.

Seeing that the officer was getting impatient she offered to show him the room that she was renting to the suspects, continuing her clamouring all the way up the staircase until the officer hissed at her to shut up or be sent to jail herself.

The group of soldiers reached the door of the room, muskets pointing at the door, swords ready. They knocked, but nobody answered. They were greeted by total silence. The officer made a sign and three men pushed their full weight against the door, tumbling into a small room – but the room lay empty and deserted.

"Are you crazy?" howled the landlady. "You stupid fools, I could have told you straight away that they're not inside. There was no need to ruin a perfectly good door! Who's going to pay for that?" Her voice rose hysterically and it was impossible to extract any additional or useful information from her.

The birds had flown, orders needed to be given to control the port, ships and the gates – if they were still in Calais they'd get them. The commander was disappointed but he remained confident of his men.

Pierre and Armand had spent a peaceful night in the hay stored in the attic above the stables. It was fresh and soft and held the fragrances of summer. The groom had showed them a remote corner where they could hide safely, assuring them that his colleagues never ventured up there if they could avoid it.

The next morning he brought them some bread and fresh milk. Lingering, he cleared his throat and remarked casually, "There's a mighty lot of trouble out there, constables and musketeers everywhere, all over the place."

Armand was still a little sleepy but when the full significance of this message penetrated his brain, he leapt immediately out of the hay.

"Why? What's going on?" he exclaimed.

"Dunno," answered the groom. "Seems they're looking for two young men, one blond, one dark." He looked at Armand in a non-committal way, apparently waiting for his reaction.

Armand hesitated as to whether he should confess the truth or not and decided to show his cards. "All right, they're looking for us!" Armand answered, looking at the groom with wide eyes. "We escaped from our monastery school; we simply couldn't bear it any more. Will you report us now or will you help us?"

"I ain't seen nobody," said the groom. "I never mix with them government lot, let them musketeers have their own fun."

Armand sighed with relief and kicked Pierre who was still sleeping innocently next to them. "Get up you lazy bones, the musketeers are searching for us, it's time to put our plan into action!"

Pierre just groaned. Sleep seemed to be a much better option.

Armand asked the groom to take a message to Marie and added, "If we get on the ship with your help, I'll make sure that you get a reward, I promise!" The groom just nodded and left with the message.

Armand was very nervous. He didn't know how far he could truly rely on the groom's honesty or reluctance to mix with the authorities. He listened tensely, expecting any minute to hear the sound of musketeers' boots racing up the ladder to the stable attic. After a good hour – time that stretched slowly and endlessly – they heard the sound of a small group of people. They had built a hiding place in the stacks of hay and Pierre and Armand bolted into their hide-out.

Through the curtain of the hay they detected first the familiar head of the groom, then Marie and afterwards a tall woman, still young but definitely past the first flush of youth. She was carrying a bundle of clothes. Marie had some water and the groom held another bundle in his hand.

Armand left his hiding place and greeted Marie and the unknown lady with perfect courtesy, notwithstanding that he was covered with strands of hay – not even a stable could ruin his elegant poise, Pierre thought jealously. Pierre then appeared and tried his best to live up to the manners and elegance of his friend. The tall lady gave him a friendly smile; they liked each other at first sight. When he looked at Marie his bow was less than perfect. He was stunned; she looked even more beautiful than he had remembered in his dreams.

Marie saw his look of admiration, and being a true woman she relished that look and basked in it. But looking closer she also detected a change in Pierre. Not only had he grown somewhat, he looked and moved like a well-trained athlete after three months of riding and exercise. It came as quite a shock: she had left a boy and found a man. With the sixth sense of a woman she sensed immediately that the two friends had not been on the road for three months without having enlarged their experience beyond riding and hunting and a wave of jealousy for her unknown female rival – or worse, rivals – washed over her. Even worse: she had to admit that she liked this new Pierre even better than the old one. The boy had made her fall in love, but now she found him devilishly attractive to boot.

147

All of these thoughts went through her mind in a flash and Pierre, having no idea of this, lifted his eyes to meet hers and gave her a smile that nearly knocked Marie off her feet.

Now I fully understand why she moved heaven and earth to come and meet him again, thought Céline, looking at this attractive, young, blond man. *It's unbelievable, he doesn't even seem to have the slightest idea of how attractive he really is. Poor Marie, she'll have to guard him well!*

Marie had decided that playing hard to get would probably be her best strategy. She wanted him badly – but she wanted to be sure that he felt the same, and not only today. She answered the smile and expressed her delight at seeing him – but she seemed to welcome Armand in the same familiar way, thus sending Pierre into despair. He looked at her like an eager puppy and she had to muster all of her resolve not to melt here and now.

Armand had seen the exchange of glances and suppressed a smile. Those two were head over heels in love, even if Marie was the more accomplished actor and could conceal her feelings much better. Pierre was hopeless, of course. Marie could read him like an open book. Armand would have to talk with him – women also liked to conquer a man, he shouldn't make it so easy for her.

Céline introduced herself and Marie inserted, "She's my best and trusted friend, we can rely on her, she's part of our adventure now. Let's hurry, my father will be searching for me soon. We'll have a last lunch together and then leave together to board the ship. The owner of our hotel told us that some escaped villains are hiding in the town," she giggled. "Funny, their description could fit you perfectly!"

Becoming serious again, she continued, "We have to act fast now! Armand will replace one of our footmen, I paid him handsomely to remain in Calais. With his new appearance," and she gave a quizzical look at Armand who pretended not to notice, "there shouldn't be a problem, he blends in perfectly with the commoners."

Armand just grinned, he knew his worth.

Pierre found himself sitting on a bale of straw as the groom started to shave him until his skin hurt, but after this operation there wasn't a hair left. Céline gave him the bundle of clothes; she had in fact offered to sacrifice one of her old and less fancy dresses as she was unusually tall for a woman and had hoped that she could make it fit Pierre.

Pierre disappeared to their hiding place that had now become a dressing room and after some minutes he wailed from behind the screen that this was impossible, no person in their right mind could wear such clothes with all these buttons and ribbons.

Armand rolled his eyes in despair and disappeared to give him a hand.

148

Armand seemed to have more experience with women's clothes as he managed to get Pierre into the dress fast, dealing with buttons and ribbons like an expert. They all held their breath as Pierre emerged, managing to look stunning – even as a girl.

Céline had brought a comb and she arranged his shoulder-length hair in a more feminine way. Ignoring his wild protests she added a final touch of some coloured ribbons – but not too many, as Pierre was to play the role of Marie's chamber maid. They had even thought about bringing shoes with buckles along from Anne, Marie's dragon of a maid. The shoes were slightly too large, but at least he could walk in them without too many difficulties. He walked up and down the attic as if he was out for a promenade and having made his peace with his disguise, Pierre took to his role and even pretended to send coquettish glances and kisses to Armand, to the delight of Marie and Céline.

Céline applied a last artistic touch by adding some subtle rouge to lips and cheeks and the new maid was ready to take up her duties.

Time was suddenly racing on. Marie enjoyed a last lunch in the company of her father – at least she pretended to enjoy the meal, as their impending departure was making her heart sink. Far too soon it was time to leave. Although their hotel was close to the port they still needed two coaches and several horses to transport their luggage and the servants chosen by her father to accompany her. Luckily he was to such an extent upset by her departure that he failed to notice that one of his footmen had changed his appearance.

Céline had already enquired two days before if Marie's father would mind if she engaged a maid to sail with her. She could stay in her cabin and she wouldn't be a burden!

He had accepted this idea gladly as this could only mean additional company and security for his daughter.

The port was teeming with soldiers and musketeers. All movements were controlled heavily and the soldiers made a great show of their importance. Something special must be going on!

However, Marie's father's group didn't arouse any suspicion, as a provincial gentleman travelling with his daughter and retinue could not possibly be hiding any villains.

Inspecting their little group was therefore a mere formality. Nobody could possibly imagine anything untoward, seeing his beautiful and delicate daughter, chaperoned by her three tall female companions. They screened the footmen – all were dark haired, the big fellow with the beard looked particularly stupid, and not one single blond man could be detected in the whole party. The officer had told them that the blond man should be found as a priority; he didn't seem to be especially bothered about the other one.

Having passed the scrutiny of the officer, Pierre vanished rapidly into a cabin with Céline, pretending to store away and tidy up her belongings. His heart was still thumping – he had been convinced that the officer would unmask him as soon as he glanced across at him, hiding behind Anne and Céline. But Pierre was amazed – not only had their ruse worked, the officer had even winked at him! Once more Marie's idea had saved them.

Although Marie had been so looking forward to sailing to England, now she had a big lump in her throat and tears sprang into her eyes when her father embraced her for the last time on the boat. Her father could barely speak; all the admonishing, advice and warnings that he had wanted to get rid of remained unsaid. They stood for two minutes, embracing in silence, then he kissed her forehead and blessed her.

Turning back again he left the ship. At the quay he halted and waved until he stepped into the sedan chair that was waiting for him. They had agreed that he wouldn't wait for the ship to sail; the sight of the ship leaving the harbour would probably break his heart, he had told her, with tears in his eyes.

Marie still lingered outside, knowing that Anne would take care of her luggage and prepare the cabin. Her father had been able to retain two cabins, so her footmen and guards would have to sleep in the crew's quarters.

She still had tears in her eyes, but there was so much to see! Provisions were still being loaded, fresh water brought on in huge barrels, baskets with loaves of bread, fruit and vegetables unloaded by beefy stevedores. The seagulls were circling around the ship in greedy anticipation, ready to have their pick of anything that might fall. Marie couldn't believe her eyes, so many things were loaded for a short trip of one day only – if the winds stayed favourable.

Horses panicking in fear were led across swaying gangways into their makeshift stables on board. Marie was still standing there watching in admiration when Céline, who had joined her, exclaimed, "Look, who's that over there!"

Marie turned her face in the direction Céline had pointed to. Six musketeers on horses were preceding a gilded coach with a coat of arms that she had never seen before. The coach stopped and a footman alighted to lower the staircase. "This must be the villain cousin," Marie whispered. "Do ask Thérèse to come and have a look!" Céline nodded and smiled – Thérèse was Pierre's new name and it gave them much fun to call him that.

She hurried down to the cabin, taking care not to bump her head on the low ceilings of the decks, as she had experienced the first time she went down to the cabin – these beams formed painful obstacles for a tall person like her.

Soon she returned with Pierre, just in time to see the elegant gentleman who had alighted from the coach. Henri de Beauvoir had dressed splendidly, according to his new position as special ambassador. His tall boots were shining in the sun, and his dark red velvet waistcoat shimmered with golden threads, jewelled buttons gleaming in the rays of the sun. A magnificent collar completed his appearance to perfection. When he turned his head to examine the ship with an arrogant look, all three onlookers gave a sharp intake of breath. They couldn't believe their eyes – he looked like the twin brother of Pierre, only older.

"Now I understand why Armand wanted you to stay disguised!" Marie exclaimed softly. "I'm afraid, Thérèse, that you'll have to become sea-sick until this gentleman has left us. Unless he's blind, he'll recognize you immediately!"

Pierre didn't even protest, he was lost in thoughts. Here he was, standing on the same ship together with his cousin who seemed to have become his worst enemy, the person who wanted to take his place – and the only way to do this would be to have him killed. What a coincidence of fate that his foe and only known relative should resemble him so much. Pierre wasn't frightened or nervous; on the contrary, he felt quite confident. If luck had held for him until now, why should it suddenly desert him?

But this elegant and refined enemy looked dangerous and competent. Armand had warned him that Henri had the reputation of being one of the best duellers in France, with both sword and pistol. His record of defeated opponents was legendary.

Armand had taught Pierre how to use a sword, but instinctively Pierre felt that he was a mere amateur compared to his cousin. It wouldn't be courage, but sheer madness to take him on him now. He'd need to find support from his mother's relatives first and learn to fight better, indeed, he would need to train intensively. But he swore once more to himself, he wouldn't let go, he was going to claim his heritage; he had to fulfil the wish of his dead parents who had sacrificed so much to protect him, their only son and heir, not this arrogant and greedy cousin.

Thérèse, alias Pierre, bobbed a short curtsey and went back into the cabin. It was agreed that he was to stay hidden until they reached Dover. The wind had become stronger, and profiting from the long daylight, the ship left Calais the same afternoon. Marie and Céline were invited by the captain to share dinner with him and, respecting convention, they obliged. They were not surprised to find the second guest of honour, Henri de Beauvoir, sitting next to the captain. The dinner was sophisticated (no surprise as he had clinched the deal of his life by charging twice), served on expensive silver plates, and the captain offered wine from Bordeaux, which both ladies declined but Henri consumed in remarkable quantity.

To Marie's surprise Henri didn't start flirting with her although she had dressed to look her best. She intended to get to know as much as possible about Henri and had been prepared to flirt with him to make him talk. When she saw Henri's eyes lingering a long time on the young muscular sailor who served at table, a suspicion formed in her mind as to why he didn't respond to her overtures. All the same she did her best to make him talk and as the wine started to loosen his tongue she got to know that he intended to leave immediately after their arrival in London in order to stay at the French embassy and be introduced to the royal court.

When Henri enquired about her plans, she told him that she was intending to visit her uncle and that she was really looking forward to being introduced to the court of Whitehall by her aunt.

Céline had lived a good part of her life in the Parisian circles that were close to the royal court. Feeling that Marie was running out of topics she cut into the conversation and made Henri gossip about the King of France, Richelieu and their complicated – often hostile – relationship with the Queen, who was known to favour the enemy Habsburg party. Henri confirmed that the Queen's position had strengthened once she had recently borne – after many years and against all expectations – the heir to the throne. France finally had a Dauphin and the Queen had become a factor to be reckoned with. Marie's head started to spin with all the names and connections but she could see that Céline was perfectly at ease. Céline managed to find out that Henri's mission to London was being conducted on behalf of the Prime Minister, the famous Cardinal, Duc de Richelieu, but he remained mysterious about the content of his mission.

They left on good terms, both sides assuring each other with fake enthusiasm how much they'd look forward to meeting again at the court of King Charles at Whitehall. Henri had drunk much wine and washed down his cheese at the end of the meal with a strong wine from Portugal, called Porto, a wine offered ceremoniously by the ship's owner. This wine was becoming very fashionable, he ascertained proudly.

Henri therefore left the table still walking straight ahead, but the wine had made his head spin and when he opened the door of what he remembered to be his own cabin he saw a tall maid standing there with half of her clothes removed, her bare back turned towards him. Most likely this wasn't his cabin after all – but if fate was offering him an opportunity, why not grasp it!

He still felt excited from watching the sailor who had served him at table and was willing to have a bit of fun – maid or boy, he didn't really care right now. Before Pierre could react, his cousin had grabbed him hard, kissing his mouth brutally, his hands fumbling already with his buttocks, trying to enter the dress, whilst Henri's knees were trying to open his legs. Pierre fought hard but was totally taken by surprise. After a second of panic he rammed his knee into his cousin's private parts. He knew from his monastery days that this was a highly effective defence against unwanted overtures.

Henri howled in pain, but strangely enough this action seemed to excite him even more and he held on, his arms like iron pincers around Pierre, trying to insert his tongue into Pierre's mouth. Pierre looked desperately around to see if he could find any weapon; his cousin's grip was like a vice and he could hardly breathe.

"I do think that I heard some noise," Céline's voice suddenly twittered next to them, as if she hadn't remarked anything unusual and continued, "Thérèse, would you mind letting His Excellency get to his own cabin, you're far too forward for my liking," admonishing her maid with a stern voice.

Henri dropped his arms immediately, made a bow to Céline and retreated. Pierre wanted to grab his sword and follow him but Céline had already closed the door and whispered, "Don't play the stupid hero. He's so drunk, he won't remember anything tomorrow. Let him go, you'll get your revenge later. We all want this rat to be dead, but give it time! We don't want you to spend your life in a British or French dungeon!"

Pierre's anger abated and he had to accept the sense of Céline's words. He dropped the sword and just replied wildly, "I won't just kill him one day, I'll skin him alive!"

Céline sneaked into Marie's cabin after this incident. She gave Marie a short account of the scene she had just witnessed and Marie didn't know if she should laugh at the funny side of the drunken cousin trying to rape his own disguised relative or panic when she thought what might have happened to Pierre without Céline's intervention.

Their ship was built for transporting freight and not for speed but the captain was optimistic that they'd see the white cliffs of Dover latest at sunrise.

Marie settled in her bed, too exhausted now to talk or gossip. Her maid, Anne, and Céline were trying to make themselves as comfortable as possible on a large upholstered bunk that was built into the corner opposite Marie's bed.

They wouldn't get much sleep, Céline thought, as she moved uneasily, trying to find a comfortable position on the bunk but the strain and excitement must have been more tiring than she thought and she dropped into a deep slumber in no time. Only Marie couldn't sleep; she kept listening to the noises outside, scared that somebody would cross the floor, afraid that Henri could try once more to harm Pierre.

Armand sat in the crew's quarters in the centre of a roaring crowd playing cards. He hadn't fancied sleeping in one of those hammocks with stinking blankets, worn from use, which had probably never even been cleaned. He could easily imagine how many generations of fleas and bedbugs were just waiting for a new juicy victim.

Inviting the crew and some servants from Henri's retinue to join him for a bottle of rum, they were best friends in no time. He skilfully managed to lose small amounts of money and with the second bottle of rum he paid for, he had become their hero. Soon tongues were loosened and it became apparent that Henri was a feared master, impatient, choleric and brutal. His valet with the beautiful bronze-coloured skin seemed to hate him from the bottom of his heart.

Good to know, Armand thought. *You never know when we'll need his help. He'll do everything to get his revenge, that's for sure – I wonder why he's so bitter?*

They enjoyed a smooth crossing and the light wind helped to make quick progress during the night. The bright moon and a cloudless sky studded with bright stars had made navigation easy. None of the dangers, ranging from bloodthirsty pirates to shipwrecking thunderstorms that had haunted Marie's father had materialized, and their journey had been smooth and agreeable.

The sunrise witnessed from on board ship was spectacular. As soon as the golden ball of the sun started to rise above the sea, the rays of the sun – first shimmering in a glorious pink and then turning quickly to a bright fiery gold – were reflected by the vast surface of the sea. Dancing waves broke the reflection of the sunlight as if the sea was composed of thousands of crystals, moving and sparkling under the sun.

In the early morning haze they caught sight of the coastline, gleaming a surreal, pristine white against its frame of green pastures.

Pierre had insisted on being woken up before they reached England. He wanted to be awake when they approached the country where his mother had been born. Carefully avoiding any new encounter with his cousin he climbed silently with Marie to the bow of the ship. When the sun rose and the famous cliffs appeared in their full splendour, he didn't say a word and in a trance he took Marie's hand and held it tight.

Marie would never forget this moment she shared with Pierre. They didn't talk, they didn't do anything particular, but both had the feeling that a lasting bond was being forged, between Pierre and England, and – as she fervently hoped – between both of them.

Pierre then disappeared once more into Céline's cabin and stayed hidden. They had agreed that his cousin should depart first, then they would disembark and wait in the guesthouse that Marie's father had booked in advance for the meeting with her uncle.

A tired but upbeat Armand said goodbye to his new friends from the crew and joined Marie and the rest of her delegation, ready to disembark.

To their great surprise, they were greeted by coaches and luxurious sedan chairs for the ladies. Marie's uncle had lived up to his promise and had not only come himself to greet his niece but he had trailed his wife and eldest son with him.

Greetings were exchanged, courtesies offered and Marie had the opportunity to get to know her relatives with whom she was going to spend several months.

154

Her uncle was tall and resembled slightly her mother's family line, more fair than dark, with alert brown eyes and a prominent nose. He wore the kind of trimmed beard made popular by the English monarch. Marie thought that the beard made his face look too long, she didn't like this fashion. He was very polite and obliging but Marie found it difficult to judge how far his welcome truly came from his heart. He was most probably a very skilled diplomat and wouldn't let someone see his true face or feelings easily.

Her aunt looked like a ball, short and plump, dressed according to the latest fashion in expensive velvet dresses with rich embroidery. To Marie's great relief she had a very warm personality, sharing confidences with her from the beginning and heaping praise on Marie for her beauty. She was of Italian origin and spoke French with a warm and sometimes slightly funny accent. She was very kind toward Céline as well and the three ladies decided that they would get on with each other very well.

Proudly she presented her eldest son, Arthur. Unfortunately Arthur had inherited his physique from his mother and was rather short and portly with an unruly mop of dark hair. All the same he was very charming and soon had Marie laughing at his side when he imitated the way those stiff English tried to speak French, making impossible faces whilst he imitated their desperate efforts to pronounce words like 'grenouille'.

In the evening they partook of dinner in a private dining room. As soon as Marie and Céline entered, both men immediately left their seats to welcome them. The food was different and heavier than the food they were used to eating in France, but Marie was hungry and ate from most of the dishes that had been served, trying to repeat the English names for each dish until she felt that she would explode.

"Dear Uncle, what's the plan for our stay, shall we be leaving immediately for London?" Marie enquired curiously. Her uncle hesitated slightly and before he could answer, his wife took over.

"There's a problem, my dear," she replied, patting her hand. "In fact, soon after we had received your kind letter and confirmed our invitation to your parents, the plague broke out once more in London. It's quite frequent in the big cities, you know. I didn't want to call off your visit as we all felt so excited about you coming here," and looking very indulgently at her eldest son she continued, "Arthur especially was looking forward to your visit very much indeed! Therefore your uncle decided to stay some time in our country estate in Hertfordshire, meet some of our friends and take you there first to avoid any risk. We'll descend to London and present you at court as soon as the plague leaves the city and it's safe to return. I understand that even the King and the Queen are planning to leave London. I hope you don't mind?" she added anxiously.

Marie felt disappointed at this complication but she understood the sound logic of her aunt's proposal. She didn't really fancy spending the next weeks in a country house, confined far too intimately with her cousin for her liking. If his parents were planning a marriage she would have a hard time keeping him at a distance. These thoughts flashed through her mind but she answered with a charming smile, "Oh, please don't worry, dearest Aunt, this is exactly what my parents would have asked you to do. We'll have a marvellous time, I'm sure!"

Her aunt felt relieved that Marie didn't mind their detour and in a spontaneous manner she placed a kiss on Marie's cheeks. "I am sure we'll have a great time there," she continued in a confident tone. "We'll have parties, picnics and you'll get to know the family really well!" she beamed.

That's exactly what I feared, Marie wanted to retort – but she swallowed her reply and put on a brave face.

Later in the evening Marie and Céline managed to meet with Pierre and Armand. In the commotion of numerous people arriving or returning to France, nobody had noticed that Céline's tall maid had been replaced by a newly arrived blond footman. Their whole group was reduced to six persons now: Marie and Céline, Pierre and Armand, and Marie's maid Anne, who had brought along her husband who was serving as footman, groom or valet, whatever seemed necessary. He and Anne knew, of course, about the whole story and Marie didn't need to worry about their loyalty.

Marie briefed them on her aunt's decision to stay in Hertfordshire first. She had described the house where they'd be staying as a fairly elegant manor house built in the style of the Tudor monarchs with extensive parks and gardens bordering a huge estate which belonged to the Neuville family, Hertford Castle. Putting on a brave face she said "We'll have fun there, we can hunt, ride…" She didn't finish as she saw Pierre's face. He looked very downcast, he had longed so much to be able to leave straight away for London, reunite with his English family and find out about his mother's background.

Nobody had noticed Armand until he cried out excitedly, "Did you say that this place belongs to the Neuville estate?"

Marie was confused. "Yes, that's what I heard. She even said that she'd try to socialize with them and invite them for a dinner party, but she didn't seem to be very optimistic as they're one of the great families of the realm and, being in mourning at the moment, they probably wouldn't be attending any official parties."

"Who died?" Armand asked sharply.

"How should I know!" Marie exclaimed angrily. "Maybe your arrogant Excellency remembers that I have only just arrived from France?" Marie's furious eyes flashed at Armand who responded with a fencing gesture.

"Touché!" he replied. "Sorry, you're right. I'm so excited because Pierre's mother's maiden name was Lady Margaret Neuville, she must be linked to the family owning this estate and, although I'm not a specialist on the British aristocracy, if I remember correctly, her father carried – amongst other titles – the title of Duke of Hertford. This means leaving for Hertfordshire is wonderful – we couldn't have asked for better! We'll accompany you and try to meet the Duke as early as possible, maybe we can convince him to acknowledge his grandchild officially – this would be fantastic!"

They looked at him, stunned; this plan sounded just too good to be true. Pierre felt slightly stupid – it was his friend who had remembered the name of his mother, whereas he hadn't! The shame of it!

Armand saw the abashed expression on his friend's face and understood immediately. Quickly he added, "It's no miracle; I remember all of these details. Pierre saw his family documents only once very quickly after we had pinched them from the monastery archives with Marie's help," but before he could go on, Céline, looking curiously at Marie, interjected, "Marie, you never told me this story, you'll have tell me later today, I insist!"

Armand went on, "Actually, I'd love to get rid of them, they're too dangerous to be carried by one of us. Céline, would you safeguard them for us?"

Céline agreed readily. She felt so much part of this adventure that she didn't hesitate for a second.

Marie was immediately in high spirits. She had dreaded saying goodbye to her two friends so soon after they had reunited and after they had overcome so many obstacles in Calais only days before.

The vision of spending more time, maybe even several weeks together, was most appealing to her – a dream that suddenly had come true. Furthermore she had dreaded the idea of Pierre and Armand leaving for London, being exposed to all kinds of dangers. In her nightmares she saw Pierre as a victim of the plague or duelling with Henri. She saw Céline's glance and her understanding eyes told her that she could read her like a book. But she didn't mind any more. Since she had been with Pierre on the ship, holding his hand, she knew that she belonged to him. And she was sure now that he felt the same.

*****

The journey to Hertfordshire took only a few days. In fact they could have moved much faster but Marie's aunt had precise ideas about the level of comfort she was prepared to accept when travelling. She insisted on making frequent breaks, claiming that fast coach travel was ruining her fragile health. Their stops were invariably accompanied by lavish meals, and on one occasion a picturesque inn serving delicious cakes with clotted cream pleased her so much that she decided to stay an additional day. Arthur made faces behind his mother's back and

157

made Marie and Céline laugh – but the family was under the iron rule of her aunt, there was no doubt about that.

Marie's uncle had already left for Whitehall as he was afraid that his prolonged absence for private reasons might be looked on unfavourably by His Majesty's Government. His farewell had been tearful towards his wife, but Marie couldn't fight the feeling that her uncle didn't really mind returning to London and being back in the centre of life at court – despite the vague threat of the plague.

He had just shrugged it off. "In London, there's always some sort of plague, it's like Paris, actually. If I start running away every time some scaremonger tells a story about the plague, I might as well leave my position and go back to Savoy with your aunt and my son!" And off he went, leaving them under the care and supervision of his son and most of his footmen.

The final leg of their journey had started with a pleasant enough day and nobody had foreseen the heavy, dark clouds that had suddenly gathered, taking everybody by surprise, obscuring the sunlight. When the rain started – commencing timidly with some scattered drops, then fast turning into wild rivers of water pouring from the sky with unbelievable force – it had been too late to turn back. They had dragged on, the two friends stuck on their horses as was expected of faithful grooms. Even Arthur had decided to join them after some time, as it seemed to him that riding and getting completely drenched outside would be better than the constant nausea he felt as soon as he travelled inside the coach.

But their horses sensed quite early the approach of the storm and anticipated the arrival of thunder and lightning. It took all the skill and horsemanship of the grooms and riders to control them.

After rain there followed hail, hammering loudly on the roof of their coach. They stopped briefly under some trees as it was impossible to continue their journey amidst this apocalypse. Then lightning and thunder set in as if the end of the world was nigh. Marie and Céline feared for their lives, Marie praying fervently to her patron, Sainte Marie, and even Pierre and Armand, sitting without shelter on the horses secretly begged for heavenly support. Arthur silently cursed his mother, as it was her addiction to cakes that had delayed their arrival.

But the ordeal was over now and the small group stood dripping wet in the entrance, all of their noble splendour and decorum gone. Make-up was ruined, feathers drooped listlessly and clothing clung heavily to their bodies – hardly an impressive image of beauty and aristocracy. They looked at each other, relieved to have survived this nightmare and started to laugh.

"You look like a drowned cat," Céline said to Marie, tears of laughter streaming down her already wet face.

"And you look like a drowned corpse freshly recovered from the village pond," Marie retorted, laughing.

Arthur looked down at his ruined leather and velvet waistcoat. "Maybe a new fashion – the wet look?" he proposed. Having arrived safely, he had already forgiven his mother and had regained his usual good mood.

Nobody refused the offer of a hot drink from the housekeeper who was buzzing around them like a friendly bumble bee. Afterwards they all decided to retire in order to change their clothes – with the exception of Armand and Pierre who had tried to maintain expressionless faces (servants were not supposed to laugh). They needed to help unloading the coaches and only much later were allowed to withdraw to their tiny room in the servants' quarters to have some rest and dry their wet clothes.

Pierre felt excited and worried at the same time. They were so close to his family now, and most probably very soon he'd have the opportunity to meet his grandfather! Would he finally become part of a genuine family? Would his grandfather refuse to talk to him? Would he consider him a bastard with a French father? What could he do if his grandfather wouldn't help? Question after question was passing through his mind whilst he was mechanically handing down chests and trunks from the coaches, as Marie's aunt had not only brought clothes but everything she deemed necessary for her comfort from London – and what a lot of it there was!

THE NEW AMBASSADOR

Henri de Beauvoir sat in an elegant coach speeding towards London, his face relaxed. He had to admit that he loved his new position, and the recognition and pomp that came with it. For the first time he was not just a mere member of the aristocracy, and a younger son of a great family, a position he had always found ambiguous. He was certainly envied by the commoners but almost ignored by the highest members of the aristocratic circle who ruled France and dominated life at court.

Henri had been treated like a celebrity since he had arrived in Calais. The reception on the ship had been first class, in Dover a coach from the embassy accompanied by musketeers had been waiting for him, greeting him deferentially with all honours. He was important now. His face hardened. He had to get rid of this cousin, otherwise this would remain a passing episode and he would have to return to France, financially ruined, a mere nobody. His heart beat faster and a cruel smile appeared – yes, he would destroy this little dirty bastard, with pleasure, in fact, he was looking forward to it.

He closed his eyes and savoured the enticing vision of drawing his sword out of the twitching body of his cousin, blood gushing from the wound and oozing into the grass.

Duels were his specialty; he'd just need to offend his cousin in public so that he'd have no option but to accept. Yes, he'd have a lot of fun killing this imposter. Life would be sweet!

He must have fallen asleep in the coach as they reached London in no time. He was greeted in style by the French ambassador who had received detailed instructions from Richelieu and ushered him into his private apartments. Henri looked at the high wooden panels with their rich carvings, the stately bed in the middle of the room with the green velvet curtains to keep away the cold during winter. Rich tapestries hung from the high ceilings, glorifying the kings of France.

Jean unpacked Henri's luggage and lay out fresh clothes, as an official dinner was planned in the evening with the ambassador and his spouse and Henri planned to look his best.

During dinner the ambassador mentioned that the court of Whitehall was planning to retreat to one of the numerous royal castles in the countryside as more and more cases of the plague had been reported in the city. This would probably delay Henri's introduction and the meetings that had been planned. Henri felt afraid; the only thing he really dreaded was illness! "What are you going to do, Your Excellency?" he enquired nervously.

"We will of course follow the court to the countryside if His Majesty, King Charles, should decide to relocate to one of his more spacious residences; if not, we'll move to some estate outside London. Does this news upset you, Your Excellency?" he asked maliciously.

Henri sensed a trap and reassured him with false cheerfulness, "Not at all, not at all! We're all in God's hands, in any case!"

Both men exchanged smiles as bright as they were bogus and toasted the health of His Majesty, King Louis and his heir – and the success of Henri's mission.

The next day, Jean announced a visitor, a man apparently from the service of his Eminence, the Cardinal Richelieu. Henri rapidly scanned the letter of introduction and nodded his approval to Jean to let the visitor enter his apartment. The man had all the bearing of a religious background, a monk probably, but was dressed in the unobtrusive garb of a travelling merchant. He greeted Henri with all decorum and asked if he had found the arrangements made by the office of the Prime Minister to his satisfaction. Henri confirmed that his travel had been satisfactory and feeling that he needed to be polite to a messenger of the great Cardinal he expressed his gratitude for the lodgings and the smooth organization.

His visitor answered, "My Lord, you seem somewhat worried, if you will pardon my speaking freely. I've come here on behalf of the Cardinal, who wishes you well. Please let me know if there is anything that I can do to assist you in your task?"

Henri looked at him and decided that he wouldn't risk speaking his mind openly. "Yes, indeed, I am worried. His Excellency, the ambassador, informed me that the royal court may leave Whitehall and move outside London shortly as there are cases of plague reported in the city. This would mean that my mission may be delayed for a long period of time and I'm anxious to find and reunite with my cousin."

The visitor allowed himself a thin smile and asked, "May I ask your permission to sit down, my Lord? I would like to give you some important information that you may find useful in the accomplishment of the task of, well... let's call it a family reunion." He seated himself on the opposite side of the desk and continued talking whilst he extracted a document from the folds of his waistcoat.

"I happen to know that the court will indeed move to Windsor Castle next week. As this castle is one of the biggest of His Majesty's castles, life at court and Government will not be disrupted for long, and it offers better accommodation than Whitehall Palace, which can sometimes seem like an ant hill. Consequently there's nothing to worry about in this respect, and you'll be able to be introduced to court in a reasonable period of time. As you, my Lord, are accustomed to life at court in Paris, you know as well as I do that this can reasonably stretch from three weeks to three months." Again a thin smile appeared: "But we'll cooperate, of course, with our men to get you introduced to court as fast as possible!"

The visitor's face then changed and he became very serious. "I need to bring to your attention some new circumstances that we have discovered only fairly recently," the visitor continued, apparently treading with care now. Henri wasn't sure if he liked that this unknown visitor had taken the lead in the discussion, but there wasn't much that he could do or object to. Therefore he listened and curiously observed that his visitor nervously straightened the document that he had just put on the desk between them.

"Your cousin's mother was Margaret Neuville. She herself was the only daughter of His Grace, the Duke of Hertford, who passed away unexpectedly last month."

Henri swallowed. He had known of course that his 'bastard' cousin as he liked to call him, had a mother from the British aristocracy, but he had ignored the fact that Lady Margaret was the daughter of a Duke.

His visitor continued. "His Grace, the Duke of Hertford, had two sons, natural heirs to the title and a considerable fortune. Unfortunately the first decided to break his neck in a brothel row, the second unexpectedly succumbed to a virulent disease early this year. The Duke had two brothers, by now also deceased, each of them had a son, living and enjoying good health and therefore…"

Henri cut in, rather bored by the long explanations. "The eldest son of the eldest brother will become the new Duke and head of the family."

The visitor shook his head and said solemnly, "This is how it should be and the law of nature commands it, and this is what everybody supposes – even here in London. But His Eminence has instructed us to be very thorough in our research and when we checked, we found out…"

The visitor now looked pointedly at his finger tips, as if he was about to say something outrageous. He cleared his throat and continued. "The fact is, however, that the ducal house of Hertford obtained a special and very rare royal derogation of this rule two generations ago – actually under the reign of Queen Elizabeth. The Duke of Hertford was a close friend of the Queen. He did not succeed in siring a male heir, but he had several hopeful daughters – and he truly hated his brother who had sired several sons. He offered two fully armed ships to the Queen and paid for their upkeep to fight against the Armada. As a special royal favour and as recognition of this he obtained the right for the ducal title to be conferred in primogeniture to the sons of the Neuville family but to be inherited by the eldest daughter in the direct line if no sons are available to carry on the title. As both sons of the late Duke died without offspring, the future Duke of Hertford will therefore be…" and after a short pause he uttered, "your cousin!"

Henri was devastated but managed to control his face, keeping it unmoved solely by means of his iron will, his polite smile frozen like a mask. He would not show his emotions to this strange visitor, as he knew that every detail of this

162

meeting would be reported to the Cardinal – including any weakness he might show.

But deep inside his emotions were boiling – this rotten bastard cousin not only had inherited the title of Marquis de Beauvoir but was set to become an English Duke – ridiculously through his heretic mother! This simply couldn't be true, how could fate be so cruel!

Henri held a quill in his hand that he had picked up at random from the holder on the desk. The room lay in total silence once his visitor had finished his narrative; only the cracking sound of the shaft of the feather cut into the silence as it broke in his palm.

His visitor pretended not to have noticed the cracking sound and continued his speech. "We would like to suggest that you try to contact as fast as possible the presumptive heirs. Your interest matches theirs: Pierre de Beauvoir is your common obstacle to ascent to the title and fortune. We can safely assume that it will take him several months at least to obtain confirmation from the House of Lords; this is all the time you have at your disposal. We know already that Parliament will be difficult as the Dukes of Hertford have been staunch supporters of the heretic Anglican Church – but your cousin is a Catholic and this will not please Parliament at all. This sinful kingdom is dominated by the enemies of the true Faith," and he spat out this last sentence, showing that if there had been any doubt about the position of the visitor, he was clearly a man of the Church.

"The position of His Majesty, King Charles, is unclear. He secretly may wish to increase the influence of the Catholic party in Parliament as he has sympathy for the true faith." He paused. "But it is reported that your cousin is young and handsome, which is an important asset when it comes to the Queen, who likes to meddle in the affairs of the State," leaving the meaning of his words open to interpretation.

Henri cleared his throat. "Do you have any idea where my dear cousin is staying at the moment?" he asked.

His visitor's face became opaque. "I'm afraid that we lost trace of him in Calais. We do know that he stayed in Calais, preparing to leave for Britain but when we tried to arrest him, he had disappeared. This happened a good week ago and we don't know yet where to; it's an enigma how he succeeded to escape, as the port and gates were heavily guarded and every single man moving in and out has been searched. But His Eminence operates a very efficient network of intelligence, it will be only a matter of weeks and then we'll know, that much is certain!"

The visitor gave Henri a document with the names and details of Pierre's two cousins – who logically should become Henri's allies in England. Furthermore he promised to come back immediately as soon as he had obtained a date for Henri's

163

audience at the English court or any new information where he could find his cousin. Bowing deeply and profusely, he left.

Henri made sure that his visitor had descended the stairs before he let his feelings go – but then he simply exploded. In his first rage he took a heavy, decorative faience jug and threw it wildly against a ludicrously expensive Venetian mirror on the wall where it exploded with a loud crash into hundreds of pieces with a deafening noise and a shower of splintering glass.

Embassy footmen and Jean hurried into the room in a panic to find out what was going on. They found Henri standing with a face that looked like a mask, chiselled from stone. He turned and looked at them furiously, then barked at them to clean up the mess and not stand there looking like stupid idiots.

In his head he kept repeating the same thoughts over and over again: *I have to change this! I must get rid of this bastard!* Jean had brought a glass of brandy, hoping that this might calm down his master – and make him tired. Henri took a large gulp, cherishing the warmth of the fire that spread in his body.

Starting to relax and feeling the effect of the brandy he concentrated on his task and tried to be positive. If the envoy from the Cardinal was right he could find one or two precious allies – and a thought suddenly flashed through his mind – if he played it right, he could be paid handsomely!

He started to like this idea; probably a lot of money could be gained if the legal heir of a Duchy were to meet a fatal end and at least one of his loving cousins would be prepared to pay a fortune to make it happen.

He, Henri, would be master of this game! Henri started to laugh and Jean thought that his master was definitely going insane. No surprise, really, it was bound to happen – sooner or later.

The Cardinal's brow was set in deep lines but mellowed once he noticed the latest visitor enter his study. The prelate who had crossed the room and now bowed to kiss his ring was his absolute favourite, in fact all his hopes of one day passing on the office of prime minister were concentrated on this young, energetic and talented man, Jules Mazarin.

Mazarin sat down and amicably they exchanged some remarks and views on the daily matters of government and – most importantly – discussed the latest moods of the King. Both men knew that they were without doubt the most powerful men in this kingdom, probably even in Europe – but one wrong move and they'd sink into oblivion. Keeping the King happy and satisfied was the most daunting task they faced, day after day.

Richelieu had watched Mazarin perform several missions during recent years and held him in the highest esteem. Mazarin had a natural talent for negotiation – he understood the rules of power and how to exploit it.

They only disagreed about the Queen. Richelieu had worked against the Queen all of his life – when the young Habsburg princess had arrived from Spain, he knew immediately that she'd act like a puppet controlled by the Spanish enemy. How stupid she had been to make cow eyes at the English envoy, the Duke of Buckingham, how foolish! Even today, many years later, Richelieu still became angry when he remembered that the Queen of France had debased herself for a low-born stranger, a man without principles and character.

But now she had borne the heir to the throne – and consequently her position had changed. The scales of power were changing and reluctantly Richelieu had to accept that the Queen had to be taken into account as an important element in the future game of power.

Mazarin was already playing this card to perfection. Winning a fortune at the gaming table some weeks ago he had, apparently spontaneously, offered the largest part to the Queen, as he claimed that it had been Her Majesty who had been his harbinger of luck. The Queen had accepted gladly after a coy pretence of reluctance – the King wasn't generous and she could do with the money.

Yes, Mazarin was bright and would survive at court even without his help, Richelieu was sure of that.

Mazarin looked into his eyes and smiled. "I had the privilege to be informed by Brother Joseph of your dealings with the presumptive heir of the Marquis de Beauvoir," he said. Richelieu raised one eyebrow; he didn't remember that he had given permission to the monk to talk about this matter.

165

Mazarin read his thoughts and smiled. "Please don't be angry with him, he needed some advice whilst Your Eminence was on more important business and not available."

Richelieu liked this diplomatic allusion to his latest bout of renal colic. He made no move and waited for Mazarin to continue and show his cards.

"I understand that Your Eminence is making sure that this important title and the fabulous de Beauvoir fortune will not be spoilt on an unknown youth, a total stranger, but that the Crown and the Church profit from what can only be labelled a unique opportunity. The territories of the Marquis de Beauvoir will be a perfect fit with the royal and the ecclesial domains and your deal with Henri de Beauvoir is, if you will allow me, simply superb, as he will always remain in your hands – unless a fatal accident should also befall him."

The two men exchanged a significant glance, both knowing that Henri's life wouldn't be worth much as soon as he'd dealt with his cousin.

"I did however take the liberty of conducting some random research into this matter," Mazarin continued, "and I'm happy to propose an additional line of thought to Your Eminence, if you will excuse my meddling?"

Richelieu was in fact quite keen to hear the proposal of his favourite; Mazarin must have an ace up his sleeve if he was interfering.

"Of course not," he said with a benign smile. "I expect a brilliant idea from you, as usual."

Mazarin smiled. He had some well-known weaknesses: he liked women and gaming tables and was an easy victim of flattery.

"As Your Eminence knows, I had the privilege of a legal training before God led me on the path of serving Church and Crown."

Both men looked at each other knowingly; they both knew that it was less God's guiding hand and more Mazarin's burning ambition that had brought him here.

"When I was young I used to read and sometimes – to the surprise of my adversaries – dig up and use to our advantage centuries-old and seemingly forgotten legislation or jurisdiction. I thus at my leisure read some judgments related to those noble families who were sentenced because they were engaged in the heretic Catharist uprising in the fourteenth century in the South of France." Mazarin's face had reddened, he apparently loved this subject.

"They make fascinating reading. Our Holy Church dealt admirably with these heretics, burning them and purifying our country of this pest. Only decisive action preserved the unity of the Church and made it possible to continue expanding this proud Kingdom. I will be brief: the interesting point for us is that the States

166

General confirmed a vital judgment – and now comes the important point: never revoked, thus still valid today – that any French aristocrat convicted of active heresy by a court of the Church can be condemned to forfeit his titles and lands to the profit of the crown!"

Mazarin paused and then continued. "It was, however, expected and good practice that the King would hand back a large chunk of these territories to the Church and often to those relatives of the sinners who swore allegiance to the Crown and the Church."

Both men looked at each other meaningfully and Richelieu remarked, "Fascinating. I had thought about addressing myself to the Pope to have Pierre de Beauvoir declared an illegal bastard. The problem with rulings from Rome is that it will take years and the outcome is insecure; Rome can be bought, we all know this fact and use it. Sometimes this is helpful, sometimes not."

Mazarin smiled. "The court that can judge matters of heresy was set up by the Pope centuries ago and this institution has never been rescinded. Until today the Grand Inquisitor of France has had the power to set up a special court and sign the judgment in lieu of the Pope. It's all still perfectly legal. The problem will be our Protestant aristocracy; they'll howl in protest and may start a revolution immediately if we use this instrument too bluntly. What we need – and I'm sure that this will be found – is an undeniable statement that the mother of the present Marquis committed sacrilege while she gave birth, like cursing the name of our Lord. In this case her protestant faith will not be mentioned and the judgment will cause some unpleasant commotion but no revolution – and the titles and land will be at the disposal of his Majesty, the King – and of course the Church!"

Mazarin smiled. It was obvious that he was convinced that his proposal was brilliant.

Richelieu looked at him thoughtfully and started to speak. "Yes, that's excellent. I didn't expect anything else from you, by the way. The position of Grand Inquisitor has become a mostly honorific title, but the office still exists. How much will it cost to make him start the proceedings and how much time do you think it will consume? Can we proceed secretly?"

Mazarin smiled again; he was well prepared. "I took the liberty of mentioning some hypothetical case to the Grand Inquisitor. He's willing to take up the case if three of his illegitimate children become high prelates in the Church with yearly incomes of 10,000 livres or more and if he is promoted to cardinal at the first opportunity France has to choose a new cardinal."

Richelieu laughed almost silently; only a slight crackle could be heard. "Oh, yes, that's him, always greedy. Well, promises come cheap, he'll be happy if we fulfil half of this."

Mazarin nodded in agreement and continued, "The time span would be between six months and one year. We'd need signed statements of witnesses confirming the sacrilegious behaviour and normally the accused party must be questioned by the tribunal – but we'll represent the deceased mother by an advocate in favour of the Church, so that will be plain sailing, yet legally and formally correct. All will be debated in Latin in an ecclesial court in Avignon – in private sessions. The judgment will come as a complete surprise, but must be confirmed by the legal chamber of the States General," but before he could continue, Richelieu interjected, "How much?"

Mazarin paused to draw breath and continued. "I'm still bargaining, I estimate between thirty and fifty thousand livres – for each member who needs to sign."

Richelieu calculated quickly. The whole enterprise would cost roughly three to five hundred thousand livres once all expenses were paid. The de Beauvoir fortune was far beyond this amount, its value expressed in millions in pure gold. An expensive, but still an excellent, deal.

He looked suspiciously at Mazarin. "And you my friend, what do you expect from this deal?"

Mazarin laughed, full of confidence. He smelled victory, he knew he had convinced the Cardinal. "You know all of my weaknesses: yes, I have a humble wish to make. You know that I love diamonds. In all modesty, I have probably one of the best collections in France. The Marquis de Beauvoir has owned for generations a special diamond ring – their ancestors received it as a gift from the famous Sultan Saladin when he was serving with the first King of Jerusalem. This diamond is reported to be of outstanding size and clarity."

Mazarin had closed his eyes whilst speaking the last sentence, imagining the jewel lying before him. He did not mention that this ring was reported to have special magic powers. As a man of the church he shouldn't believe in such fairytales, but the idea intrigued him. Now he opened his eyes, burning dark and full of passion, and he continued, "I have a fancy for this ring, I dream about it, I'd be eternally obliged if you would help me to acquire it!"

Richelieu took the cup that stood in front of him and toasted him: "To my brilliant scholar, Mazarin, and to the glory of France! Go ahead, get me the land and the title of de Beauvoir and this diamond will be yours!'

Mazarin got down on his knees and kissed the scarlet robe of the Cardinal with passion and reverence. Very soon, he knew, he'd be promoted to cardinal himself. How much he loved this colour – and the power that came with it!

168

HOW TO MEET YOUR RELATIVES

Marie had settled comfortably with her aunt and her cousin on their charming estate. Once the thunderstorm had passed, the weather changed and a beautiful sunny autumn set in.

The Tudor manor house had been erected about a hundred years previously and was surrounded by a truly magnificent garden. It was called Sevens because a group of seven oaks standing close to it – rumour had it that the first squire had claimed to have possessed seven mistresses and had planted a tree in remembrance of each of them.

The walled gardens had originally been set up in the fashionable French way – perhaps to impress the neighbours or simply because the owner had fancied the foreign style. But as the gardens had been neglected for decades, nature had taken over and their former geometric patterns and formal shapes had mellowed into a hollow echo of their glorious past.

Roses spilled over the formal stone borders in triumphant abundance, dotting the green bushes and low hanging trees with magnificent accents of red, white and pink. Daisies, lilies and sunflowers fought with wildflowers in shades of brash yellow and purple for the best spots in the sun, greedily taking over the mossy alleys and pathways. The riot of flowers and untamed vegetation left the random visitor spellbound by its magical atmosphere.

To Marie it looked like the incarnation of her romantic dreams, a setting come straight from a fairytale. It seemed that a unicorn must surely be hiding behind those bushes, just waiting to appear – luckily her prince charming wasn't far away, she mused.

A large pond lay undisturbed in a secluded part of the garden. Located close to the neighbouring woods, it had turned into a complete wilderness, like a world apart. Watching the still water and the reflections of the clouds drifting slowly high above in the sky, the stray visitor was seduced into just standing there, watching and dreaming.

To Marie's great delight she could detect from time to time the shadow of a fish shooting from the thicket of reeds into the shallow part studded with water lilies. But she was to discover soon enough that mosquitoes adored this part of the garden probably as much as she did and, enjoying a new source of fresh blood, were prepared to defend their territory against the enemy. It did not take much reflection to run away and avoid further visits before she was eaten alive and covered with red blotches all over.

It was still warm enough for long leisurely rides with bucolic picnics stretching into the early evening. Marie would have enjoyed her time thoroughly if only the

169

man sitting next to her during the picnics could have been Pierre and not the sturdy Arthur.

Today they had decided to ride and visit St Albans Cathedral – a cathedral dedicated to a saint of local renown. The building – reportedly of Norman origin – was a popular place for excursions. Although most people in Britain had converted to the Anglican faith, the impressive cathedral was still worth a visit and a magnet for many pilgrims who were convinced that paying their respects to the old saints could only broaden their options once they crossed the threshold of heaven.

Pierre and Armand, acting as faithful grooms, saddled the horses and helped the ladies and Arthur to mount them. Marie looked stunning in a velvet riding gown with rich trimmings, a pert hat sitting on her curly auburn hair. She loved to see the admiration in the men's eyes and allowed Pierre to hold her hand just longer than was necessary to help her to mount her mare.

They had separated into small groups as the road was narrow and Arthur had skilfully managed to ride alone at her side. The faithful grooms were riding ahead, at a suitable distance. Marie started to become nervous. Until now she had always succeeded in avoiding being alone with Arthur, although she rather liked him. She knew of course why she had been invited to England and dreaded that her aunt would be trying to tie the knot and secure their engagement before she had the opportunity to go to London. For Marie's aunt was anything but stupid – Marie could quite easily meet other and even more eligible potential husbands at court.

Marie therefore put on a brave face, but was expecting Arthur any minute to become romantic and push his case, now that nobody could interfere.

Arthur looked at the sky and pointed at some white clouds, scattered like abandoned sheep in the blue sky. "Look Marie, the big cloud in the middle looks like a heart. Could it hold a promise for me?" he asked, provocatively.

Marie lifted her eyes to the sky and indeed she did see a big, fluffy cloud resembling a huge, if slightly blurred, heart. To her amazement the heart-shaped cloud started to drift slowly but surely, and broke apart.

"Well it does!" replied Marie, and not really hiding her satisfaction she continued, "But it looks more like a broken heart, I'm afraid."

Expectantly she watched Arthur, waiting for a flirtatious answer but to her great surprise he spared her any further shallow gallant statements. His face suddenly became serious. It came as a shock, but apparently he had decided to jump into the cold water and get straight to the point.

"Marie, truly I adore you, but I feel that you have been avoiding me. I am aware that I'm no Adonis, but I sincerely hope that I'm not that ugly either. Maybe I'm being conceited but I was convinced I was rather pleasant company. You probably know that our parents would like us to marry. I must apologize that my

170

mother used as an excuse the rather convenient plague in London to arrange our stay in the countryside. But please believe me, she meant well, she wanted to give us the opportunity to get to know each other well before we rushed into any decision that we might regret later. People of our position do not marry for love, it's business, it's a deal between families and fortunes, and we both have considerable fortunes that make us perfect partners."

Arthur drew breath; it had been a long speech and his alert eyes watched Marie, trying to guess her reaction.

Marie's face didn't move and as it was impossible to see behind this aloof façade, Arthur sighed and continued.

"But I must confess that I don't want to marry a wife who doesn't like me and if you feel that you don't like me enough to contemplate such a move, I would understand and will ask my mother not put any pressure on you. I really would like to remain your close friend though. I do feel that we have many things in common and could be excellent friends!"

Marie was stunned by the unexpected openness of his speech. She had expected drama, romance or false vows of eternal love, not this nearly brutal honesty and definitely not this moving and kind offer of genuine friendship.

She looked thoughtfully at Arthur who looked back at her with his sincere and friendly eyes, waiting for her answer. Her cool façade started to break down. Should she be open to him as well? If she made a wrong decision, this could become very dangerous for Pierre and Armand but she didn't want to rebuff this precious offer of friendship. She also felt that Pierre desperately needed friends if he wanted to have any chance of succeeding with his mission.

"Come on, tell me the truth, you're hiding something," Arthur prompted her gently. "You can confide in me. I chatter a lot but I learned from my father that a good diplomat is someone who talks a lot but keeps the important things for himself. Let me be your true friend and tell me what's in your heart!"

Marie couldn't resist the pleading tone of his voice and his eyes. Still cautious, and on her guard, she answered, "Arthur, please believe me, I do like you very much and I hope that we can become best friends. But my heart is taken by someone else and I'm really sorry if I should cause you or your mother any pain."

"So, who's the lucky man?" Arthur asked. "I'd like to congratulate him. Don't look so distressed. I like you very much, but" – and he grinned broadly – "I must confess I love plenty of women!"

Marie laughed. "What about being honest then? You just proposed to me and now you seem to be relieved that I declined your offer. I may even contemplate marrying you, just to punish you! You men are all the same, faithful only for one night!"

Arthur laughed and feigned being struck by a rapier.

"Touché," he exclaimed, "but better to see me laughing than crying. Now tell me, who's your sweetheart and can I do something to help you?"

"Swear to me by the saints and the life of your mother that you'll keep this secret," Marie insisted with all seriousness, and only after Arthur had made a solemn oath she inhaled deeply to gather all her courage before she continued.

"I'm in love with Pierre, the groom that is accompanying us. I swore to myself that I'd marry him – for better or for worse."

Arthur looked scandalized. "Marie, I'll keep this secret as I promised, but people of our class cannot fall in love with servants, *it just isn't possible.* You should know this!" He looked at her with grave eyes and said, "Wake up, this will never be possible – and let's never mention this again!"

Marie laughed and answered, "Oh Arthur, I haven't lost my senses – yet. Pierre and his friend Armand are here in disguise. Pierre is in reality a Marquis, his father was the late Marquis de Beauvoir and Armand is a younger son of the Marquis de Saint Paul. Their social rank is not the problem. The moment Pierre is reinstated as the rightful Marquis, all the ladies of the realm will be throwing themselves at his feet; that will be one of *my* problems in the future," she added dryly.

Arthur's jaw dropped and his eyes became as wide as saucers.

"Marie, are you telling me that I chided a Marquis this morning because he was too slow with the horses? God in heaven, a Marquis as a groom, am I dreaming? Why this charade?"

Marie smiled as she saw his distress and started to explain the whole story, starting from their first meeting in Reims and finishing with the narrow escape from the encounter with Pierre's cousin on the sailing ship.

"The point is," she continued, "that Pierre needs help and money from his mother's relatives before he can return to France. Armand is convinced that Richelieu – we actually started calling him the evil Cardinal – is pulling the strings behind all of this and has put his cousin on his trail to get rid of Pierre – but we don't understand yet why the evil Cardinal wants Pierre to be eliminated. But we do know that there's no hope of fighting Richelieu if you don't have money or influence. I guess you'd agree now that it's absolutely necessary for Pierre to meet his grandfather, the Duke, and be acknowledged by him. Until today he doesn't have a penny of his own and he's too proud to accept my money!"

Arthur looked at her, eyes burning with curiosity and said, "Let's move on. We'll reach a nice spot to rest and have a picnic soon. I'll find a pretext to send my grooms away to fetch us some ale from the next village and we'll use the time to speak openly." He suddenly gave a boyish laugh. "What an adventure! I didn't

172

realize how boring my life has been until now. None of my numerous cousins has been chasing me – they're a boring bunch of people compared to Pierre's loving kith and kin. Well, let's make the best of this!"

They spurred on their horses and caught up with the rest of the group. A murderous-looking Pierre greeted them – of course he had noticed that Marie and Arthur had remained on their own for most of the time, isolated from the rest of their small group. Marie had to hide her amusement and, playing the haughty aristocrat, she even chided Pierre that he had abandoned her. Luckily looks cannot kill, or she would have dropped dead on the spot.

Arthur got the hint and pretended to flirt with Marie. Within Pierre's earshot he praised her wonderful eyes and called her his divine princess. Marie played the coy maiden, but gleefully she imagined Pierre's teeth gnashing in anger.

They reached a pleasant clearing where the wood yielded to pastures, close to a small stream of water purling peacefully under willow trees. The friends unanimously decided that the spot was ideal for a picnic – Arthur even questioned why they should move any further. After all, why should they bother looking at an old cathedral and a bunch of sad-looking statues? This spot was so beautiful and just perfect for their picnic! Wouldn't it be nicer just to have a long rest and then ride back? People who were fond of ancient history and old stones must all be mad…

He tried to impress Marie and Céline and told the story of the Cathedral's saint. Legend had it that the constable who had ordered the beheading of the saint had his eyeballs popped out of his head as a punishment by God as soon as the sentence had been executed!

But to Arthur's disappointment this gruesome story didn't really cut any ice with the ladies. All the same, they agreed that a picnic would definitely be the better option compared to visiting a cathedral with a headless saint.

Arthur gladly accepted the ladies' verdict and ordered his own two grooms to ride to the nearest village and fetch some ale. "I'm terribly thirsty from the hot sun and I'm afraid we've only some wine left."

Arthur's grooms didn't mind at all and obliged on the spot. The lovely vision of a good drink of cool ale for themselves floated in front of their eyes and they left in good spirits.

Pierre dismounted from the horse and held out his hand to help Marie to step down. To his great surprise Arthur had already moved swiftly forwards, and taking off his hat, he bowed ceremoniously towards Pierre and Armand.

"Greetings, my lords," he addressed them formally. Pierre's eyes widened in shock. He stood frozen; nothing had prepared him to be recognized here and now.

173

"Marie has told me your story," Arthur continued quickly, "and first of all, please don't worry. I admit that I wanted to win Marie's hand – but now that she told me that someone else has stolen her heart, I can only congratulate you and tell you that I sincerely want to gain your friendship and will do whatever is needed to help you!"

Pierre blushed crimson and Armand grinned broadly; he, of course, had known all along what was going on.

"Let's be practical," Céline proposed in her cool voice, "and settle down with some of this excellent food we brought along and a sip of wine and fresh water. I'm terribly thirsty and hungry! I always find that whatever I want to discuss, I'm simply better at it when I'm not starving!"

Arthur laughed. "And they say only the English have common sense! You have plenty of it. I fully agree, let's sit down and have our picnic. I sent my grooms away so we could discuss things in private. They'll be gone for at least one hour and will make the most of their freedom. We'll have plenty of time to discuss this incredible story of yours; I still think I'm in the midst of a novel, not in reality."

Pierre had started to thaw and once more Pierre and Armand told the story of their extraordinary adventures but soon Armand took over – he was a natural born story-teller. Marie and Céline listened with growing excitement and discovered many episodes that were new to them. When Armand reached the night of their dangerous escape from France (leaving out those details that might risk upsetting the ladies, of course) Marie sneaked her hand into Pierre's and her eyes were wide with anxiety.

"In essence we must go and seek Pierre's grandfather as fast as possible," Armand concluded.

Arthur nodded assent, evidently fascinated. "I'll help you. I promise!"

He paused and then he exclaimed, "I know now how to proceed. My mother has been chasing me for the last few days to make social calls on our neighbours. I'll be a good son now and go tomorrow to Hertford Castle, leave my compliments and see if by any chance Pierre's grandfather is in. I know that he has been ill for some time and hasn't been seen at court for months, but maybe we'll be lucky and he'll receive his humble neighbour."

It was decided however to keep up appearances in order to protect Pierre and Armand. Hence the two friends immediately switched back into their role of humble servants when Arthur's grooms finally arrived with the ale, their breath stinking of booze and their mood surprisingly gay after what should have been a tedious journey, riding a long distance just to serve the whims of their master.

Pierre respectfully helped the ladies and Arthur to mount their horses and then rode together with Armand at an appropriate distance. The party dissolved once they were home but they had decided to meet up again secretly after dinner in the garden to discuss the next steps.

In the evening Arthur knocked at the door of his mother's room. She was preparing herself and dressing in style for dinner. Her maid was buzzing around her, arranging her hair and putting on her jewellery. Arthur, being a good son, paid her lavish compliments on her beauteous looks and the fashionable gown she was wearing.

His mother was flattered but she was not stupid and with an attentive glance she remarked, "I always tend to be a bit sceptical when you heap so much praise on me. The gown is old by the way, but I tend to like it all the same. I used to be a beauty, but I know that there's no comparison between me and Marie nowadays!" She paused briefly, as her maid was applying some make-up, before continuing, "How was your riding party, how did you like the cathedral?"

Arthur admitted, full of mischief, that they had never even reached the cathedral as they had changed their mind and chosen to have a leisurely picnic at a charming site close to the river instead of looking at boring historic monuments. His mothers' eyes scrutinized him carefully and she said, "So how did you get on with Marie? Was she still playing the shy maiden, difficult to get?"

Arthur admitted truthfully that Marie had still kept her distance and that he hadn't been able to advance his case.

"Arthur, I must confess, I am starting to be worried about this girl," his mother confided in him. "She's behaving like an iceberg to you, but I find that she grants far too many liberties to those extremely good-looking grooms. I don't find this behaviour fitting for a lady who may one day become my daughter-in-law. I don't even know if I should still recommend this union."

Arthur saw that his mother was truly upset and he had to suppress a smile. Unbelievable how she had hit the bull's eye! Women really did have a sixth sense... He hastened to say, "No, I don't think she is of lax morals. But I do feel that her heart is not as free as her parents made us believe!" Changing the subject abruptly he continued, "You told me yesterday that you wanted me to pay a courtesy call to our neighbour, the Duke of Hertford. I gave it some thought and believe that you're right; we really should try to get acquainted with him. If we don't gain some new acquaintances here, your famous dinner parties will become very boring. If you write me a short letter of introduction, I propose to ride over tomorrow and if I find him agreeable, I'll invite him for an informal dinner."

"Why do you want me to write this letter?" his mother asked in surprise. "You can write, at least this is what we paid your teacher for – and they charged your father a fortune!"

Arthur laughed and answered, "That's very simple. You're a born Principessa di Colombare. Your maiden rank is the same or even higher than that of the Duke

175

– if I write as a mere Viscount he may not even condescend to meet me, or even bother to reply to me!"

He knew that he had hit the right tone. If there was one point of regular dispute in the family it was his mother's pride about her princely origins. His father then usually retorted sharply that her father, the proud but regrettably not very affluent Italian prince, had been more than happy to marry off one of his seven daughters to a mere foreign count – but a count who could afford to pay his father-in-law's debts. At this stage the arguments usually stopped.

Today his father couldn't dampen his mother's pride and with flushed cheeks she continued, "You're right," purring like a cat. "My family tree is probably older than those of most of these English dukes or even this funny man they call their King, however arrogantly all these men may behave. When their ancestors were still peasants toiling in the English mud we Colombares were already governing Rome. You, my son, have inherited from my side the blood of Roman nobility. Rome governs the world. Never forget this!"

Making her little speech, she had risen from the chair and was standing in the room like a queen, every inch living up to the glory of her ancestors.

Arthur suppressed a smile; he tacitly agreed with his father's point of view that pride can't buy bread and preferred the comfortable knowledge that his father had accumulated fabulous wealth by dealing secretly with the Venetian enemy through lucrative trade. His position as an ambassador was not very time-consuming, as the tiny principality of Savoy had next to no influence in British politics, even if his government was trying desperately to receive British support to survive and keep its independence from a greedy neighbour like France.

Staying in Britain gave his father valuable access to all kinds of information, information that paid handsomely – once used in his trading business. No true aristocrat was allowed, of course, to trade – but his father had confided in him that circumventing this law only added additional spice to his dealings.

His mother – who had no idea about the flourishing business of her husband – sat down immediately to oblige Arthur and write the letter of recommendation. During dinner she handed him a document introducing herself to the Duke and requesting the honour of meeting the carrier of the message. Arthur was delighted; this was even better than he could have imagined, and was exactly what he needed for Pierre. His mother was rewarded with a big kiss.

He met the small group of friends after dinner outside in the garden where they held a short council. The sunset had painted the sky in fabulous colours, but Mother Nature's splendour was wasted and went unnoticed. They had more pressing matters on their minds.

It was decided that Armand and Pierre should ride instead of Arthur and use this letter of introduction, as this might give Pierre a chance to meet the Duke personally. Pierre was stunned that Arthur had really lived up to his promise. He silently shook his hand to thank him, unable to talk, as he had a big lump in his throat. Armand spoke for both of them and said, "You're really our true friend now, Arthur. We don't know how to thank you, but please be assured, if ever you need a service from us, we'll there for you!"

He embraced Arthur to underline the sincerity of his words and Marie kissed his cheek to show her gratitude as well. Arthur grimaced – of course he liked to be kissed by Marie, but this kiss was far too sisterly for his taste.

Tomorrow would be a very important day and they parted, wishing Pierre well and keeping their fingers crossed that he should finally meet his grandfather and be well received.

Pierre didn't get any real sleep that night, as he was far too excited. As he shared a small room in the servants' quarters with Armand, Armand also had no sleep, as his friend was tossing and turning in his bed, moaning and babbling frantically in his dreams.

They left in the early afternoon under a cloudy sky. Luckily the weather held and they were spared having to arrive dripping wet. Pierre was so nervous that he had no eye for the beauty of the forest that surrounded them and when they reached the open road he barely noticed the enchanting landscape with its well-kept hamlets dotted with picturesque farms that unfolded around him. All he knew about farming was the little knowledge he had acquired when he was working in the monastery gardens or fields. Pierre wouldn't be able to tell if the soil was good, what kind of harvest had already been gathered or was about to be brought in, or if the fields were in good shape. He just saw fields, cattle and farms, wondering why this road stretched endlessly, feeling both fear and eagerness at the thought of reaching the house of his grandfather.

Armand, on the contrary, had grown up in a castle in the French countryside and could tell immediately that the peasants and cattle were well fed, houses and fields well tended. The Hertford estate was by all appearances in excellent shape. Pierre's English family therefore was rich; this much became evident to him the deeper they entered into this vast estate and – unless this Grandfather turned out to be really thrifty or mean – he'd definitely be able to help Pierre and give him the means to claim his father's inheritance.

All of a sudden the road turned and a huge castle with high towers and a rose-hued brick façade with beautiful trimmings of creamy sandstone came into sight. They had of course expected a castle fit for a Duke, not merely a modest estate or manor house, but this vast and imposing palace of royal dimensions filled them with awe. Even the dashing Armand had a dry throat when they rang the bell. The gate was opened and they had to pass the scrutiny of a high-handed gatekeeper. An imposing coat of arms with a ducal crown and its heraldic strawberry leaves adorned the front of the building. Both friends felt awed by the imposing architecture. Strangely, a large piece of black velvet was wrapped around the doorknob. A member of the family must have died recently, but as noble families were often extensive, such an occurrence was nothing unusual.

They were handed on to the butler who answered their call at the main entrance. He encountered two handsome young gentlemen standing in front of him with alert and eager faces.

Armand had insisted that they bring their swords along and Arthur had given them the best riding boots he could find, and donated two expensive Flemish lace collars of his own to smarten their appearance, plus dashing feathers to crown their hats. To Arthur's satisfaction he had waved good-bye to two young men who looked very presentable and every inch the gentlemen of good ancestry that they wanted to represent.

The elderly but still very impressive butler looked at them, scrutinizing slowly both young men. But his glance returned quickly once more to the blond gentleman. He must be around seventeen to eighteen years old, quite young and strikingly handsome. He bore a slight resemblance to someone he knew but he couldn't quite place him. He searched his memory but could not come to a satisfactory answer.

Maybe one of the bastards of the old Duke, he concluded secretly; the surrounding villages had many of those, but – he corrected his thoughts – they wouldn't be aristocratic. These young men were undoubtedly of noble birth; he hadn't served for decades as a butler without knowing such things. This was a riddle indeed and it made him extremely curious. They now addressed him in the purest French which only added to his curiosity. There had only been one member of the family married in France as far as he knew and that had been poor Lady Margaret. He looked at the blond visitor once more; yes, there was a resemblance, very interesting indeed!

He ceremoniously took possession of the letter of recommendation that Armand presented to him and, noticing the impressive coat of arms and the title of a princess, he asked the gentlemen to take off their arms as was customary and follow him to the reception room. When Pierre announced his full name, the butler's eyes widened; this would come as a *real surprise* to his lordship, he was sure of that now.

The dignified butler led the two friends through endless galleries and they started to realize that the building was even more impressive and extensive inside than it had looked from the outside. Although of fairly recent construction, new wings had already been added, and at least two generations had left their traces by paying respect to different styles and fashions.

Pictures of regal-looking ancestors hung on the walls, most of them frozen in unnatural poses with blank and arrogant faces, proud coats of arms painted in the corners to proclaim title and name. Richly dressed with embroidery, jewels and feathers, the gallery seemed to Pierre like an endless display of conceited people, of proud and narcissistic peacocks. As the butler walked slowly they had ample time to study what seemed to represent Pierre's entire maternal line of ancestors.

"What a bunch of unfriendly and ugly folk," Pierre whispered to Armand. His friend grinned and answered, "They all look like this in paintings. You should see the painting of my father at home, he looks terrible; the worst thing is, they all claim I resemble him!"

The procession finally reached the reception room. Designed for official functions, it was crowned by an impressive, dark wooden ceiling with richly gilded carvings stretching high above them and adorned with a white and black chequered marble floor. The marble made their booted steps resound with a boisterous echo – they sounded like intruders entering the Duke's inner sanctum. Formal chairs made from heavy dark wood with red velvet cushions were grouped around a single high chair that appeared to represent the ducal version of a throne.

This castle might not be a royal one but it certainly came very close. Oversized iron candelabras were inserted in the walls and chandeliers hung from the high ceiling, but as they had arrived in daylight the butler just ceremoniously lit some candles on the desk standing close to the high chair. This done, he excused himself and disappeared at his dignified pace, leaving the friends on their own.

Pierre sat down and exhaled. "This room is as cosy as the chapel in our monastery in winter. All I need is a confessional – I already feel the need to repent."

He looked at Armand and spoke from the bottom of his soul. "I'm so happy that I won't ever need to live here. This building is truly oppressive!" His glance roamed around the dark wooden ceiling and panels and he shuddered.

Armand laughed. "From orphanage to castle! When you're old you can ask your poor secretary to write your memoirs. In the meantime, let's pray that your grandfather doesn't look as sour as these gentlemen in the picture in front of us and that he'll be nice enough to help us. I'm thinking about an alternative if he doesn't, but I'd prefer that he did."

After this remark there wasn't a lot to be said or discussed and they sat rigidly on their chairs, fighting their mounting tension and trying to look as poised and presentable as possible.

The butler came back, carrying with visible effort a heavy silver tray loaded with finest Italian glasses and a carafe of red wine. Panting, but still in a pompous voice, he announced that his lordship had been kind enough to accept to meet them shortly. Armand frowned and when the butler had left the reception room hall at his slow pace, he said to Pierre, "What a pompous ass. I can only hope that we'll meet your grandfather. It's strange that he didn't call him 'His Grace'. Can't imagine him not using the proper title! I hope we'll see your grandfather after all and not some other stuffed relative of yours who looks after this estate. I also don't like the way he looks at you, it seems strange... or maybe he just has a penchant for blond boys?"

Pierre made an explicit gesture to show Armand what he thought of this last remark but then he looked around gloomily and digested this information; all he needed was yet another obstacle, especially when they had been so close to success! He desperately wanted to meet his grandfather – today, and not some weeks later!

After a good quarter of an hour spent in nervous waiting and only comforted by the excellent wine to calm their mounting tension, the door opened and to their surprise a giant of a man in his early thirties entered the room. He was extremely tall, towering over his young visitors and forcing them to lift their faces to be able to see him.

He had a pleasant face, and reddish blond hair cut unfashionably short. His clothes were of excellent quality but had been cut for comfort not for style. His eyes were disconcerting; one was olive green, the other dark, and it took some time to get accustomed to his face and not be distracted by his eyes. He strode into the room with the lope of an athlete; despite his size and weight it was clear that this man would be good at arms and a force to be reckoned with.

He approached them unceremoniously but bowed politely and introduced himself as Charles Neuville, not mentioning any title. He strode directly and confidently to the highest chair and sat down, apparently used to representing the Duke during his absence. The chair squeaked in mild protest as he sat down and Charles grinned broadly at his visitors and remarked, "I know, I'm somewhat heavy."

Shooting a sharp glance at Pierre from these strange eyes he said in a more formal tone, "Please do explain to me, Sirs, why two French gentlemen seek a meeting with His Grace by presenting a letter of introduction from the Princess di Colombare? What could you possibly desire from His Grace?" His French was fluent but he had a broad English accent and it took Pierre some effort in order to understand his question.

He was flabbergasted. He had rehearsed a thousand times what he would say and how to greet his grandfather but this man was neither his grandfather nor did he bother with conventions or the usual flowery speeches that were the hallmark of a true aristocrat; he got straight to the point, clearly unbothered by conventions.

Armand laughed. "You get straight to the point, Sir. May we sit down?"

Charles waved his consent and replied good-humouredly, "Of course, the chairs look a little odd, but they're only half as uncomfortable as mine, so don't worry." He helped himself to a glass from the silver tray, sipped some wine and closed his eyes to savour the taste.

180

Armand waited until their host had finished his private tasting ceremony and as Pierre was still frozen in silence, he decided to move on, plunging in and telling their story instead.

"We're here to ask for your help, my Lord. We apologize for using the letter of recommendation from her Highness, the Principessa di Colombare, but we wanted to be sure to be received by His Grace, the Duke of Hertford, and," he took a deep breath, "to present to him Pierre de Beauvoir, his grandchild by his daughter, Lady Margaret de Neuville."

Their host looked at them in a peculiar way, his strange eyes focusing on Pierre and he replied, "Are you sure that you're Margaret's son, you're not an imposter?" His voice was pleasant enough but held a steely note. "I can become extremely unpleasant if someone tries to outsmart me!"

Pierre jumped up from his chair, his face the palest white. The chair lost its balance and crashed behind him with a loud bang on the marble floor, but Pierre didn't care.

"I don't know how you're related to me, Sir, but I am Pierre de Beauvoir and ready to defend my honour here and now!"

The giant made some noises that could be interpreted as suppressed laughter. He also sprang up from his chair with the agility of an athlete, took two swords hanging across the open fireplace and said, "Show me then what you're worth, Pierre de Beauvoir!" whilst managing to convey his invitation with an offensive hint of irony.

Pierre was now enraged; all the tension that had built up over the past few days and hours needed some outlet. He took the sword and started to fight but he soon realized that he was no match for this giant who fought with effortless elegance. In no time at all Charles's sword was pointing at his throat and whilst Pierre was panting hard, his enemy was breathing as evenly as if he hadn't moved at all. It had all happened so fast that Armand was still desperately trying to find a weapon in order to help to defend Pierre when the fight was already finished.

"Pierre de Beauvoir," Charles said, grinning. "You have much to learn, much indeed!"

Pierre just hissed like a snake, "Make it quick, kill me here and now. I lost, do what you want, but I'll never give up my honour or my name!"

The giant removed his sword from Pierre's throat and to Pierre's and Armand's great surprise, the huge man suddenly drew Pierre close to him and embraced him with the words, "Welcome home, Your Grace! I'm sorry for the test but I couldn't risk accepting an imposter or a coward."

181

"Would your lordship please have the kindness to explain what is going on here?" said Armand, still in shock from the previous scene. "We wish to meet His Grace, so who are you, and why can't we?"

Charles made a sign inviting them to sit down and he offered them fresh wine. "Let's trade stories then, yours against mine."

Pierre had reached a stage where nothing could surprise him anymore. He decided to play it straight with this man; despite their strange encounter he had the feeling that he could trust this giant and perhaps even become his friend. Pierre sat down and following Charles's invitation he told his whole story from the orphanage to his escape, even mentioning his cousin Henri who was following his trail with the intention of getting rid of him and claiming his French inheritance. Charles listened attentively, evidently enjoying this story and encouraging Pierre to tell more and more and go into details, slapping his thighs in delight when Pierre reached another hilarious or spicy episode in his journey.

Charles rang the bell and the pompous butler appeared immediately. He'd probably been listening at the door, Armand thought to himself, judging by his surprisingly quick appearance.

"His Grace and His Grace's guest will stay tonight," Charles said. "Please have dinner prepared and their rooms made ready."

Once the butler had bowed to them, most deeply to Pierre, and had turned his back to leave the room in his slow and dignified manner, Charles added in a soft voice, "And would you mind not eavesdropping please, even if I must admit it's been most entertaining."

The butler's face didn't move – some comments were simply beneath his acknowledgement – and they just heard the soft closing of the doors.

Pierre grinned at this exchange but was still wondering about these strange instructions. He hadn't finished his narrative yet and after a short pause to remember where he had been interrupted he reverted to his story, describing their narrow escape from Calais in disguise.

Charles laughed out loud when Pierre went on to describe how he had barely managed to escape the amorous attentions of his drunken cousin. Armand took the hint and good-humouredly added some zesty comments. The poor chair started squeaking again as Charles was drumming on the armrests in irrepressible pleasure.

"Oh, that's hilarious!" he gasped. "I'd give a fortune just to have been there and seen his face when this lady came to your rescue, she must be very courageous! Well, at least that's one experience you missed."

When Pierre finally finished his long story Charles exclaimed, "What an adventure you had! Amazing, really!" He jumped out of the chair and walked to the fireplace.

"All right, now I owe you my part of the story. I will need to see the documents you mentioned, although I believe every single word you say, but you'll understand quickly why I need proof beyond any doubt."

Armand looked at Pierre, who nodded, and he carefully took out the hidden documents from his waistcoat. The giant cousin scrutinized them with his strange eyes, seemed to struggle from time to time with some phrases but apparently found them satisfactorily convincing.

"First, I regret that I must be the bearer of sad news," Charles started in a low voice. "Pierre, if I may call you that, I am sorry but your grandfather passed away some weeks ago. I'm sure that he would have been proud to get to know you, he was very sad that he had never seen his grandchild in France and was convinced that you were dead. We are still in the official period of mourning as you might understand." Pierre looked crestfallen but added hopefully, "Then I suppose that it is you who will become the next Duke? Can you help me at least?"

"Well, no, not really." Charles paused and looked at Pierre with his disconcerting eyes, smiling strangely. "I was in fact supposed to become the next Duke as I'm the eldest son of your grandfather's eldest brother, your uncle. To make it short, I'm your cousin. But the Dukes of Hertford are one of the few families in the realm where the title – by royal charter – is passed on in the male and the female line, and as your two uncles also died recently your sudden appearance means that you are the legal heir now. This may come as a shock: you are now the head of the hopeful Neuville family."

He paused and looked at a completely bewildered Pierre and speechless Armand.

"Yes, you did hear correctly, I mean what I say: by royal charter you should now become the fifth Duke of Hertford with all associated rights."

Pierre's head was spinning. "It's impossible, there must be an error! You must hate me then, I'm taking your place. I'm an imposter in your eyes! Why didn't you kill me with your sword? You had the opportunity right then?"

The words streamed out of his mouth, his whole face one big question mark.

"Maybe I was tempted to kill you when you were buzzing around me like an angry wasp. But let me clarify something, Your Grace," Charles said mockingly. "If you think that being a Duke is a godsend, you're completely wrong! I'm in the lucky situation of having inherited enough money from my parents, as my father had the brilliant idea of marrying a very rich bride. I have estates of my own, I'm even an earl in my own right. I lead a very comfortable life and have no aspirations

183

to exchange my peaceful country life for a life at court, squabbling with these Puritans who seem to be meddling everywhere in British politics, administering these huge estates, and last but not least, fighting for my life. I'd be expected to marry some lady from an influential family to breed new and promising ducal offspring. Believe me, I love my comforts; to me you're a gift sent from heaven, I leave all of this fun for you! This pompous family butler actually guessed it right from the start. He told me, 'My lord, we have a new Duke, Lady Margaret's son is downstairs.' Small wonder I was curious to meet you."

Armand had stood by silently, but now he exclaimed, slapping his forehead, "I can't believe it, six months ago you were an orphan with no future, and now you're a Marquis in France and a Duke in Britain! God in heaven, Pierre, can this be real! Will we discover next week that you have inherited a kingdom somewhere else in the world?"

"It is insane," said Pierre, "it really is. But I'm a nobody in reality! I'm a Marquis by title, but my heritage is inaccessible, blocked by Cardinal Richelieu, and I have a loving cousin who wants to kill me, apparently with his assistance. I wouldn't be astonished at all if in England there's some other kind cousins just ready and waiting to get rid of me!"

Charles cleared his throat. "Well, to be perfectly honest, there's the frog."

Pierre and Armand looked at him. "Frog, *grenouille*? What do you mean?"

"The family likes to call him that. He's the son of your second great uncle, the former Duke's second brother. He's got a flat chin and becomes greenish when he drives in a coach, so we nicknamed him 'the frog' and although, or maybe because, he hates this name, it stuck. He'll do everything to get the title and the estates as he's nearly broke. He's addicted to gambling. And he's dangerous, as he's licking at the feet of the Roundheads and trying to convince them the Duchy of Hertford must go to a follower of the radical Protestant faith and follower of these new upstarts in Parliament."

"Roundheads?" Pierre asked. "What's that?"

"You should be asking, who are they," Charles answered. "Those men are the new breed of radical Protestants. All work and prayer – never any fun. They all wear the same ugly haircut to recognize their brothers in faith. They're fast becoming the most influential political party now in England and will soon govern this kingdom if our King, may God bless him, is not more cautious. He's dreaming of becoming a powerful Monarch like Louis XIII, but he has no Richelieu to keep his back covered. But let's discuss politics later. I'll ask the butler to take you up to your rooms and we'll discuss more at dinner. Do you have any special requests?"

"Not for the lodgings," Pierre answered, "But I'd like to send a footman with a short note back to Sevens and my hostess, the Principessa, to let her know where we're going to be staying…"

And one to Marie… Armand added in his thoughts.

Dinner was served quite early as was customary in the countryside. They met in a huge and formal dining room. At least, that is what Pierre thought. Later he was to learn that this dining room was considered to be private and cosy compared to the stately dining room that could easily seat more than a hundred guests and dignitaries at a seemingly endless table. The butler had knocked at the door of their bedroom to guide them through a labyrinth of galleries and rooms to the dining room, addressing Pierre as 'Your Grace', as if his arrival was nothing unusual and had been expected for a long time.

His giant cousin had already been waiting for them, sprawled in his chair, but he rose immediately when Pierre and Armand entered and led Pierre to the chair reserved for the head of the family. They kept a conversation going but chatted about minor subjects as long as a small army of footmen was waiting on them under the guidance and critical supervision of the butler.

When finally they were left on their own, Charles looked at Pierre with a serious face. "I've been thinking about your story and I'm still amazed how you managed to arrive here unscathed. There's one thing though, I cannot let you carry on like this, unprotected like a newborn kitten. It's far too dangerous. You only survived because you have marvellous friends you can trust who are ready to risk their lives for you," and he bowed to Armand who flushed with delight at this compliment.

"Really, I do envy you such friends! But you cannot fulfil the position of your grandfather without additional education. You need to learn English, the game they call politics, manners at court, you must know silly things like how to dance properly and important ones like what to say to others and – most important – when to be silent. You must learn how to fight with the latest techniques and become a duke for real, not just by title. Are you ready to do this?"

Pierre looked at him and then at Armand. "Yes, but who will do this? Who's going to teach me? And," he paused, his face becoming determined, "I'll have one condition."

Charles replied, watching him closely, "It would be my honour to be your teacher, as far as politics, court life and administration of the estates are concerned. For the rest, we'll find more suitable teachers. It will be an intensive training course from morning to night as you must be able to join the court in winter in order to be recognized by the King and by Parliament and to prevent your dear cousin frog from occupying your position. Be under no illusions – it will be extremely hard work!" He looked quizzically at Pierre, who didn't budge.

"Well, I can see in your eyes that you're not scared – apparently you love a challenge. Maybe after a life at a monastery it won't be too hard after all. But tell me, what's your condition then?"

"I wish for Armand to join in everything I do and learn," Pierre said.

Armand looked at his friend. " If you want this, then of course I'll join you, perhaps you need someone to hold your hand or have a handkerchief ready and mop your precious face when you perspire?" he joked. "But why on earth would you want me to join you in learning English or discussing British politics? I'll go back to France sooner or later, even if I never become a bishop after this escapade: I guess – luckily – I've ruined that as a career option!"

Pierre looked at him and smiled. "Because, my dear friend, whilst you were having a nap, I interrogated the butler in detail about my future inheritance. He was only too willing to oblige and recited all the titles and estates that come with the Duchy of Hertford. He reverently informed me how rich and powerful I'm going to be, probably the second most important man on earth, right after the butler."

Charles grinned; he could easily imagine the scene.

Pierre continued, his tone firm and severe. "Armand, you saved my life and helped me to find and gain my heritage. If I ascend to the rank of a Duke with all the whistles and bells that come with it, I hereby promise that I'll find a way to confer my title and estates of the Earl of Worthing on you. The butler told me that among my estates that are not bound by fideicommissum, the title and estates of Worthing seem to be of the greatest value. Charles is right: without you, I'd be nothing. So either you accept my proposal and become an English earl – and I'll become a duke – or we feed cousin Charles to the greedy frog, the pleasures of poisonous court life and take our leave and go back to France immediately!"

Charles and Armand were stunned. Armand was – probably for the first time in his life – incapable of saying anything. He just looked at Pierre in a daze and nodded slowly to show his approval as Charles raised his glass and cried:

"Santé! To your health! Cheers to the Duke of Hertford and cheers to the future Earl of Worthing ! The moment I saw Pierre I thought that he could make an excellent Duke, now he just proved it – at least if we forget his fighting skills!"

The ice was broken and they passed a thoroughly enjoyable evening; luckily the butler showed them the way back to their rooms that night, otherwise they'd never have made it!

Charles proved to be true to his word and he was an excellent – if very demanding – teacher. For Pierre had to learn from early morning until late evening and sometimes felt as if his head would explode. Learning English was one of the easier tasks, he found. Once he had overcome his first reluctance to pronounce–

186

what seemed to him – very strange sounding words and an awkward way of twisting his tongue, he finally succeeded in speaking more and more fluently whereas Armand retained a decidedly French accent, but he didn't seem to care, and in truth it only added to his charm.

Learning to understand the subtleties and intrinsic entanglements of British and European politics was an entirely different matter. Armand easily excelled in this field and often helped to clarify the broader picture by adding the French perspective or citing practical examples. Coming from the background of one of the great and noble families of France, Armand had grown up with politics since he could talk and he instinctively understood the networks and pitfalls of power.

Charles opened Pierre's eyes: questions of faith could be seen and judged from different perspectives. People in England had started to question the role and absolute power of their sovereign, resulting in almost constant conflict, if not a state of war, between King and Parliament.

What made matters even more complicated was that appearances were deceptive. Protestant countries would support each other officially but went to war against their brethren in faith on the first occasion if trade and money were at stake, such as Britain and Holland, ready to cut each other's throats for the stream of gold coming from the new colonies.

France would happily deal with their religious foes if this could harm Spain, although both countries were linked by a sacred bond of marriage and religion. The blatant truth was that any king in the world would marry a royal princess from a rival country to ensure eternal peace, yet be happy to the break the solemnly sealed alliance at his first convenience.

Pierre discovered that the world was changing fast, a world that had seemed so easy to understand, so long as he had stayed in his monastery school. To Pierre, this revelation was frightening, but exciting at the same time.

Parliament in London was a much more powerful institution than in Paris where Richelieu had skilfully manipulated it until it had become a mere stage for his obedient puppets. In total contrast the English Parliament was alive and kicking and the King needed its consent to levy taxes. Of course Pierre had learnt about British history and sovereigns in the monastery school, but naturally all stories had been taught with the sole intent of glorifying French history. Pierre remembered that Queen Elizabeth had been depicted by his teachers in Reims as a heretic bastard whore who practised witchcraft and it was fascinating now to hear stories about her reign from Charles – so different from what he had heard before.

Queen Elizabeth, Pierre now discovered, had managed against all odds not only to keep this kingdom afloat against an enemy who had seemed almighty. She had also united the old foes of England and Scotland to become Great Britain. It took exceptional skill, courage and dedication to achieve what she had done, Charles told him, with awe and admiration in his voice.

Luckily a young duke had to excel not only in politics but also in martial arts and to Pierre's and Armand's delight, a lot of their time had been reserved for practising their skills of riding and fencing.

Sword fighting was fun but exhausting. Charles found an Italian master willing to teach them the latest techniques from Italy, the country universally regarded as the cradle of the art of fighting.

Once Charles saw how fast the two friends improved their skills he decided also to participate from time to time. "Always good to brush up my technique," he commented, whilst panting hard under the attacks of Pierre, who had become a master with the rapier. Pierre simply loved this sport now.

They continued their fighting and Pierre laughed and continued his pressure. Charles was a dangerous enemy to have but Pierre was lighter and faster and he had realized that speed had become his asset against Charles's athletic prowess. Like an elusive wasp he buzzed around Charles and the day he won for the first time against his cousin he could have embraced the whole world.

One day Charles had shown Pierre the chamber where all the family weapons were stored and maintained. Pierre had immediately fallen in love with a rapier that had belonged to his grandfather; it had an elegant and light handle, an intrinsic part of the weapon, crafted by a German master. The blade was made from a secret blend of steel and was of a bluish shade. It sported a proud inscription – 'I serve well' – and was a dangerous weapon of deadly elegance, now his biggest treasure.

In the afternoons he spent hours learning about the Hertford estate and its administration. Charles was very popular and widely respected by the servants and tenants and, as was to be expected, in the beginning Pierre faced an atmosphere of polite but firm hostility as soon as word had spread that he was to follow his grandfather's steps and would be addressed as 'Your Grace'. Charles had been regarded as the natural heir and was widely respected.

Pierre was taken aback at first when he sensed this reticence, however he decided not to back down but to accept the challenge. He resolutely delved into the different subjects and soon earned the acceptance of his stewards who started to understand and to appreciate that the young duke might be very inexperienced indeed but couldn't be intimidated and had a sound head on his shoulders.

The day came when Pierre decided that it was time to show his mettle and impose for the first time his own decision on some matters, albeit not very important ones.

They had been discussing the case of a tenant. The steward objected to Pierre's decision and made it clear that he wanted to move forward with his own proposal. But when he looked up, he detected an icy look in Pierre's blue eyes. Pierre simply said in an even tone, "I think he had better execute what I have just decided; I won't say it again."

His steward realized immediately that he had better give in and be careful in the future. Later he told his secretary, "I knew that it was time to give in. His Grace cannot be fooled, that's for sure; he looked just like the old devil, his grandfather, when he looked at me."

Charles watched this development with amusement and growing satisfaction. Soon his cousin would be ready to face the challenge of presenting himself at court, he was becoming daily more confident of that!

Back in Sevens, Pierre's note had been received with great relief by most of the inhabitants – with the exception of one.

Two days later Armand rode over to meet his friends who were bursting with curiosity. Armand was an excellent story teller and his highly entertaining version of the latest events matched the performance of any professional entertainer.

His story was met with exclamations of surprise and joy. Marie was terribly thrilled, she couldn't sit still on her chair any longer and jumped up in excitement. Unfortunately a small table standing next to her toppled over and a beautiful green marble plate smashed into a thousand pieces.

Marie couldn't care less. She danced around the room, shouting, "He's a duke, now, a genuine duke! Now we can take on the evil Cardinal and kill this monster of a cousin!"

She wouldn't listen to Céline's mild reproach that a lady shouldn't destroy furniture, dance around the room and propose murdering people. Marie's eyes glittered. "*Je m'en fiche*, I don't care! We'll crush this Henri like a cockroach!" and the gesture that accompanied her words was as explicit as it was unfitting for a lady.

Armand had delivered a formal invitation for the whole party to join them in Hertford Castle for lunch but to his dismay Marie's aunt wouldn't hear of it and, speaking to Marie, she flatly refused any such idea.

Truth was that the proud Principessa had been very upset when she had discovered the charade that had been played out right under her nose. She viewed the disguise as nothing less than a *lèse majesté*, a personal insult. Having the highest opinions about her own position in the world, she couldn't accept that what she called a vicious joke had been played on her. It took a lot of persuasion from Marie and Arthur to make her agree to at least meet Armand and not to withdraw into her chamber as she had intended to do. Tearfully she announced that she could feel a serious migraine coming on.

Armand was kept waiting for her in the beautiful salon facing the lovely rose garden. The French doors had been opened, fresh air and sunlight were streaming in, giving the room a welcoming and friendly atmosphere filled with the scent of the last autumn roses. A large black cat with white paws lay on a comfortable chair

189

fitted with inviting cushions. The cat made it clear that she owned this chair. She looked extremely belligerently at Armand, disturbed by this strange intruder, ready to defend her place. Armand opted for peace and chose a less comfortable seat. He sighed and looked out of the open door into the garden.

What truly beautiful scenery, he thought, as he looked out into the enchanted-looking garden.

Regrettably the garden's sunny spirit and peaceful atmosphere didn't reach Armand's hostess. When she entered the room accompanied by Marie, Céline, and her son, Armand's heart sank as he realized immediately that she had decided to make him pay for what she had apparently interpreted as a grave insult to her dignity.

Marie's aunt barely replied to Marie's and Arthur's numerous attempts to launch a conversation and flatly refused any suggestion of riding over to the Hertford estate or allowing any meeting between Marie and Pierre.

Marie was still wondering how she could convince her aunt that this disguise had not been made with any ill intentions when Armand decided it was high time to break the ice. He strode through the room and seated himself next to the Principessa, then he started to chat with her in his nonchalant way, pretending that he hadn't even noticed her obvious fury.

It was very rare that a woman could resist Armand's considerable charms and soon – very much against her firmest resolve – she started to thaw. When he confided to her with a wistful glance of his beautiful dark eyes from under adorable lashes (those long lashes being the secret envy of many a girl) that his only regret was to have been born twenty years too late and to have missed the opportunity to meet her when she was still free, she laughed out loud. She slapped his arm reprovingly with her fan, but she did consent with a charming smile that she had been a first class beauty when she was young.

Armand shamelessly continued his offensive and Arthur could only marvel at Armand's masterly skills of courteous flirtation. Finding his hostess more responsive Armand moved delicately to the touchy subject of their disguise. Dextrously he managed to make it obvious that their disguise had been chosen with the pure and sole intention of avoiding any potential harm to Marie's and her hosts' reputation as their situation had been delicate, very delicate indeed. He did not want to go into details but she, a Princess and a woman of the social world who mattered, would understand instinctively that a case where the great Cardinal Richelieu was involved was a very delicate one and needed to be treated with the highest degree of caution and discretion.

Céline immediately took the hint and made her opinion known, that she could only agree that this had been a very smart move. Potentially delicate questions and complications – especially harmful for Marie but also for the household and reputation of an ambassador – had luckily been avoided.

The ruse worked and after a short pause for reluctant deliberation their hostess had to admit that – seen from this perspective – their action was just about defensible and that she might consider forgiving Pierre for having abused her hospitality. It only took ten more minutes and she had forgotten all about her sorrows, let alone her approaching migraine. Curiosity taking over, she happily started planning to come over with Marie and Arthur to visit Hertford Castle. Armand winked at Arthur, who had followed these manoeuvres in astonishment.

Later he accompanied Armand to fetch his horse which the groom had brought from the stables and said, full of admiration, "You know, you shouldn't bury yourself in the countryside; the way you handled my mother was brilliant, you'd make a first class diplomat or minister!"

Armand smiled. "For the moment Pierre is planning to keep me in England. Your mother did indeed give me a hard time, but she reminded me so much of my own mother when she used to be upset with me – and I'm afraid that happened often enough to give me a lot of practice. I wasn't really intimidated by her. It will be wonderful to have you over with us, we have missed you!"

"So have we," answered Arthur. "It's become pretty boring since you left, we could do with a bit more adventure."

"You never know what life has in store for you," Armand answered good-humouredly and waved goodbye.

A RAINY DAY IN LONDON

Henri was gnawing at his fingernails with frustration. He had been sitting idle in London for several weeks now as he had remained stuck without news from Richelieu. He had been spending precious time and money – money he didn't have. His financial situation was becoming tight, and soon would be desperate. Money seemed to ooze out of his pockets with steady but frightening speed.

An ambassador was expected to reside in style, hire expensive coaches and have plenty of footmen to impress; he hadn't even started to throw lavish parties or to attend the most famous gaming tables in the city where the inner circles of power met; there, fortunes were made or lost over night.

Sooner or later he'd need to make himself known in London but Henri had used the fear of the plague as a welcome excuse for an unusually secluded lifestyle, preferring to live unobtrusively until he had been able to dispose of his cousin discreetly. He had been patiently waiting for the right opportunity but now he started to realize that this might have been in vain and if nothing happened, soon, very soon, he'd need to return to France, ruined and broke, his mission a failure. His mind was racing. Was Richelieu playing games with him? Had this been just a ruse to remove him from Versailles?

At first the royal court had decided to leave London and move to Windsor Castle, a decision made in panic as soon as the first serious cases of plague had been reported and the number of deaths seemed to grow daily with frightening speed.

The well-oiled machine of Whitehall had sprung into action. Heavy coaches full of furniture, weapons, clothes, paintings, servants, food, jewellery and everything imaginable had been sent to Windsor, carriages shuttling back and forth. During those weeks of busy removal, no official audiences had taken place. The King had only received his ministers in Privy Council and rarely granted any but the most pressing private audiences.

Two weeks later news filtered through that the reports of casualties had been grossly inflated and that the plague had not been spreading beyond the quarters of the poor as previously feared. And who seriously cared about the fate of the poor? Even the Church had more important matters at hand!

The King had been reluctant from the beginning to leave London. He was afraid to abandon a city that was – once again – boiling with tension.

King Charles had dissolved the previous Parliament only some months ago, after only three weeks of session, but he was under intense pressure to call a new and longer lasting session. The plain truth was that His Majesty, the all powerful King of Great Britain, was bankrupt, and a beggar: his last war had depleted all his reserves. It was a matter of survival to organize a Parliament – but he needed a Parliament favourable to his pleas, ready to vote for new taxes. Consequently he decided to stay in London to show his subjects that His Majesty, King Charles, was a person of great courage and resolve, caring for the people of London, a true defender of his subjects.

The machine organizing the royal removal to Windsor thus came to a grinding halt and was put into reverse mode, moving back to London all the goods and persons that had been deployed to Windsor already.

Once more all receptions, audiences and balls were cancelled or delayed until Whitehall Palace would be fully operational once more.

Henri, thus having plenty of time on his hand, had visited everything and everywhere in London that had been recommended to him. He found a city even dirtier than Paris – if this was possible. He judged London shabby and definitely outdated compared to the modern splendours of Paris. London streets were narrow, only a few of them paved properly, the houses built low and their style unassuming with the exception of a few impressive noble mansions. The majority of London houses, built practically one on top of the other, were made from wattle and daub, and many were still thatched. Fires therefore were a daily occurrence and formed a perpetual danger as they often spread fast. Luckily it rained often – too often for Henri's taste – otherwise London would probably have already burnt down to its foundations several times over.

London did not have any proper avenues like Paris that allowed the display of regal power, or splendid parades to ease the flow of traffic. If the King or his nobles wanted to travel fast, their obvious choice would be to use the River Thames, as London city, its traffic and population, were in a state of pure chaos from sunrise well into the night.

Henri had of course toured the excitingly seedy taverns close to the Thames ports and found to his delight that they catered for every taste. A local hero playwright, William Shakespeare, had long ago written comedies and dramas full of action, passion and love, very different from the tamer and less explicit French plays Henri was acquainted with.

Henri loved to watch Shakespeare's comedies and dramas with their bold displays of love, jealousy and hatred. Fake blood was spilled in abundance in plenty of scenes before a captivated audience that came from all parts of the society. They craved action; boisterous and rude, they'd criticize or praise the performance of the actors and the action on stage – and nothing would escape their attention. Henri was still at odds with this funny language – but he loved the atmosphere in the small theatre built especially for the performance of Shakespeare's plays.

Some of the young actors who played the female parts were more than willing to join him after the show and he soon became intimate friends with a young actor.

He had reddish hair and a reckless freckled face – once his wig and the white lead powder had been removed and his true face appeared. Soon on best terms with Henri, he had made it clear that he'd take on any job to improve his meagre income – in bed and out of it.

Good to know, Henri thought, while he watched the young actor undress, feeling the pleasant ticklings of desire. *He might come in very useful when I need to set up my trap for Pierre, he seems to be delightfully ruthless.*

Henri would definitely cultivate this relationship and opened another bottle of wine to cement their intimate friendship.

But in the end, all of his nightly activities couldn't appease him anymore. Henri knew that time was running out; maybe his cousin had already discovered that a great destiny was waiting for him. Getting rid of a duke and a peer of the realm would be much more difficult and dangerous than having a random French visitor 'disappear'. He knew that he needed to act fast but the fact that – once again – the trail of his cousin had been lost, was quite maddening.

On top of all his worries, true English autumn weather had set in: wet, cold, often foggy with only occasional spells of sun. He had never experienced such a fog before in his life, the cold dampness mixed with the fumes of thousands of chimneys clogging his throat, his lungs and his brain.

Henri yearned to return to France, to stay on his estates close to the lovely Loire where autumns were mild and sunny and the new wine would soon be waiting to be sampled.

Richelieu's messenger, whose duty it was to call on Henri and report regularly, found him one day highly strung, ready to pounce and in an extremely dangerous mood.

Nervous as a caged lion, the monk thought.

Henri didn't even bother to greet him properly and just barked at him, "Have you come once more to tell me that you have no idea where my cousin is staying and that I need to be patient and pray to the Lord? I'm fed up with this and your incompetence. You can tell His Eminence straight away I've had enough of this stupid waiting, it's finished, I'm returning to court in Paris!"

The monk didn't reply immediately but made a sign for Henri to calm down. Henri paced the room up and down and replied, "All right, go on then, tell me the latest news, but my decision is firm!"

"My lord, finally I do have news. The time of waiting is over! We've found Pierre de Beauvoir. Somehow he managed to reach Hertford Castle. Your cousin is residing there, presenting himself shamelessly already as the new Duke of

Hertford. According to our sources he's planning to attend court at Whitehall no later than November."

Curiously he watched Henri, who had listened impatiently, and saw that his face had turned crimson. The monk hastened therefore to go on with his speech as he was frightened that Henri would explode any minute. Worse, his host looked as if he was ready to strangle the bringer of bad tidings.

"As a duke he's now travelling accompanied of course by a whole army of servants and footmen, which means that our initial plan to abduct your cousin has become too risky."

Henri stopped, his handsome face distorted by anger and hate. "I may guess then that you probably recommend me to show true Christian charity and send him my congratulations and everlasting love as his cousin?" he spat in the direction of the monk.

The monk moved a step backward when the full heat of Henri's anger hit him.

"Please listen, my lord," he implored Henri, "with your permission, we have developed a new and in my humble opinion, very efficient plan. Our agents tell us that your cousin is planning to become betrothed to a young lady of French origin staying in a manor house called Sevens, close to Hertford. We propose that this lady should become the centre of our attention."

And while he continued to explain his plan in detail, he watched how Henri's countenance suddenly changed completely. When the monk had laid out all the steps of his devious plan, Henri pretended to give it a good minute of thought before he answered, "I must admit, this plan seems simple enough," in his mind adding, *Actually, delightfully evil.*

"You have my consent. I propose to bring along one person who has my trust and who can be of great help. He's an actor and used to disguising himself."

The monk nodded his consent; of course he knew with whom Henri had been meeting regularly as Richelieu had given order to keep track of Henri. Every single step had been followed and recorded. The young actor was a part of their web of spies dextrously planted under his nose, but Henri apparently had no clue as to this. This arrogant aristocrat no doubt thought that he was very clever, but nobody could beat Richelieu, the great master of all secrets, that much was certain.

The monk bowed, made the sign of the cross and retreated, satisfied that his mission was finally yielding results.

For the first time in weeks Henri felt what could be described as his peculiar version of happiness and contentment; the hunt for his cousin could start and there would be success, he was sure of that – this brilliant plan couldn't fail! If there was any human being more devious and reckless than Henri de Beauvoir, he had to admit, it was the Cardinal Richelieu.

195

HUNTING IN HERTFORD

Pierre had settled quickly and, to his surprise, very comfortably into his new position and lifestyle. Being addressed reverently as 'Your Grace' didn't irritate him any longer. In the first few days he had woken up early in the morning and sometimes even at night, worried, convinced that he'd find himself back in his old life at the monastery school. Maybe all of this amazing adventure was only part of some wonderful but fundamentally crazy dream, and on the miraculous spell being broken, he'd wake up and find himself an orphan once more, under the care of terrible Brother Hieronymus – a true nightmare!

But as soon as he opened his eyes and found himself lying comfortably in his immense bed with those wonderful soft cushions, his skin caressed by the softest linen he had ever experienced, the curtains of his bed carefully closed by his personal valet to spare him the slightest inconvenience of chilly draughts, his sleepy brain realized with joy that this was reality and to his great relief no dream at all – and that another day full of new and exciting experiences was waiting for him.

The orphaned pet dogs of his grandfather, the late Duke, had attached themselves to Pierre; actually, it had been love at first sight on both sides. Pierre could be seen moving through the castle followed by the trail of three eager black and white spaniels. Each of them was trying relentlessly to attract their new master's attention, pink tongues hanging out of their mouths in hopeful anticipation. He looked very much like the late Duke, who had never been seen without his dogs when he resided at Hertford. Funnily enough, this small detail had convinced even the most reluctant and sceptical of his servants to embrace him fully as the legitimate heir – papers or documents could be forged, but dogs couldn't be fooled.

Charles was amazed to see how the tide had changed in such a short time. The late Duke's personal valet served Pierre initially with the greatest condescension and reluctance, hardly hiding his contempt for this boyish newcomer who had no bearings of a true duke in his eyes. He delegated as many tasks as possible to his footmen, letting the butler know in confidence that he probably wouldn't stay on to serve somebody he considered to be a mere child and an adventurous imposter of uncertain ancestry and – even worse – of foreign origin, unworthy of his sophisticated services. The butler, being a staunch supporter of Pierre since he had set eyes on him the first day merely replied, "He's so much like the old Duke, if you can't see this, you must be blind!"

But – very much to his own surprise – it had only taken a few days for the valet to become convinced that Pierre was the true heir and grandchild of the late Duke and consequently he changed his mind completely. In no time he had become attached to Pierre, castigating himself for his previous attitude.

Soon he'd stay up late, as he couldn't bear the thought that a servant of lower rank should undress the young Duke and prepare his bed. When Pierre told him curtly not to bother, he had tears in his eyes and pleaded with Pierre not to punish him for his previous attitude and to let him serve Pierre as diligently as he had been allowed to serve his grandfather.

Pierre's daily routine of lessons and studies or perfecting his fencing skills was agreeably interrupted by inviting Marie and her relatives over to Hertford from time to time, but more often he would ride with Armand over to Sevens, soon to be joined more and more frequently by a good-humoured cousin Charles.

He had remarked to Marie casually that he didn't really understand why Charles joined them so often: "Armand and I are already travelling with at least five to six footmen and grooms! Charles was shocked when I wanted to ride on my own on the first day; apparently a duke must never ride on his own or he'll lose his reputation. So there's no need, does he think I'll get lost without him?"

Marie just laughed. "Men can be so blind! Don't you see that he's courting Céline?"

Pierre looked at her, bewildered. Of course Céline was a fine-looking lady, but she had seemed so tall and – to his seventeen year-old mind – far too old to be involved in a romantic affair. He grinned at Marie sheepishly. "That could explain it. I really did wonder why he proposed joining us so often and this morning he made a big fuss as his valet had prepared the wrong waistcoat and we were delayed because he insisted on changing." He laughed, remembering the scene. "And once he had managed to put it on, he rushed to a mirror and was shouting that the tailor was an idiot, he complained that he looked like stuffed bear in it!"

Marie watched Pierre playing this little scene in front of the mirror, moving right and left and looking critically down his waistline and she roared with laughter. Charles was already impressive but clad in a quilted waistcoat he must have looked as if he'd been positively inflated.

Pierre looked at her, still smiling. "It seems strange to me, but of course you're right, he must have fallen in love. I hope she's not upset!"

Marie just grinned, remembering a scene from yesterday evening. The ladies had been sitting comfortably in the large sitting room, and a cosy fire had been lit as the evenings had already become quite chilly. The dark red brocade curtains with their pattern of embroidered unicorns had been drawn and a comfortable silence had reigned. Arthur had left the room, pretending a need to study some documents and had looked at the group while he was closing the door.

Marie looked lovely – as usual – in her light blue dress with golden trimmings, the silk shining in the light of the fire, as did her hair. A shawl of golden coloured silk complemented her dress to perfection and matched her amber eyes. Céline and Arthur's mother had also dressed up, as they had dined with neighbours who had

197

just left. Marie's aunt wore a necklace with diamonds that sparkled around her neck as if the fire had set them alive. What a lovely picture; a shame that Marie's heart had been taken by Pierre, he thought, she would have made a lovely bride.

The ladies sat gathered around the fireplace, stitching listlessly while holding an embroidery frame and colourful silk threads in their lap. Needlework for charity or church was supposed to be a fitting pastime for noble ladies. Marie's aunt hated silence and as soon as the door had closed, she had started chatting about various subjects. Marie answered mechanically when suddenly her aunt changed the subject and to Marie's surprise started to praise Pierre's qualities lavishly.

"He's so handsome, Marie, I understand now why you fell in love with him. I must confess that I was a little upset in the beginning. It was rather naughty of the boys though, to come in disguise, but of course now I understand that all of this was done with the *best* of intentions!"

She emphasized the word 'best' to underline why she had forgiven Pierre and continued with a satisfied sigh, "But it has all been so romantic! Of course one shouldn't disregard the fact that he'll be one of the wealthiest men of England with two enormous heritages just dropping from heaven upon him; I imagine your parents will be very pleased."

Marie was fascinated. Her aunt had developed a technique that allowed her to talk nearly without a break, therefore she continued without interruption. "Not that my Arthur wouldn't have been a good match either, he's really a nice boy and will make an excellent husband, but don't worry, I won't ask you to reconsider your choice." Now her voice sank to a confidential whisper. "Although he'll be an excellent match as well, I have always suspected that my husband has considerably more money at his disposal somewhere than he wants to confess to me. He probably thinks I'll spend it all if I know about it," ending with a good-natured giggle.

She had looked up from her needlework while she kept the flow of conversation going smoothly, then once more changed the subject of conversation without prior warning. "Well, as I'm certainly not blind, I can see there seems to be second match in the making," her bright eyes now directed on Céline who pretended to have overheard this hint and seemed to be totally involved by some intricate pattern she was about to stitch.

Marie's aunt giggled again and decided to become more outspoken. "Céline, you don't need to hide behind your needlework, my dear! I've been watching you these past ten minutes and you haven't really done a stitch. Daydreaming about a certain handsome earl in the neighbourhood, that's what you're doing. But you can confide in Aunt Carlotta, your secret's safe with me! Trust me, he's head over heels in love with you, listen to an expert, in no time you'll be an English countess."

Céline had protested of course, but even to Marie's ears this didn't sound very convincing. Her nosy aunt had been on the right trail. Well, next time she'd definitely watch Céline and Charles more carefully!

Céline had to admit to herself that she had been daydreaming, and the Principessa was right, of course. Even worse, she had to confess that daydreaming had become a bad habit during the past few days. She had never thought that she would ever return to this stage of life, being in love, hopelessly, her heart beating violently as soon as Charles appeared.

It had happened almost immediately she had set eyes on Charles for the first time. What a comfort to finally be able to look up to a man and not down on him. She had liked everything she saw, his unruly hair, his freckled face and his loud and melodious voice – even his strange eyes. And how she adored his funny accent when he spoke French with her!

Maybe Charles wasn't the most handsome man in the world but he had stolen her heart – and she couldn't help it. There were the moments when she was alone in her bed, sleepless, when she started fantasizing about the possibility of a marriage, a truly seductive dream of the fairytale happiness every woman dreams about. But in the cold light of day the likelihood of it seemed remote, even impossible – even if he had, surprisingly timidly and in a very courteous way, shown his interest in her as well.

But Céline was painfully aware that her father had left her no dowry. Marriages in noble families were first of all decisions to do with money and business, not affairs of the heart or sentiment. She was of good ancestry – nothing outstanding – but she didn't have a penny to offer. It would be unreasonable to imagine that an Earl who had just given up a huge heritage for the benefit of his newly arrived cousin could afford to marry a pauper, an over-tall lady past her prime. Her reasoning might sound brutal but Céline had always tried to remain honest and true to herself. She had to be brave and look at reality objectively – there was no place for romance, and apart from her pretty face, she had nothing to offer.

Every morning she firmly decided to become her old self once more, detached and formal, and to turn a cold shoulder to Charles – only to postpone this painful decision to the next day as soon as she set eyes on him, and then again to the next day, secretly cherishing every day she saw him, forgetting that there could be no future for the two of them.

Charles had no experience of courting a lady, even if this might sound ridiculous to him at his age. Until now he had been convinced that he'd remain a bachelor forever, happy to have a comfortable home with servants, dogs, horses and his friends coming over for long weekends to play cards, savour the wonderful and plentiful supply of wines that he usually bought straight from some dubious smugglers in his county and no wife to criticize his relaxed lifestyle and lack of ambition to attend court more often than the strict minimum that was demanded of a rural squire. The vision of succeeding the late Duke of Hertford had been a nightmarish prospect for Charles and he had gladly accepted Pierre's claims, looking forward to the day he'd be able to turn his back on this huge and imposing estate and revert to his former comfortable lifestyle.

But as soon as he set eyes on Céline, his heart had stirred and immediately he knew she was the one with whom he could imagine sharing his life. He couldn't explain why, the feeling had come upon him, and each time he met her, this feeling had grown and he carefully and slowly had started to court her. In fact, she rather puzzled him. He could read in her eyes that she liked him – how often their eyes would meet and they would laugh about the same things – but then, suddenly and unexpectedly, she would retreat into a shell of polite indifference, making it clear that she didn't want him to move closer. He was bewildered, he knew instinctively that she was not one of those ladies who would deliberately employ a strategy of giving the cold shoulder, thus there must be a reason! One day he had been surprised to see a desperately unhappy look on her face, full of longing, and it had taken all of his good manners and resolve not to rush towards Céline and take her into his arms, there and then.

He must a find a way to declare his intentions – but he was suddenly afraid that she would reject him and he racked his brain to find the best way to do it, and a fitting occasion. He had no idea that Pierre and Armand could read him like a book and had already exchanged bets as to the day he'd finally make his move.

Autumn rain and unpleasant cold weather had set in. Thick and heavy clouds of a leaden colour hovered above the wet countryside like a quilt of dirty grey spread across the sky. Trees shed their useless burden of dying leaves, preparing to hibernate. Only from time to time would the sun chase away the clouds for a short spell of sunshine – and then rarely for a full day, but more often for a few short but immensely precious hours only. During these magic moments the depressing colours of autumn would suddenly lose their pale complexion, transforming the forest and the countryside into a fairytale landscape of warm and glowing tints. Yellow and dark red leaves fell from the trees, dancing in the rays of the sun like petals strewn for a late bride.

The time for leisurely late summer picnics was definitely over, but the pleasures of the hunting season were in full swing. Pierre and Armand had an exciting time accompanied by Charles, who, despite his considerable weight, was a master at flying over fences with his gigantic horse that would carry his heavy master as if he were no burden at all, Charles and his horse still fresh when Pierre and Armand were spent, longing desperately for a break.

Armand sometimes felt rather awkward in the presence of Charles and Pierre who showed all the signs of being fully and – in Armand's personal opinion – boringly in love. All the same, he was truly happy at having accepted Pierre's invitation to stay on at Hertford.

Armand had always considered himself a good fighter, especially with his sword, until the day their Italian teacher had shown him what real mastery of refined sword fighting was about. Armand had even started to talk English fluently – the fact that one of the chambermaids often visited him at night in his bedroom had probably contributed much to his motivation in this area. He couldn't, however, pronounce this funny language in the way his teacher wanted him to, retaining a distinct, but very charming, French accent.

One day in mid November they came home, boots and trousers covered in mud, the dogs rushing around them excitedly, leaving a wet trail of dirt behind them. It was the usual chaos after returning from a long excursion, their leather waistcoats glistening from the rain, all of them just longing to get into some clean and dry clothes and drain a good jug of ale to satisfy their thirst.

The butler waited until the first commotion had died down before he approached Armand. He bowed discreetly and handed him an envelope that had apparently arrived the same day. Armand recognized the seal and forgot about his thirst; the letter showed the coat of arms of his father, the Marquis de Saint Paul. He had dreaded this letter arriving as he had taken the initiative some weeks ago and sent, after long deliberation, a message to his father. He had carefully worded an explanation of his hasty decision to leave the monastery without his father's consent, assuring him all the same of his filial love, respect and eternal devotion. Armand had drafted letter after letter, and was still not sure if he hadn't overdone it – he knew his father well enough to recognize that he probably wouldn't be at all impressed by any of his carefully worded excuses, and could only hope that his mother might have a mellowing influence on the tone of the reply – if she bothered at all to interfere on behalf of her lost son.

Armand went slowly upstairs into his rooms, dragging his feet; he wanted to confront the unpleasant task of opening the letter as late as possible. First he wanted to undress and wash, steeling himself for the unavoidable. What a pleasant surprise to find the charming maid waiting for him in his bedroom – news of his arrival must have travelled fast.

With a skilful display of false timidity, offset by a seductive twinkling of her blue eyes she demurely offered her help. It was decidedly difficult to decline her kind offer – especially as she had taken the precaution to make sure that they were undisturbed. Armand grinned and gladly accepted the services that were so kindly and generously offered to him. He didn't mind the added benefit of the dreaded moment being delayed for when he would have to open the envelope that lay on his dressing table.

As soon as the maid had left the room, Armand sighed deeply and took the envelope in his hands. He looked at the seal with its coat of arms that was so familiar to him. He was just about to tear the envelope open when he hesitated – something seemed wrong... He scrutinized the seal once more. He remembered that he had noticed a polished crystal that served as a magnifying glass on the desk. He took it and studied the seal carefully. It showed cracks where there should have been none; a faint trace of red wax showed that it had been glued or repaired after opening. Clearly somebody else had shown a keen interest in this letter and opened it before him.

Armand deduced that a copy of this letter must be on Richelieu's desk already. He stared at the letter, with a sudden feeling of foreboding that the peace and quiet of the last few weeks would soon be over.

To his surprise the envelope contained not only one, but two letters. The first letter showed the bold signature of his father, and was short and concise. Armand was ordered to come back to France. The letter continued that he had brought shame on the honour of the family and had disobeyed the strictest and clearest instructions of his father, the head of the de Saint Paul family.

Armand was stunned. He had indeed expected a formal letter and to be scolded severely by his father! Well, he had to admit that he had merited some harsh punishment, that much was certain. But this document was not like his father at all, who was a known choleric – this letter had the bureaucratic charm of a royal ordinance, a damnation written with cold detachment! And why didn't his father order him to come back immediately? He read the letter again, but there was no deadline. It didn't make sense. He was most puzzled.

While his brain was still working to find answers to all of these questions, he unfolded the second document. It was much longer, signed by his mother. It started 'My Dearest Son' and now Armand's nerves were pricking; alarm bells were ringing in his head. His mother had used the old language the family used to speak at home when they wanted to be sure not to be overheard, the language of 'Languedoc'.

The de Saint Paul family used a secret code; whenever they sent each other a message containing phrases in this almost forgotten and officially spurned language, the content had been encrypted. Richelieu – named in the family language 'the evil one' – had installed an omnipresent network of agents and spies all over France and Armand's father had warned them again and again that all of his letters would be copied and read by the enemy. Armand read through the sentences of apparently motherly concern, warnings not to get involved in evil, mixed with gossipy news about friends and family and questions about his stay in England. She asked if he still had the precious family ring and added stern warnings to avoid any dealings with heretics and freemasons such as the heretic Templars – all very puzzling and very unlike his mother, who had never really bothered about her younger children and certainly wouldn't bother about heretics.

Finally he found the key; his mother piously instructed him to be a good boy and read his prayers at night citing page 10, verses 2, 3 and 7. This meant that he had to use only each second, third, seventh and tenth word from her letter.

Armand felt like a bloodhound on the scent and took a fresh sheet of paper and a quill, in his haste splashing ink across the empty page. He quickly copied the words that needed to be extracted. After a good twenty minutes he had rearranged the puzzle of words into a message that started to make sense, the result of which made him gasp:

Armand, I understand why you joined Pierre and why you had to leave the monastery. His father was my best friend. I always wanted you to protect him, this is why I sent you there. I knew you had neither the intention nor talent to join the clergy. Pierre will need more of our help. The evil man in Paris has secretly started litigation in a Church court to declare him a bastard and heretic. His cousin is already in England and wants to kill him. He's in danger! Go to the Templars in London as fast as possible, they will help. Further instructions will be waiting there. Show your ring for identification. God bless you. In love, your father.

Armand stared at the paper for at least ten minutes, the words dancing in front of his eyes, trying to digest the message and the sudden turn of events. His father had been Pierre's father's best friend?

He remembered vaguely how his father had pointed to Pierre when they had arrived at the monastery in Reims telling him, almost giving him an order, to attach himself to this frail blond boy, as he looked particularly bright and kind. But since then he had never mentioned Pierre again, knowing probably all the time that they had indeed become best friends – like their fathers. But the essential message was clear; Pierre was in great and immediate danger – once again.

They would need to go to London as fast as possible and find out what the Templars would know and how they could help. The worst thing was that Armand had no idea where to go or how to find them! He tried to remember the history, cursing himself that he hadn't paid more attention. He had a vague memory that the order of the Knights Templar – or Knights of the Temple – had been defeated hundreds of years ago. Why did this matter now? Their organization had been outlawed and dissolved everywhere in Europe, their members tortured and their fortunes seized by a coalition of the greedy kings of France, Spain and of course, England. Even when their history at the monastery had been taught, their names were never openly mentioned, and whenever the subject of the unfortunate knights was touched upon, the monks did so in awe and fear, for an order so rich and powerful must have had the devil as their true master.

The Templars had gone underground and disappeared, leaving only a powerful legend; it seemed perplexing that Armand should turn to an association as secretive and shadowy as the medieval Knights Templar to help Pierre to survive and claim his heritage in France or England. But his father would not write such a letter without deep reflection; his cunning had saved the de Saint Paul estates already many times from the grip of the Cardinal. The message was clear; they'd need to leave for London, and fast!

203

When Armand lifted his eyes he saw that the dim light of the sunset had disappeared and it was completely dark outside. He gave a low curse, he'd be late for dinner, which in England was served much too early for his French taste. Charles and Pierre would be waiting for him impatiently, as they'd be hungry from a day of hunting in the woods.

He looked quickly into the polished silver mirror that hung above his washstand and saw to his annoyance that his face looked flushed and excited. He hoped that he'd regain his normal appearance as soon as he had passed the endless galleries leading from his wing into the main building, as they would be dining, as usual, in the 'private' dining room.

Armand had already hurried down the first sombre gallery and was heading for the long corridor linking the left wing with the main building when he remembered that he had left the letter and – even worse – his own decoded version lying on his desk. He cursed, as he'd wanted to discuss it privately with Pierre and Charles after dinner and turned back immediately on his heels, heading to his room.

The gallery was fitted with a marble floor but his fine leather shoes with their suede soles made almost no sound. He approached the door of his room, pushed on the latch and rushed into his room.

He saw that the curtains of his rooms had already been drawn after he had left, but he was amazed to find a new valet on duty. It was obvious that he had been snooping around, as the valet jumped as soon as Armand entered the room, showing confusion and guilt, thinly masked by an air of defiance.

"What are you doing at my desk?" Armand shouted at him angrily in his accented English.

"I was looking... I mean I was going to change the candle, my lord," the valet answered, pointing to the candelabra on the desk, trying to look meek and reverential as was expected from a mere servant.

Armand looked at him critically, but the excuse was a credible one; the candle was smoking and had burnt down, only Armand was sure that he had extinguished it before he had left the room.

Armand gave the valet a thoughtful look, gathered his documents and headed once more back to the dining room, but this time he was more running than walking. The incident with the valet kept his mind busy; he didn't like at all what he had seen – nor the mendacious face of the valet. If this man wasn't sent and paid for by Richelieu, his name wasn't Armand. His father was right, they'd have to leave and seek support against the enemy, and do so as fast as possible.

The dining room was brightly lit by a multitude of candles; no expense had been spared. The walls, furniture, and frames of the paintings were all heavily decorated with pure gold, shining warmly in the soft candlelight. The decorative silverware, polished to perfection, was gleaming. The heavy wine from Bordeaux served in the finest Venetian glassware projected sparks of deepest red that stirred in the flickering light of the candles, dotting the snow-white table linen with its reflections.

When Armand rushed into the room, Pierre and Charles had already started eating. Hungry as a pack of wolves, they had unanimously decided to discard the rules of etiquette and to start dinner on their own.

"Who knows what has delayed Armand, I'm hungry as hell," Pierre had said, rubbing his stomach, simultaneously giving a wink to underline that he had actually some very precise ideas about the most likely cause of Armand's prolonged absence.

The delicious pheasant soup – a result of their own hunting skills – was finished and they were greedily eyeing the next course when Armand rushed into the room. He listened to their good-humoured hints about the reason for his late arrival, which was apparently important enough for him to forget about his best friends. Armand grinned complacently, uttered some words about some people who have it and some who don't, and tackled the difficult task of choosing from the huge selection of tasty dishes that was offered to him by a servant, undisturbed by their chit-chat.

After dinner they usually went to the library just to talk or play cards, so Armand had to wait impatiently for the meal to finish and to be able to speak openly as soon as they were on their own and could discuss matters in private.

Having finished the last course of the meal with some excellent cheese and sweet pastries, Pierre said that he would explode if he ate another crumb and proposed moving to the library to share a drink. Armand quickly grabbed a last piece of apple pie and – still munching the delicious pastry – pronounced in a slightly slurred voice that having something stronger than wine would be a very tempting idea, so the small group marched through the gallery into the garden wing, where the library was situated. The butler had already made sure that a fire was burning invitingly and a tray with liqueurs and some sweetmeats was waiting for them, as it was well known that Charles had a sweet tooth.

This evening though, Armand had no eyes for the library's wonderful panels and shelves, skilfully crafted from solid and costly timbers. He didn't bother about the impressive-looking books, bound in leather with stylish gilt imprints in English, Latin, some even bearing titles in French or German on their spines. Next to its cosy fireplace there stood an impressive globe of gigantic proportions. He never could walk into this room and escape the fascination of this globe, a quite recent and probably very expensive addition to the late Duke's collection.

France seemed hideously small on this globe whereas unknown continents like Asia, Africa and the Americas looked huge, all of them floating in dangerous oceans, the frontiers blurred. What a wonderful but scary part of the world this seemed to be, guarded by greedy sea monsters also depicted on this wonderful globe, stretching their fearsome tentacles towards fragile-looking sailing ships. The artist had painstakingly painted every detail, even the frightened faces of panic-stricken sailors being grabbed by the terrible monsters.

Pictures of the wild-looking heathens of Africa, Asia, America and India had been lovingly painted by the unknown artist, showing in vivid detail dark-skinned natives clad in apparel he could never have imagined – some even naked – waving their spears and daggers angrily against the brave missionaries and soldiers who were diligently carrying the cross to enlighten the world.

In Armand's mind – and that of all his teachers – France had undoubtedly been the biggest and most important nation on Earth and it was quite sobering to discover that France and England were in fact two relatively small plots of land on this big globe. As soon as he had set eyes on those wonderful maps he had decided that he wanted to travel and see this fantastic world with his own eyes, and how much he longed to share this adventure with Pierre – they'd just need to work out how to avoid the sea-monsters!

But today Armand had other issues on his mind. He surprised Pierre and Charles when he insisted on opening the library door and checking carefully that no servant was listening; he even checked that the heavy curtains had been drawn shut to make sure that nobody was hiding behind them.

Pierre started to feel uneasy; he knew Armand well enough to realize that he wasn't joking. He wouldn't take these precautions if there were no need.

Armand walked to the globe and spun it around, lost in thought until he stopped it abruptly, looking absent-mindedly at France while he tried to find the best way to explain the situation. Finally he cleared his throat and started to speak.

"I hope you don't mind travelling, in fact, as soon as possible. I'm afraid we have to leave this hospitable place."

But Charles didn't think that this was very amusing and interjected, "What's going on, Armand, can you please be more clear? What's the matter? Is it related to the letter that you received today?"

Armand nodded and continued, "My dear Charles, you fill me with admiration; this impressive body of yours harbours a sharp brain: you have hit the nail on the head. I received a letter from my father today and want to show it to you; it's probably easier to understand what I'm talking about, if you read these letters here."

"Letters, you mean you received several today?" Pierre asked.

"Two of them, to be precise, but let's start with the first one."

He showed the first letter to Pierre and Charles, who, curious as to its contents, leant over his shoulder to read it at the same time. Pierre finished much faster, and looked at Armand questioningly.

"The Marquis seems to be very upset, well, I suppose this had to be expected, but why should this concern me – and what's your decision, will you leave us, do you want me to come with you?"

Armand didn't answer directly but handed them the second letter, commenting, "Now read this letter and then I'll answer all of your questions."

Pierre and Charles ploughed through the stream of motherly concerns and recommendation, totally puzzled by now.

"Armand, you're joking, this letter has nothing to do with me," Pierre exclaimed.

"Pierre, didn't I tell you before, my mother isn't really the caring type?" Armand said softly, "I suggest you become a little more sceptical and not take everything at face value if you really want to enter politics as a duke!"

Pierre answered hotly, "Don't play games with us, Armand, tell us straight, what's behind all of this?"

Armand raised his hands as if defending himself from Pierre's attack. "All right, I admit, a little too much drama, but it took me some time as well to understand what this was all about. Here I have the key to the mystery: this is the decrypted version of the second letter."

Like a conjuror he handed them the third document, explaining that his family had the habit of communicating in coded language, being aware that Richelieu and his agents would be checking all their correspondence.

"This third document has been written by myself, in fact I was working very hard during the time you were already stuffing yourself with delicacies in the dining room."

Pierre grinned. "Touché! We apologize for any indecent thoughts that might have crossed our minds… although our explanation seemed probable enough." Armand grinned back at him, thinking about the pleasant time he had spent before toiling at deciphering the letter and decided that it was probably best to drop the subject.

This time Pierre and Charles sat in mutual silence for some minutes, Pierre, because he had to digest the content of the letter first and Charles, because he had to fight with two obstacles: the decrypted version was not only in French but Armand's handwriting was simply appalling, not to mention the spots of ink liberally scattered across the page, making it hard to decipher the words.

Pierre was, of course, used to his friend's sprawling hieroglyphs and had seized the content of his father's true message almost immediately.

Looking at Armand with wide eyes he stammered, "Why would your father bother about me? I mean, why would he take the pains to write to you like this? It seems that he really cares for me, although he never even got to know me. Isn't it fantastic that he should have been as close to my father as I am to you now – and need I guess the 'evil one' to whom your father is alluding?"

"Yes, it seems too much of a coincidence, but apparently it's true that they were best friends. Your guess is right by the way, in our family 'the evil one' is our code name for Cardinal Richelieu."

Armand moved away from the globe, poured himself a good measure of the brandy of dubious origin and sat down in front of the two, watching them with alert eyes.

"The fact is, Pierre, you're in danger once more. Let me add just another point that's bothering me. I left my room to join you at table and suddenly remembered that I had forgotten the letters on my desk. I returned to my room and found one of Your Grace's numerous valets leaning over the desk. I had the impression that he was trying to snoop around. If this man hasn't been set by Richelieu on us, then my name is no longer Armand." He looked at his friend sitting motionless in his chair.

"I don't understand though, to be honest, what kind of game is Richelieu playing?" Armand continued. "Our family does not call him the 'evil one' just for fun; he is a truly dangerous enemy to have. I'm convinced that he set Henri on your trail – but what's the use of accusing you secretly in a court of heresy and proclaiming you a bastard?"

He looked at Charles to see if he had any idea, and indeed Charles answered immediately. "I'm not entirely sure, but it rings a bell. I remember a story about some relatives in Scotland, more than a hundred years ago. It was still under the reign of Mary, Queen of Scots; she was pushing hard for the Catholic cause, as you may remember. She once played with the idea of using the indictment of heresy to confiscate the estates and titles of her most recalcitrant lords. The idea was to distribute their estates to her faithful followers. I imagine Richelieu is playing a double game, setting Henri on Pierre to get rid of him and secretly moving forward to dispossess Pierre in favour of the Crown – or the Church – which is, I would guess, the same as his own personal interests."

Charles paused, and then continued, "I hate to admit it, but Richelieu seems to be a political genius; your father is entirely right to warn us. He is also right about Pierre's situation in England. Pierre's title has to be recognized by the King and by Parliament, as he's not a direct male heir. I have just heard that a new Parliament has been called – and this time the King has to make a big concession, and if you ask me, a foolish one – he'll regret it soon enough! He will no longer be able to dissolve Parliament at his sole request. The balance of power in this kingdom will shift from the King to the new mad men in Parliament and Pierre, you'll be facing strong headwinds."

Charles looked very worried now as he continued. "Parliament will be totally under the sway of the aggressive protestant roundheads; a new upstart called Cromwell is stirring up a lot of trouble. We must go to London and find support for Pierre before it's too late; if the Marquis de Saint Paul is correct, there's no time to lose!"

"All well and good," exclaimed Armand, "but where the hell shall we find the Templars? I thought they were all dead, buried and long forgotten. If I remember correctly their order was dissolved three hundred years ago! We're living in modern times, how can a medieval order help us? But if my father says that we need their support, there must be a reason, he's a clever old devil!"

Pierre was looking downcast from one friend to the other; they were busily discussing his fate, too busy actually to consider his wishes or his position. Leaving Hertford meant leaving Marie, and this seemed a high price to pay to become once more a pawn in the game of political chess that Richelieu or somebody mysterious was playing with him. He had enjoyed his stay here so much. Secretly he had to admit that he had enjoyed enormously playing the Duke and being important – but what had pleased him most had been the feeling for the first time in his life of belonging somewhere and having a real family, being able to put down roots.

However, before Pierre could finish his morose thoughts, Charles cleared his throat and started to speak. "Well, I suppose that I can be of service to you here. The Templars have, in the course of time, become clandestine brotherhoods, spread everywhere across Europe, passing on their secret wisdom from generation to generation. Here in England, after the reformation, they converted to a Masonic Lodge, and their Grand Master is based in London. Of course it's very hush-hush and strictly forbidden by the Government, and condemned by the Church of England under threat of excommunication. It happens though that Pierre's grandfather was a leading member, in fact we Neuvilles have been attached to the Templars in some way or other since the first of them joined King Richard the Lionheart in conquering the Holy Land. I was to be introduced and follow Pierre's grandfather when his failing health intervened – but it won't be difficult for me to arrange a meeting with the Grand Master as soon as we arrive in London as he knows and trusts our family."

Pierre and Armand looked at him in amazement. Pierre exclaimed, "Would you have any idea why they should be able or willing to help? Who is the Grand Master?"

Charles shook his head. "I'm sorry, I cannot disclose to you the identity of our Grand Master without his prior consent. For the rest, I have no idea at all! I'm as puzzled as you are. I know that they still have enormous influence at court and in

Parliament, and this could certainly help to solve Pierre's problems here, but how they come into the picture regarding the issues your father raised which threaten Pierre's French heritage, I must admit, that's a complete mystery to me!"

"In any case, I think we're all in agreement that we have to leave for London as soon as possible, even if I can see that Pierre doesn't like the idea, in fact he looks as if he hates the thought of leaving Hertford," concluded Armand, summing up the discussion.

Pierre flinched but knew of course that Armand was right and he nodded in agreement, even if he loathed the idea of leaving Marie and his new home.

"Let's prepare everything this week then," Charles concluded. "Armand's story about this obscure valet must be taken very seriously in the light of this letter but we can't possibly hide our departure – on the contrary we'll need to prepare Hertford House in London and Pierre has to arrive there in style with all the pomp befitting his rank. We must not leave the smallest room for any doubt or rumour that his claim to the title could be questionable. He has to arrive like the true Duke with an army of footmen and servants, expensive clothes, loaded with jewellery, splashing money around to create groups of staunch supporters, first at court and later in Parliament. You'll need to lose a small fortune at the gaming tables – but lose it to the right persons, and I'll guide you."

He looked at Pierre and laughed when he saw his reaction and unhappy look. "Come on, don't make faces! The time of hunting, comfortable boots and worn breeches is finished, wake up, Your Grace! It's silk, velvet and lace now, fancy dinners, no more cosy picnics with Marie! How glad I am that it's no longer my duty to play the Duke!"

Seeing Pierre's miserable face he continued, "Let us organize a farewell party with the ladies at Sevens and invite them over for a day. And Arthur of course," he added lamely.

"I am fairly certain that our ladies will move to London shortly after us," Armand said, in an obvious effort to console Pierre. "I simply don't see our glamorous Principessa residing in the countryside with no more diversion than dining with the drab local squires. She'll be back in London in no time, believe me!"

Pierre's reaction was amusing; his eyes, which had lost their entire lustre while Charles had painted a daunting picture of his new life waiting for him in London, suddenly started to gleam and he participated in an animated conversation with Charles planning a sumptuous invitation for their friends.

To the great surprise of the servants, all valets and footmen were called forward the next morning to present themselves to Armand and Pierre but the strange valet who had been discovered in Armand's bedroom couldn't be identified. Charles looked grim; this was no coincidence! He was quite sure now that an agent of Richelieu had been planted among them. Consequently he was quite keen to leave for London and try to find out why the Marquis de Saint Paul proposed meeting the Grand Master of the Templar's Lodge – it seemed very mysterious.

But if they were to do battle with the ingenious Cardinal Richelieu, they would need powerful allies, there could be no doubt of that.

A MONK IN LONDON

The groom requesting humble passage through the London city gates had a nondescript face, and was dressed soberly in dark colours with dark cropped hair as had become the latest fashion. Many Protestants living in rural England demonstrated their contempt for the colourful, corrupt and sinful aristocracy and a King who had never been able to reach the hearts of his subjects, by wearing the clothes and hairstyle of the Puritans.

To any passer-by he looked like any one of those who were swelling the ranks of the supporters of the new strong men in Parliament. The city was buzzing with expectation. King Charles, desperately needing money to avoid bankruptcy after his failed bishops' war, had at last given in to pressure. The King had called a second Parliament that would certainly sit for a long time, its members willing to fight for real power – they were no longer ready to play the submissive lapdogs of his Majesty.

Expectation of change – some even murmured about revolution – was tangible everywhere. The proud King, who had wanted to establish absolute monarchy like his French brother-in-law, had not only failed miserably, but was desperately clinging to the last threads of his former power.

The groom reached the street leading to the French embassy without any further delay, ignoring the tempting smells of the food stalls and skilfully navigating through the dense traffic and the labyrinth of cobbled streets. Luckily the distance from Hertford Castle to London was easy to cover in a single day, and he rode comfortably onwards without hurrying, as he didn't want to attract any undue attention.

What a provincial city, he thought, sending a condescending glance over the crowded streets and small houses that were crouched close to one of the many churches he had passed on his way. Only the new Covent Garden district with its Italian style arcades could dare to compare with – but never ever live up to – the impressive buildings that Paris and other cities in France had to offer. Even the royal palace was an old and sinister place, where the unhappy sister of King Louis XIII spent her miserable days, bound in marriage to a King who chased every woman that came close to him, surrounded by hypocrite heretics who hated her.

Looking carefully around in order not to be caught by a protestant zealot, the groom spat contemptuously in front of the small Anglican church he passed on his way. He felt personally insulted, a former sacred Catholic church had been desecrated to serve this abominable heretic cult of the Protestants. What a joy to be back soon in France where the Great Cardinal had defeated the heretics and the true faith would soon become the sole religion allowed in the kingdom. He sighed with joyful anticipation; only a few days more in this depressing country and he'd be back in civilization.

His arrival was expected and he was ushered immediately into the office of his superior, a monk and intimate of the great Cardinal, waiting impatiently for his return. The false groom knew that his superior wanted his reports to be precise but concise and limited his narrative to the essential points. The monk listened with full concentration, only his eyes betraying his keen interest.

"You're absolutely sure that the Duke will leave for London soon?"

The false groom nodded. "I'm absolutely sure; this letter must have contained a code because I noticed some notes written apparently by Armand de Saint Paul himself, the ink was still fresh. I was just about to start reading them, when unluckily Armand de Saint Paul returned. But I could decipher the words 'leave for London immediately' and 'danger for Pierre'. Later I heard the butler talking with the private valet of His Grace, sorry I meant the imposter, that he wouldn't be surprised if we'd be leaving for Hertford House in London shortly." The groom opened his pocket and with great care produced a document that had been stored safely inside. "I have also been able to procure for you a document in the handwriting and with the latest signature of Pierre de Beauvoir as you had instructed me to do."

The monk drummed his fingers on the oak desk, his face still showing full concentration while he scanned the document that the groom had placed in front of him. He looked at the groom and suddenly a smile transformed his ascetic face. "You have done a remarkable job, my Brother, I therefore grant you permission to return to your monastery in France and will recommend you personally to my friend, the abbot."

The false groom bowed thankfully, taking care not to betray any pleasure at this unusual praise. A monk had to be modest and never indulge in the sin of pride; he had learned this essential lesson early on.

As soon as the false groom had left, his superior decided to see Henri de Beauvoir immediately. If the spy was correct in his assumptions, they'd need to act immediately. It was time to place the cat among the pigeons.

213

A CAT AMONG THE PIGEONS

The day had been cold and rainy, a miserable day, like so many lately. November in England was always depressing, Aunt Carlotta had already told her. Marie sighed; the rain had been pouring down for days now, gushing down the gutters, creating deep pools of water everywhere in the garden. Their garden, so beautiful and inviting still in autumn, had lost its glorious lustre under the constant onslaught of cold winds and rain. Gusts of wind were rattling the window panes at Sevens, dead leaves in doleful brown and morbid yellow were floating in the muddy streams of water that flowed like tiny rivers in the garden. The daylight was all but obliterated by the grey, menacing sky. The once beautiful trees had been stripped down to pitiful naked skeletons, gone and forgotten their lush green of summer.

The ladies had gone to bed early that evening. The heavy winds made the fires in the living room smoke profusely producing anaemic bluish flames that fought against the cold draughts to no avail. The terrible weather had been a fitting backdrop to their states of mind. Armand had been chosen to be the bearer of bad news and had come over to inform Arthur and the ladies that they'd need to leave for London almost immediately. His invitation to join them for a last dinner party in Hertford Castle couldn't console anybody; they all understood immediately that the relaxed period of casual visits and easy friendship was going to end.

They had all put on a brave face and comprehended the urgency as soon as Armand had explained the content of his father's letter – at least those parts that he deemed safe to disclose to them. They maintained this attitude towards each other, even once Armand had returned to Hertford, assuring themselves that they would meet again soon in London, depicting most vividly the delights and festivities that would be waiting for them at court, but somehow their tone was false and only enhanced the morose atmosphere.

After dinner they had all pretended to be particularly tired, nobody having any desire to prolong a spoilt day by playing cards, or listening to Céline dutifully playing the clavichord for the Principessa, who loved music and often felt nostalgic, longing to be back in Italy where during meals musicians would play merry songs in praise of love and beauty.

Marie woke up in the middle of the night; why, she couldn't really tell. She lay in her bed, curtains closed to keep the cold air out, her mind curiously wide awake, her body still tired. Trying to go back to sleep she tried to remember her mother's advice: "Always think about something nice, my girl," she had used to say, hugging her and humming softly into her ear whenever Marie had cried out for her, waking up after a nightmare or a bad dream.

Suddenly she longed to have her mother beside her, to be able to share her feelings about Pierre and to appease her anxieties – what would happen to him in

London? Panic started to engulf her; how on earth would Pierre be able to escape confrontation with his ruthless cousin?

Marie started to perspire with trepidation; men were so stupid! If Henri challenged him to a duel, Pierre would definitely accept and be killed – this was the gentleman's accepted code of honour. Or Pierre might meet a beautiful lady at court, with the right connections and ancestry to suit a Duke, polished and sophisticated, not a simple girl like her from the French provinces.

The curtains that were meant to protect her suddenly looked stifling and menacing. Marie had to get out of her bed; she desperately needed to get some fresh air or she would go mad. Groping for her slippers, she slid out of bed and rushed to the window. Even if it was cold outside, she needed to breathe!

Fumbling with the latch, she managed to tear open the window overlooking the garden and the borders of the dense woods that stretched all the way from Sevens to Hertford. Marie didn't really expect to see anything but darkness, as during the past nights the moonlight had been completely swallowed by the thick clouds. Opening the window pane and peeking out, she gasped with surprise. The garden had been completely transformed into a ghostly scene, strange and menacing, aggravating, not alleviating, the agitated state of her nerves.

The clouds had been ripped apart into the strangest of patterns, black tatters floating in the sky, chased by a ghoulish wind. The full moon shone brightly, pale silvery light pouring across the wet landscape. The puddles of water that dotted the garden mirrored the eerie moonlight. Marie gave a shudder. Under the pale, cold light they resembled dead, sightless eyes. Marie looked at the eerie scenery, her skin turning to gooseflesh.

Barn owls screeched in the darkness – whether they were hunting or looking for mates, Marie didn't know and didn't care, but their piercing cry was haunting and frightening. Hadn't her nurse told her that owls were the restless souls of the condemned, buried in eternal sin without the blessings of the Church?

Marie slammed her window shut and fled back to her bed which suddenly looked warm and inviting, a safe haven. But it took her considerable time to sink into an uneasy slumber; a feeling of foreboding had firmly settled upon her. The next morning, still tired, she awoke with a strange and unpleasant notion of anxiety.

Her aunt was already sitting in the cosy breakfast room chatting with Céline about the programme for today. The room was lit by the sun, the clouds and the wind had disappeared. When she looked up and saw Marie's haggard face she exclaimed, "Good Lord, Marie, are you ill, my dear? You look ghastly!"

Marie answered that she was absolutely fine but her statement was met with a glance of total disbelief from both ladies and she was gently made to accept a cup of this new and exotic steaming drink that Aunt Carlotta had brought with her, called chocolate, the latest fashion in chic Paris.

"You must try it, it is most delicious and will bring the colour back to your lovely cheeks in no time!" the Principessa told her, while she lovingly patted a cushion waiting to be placed behind Marie's back.

"Don't spoil me, dearest Aunt!" Marie protested, but to no avail. Her aunt's motherly instincts prevailed. Aunt Carlotta not only made her drink the chocolate, but Marie also had to eat some bread to show her aunt that she was a good girl and feeling much better. Marie first made a face when she swallowed the first sip of hot chocolate; it had an extremely bitter taste. When she grimaced, her aunt added generous amounts of honey and the taste became bearable, even delicious once she had got used to it.

Céline watched the scene with amusement, happy not to be at the centre of Aunt Carlotta's administrations but the closer she looked at Marie, the more Céline started to worry whether something was amiss. After breakfast she proposed to Marie to profit from the spell of sunshine and accompany her for a short walk in the gardens. Marie was glad to accept; she still felt queasy, a sentiment that was difficult to describe, a brooding sense of unease that had settled upon her and wouldn't fade away, although she had to admit that the chocolate had done her good. They agreed to meet in front of the door in a quarter of an hour, taking the time to change into some more comfortable and warmer dresses, as it was still very wet and cold outside, despite the rays of the late autumn sun that made the water steam and made small clouds of mist hover above the lawn.

Marie closed the heavy door when she stepped out of the house and she greedily inhaled the crisp fresh air, laden with the autumnal scents of decaying wet grass, the damp smells of the nearby forest mingled with an acrid note of the charcoal and wood fires that were burning day and night inside the house. She walked down the flight of sandstone stairs to the gravel-covered driveway that crunched under her shoes, totally lost in her thoughts.

Small wonder that she was utterly startled when she looked up and all of a sudden a groom, wearing the livery of the Duke of Hertford, materialized in front of her. Marie couldn't remember having heard the noise of any horse or coach approaching the driveway. The groom had a boyish freckled face with reddish hair. He bowed reverently towards her, holding an envelope in his hand as he started to speak to her.

"My lady, please accept my apologies for disturbing you. His Grace, the Duke of Hertford, has sent me to bring this urgent message to your personal attention. My lady may be kind enough to remember my face from your last visit to Hertford Castle. His Grace requests the favour of an immediate answer and has asked me to wait here until my lady might have the kindness to read the message and give her reply."

216

Bowing deeply once more he handed the folded and sealed document to Marie and then withdrew some paces so as to let her read the message in private. Marie was stunned; what could be so urgent to induce Pierre to send her a message so early this morning when they had been invited to come to Hertford tomorrow? Nervously she removed the seal with the familiar coat of arms she had seen so often lately, depicting three proud stags with a cross. She unfolded the letter and read:

Chère Marie, mon amour, mon cœur,

Please accept my apologies for taking the liberty to send you this letter. I have learnt yesterday that I cannot leave for London. I have to return immediately to France for matters of the greatest importance linked to my heritage. Marie, my love, I cannot face leaving without having seen you once more. Please meet me this afternoon when the clock strikes two. This is my greatest wish. I shall come alone to the chapel at the road leading from Sevens to London, you know the place, close to the house. Please also come alone, I need to see you, the thought of having to leave you soon is breaking my heart. In eternal love, yours forever.

Marie could barely read the end of the letter, tears were streaming from her eyes. She stared at Pierre's signature; how proud he was, to sign his name thus. She stood there, trying to recover her composure, when she heard the groom clearing his throat and asking, "My lady, what answer may I give to my master?"

Marie stared at the groom as if she were seeing him for the first time, and fighting for words she just uttered, "Yes, just tell him, yes, I'll be there," and she abruptly turned to run towards the garden and be on her own, drowning in tears and misery.

*****

Céline was bustling down the staircase towards the door. She was late, as she had been fighting with the many buttons on her overcoat, and the buttons had won. The top button had expressed its wish for liberty by popping out of the button hole and had rolled under the cupboard. As the buttons were made from precious mother of pearl, Céline had sighed and crept along the floor until she had located the fugitive button and had fixed it with needle and thread firmly back into position; she was still in the habit of doing such tasks herself. Therefore she wasn't really surprised that Marie wasn't waiting for her outside the door and assumed that she must have decided to walk out into the garden.

Navigating carefully around the muddy puddles in the alleys she discovered Marie, sitting forlornly on a bench, a small vulnerable child. When she approached Marie she realized that she had been crying, her eyes still swollen and red. Céline sat down silently next to Marie, deliberately ignoring the fact that the bench was still wet from yesterday's heavy rains. She took Marie in her arms and gently rocked her like a baby saying softly, "I can guess why you're crying, my darling, you're afraid that we won't see Pierre very often once he is living in London – or that you might lose him altogether. I can assure you, I have rarely seen someone so much in love, you really don't need to worry, my dear."

Marie sat still, trying to regain her composure. She was very much tempted to tell Céline about the letter and its contents that had hit her like a bombshell. But Pierre had written in confidence, she couldn't betray him. Marie was also realistic enough to know that Céline would have forbidden her to leave and meet Pierre on her own; this kind of behaviour was against all propriety and she had accompanied her in order to protect and chaperon her. As she desperately wanted to see Pierre, Marie kept silent, although she would have loved to talk with Céline, who had become like a sister to her. She tried to muster a brave smile and just nodded.

"I'll be all right," Marie answered finally, swallowing her last tears and putting on a bright face, but failing miserably to convince her friend. Céline went up and took out her scarf in order to dry the tears on Marie's face. Marie closed her eyes and enjoyed the soft touch of the scarf as Céline dabbed her tears.

Céline hesitated for a second; she had detected a crumpled piece of paper that looked like a letter poking out of Marie's pocket. She was immediately on the alert. When Marie had left the breakfast room she had looked haggard. This had seemed perfectly normal and not alarming after a bad night's sleep, but now she was definitely shattered. Something serious must have happened; this piece of paper could be the key to the mystery.

Céline's thoughts raced through her mind as she kept a flow of non-committal and soothing conversation going. She decided that she couldn't do anything immediately without losing Marie's confidence but she'd watch Marie closely; every fibre of Céline's body told her that something sinister was going on, but she couldn't really work out yet what and why.

The young ladies went back into the house and, bowing to the concerns of her aunt, who apparently had decided that she wanted to pamper her, Marie agreed to a large drink of mulled claret. Having dutifully finished her glass of hot wine she declared that she felt so sleepy that she needed to retreat to her room – probably until the early evening.

Marie, feeling slightly dizzy from the wine, then fled upstairs into her room, locked the door and threw herself onto the bed, letting her tears stream once more freely and bathing in her misery.

*****

Céline sat in her chair in the salon that faced the garden. She was still pondering how best to approach Marie and make Marie confide in her when she suddenly remembered that she had promised one of the tenants living on a farm close to Sevens to bring him a poultice. This poultice was a secret recipe from her mother, one of the few things she had inherited from her in fact. It was made from goose fat and some pretty unsavoury ingredients with plenty of herbs to cover the disgusting smell, but it seemed to help.

During a recent visit to the village she had discovered that a tenant's wife had developed problems with her swollen knee and she had offered him to try her mother's special poultice. It seemed that her remedy had worked miracles. Timidly he had thanked her and asked her if she would have the kindness to prepare a second time this miracle cure for him before she left, as word had spread that they might be returning to London. She had gladly accepted his request, happy to know that she had been able to help his wife. The poultice had been ready for several days but as the weather had been simply dreadful she hadn't found the courage to go out.

As there was no more excuse for the delay, she decided to honour her promise and leave after lunch. She went into the kitchen to tell cook to prepare the poultice for the tenant and an early light lunch for three as Marie would be staying in her room.

Lunch was an unusually quiet affair. Everybody seemed to be harbouring some secret thoughts and concerns, and consequently the flow of conversation was patchy and artificial. The Principessa wasn't really surprised to hear that Marie had retreated to her bedroom. "Well, she most definitely looked dreadful this morning, poor dear," was all she said, comforted by the thought that Marie had at least accepted the mulled wine before going to sleep.

After lunch Céline grabbed her coat, but the sun was now shining more powerfully and soon she regretted having chosen her thick winter coat. A maid followed her dutifully with a basket containing not only the poultice but also a bottle of wine she had wrenched from the unwilling butler, who had greatly disliked the idea of wasting his good wine on unworthy peasants.

*****

Marie waited impatiently in her room; she had no idea of the exact time, as the only clocks in Sevens were downstairs – a simple guest room didn't contain one of these expensive mechanical miracles. She lay on her bed and had to judge from the familiar clattering noises of lunch downstairs approximately when one o'clock was approaching, the time she had fixed for herself to set off to meet Pierre. This would leave her ample time, as the chapel was only located about fifteen minutes' walk from Sevens, but for nothing in the world did she want to be late, as every second spent with Pierre was precious.

The creaking noises of someone moving up the central staircase (hopefully after having finished their lunch) meant that soon the ground floor would be deserted. She therefore decided that it was time to get up and get prepared. When

219

Marie looked in the mirror, her face was flushed and swollen and she flinched. This was not the face she wanted to show to Pierre. If she was suffering, he shouldn't know – or at least, not how much! She splashed cold water from a jug into the basin and patted her face, relishing the soothing effect of the cool liquid. She brushed her hair and chose a gown in pink, a colour that would be a perfect match to her brown curls and her wonderful amber eyes. The gown had drawn many admiring glances already and would most probably be ruined afterwards by the long walk in the damp weather but she couldn't care less, she wanted to look her best when she met Pierre.

She unlatched the door and opened it just a crack, peeping into the long corridor that linked her room with the main staircase. To her great relief, the house was totally silent. She knew that her aunt loved to have an extensive siesta, 'just a short nap', after lunch. There was no sign of Céline; maybe she had left for a short stroll in the garden. Marie still had to be careful and must avoid Arthur and the servants, therefore she tiptoed to the back of the building, preferring to try the servants' staircase and leave the house via the back entrance. Once again she was lucky; even the servants' quarters lay dormant. She could only guess that they were still lingering in the kitchen, trying to convince the cook to be more generous in sharing out the remaining desserts.

Marie slipped out of the door, quickly hurrying across the driveway. The dense scrub stretching from the manor to the gatehouse made a perfect screen to hide her.

Once more she had to be extremely careful. The gatehouse was guarded by a huge dog, known to bark often and loudly. But her luck held, the dog came close, curious and ready to attack, but soon enough he recognized Marie and his growling changed to a friendly whimper. He nudged her to remind Marie that he loved to be stroked. Marie obliged him and patted the dog's head, then she rubbed his belly, to his great pleasure and delight, making him roll on his back, stretching his paws in the air in ecstasy.

Nobody noticed this incident and once this obstacle had been overcome, she quickly ran to the main road that led to Hertford and took the direction of the chapel that Pierre had referred to in his letter.

*****

Céline arrived at the tenant's farm accompanied by her maid, creating as much uproar as if royalty had arrived. She had learned some basic English since she had settled at Sevens but communication was still difficult, especially since she had great problems understanding the thick accent of the peasants. This didn't, however, impede the efforts of her hosts to make a tremendous display of gratitude, sitting her down in the only chair in the kitchen that looked as if it wouldn't break at any moment. If Céline wasn't mistaken, the small kitchen served at the same time as a living room and also as a bedroom for a bunch of the youngest children, a family of ducks, a dog, and other valuable members of the household. Luckily the pigs she heard grunting outside were not allowed to join in.

Her maid saw Céline's eyes growing larger and larger and decided that it was time to come to Céline's rescue.

She uttered several phrases in the local dialect which apparently brought her hosts to their senses; it sounded as if two of the dirtiest children had been admonished, as they disappeared. Céline then heard a faint sound of splashing water outside in the courtyard; the maid must have made some acerbic comments about their cleanliness. Serving as an interpreter she explained that the tenants wanted to express their immense gratitude. They had to admit that they had been very sceptical at the beginning. The knee of their hostess had been hurting badly and not knowing what to do, they had already consulted the local wise woman. Physicians – of course – wouldn't look after the poor people.

Céline was impressed and saw that her hostess was gesticulating wildly, apparently very upset.

"What is she saying?" Céline demanded, fascinated by the spectacle.

The maid smiled and continued to translate. "The wise woman came and demanded a chicken as payment before she'd start. She brought a dark potion and made some magic signs above the swollen knee. But nothing helped. The farmer's wife demanded her chicken back because she was still in pain, but the woman just replied that her charms hadn't worked because the farmer had given her the the eldest chicken and that the meat had been so tough, she had been obliged to feed it to her dogs."

Céline listened, intrigued and impressed that she was apparently now rated higher than the village wise woman. Her hostess continued in her broad accent and the maid translated.

"She admits that the chicken was a bit old, but the woman had never asked for a young one and even an old chicken still makes a good soup! Later, Will, that's her husband, brought her your poultice but told her that it had been prepared by a foreign lady, so – even if she's ashamed to admit it now – she was very scared."

Céline saw in fascination how the farmer's wife rolled her eyes to underline how frightened she had been.

"Her mother had always told her that foreigners were worse than wise women and witches."

The maid continued but with a broad smile now. "Not knowing what to do, she decided to test the poultice first on her goat, which was very complicated, as the goat licked at the poultice all the time! Their only goat also had some pain in one leg, was walking with difficulty, giving less milk every day, and then the miracle happened – the poultice cured her!"

Céline's hostess now beamed at her with delight and the maid continued.

"Therefore she decided to use it for herself and now her own knee has improved greatly. The reason why she has asked for a second box was that she had the feeling that she and the goat could use some more."

Céline nearly burst out laughing; it was simply too funny! She managed to keep a straight face, but the maid understood perfectly what she was thinking and with laughing eyes she added, "These people here are very superstitious, but now your reputation will spread. A goat is very precious in the country; if she has to choose between using your poultice for the goat or for herself, she'll probably give it to the goat as they need the milk for the children and the pigs."

The two children reappeared, faces and hands scrubbed clean. Proudly they offered a true treasure to their guest: a basket of apples, polished to perfection, shining red and yellow. Céline protested; she didn't want to take something as precious from a poor family but her maid whispered to her that she'd have to accept otherwise they'd be offended. They needed to express their gratitude and couldn't accept her gifts without giving something in exchange. Céline understood the reasoning and accepted the apples, and even ate one of them on the spot – watched by the whole family. She noticed the satisfaction in their eyes; they were happy to see that she liked and appreciated their precious gift.

Soon it was time to leave and as John, their eldest son who worked as a groom in the neighbourhood, had just arrived with his master's hunting horse, Will and his wife insisted that he accompany Céline and her maid back to Sevens.

Céline was still smiling as they walked along the road. What a pity that her mother would never know that her famous poultice worked on humans and goats! They had to walk slowly and carefully, as the road was studded with muddy puddles of water that had formed in the many potholes, sometimes deep and treacherous. All the same, Céline felt happy; this had been a hilarious experience and she was satisfied that she been truly able to help.

*****

Marie had arrived at the old, whitewashed chapel. Nervously she noticed that the door stood slightly ajar. She pushed it open, its rusted hinges squeaking frightfully in protest. The inside of the chapel was almost completely dark, with only a small, smoky flame flickering in front of a crudely painted statue of the crowned Virgin holding firmly to an unwilling child. Marie's eyes took some time to adjust to the obscure lighting until she could finally discern two rows of rough wooden benches and a small altar with a simple painted wooden cross. The chapel was deserted, but Marie wasn't surprised as she had deliberately come too early. She walked towards the statue of the Virgin Mary and sank down on her knees, crossing herself, praying fervently to her Saint to give her strength.

After her prayer she sat down on the uncomfortable bench in front of the altar, listening to the noises outside, but no horse arrived.

Marie heard the noises of the wind, the rustling of the fir trees that surrounded the chapel and the desolate cries of black crows she had seen circling above the empty fields. She started to feel the damp and cold inside the chapel, as her dress had been chosen for beauty, not for comfort. The cold air was rapidly creeping through the thin silk and her hands were freezing. By now she felt totally miserable, longing to see Pierre as soon as possible – and dreading their encounter at the same time, as it might be the last time; at best he'd be absent for months, at worst, maybe years. She had to fight back her tears as all the dark thoughts of the night before resurfaced like a black wave, trying to crush her with all their might. Marie suddenly realized how lucky she had been until now; only today did she understand that life could be very cruel.

Marie didn't know how long she had been sitting and waiting there, hunched on the uncomfortable bench, when she heard the noise of snickering horses and the iron-rimmed wheels of a coach or carriage rattling on the road. Her fist reaction was joy but then disappointment; it couldn't be Pierre as he had written explicitly that he'd come on his own. She was therefore astonished when the wheels ground to a halt. She heard voices, shouting commands at the horses and the faint noise of the opening of a carriage door. Pierre must have changed his mind, but most important, he had come! Marie leaped up from the bench, back and legs hurting from her long wait – but she didn't care!

She hastened to the door and out of the chapel to meet Pierre. Her eyes coming from the dark, needed to adapt to the sudden daylight but she could make out the shape of his slender figure and his bright blond hair. With a cry of joy she raced forward, her silk gown flying behind her like a triumphant flag. Only when she was about to fly into his arms, did she suddenly stop, frozen with horror.

The slender and sleek figure moving in her direction was none other than Henri, Pierre's cousin. Her first reaction was to bolt and run but Henri had not come on his own; several armed footmen had gathered around her in a menacing circle, rendering any idea of escape impossible.

"What a nice welcome, my dearest Mademoiselle de Montjoie," drawled Henri with exaggerated politeness. "Please do come closer, I'm so pleased at this surprise meeting with you here. Well, let's be frank, it's not really a surprise. By the way, did you like our nice little letter, I put a lot of effort into writing it?" His eyes shone ironically. He was clearly relishing the situation.

Marie's mind went blank, overwhelmed by panic, then she followed her first instincts. She started yelling at the top of her voice 'Help!' in French – *Au secours!* – repeating her cry several times until Henri reacted, jumping forward and covering her mouth with his hand, pressing hard until he hurt her.

They stood like this for some time, Marie fighting to get out of this iron grip, two pairs of eyes fighting with each other, one furious, one excited.

223

Marie's panic had finally subsided, but she was ready to fight. She stopped yelling and pretended to become docile. Henri still held her but finally let his hand relax. Marie had been waiting for this reaction and with all of her force she bit into his hand until she felt her teeth strike bone. She was disgusted and satisfied at the same time by the taste of his blood that ran over her tongue.

Henri cursed – *Merde!* – and instinctively withdrew his hand. Marie profited from the confusion and started yelling again. It took some time until the startled servants finally reacted, and even Henri was shocked, sucking the blood from his wound. Following the orders that Henri was shouting whilst simultaneously cursing Marie and the idiotic servants, the footmen went into action and bundled Marie into the waiting coach, but nobody dared to cover her mouth. Marie was still yelling when the whole cavalcade left the scene, speeding down the road towards London.

*****

Céline was watching some noisy black crows crossing above her when she heard a faint cry, repeated once or twice. She stopped talking with her maid, trying to listen, straining her ears to detect from where the cry had come and who could be in distress. Again she heard a scream, this time a more audible '*Au secours!*', giving Céline goosebumps – only Marie would cry for help in French.

Her blood froze and she thought her heart would stop beating. John indicated that the cry had come from the end of the road that they were about to take.

"Take me on your horse, John," Céline demanded, "we have to get there as fast as possible!" and turning to her maid she continued, "Please run behind us as fast as you can!"

John didn't know how it happened but in no time Céline was up on the horse behind him and they were galloping towards the road that he had indicated. The yelling had suddenly stopped, sending shivers of fear down Céline's spine. When they approached the road, making a slight turn to the right, the yelling and screaming had started again, this time much more forceful and very close. Céline made a sign for John to stop. They had a clear view of the chapel now and she discovered that a coach drawn by four horses was standing in front of it. Marie – dressed in her favourite pink outfit – was fighting with a blond man. Céline didn't need to be a *savant* to understand immediately that Henri had laid a trap for Marie and was abducting her. Her heart fell when she saw that Marie was surrounded by at least six armed bandits. Her mind was racing: any wrong decision could be lethal for Marie.

It seemed clear to Céline that attacking them with John's assistance might be a noble deed but essentially would be totally stupid: there was nothing that she or John could do against so many armed men right now to save Marie. She made a sign to John to stay quiet and they hid behind the dense shrubbery where they had

224

dismounted. Her mind was racing: how could they organize help and follow them at the same time?

She watched Marie and Henri and saw a sudden commotion, she must have done something as Henri withdrew his hand with a sudden movement and she started yelling again.

You're a brave girl, Marie, she thought, full of admiration. But when she heard Henri shouting orders, Céline knew that time was running out, and they were about to leave. An idea flashed through her mind. She turned to John, yanking out her red scarf and whispered to him what to do. John nodded and as soon as the coach had gathered speed, accompanied by the armed cavalcade of bandits, John followed with his horse, careful to stay out of sight. He was to follow the coach and find out where the coach was heading to.

Puffing like a chimney, Céline's maid had arrived in the meantime, fright and panic in her face. She had a quick mind and had immediately understood what was going on.

"Sorry, that I can't let you rest," Céline shouted while they started moving. "We must get back to Sevens as fast as possible and alert Arthur, we need all the help we can possibly get!"

And so they set off for the manor house, part walking, part running, as fast as possible, that is, as fast as their long skirts and the bad road allowed them, hoping and praying desperately to find Arthur there. Céline prayed that he hadn't gone out to visit his neighbours or hunt rabbits, as it was the first dry day after a week of nearly constant rain.

They were still labouring forward on the bumpy road and Céline kept a look out for treacherous potholes. During one of the short intervals she looked up, suddenly spotting the silhouette of a horseman galloping at full speed towards them. Céline considered for a short second running and hiding but the horseman was too fast, and apparently he had seen them already.

Her initial anxiety changed to sheer joy when the silhouette grew bigger and bigger and the sight of Charles's impressive figure became clearly discernible. She cried out with joy and relief.

"Charles, Charles, you're my gift from heaven! I need your help, oh, I'm so glad that you've come!" Sobbing and crying at the same time she continued, "Marie has been abducted by Henri, you known, Pierre's evil cousin, I can't even bear to think what he's going to do to her," and the tears streamed down her cheeks, as all the tension she had been holding back until now seemed to be finally released.

Charles stopped immediately and looked down at her, bewildered and extremely worried. "Calm down, Céline, tell me exactly what has happened!" he

225

said in his deep and reassuring voice and Céline explained to him in rapid words the scene she had witnessed. Céline couldn't say if it was the effect of Charles's soothing voice or just the fact that she knew he'd deal with the problem calmly, but slowly she started to relax and was able to recover her senses. Charles had now dismounted and was walking at her side. They had already reached the entrance of Sevens when Céline had finished telling him the last details. Charles now looked even more worried.

"How shall we ever find Marie," he said. "It was an excellent idea of yours to ask John to follow them, but how on earth will we know where they went and by the time he gets back to tell us, it may be..." Here he stopped, biting his tongue and swallowing the rest of his words, hoping fervently that Céline hadn't noticed his lapse. But of course, she had noticed it.

"Before it's too late, you wanted to say! Oh Charles, I know, even I don't want to think about it, we simply must find her today, I'm nearly out of my mind, but I'm not stupid. I gave John my red scarf and he'll rip it up. At every crossroads or change of direction he'll fix a piece of it as a sign for us! Just give me time to find Arthur and we'll get going."

"You're remarkable!" Charles said, his eyes warm with admiration. "But I'll go with Arthur, you be a good girl and stay here. It's far too dangerous for you to get involved. This cousin is a real monster."

Céline didn't reply and while Charles was entering the manor house in order to find Arthur she rushed to the stables to get her horse ready; she would accompany Charles, whether he wanted her to or not!

Some minutes later she met Charles, who was looking angry and very frustrated.

"That idiot of a butler took ages to tell me that Arthur went hunting, your aunt is out and neither is expected back until sunset. I can't afford to wait and lose precious time. I have no choice, I'll just ride with a groom."

He went outside and saw the second horse waiting next to his, loaded with an impressive looking musket.

"Whose horse is this?" he asked curiously.

"Mine!" replied Céline belligerently, "and don't look at me like that. I'm not one of these frail salon beauties you might admire but who aren't good for anything and I'm not going to use one of these fancy ladies' saddles if we have to ride fast on these terrible roads. My father taught me to shoot when I was a small girl. Don't worry, I'm a good shot, he used to slap me whenever I missed. I have sworn to her mother to look after Marie and nobody, not even you, no matter how tall you are, will deter me, is this clear?"

226

Her eyes blazed at him and Charles had to laugh. "Touché! I give in, but the day we are married I'll give you the right response to this abuse, my lady!"

Now it was Céline's turn to be silent, and trying to hide the deep colour in her cheeks she pretended not to have heard his last comment. They mounted the horses, and in no time they were gone, shouting from the saddle the last instructions to Céline's maid to inform Arthur and his mother as soon as they returned to send an urgent messenger to Hertford for Pierre.

Marie felt terrible. In the beginning she had experienced fear, shock, and an immense feeling of grief when the blonde man approaching her had turned out to be Henri and not Pierre.

What a dreadful feeling of humiliation! She had been stupid enough to enter this trap, to become a prisoner at the mercy of remorseless villains! There had been a moment when she had feared being crushed, and had just wanted to give up and die. But Marie was tough. A hot wave of anger and hate had been washing over her, keeping her sane, helping her to muster the courage to fight and bite with all her strength into the detestable hand that had covered her mouth.

Here she was sitting now, or more precisely lying helpless, in a corner of the rattling coach, her hands strapped with leather straps. She groaned, her stomach threatening revolt at any minute. She didn't know if it was the revulsion she felt when she saw this beast of a cousin sitting with a complacent smirk on his arrogant face in front of her or the mulled wine she had drunk earlier to please her aunt. It seemed ages ago that she had been sitting with Céline and her aunt in the cosy breakfast room, a safe, sheltered and privileged world now gone to pieces.

How stupid had she been to trust this letter! She should have known Pierre so much better; never would he have asked her for a secret rendezvous. She had been so naïve, and this loathsome reptile of a cousin had taken advantage of her inexperience and her boundless stupidity.

Henri looked at her and started to speak. "You're a little wild cat, but I like women wild and full of passion. Mostly they're too tame, but you'll be fun, I can feel that now!"

Marie couldn't answer as she was scared of vomiting as soon as she opened her mouth; she just looked at Henri, her eyes blazing scornfully at him.

"You don't know what to say?" he continued in a sarcastic tone, but now she could detect excitement in his voice and she became even more disgusted – if this was possible.

Henri continued, "I'll share my little secrets with you now and tell you all the wonderful things that are waiting for you. Tonight we'll have a romantic dinner *à deux* in a secluded hunting lodge, followed by a nice little wedding that will be conducted by a French priest, who, well… let's say, just happened to be in England. I found this rather convenient, indeed."

Once more she saw his smirking arrogant face and decided that if ever she managed to kill him, his would be a slow and painful death.

Henri continued. "Afterwards we'll retreat into our bedroom and I'll make love to you. Several times, my little wild cat, just to make sure that my darling Marie will become the mother of my son, the next Comte de Beauvoir. Maybe I should mention that you're about to become the most honourable Marquise de Beauvoir, and the demise of this miserable bastard Pierre is just a question of time, I'll personally take care of that. As he has spent most of his time in a monastery, heaven will be probably already be waiting for him," he jeered.

His voice had become hoarse with excitement and he leaned over her, coming so close that she could smell his hot breath, stale with the smell of wine. Marie's mind went blank. She moved forward, a gesture he triumphantly interpreted as consent to his words.

But Marie's body jerked forward and before Henri realized what was happening, Marie's stomach went into spasm and she vomited, spraying the contents of her stomach all over his waistcoat, the velvet upholstery and her pretty pink gown.

She simply couldn't stop, her body had taken control and she jerked towards him, bending over once more, spitting and choking.

Henri's arrogant face transformed into a mask of disgust and contempt. He signalled the coachman to stop, and as he left the coach he turned once more to Marie.

"You're not even a wild cat, I totally misjudged you, you're just a deplorable, stinking mess. I'll ride outside and leave you here in your mess, but don't you think that you can avoid your destiny. I'll be true to my words, even if I don't ever want to see you again. But my wife you'll become and I'll make sure that you'll regret every single day of your life that you ever met me."

The door of the coach closed and Marie sat there, still fighting to breathe normally. A strange tranquillity settled over her. Her stomach was feeling better after this ordeal and although her hands were still strapped she managed to grab Henri's coat and clean her clothes and her face. If he had intended to frighten her to death, he had picked the wrong enemy, Marie decided. Tonight he would die, and if she had to die with him, she didn't care. There would be no demure Marie to carry the child of this monster, she'd do whatever it needed to bring this to an end.

The coach rattled on, swaying dangerously as they left the main road, then they followed the bumpy side track into the woods. Marie moved to the window curtain and peeped outside. The narrow road was lined by trees and dense undergrowth. Marie reckoned that soon sunset would be upon them, which meant that they couldn't be too far from their final destination, as driving on these terrible roads would become impossible in the approaching darkness. She prayed fervently for the coach to break down and lose a wheel as the road became worse and worse, and the heavy wooden frame of the carriage groaned under the strain. They

229

crossed roots, potholes, debris and mud, moving forward only slowly and with the greatest difficulty.

Unfortunately her prayers went unanswered. When the coach finally stopped Marie was bruised all over. The door of the coach was opened and a servant dragged her out, brutally pulling at her strapped wrists. Marie suppressed a cry of pain; she wouldn't show any weakness. He made some obscene remarks to a second footman who stood in front of her, his musket ready and loaded. Marie didn't mind, as being shot here and now seemed a preferable alternative to the plan Henri had outlined to her in the coach. She was pushed forward towards a hunting lodge built entirely from timber logs in the midst of a clearing. It was surrounded by the dark and menacing forest – the ideal hide-away for all kinds of secret encounters. Daylight had nearly vanished and great torches lit the entrance, making shadows dance and faces appear white and unreal. The scene reminded Marie of a play she had seen in the market place in Reims when Italian actors had staged a drama; how long ago this must have been, probably in a different life of hers. Marie expected at any minute a magician to appear in a puff of smoke in this nightmarish scene.

The servant pushed her forward towards the entrance of the lodge, prodding her stiff back from behind with his musket so hard that it hurt. Marie turned round immediately and spat into his face; she nearly laughed when she saw his reaction. His jaw dropped; apparently he had expected a docile, frightened girl, not a lady ready for a fight.

She was pushed roughly inside the lodge, a surprisingly big and well proportioned room with a high vaulted ceiling, lit by plenty of candles and torches. A lively fire was burning in the stone-framed fireplace, dirtied by smoke and grime. It had become quite chilly and only once Marie felt the warmth of the fire did she suddenly realize how cold she had felt in her thin silk gown. The room was fully furnished with comfortable chairs and oak tables and chests. The floor and walls were decorated with skins and furs – mementos of earlier hunting glory – and antlers of all sizes adorned the walls. Polished tin tankards gleamed at the fireplace; no doubt this place had often seen wild and cheerful carousing after the hunt was over.

When Marie turned around she had to suppress a shudder. She noticed a table spread with a white cloth, bearing a cross and with a crucifix on top of it. This time the suffering figure of Christ didn't inspire confidence in her; it seemed only a foreboding of the sufferings that were waiting for her.

This was a makeshift altar, without any doubt – Henri had been true to his word, and this night was to be her bridal night. A friar dressed in a simple brown hooded habit and holding a crucifix in his hand was standing next to the altar, his zealous, fanatical eyes burning into her. Tears sprang into Marie's eyes and it took all her strength not to break down or become hysterical. She knew that she was being watched closely and instinctively she gave way to a sudden impulse and she sank down upon the floor like a lifeless ragdoll, apparently having fainted. She

230

noticed the commotion around her, and someone opened her right eye, obviously trying to see if she was pretending. Marie managed to stare with an empty look, her eye wide and motionless.

Apparently she had been a convincing enough actress, and after a short and animated discussion between Henri, the friar and the servants she was carried into the adjacent room and dumped onto the large bed like a sack of vegetables. It had taken all her strength to stay rigid and keep up the appearance of an unconscious person, but now she needed to move and breathe. She needed air! As soon as she heard the disappearing footsteps and could identify the sound of the door closing, she inhaled deeply and greedily and opened her eyes.

But it was too early. From the side of the bed loomed a man of nearly black skin in the livery of the de Beauvoir family, looking at her thoughtfully. Marie sighed, and this time she truly fainted.

*****

Charles and Céline sped down the road towards London on their horses, only accompanied by Charles's faithful groom, following the signs that John had diligently posted at regular intervals. The light was starting to fade, and riding on, Céline became concerned that they might miss the next sign, but then she spotted it, yet another red ribbon, however, this time, John had posted two ribbons and when they came closer they could see why: he had laid twigs in the shape of an arrow on the ground, guiding them clearly into the forest, abandoning the road to London. Céline was relieved; she had been terribly scared that Henri would ride straight to London where they might arrive too late for a rescue, losing precious time to search for her in a dangerous and large city at night. Of course she had kept her concerns to herself, but looking sideways at Charles's face, she was sure that the same unsavoury thoughts had crossed his mind.

If the coach had driven into the forest it meant that Henri was intending to hide Marie there and due to the darkness that was falling rapidly they couldn't be too far ahead.

Following John's latest sign they had entered the dark forest. Céline had to suppress a shudder. The high trees above her, stripped to cold nakedness by the late autumn weather, looked dark and foreboding. The road transformed into a narrow, uneven path, more and more difficult to follow on their horses, and studded with treacherous roots and potholes. Freshly broken twigs indicated the way the coach had taken, forcing its way through the brushwood and thus they barely needed to follow the red ribbons. Soon it had become so dark that they decided to dismount and guide their horses, as riding would have been too risky, the path scarcely lit by a moon that was just starting to rise above them, an immense blotched balloon, tinted reddish-yellow, not at all the serene silver moon of romantic dreams.

231

Charles paused, as his horse became nervous and halted. It must have caught the scent of other animals, maybe a fox – but no, it snorted and was clearly excited, probably picking up the scent of other horses. Charles strained his senses and made a sign for his groom and Céline to stop and stay quiet. Indeed, very faintly, they could hear voices, muffled by the distance and the thick brushwood, sounds carried by the wind, barely audible.

Charles made a sign to move on but they placed their hand on the mouths of the horses as a precaution, keeping the reins tight. They continued walking for what seemed an eternity, but in fact amounted to probably only ten minutes, when Charles heard a soft whistling sound. They stopped once more, alert. Then some branches of the dense undergrowth on his left suddenly started to move. Charles immediately pointed his musket towards the moving leaves.

Their tension turned to joy when a hand appeared and waved the remains of a red scarf at them. They had made it, John was here!

A grinning John crawled out of his hiding place and signalled for them to follow him away from the path right into the dense forest, forcing their way through the undergrowth. He had found a small clearing, ideal for hiding their horses, well protected by the dense brushwood and a wall of thorny holly trees, the latter already displaying their festive attire of red berries. They fastened the reins of the horses to some low branches and John made signs to follow him silently. The horses had to stay behind; their riders couldn't take the slightest risk that they might betray their presence. Their excitement grew as they were now close to the place where the bandits were probably holding Marie. Céline's heart started beating fast as the faint voices grew louder. The day had been long and their task daunting but now all her doubts and tiredness were gone; she felt elated, they had found Marie and she was ready to take on all the bandits of this world!

Carefully they crept through the forest towards the sounds of the noisily feasting servants. Their silhouettes could be seen moving against the flickering light of a large bonfire, lit in the midst of a clearing, close to the lodge's entrance. John had checked on the situation before and to his great surprise and immense relief, nobody had bothered to post any guards. Henri and his men seemed to feel completely secure in this secluded part of the forest.

The small group made some detours to take advantage of the low brushwood giving them cover and finally ended up quite close to the group of men who had gathered around the fire. Spirits were already high, and they were passing around leather flasks filled with cheap wine or even more potent liquor, drinking heavily and becoming merrier by the minute.

In the midst of the fire stood a large metal spit with a whole pig being rotated slowly by one of them, one hand on the crank handle, the other one busy hold his flask of wine, swallowing deeply, dark liquid running out of his greedy mouth and dripping on the soil.

There was no way to see what was going on inside the hunting lodge and Céline tried to keep her mind focused on the scene in front of her. She tried to devise a plan of how to first get rid of these thugs here, as they were blocking the way to setting Marie free, but there were at least eight of them, probably more inside the lodge, and all of them heavily armed!

Nervously she looked at Charles and to her surprise he responded to the desperate plea in her eyes not only with a confident smile, but a broad grin. He seemed to consider the prospect of a fight with a group of bandits an evening's fun! Charles gave a sign and they retreated to hold a short war council back in their hiding place where their horses were waiting patiently, happy for a rest after the long ride.

Charles made them collect all the gunpowder that had remained attached in small bottles to their saddles and he distributed the muskets and pistols between the four of them. The groom looked scandalized when Charles insisted on giving loaded arms to Céline as well – this was not his idea of how a gentlewoman should behave! Each of them received a small ration of gunpowder, just enough to reload once or twice, and the rest was evenly distributed into four small bundles, as in a low voice Charles started to explain his master plan.

Marie woke up as cold water was splashed into her face. She jerked upright and wanted to scream loudly and indignantly but a strong hand closed above her mouth and the man with the dark skin hissed at her, "Be quiet, my lady. If you trust me, I might be able to help you. If you cry out now, my master will come into the room and will force you to marry him immediately. Everything is set up and ready, the priest is already waiting for you."

Marie nodded her consent and he withdrew his hand. She had just sunk back into the bed when the door of the room was slammed open and she heard Henri's angry voice, "Jean, what's going on? Is the slut still unconscious?"

Jean's deep voice answered respectfully, "Oui, Monsieur le Marquis, I managed to wake her up for a second but she fainted once more. It would be helpful if you could have some bouillon prepared for her, I'll try to wake her up soon once more but she'll need something fortifying," and feigning ignorance, he added, "She must have had a terrible shock, I wonder what has happened!"

Henri answered angrily, "Nothing for you to wonder or think about – especially if you want to keep that head of yours fixed to the rest of your body. See that you get her out of this bed ready to join us in fifteen minutes at the latest!" and giving a long glance at Jean he continued, "You know what we're going to do here tonight. I'll have my fun, whether she's conscious or not." Henri gave him a long look and then he laughed out loud and turned back towards the main hall. "The more I think about it, the better I like my new idea, three of us together will be excellent," and the door closed behind him.

Marie nearly jumped out of the bed. "What did I hear?" she whispered hotly. "Did this monster really propose to take me into his bed and ask you to join us? Is he one of those..." and she didn't finish the sentence, not really knowing what to say.

Jean just nodded sadly. "My master is a pervert. Mostly he prefers boys but in fact he only becomes really excited when he can torment someone, it is misery and pain that thrill and satisfy him!"

Marie shuddered. She had heard that some people were perverted, but the possibility of being married to such a demon this very night made her blood freeze.

"I don't know your name, but promise me that you'll kill me before he humiliates me. Please swear!"

Jean nodded but he added, "My name is Jean, but I also want my revenge. He has humiliated me so often, I must kill him, I have sworn it. The problem is that he doesn't trust anybody since one of his servants tried to kill him some time ago in his own bed. Nobody close to him is allowed to carry any weapons."

Calmly Jean assessed the room and continued, "But the antlers on the wall could serve as an excellent weapon. I'm strong enough and if you distract him for some minutes we'll succeed. But we must be under no illusions, if we kill Henri, his servants and this fanatical monk will take their revenge, are you ready to accept this?"

Marie just nodded and said with a firm voice, "I want to see him die; this may sound terrible, but it's all I wish for before I go."

They were still discussing how to lay the trap for Henri when suddenly they heard strange noises outside the lodge. It started with the sound of gunshots, followed by loud cries of surprise, changing to cries of pain and agony and further noises and explosions in a matter of only seconds and minutes.

Outside, the four attackers had started to shoot at the men who had gathered in high spirits around the fire. They had proved to be easy targets, squatting or standing in full view in front of the blazing fire. The thugs were taken by complete surprise, unsuspecting of any danger, their minds clouded by heavy drink. Céline had thought that she might feel some qualms at shooting at a man who couldn't defend himself, but strangely enough, no remorse came when her target fell down, his head a bleeding mess. Revenge for Marie was sweet, she thought.

John had also made his shot a clean kill, but Charles's victim moved unexpectedly. The bullet smashed his shoulder and in his suffering he staggered blindly backwards, stepping with his foot on a burning log. He howled in pain, lost his balance and, crying in agony, he fell straight into the fire, crashing against the rack of the spit with the roasting pig. The rack swayed and came down on him,

234

burying the crying man under the pig, whilst sending a huge flame into the dark night, lighting the clearing with a horrific brightness.

The flames devoured greedily the fat of the pig and the victim's clothes, wrapping the poor soul in a halo of fire, plunging the surroundings into a grotesque cascade of blinding light. The fire filled the air with dense smoke and a bizarre odour, a mix of delicious roasted pork combined with the sickening stench of burning bones and flesh.

It all happened in seconds, and while his fellows were watching helplessly, frozen with horror and fear, the fourth man fell too, shot by Charles's groom. Maybe it was the effect of this last shot or the sudden silence when the cries of the victim stopped, but anyhow, the remaining bandits now tried to recover their wits and save their own skins. They jumped around, searching and grabbing any weapon or stick they could find but, blinded by the fire, they searched in vain to identify in the dark forest the number and whereabouts of their assailants.

The human torch was still burning right under their eyes when the first explosion of gunpowder created a small crater close to them, only to be followed by a second explosion.

They needed no more proof that they should lose no more time, or they'd follow the fate of the first victims.

"To the horses!" one of them shouted in despair, but there were no more horses, the groom had cut their reins before Charles had started his assault and the noise and the explosions had made them stampede off into the forest, fleeing in terror. Henri's panic-stricken servants followed, all fleeing into the dark forest, running as fast as they could, never to come back to this cursed place.

Henri had heard the first faint noises of shots, but the thick logs of the lodge had dampened the sound. He had noticed of course that his servants – meaning the scoundrels the monk had hired for this enterprise – had started to drink. He could imagine them sitting there around the fire, drinking, boasting and exchanging filthy jokes. He hadn't really bothered, the men had been picked by the friar and he had told him that they were a rough lot; for such missions one couldn't be too choosy!

But firing weapons in the forest went too far. Even if they were miles away from the next village and still comfortably out of London, these idiots shouldn't be attracting any attention.

Seething with anger, Henri left his chair and went to the chest where he had stored his arms. He loaded two pistols; if necessary he'd shoot one or two of the louts to instil some discipline – they needed rough treatment, this much was certain.

He was about to load the bullets, when he heard cries of pain, an almost inhuman high-pitched screaming sound, quickly culminating in a terrible crescendo of noise. Something dreadful was happening out there. The monk had moved silently away from the altar and stood next to him now. Henri instructed him to take a sword as well; if these men had got drunk and started a brawl, they'd need to intervene quickly and with force. What a pity that he needed to take Marie with all the comfort of her family's fortune – and as a virgin – for himself; it would have been the right punishment to feed her to these greedy animals outside. He'd have loved to watch that!

His pistols ready, he shouted, "Jean, come quickly, we need to deal with those idiots out there, don't bother with that slut for the time being."

Jean heard the command and looked at Marie with sparkling eyes. "This could be our chance, my lady. I'll leave the door unlocked, as soon as we're busy with those bandits out there, try to escape."

Marie nodded, hope flooding like liquid fire through her body. Had her prayers finally been answered?

Jean opened the door and closed it after him, fumbling at the latch, making a show of closing it properly. Henri didn't really pay attention; all his mind was concentrated on the cacophony of irritating noises coming in from the outside. There seemed to be total uproar outside by now, the terrible cries had faded away but the sound of explosions was most annoying. Henri made a sign to Jean to move in front of him and, using Jean as a human shield, he opened the door of the lodge and they stormed into the clearing lit by the huge fire. Jean nearly threw up when he saw the charred but still discernible remains of a human body in the fire, next to what had obviously been a pig on a spit. To their great surprise the clearing lay totally deserted, apart from three dead bodies lying in a bloody mess around the fire, all the rest of their servants gone, and not a single horse remaining.

Before Henri could fully understand what had been going on, he heard a voice from the darkness. "Henri de Beauvoir, your game is finished, you're my prisoner now. Drop your arms!"

Henri raised his pistol and fired into the darkness, right in the direction of the voice. The answer came immediately, a shot placed neatly and accurately, kicking the second gun out of his left hand. Henri felt a sharp pain. The bullet had lacerated the tip of one of his fingers, and dark red blood started dripping from it, creating a small pool.

"You coward!" he roared into the darkness. "If you have one grain of honour in your body, come and fight me like a gentleman."

Céline stood numbed. She had hoped that this would be the final chapter and had prayed that the bullet would kill this louse, but she knew Charles and his gentleman's code of conduct well enough by now to understand that he couldn't possibly ignore this challenge.

Henri had thrown away the first pistol as it was useless once his shot had failed. He turned back and took the sword out of the hand of the surprised monk. His hate was so intense that he hardly felt the pain from his damaged hand. He moved forward to the clearing and yelled, "I challenge you, whoever you are!"

"I am Charles Neuville," Charles replied in his deep voice and moved forward, sword in his hand.

The two fighters saluted each other shortly and the fight started. It was no elegant duel; Henri was fighting to kill, in a cold rage, not respecting any rule of combat. Charles was glad that he had polished up his fencing skills with the Italian master together with Pierre, as his opponent danced around him with the speed and accuracy of a deadly cobra.

Céline wanted to hide her face, but couldn't move; she stood there, motionless, just watching. Then suddenly, it all happened very fast.

It soon dawned on Henri that – to his great surprise – he was no match for this athletic giant, who fought with the effortless elegance of an accomplished master. He had started to perspire and the pain in his hand was intensifying. Soon he would lose his concentration. He cursed; he needed to kill his opponent fast or he'd perish.

The fire was still burning brightly in the midst of the clearing, casting a bright light on the fighting opponents. Still fighting hard, they moved with masterly grace and huge strides until they reached the left corner of the lodge. Henri moved slightly around, with Charles following him closely, pressing hard.

Henri had moved deliberately to this part of the clearing and discovered in the dark shade of the lodge what he had hoped to see.

Now he knew what to do! He sped back towards the fire where the monk was still standing watching them, his hands folded in silent prayer. Henri raced towards the monk and with a swift move he kicked him hard in his side. The monk lost his balance and tripped right into the fire.

Henri whispered softly, "Heaven, or probably hell, is waiting for you, my friend."

The monk fell straight into the fire, right on top of the remains of the first victim and his brown friar's habit caught fire immediately. Terrible cries filled the air while the monk convulsed in the intense heat, desperately trying to get back on his feet. The flames had spread from his head to his toes and the ghastly scene drew the attention of the shocked bystanders. Charles was the first to react; he sped forward to pull the burning monk out of the fire. The groom and John took off their coats trying to extinguish the flames. But it was too late, the intense heat of the fire had turned the monk's skin to a blackened mess and seeing the monk suffering so terribly, Charles made a sign to his groom. He nodded, drew his pistol and terminated the terrible ordeal with his last bullet.

Appalled by the horrible murder they had witnessed, Céline, Charles and the others turned around full of rage towards Henri.

They all shared one burning desire: finish it once and for all with him, make him pay for all of these atrocities.

But Henri was gone. Using the distraction he had created to his advantage, he had disappeared. They stood there, stunned and angry, understanding that they had been outwitted by the enemy while they heard the soft sound of quickly disappearing hooves.

Henri must have discovered or known that one of the horses had been tethered behind the lodge and cold-bloodedly he had sacrificed the monk to divert their attention from his escape. It was useless to follow Henri in the dark night. All they could hope for was that his horse should trip and fall on those treacherous dark paths and that he'd break his neck.

Charles turned back and glanced grimly at Jean. The valet stood there paralysed, his dark skin looking almost pale for once. His eyes were locked on the dead body of the monk as if he couldn't believe what he saw.

"A great master you have; are you proud that you had the honour to serve him?" Charles said roughly, pointing with his sword towards the dead monk and ready to strike at him.

Before Jean could move or answer they heard a feeble voice from the entrance of the lodge.

"Charles, I implore you, please don't hurt him! Without his help I'd already be dead or married to this monster, he protected me when I was hiding inside. He truly hates his master, he's on our side, I swear!"

"Marie! Oh, Marie!" Céline flew into her arms, sobbing and laughing at the same time as she embraced her friend. Then Marie moved towards Charles, still walking as if she were in a dream, scared of waking up and finding herself back in Henri's sway.

Tears of joy streamed down her cheeks. "How can I ever thank you, my dearest friends. I was so foolish and I put all of you in danger, I'm so sorry!"

Charles looked embarrassed and fumbled in his pockets, trying to find a handkerchief or anything suitable to dry this river of tears. Charles possessed the natural British aversion to emotional scenes.

"Marie's still very French, you know what I mean!" he would remark later to his groom, who just nodded his assent. Luckily he never spoke much.

Charles took command now. "The two ladies go inside; we don't know if Henri and his scoundrels will try to have another go at us later!"

Then he ordered his groom and John to fetch their horses from the hiding place, tether them close to the lodge and then to take over the gruesome task of burying the remains of the first victims and the charred monk. Charles would inspect the clearing to see if any weapons were still lying around and make sure that nobody was hiding in the bushes.

Jean accompanied the ladies inside the lodge. It looked cosy and idyllic, like an island of peace far removed from the horrible scenes that they had just witnessed outside. The fire was still burning, radiating a comfortable heat and bathing the room in warm light. They noticed an abandoned table, set for two persons, dressed lavishly with tin plates, candelabras and plenty of mouth-watering food presented on vividly painted ceramic plates and bowls.

"Apparently this was to be my bridal meal," Marie said, putting on a brave face as tears started once more to run down her cheeks, still shaken by her ordeal of the past hours. Céline looked thoughtfully at the table and when she detected the makeshift altar in the corner, the sheer thought of what would have happened here without their intervention made her shiver. She whispered some instructions to Jean and the two ladies retreated into the bedroom. Céline led Marie inside, guiding her and holding her firmly in her arms.

Céline felt Marie shaking and she wasn't surprised; apart from the effects of the shock, her clothing was far too thin for a chilly and wet late autumn evening. She guided Marie to the bed to get some warmth. Then she started searching around in the bedroom. Full of curiosity she opened all the chests and cupboards. To her great joy she found one of the chests filled up to the brim with costly velvet gowns, complete with linen undergarments. She made Marie take off her soiled silk gown and after freshening up, Marie and Céline tried on the clothes that had been stored in the chest. It became unmistakeably clear what kind of women these clothes had been tailored and stored here for – the velvet was a vibrant red combined with the most vivid blue, with necklines cut extremely low. There was a small polished metal mirror on top of one of the chests and the two looked at each other, amazed by their transformation from ladies to women of easy virtue. Marie started to giggle and Céline joined in, swinging her hips as if she were going to serve an imaginary customer. As they giggled together, Marie started to recover her normal happy self.

Digging further, they found some horrid green scarves adorned with glittering golden embroidery and coloured glass beads.

"We'll look like silly parrots," Marie said and first wanted to refuse but relented, as Céline was most insistent; the scarves would at least serve to cover

239

their décolletage, which was rather too much exposed for a true lady. Marie's gown was a size too large, as the unknown owner of her gown must have had a more imposing figure, but this could be adjusted. Céline's was too short as she was unusually tall; it ended above her ankles (truly scandalous), but at least her new gown was warm and clean, so she decided to ignore its shortcomings.

By the time they had finished dressing, Céline looked up and said, "I have a terrible and most unladylike hunger; I imagine you feel the same! I can hardly wait until we can start. Did you see that there was even a cake on the table when we entered? The last bite of food I had was for breakfast this morning. I think that I could eat a complete pig!"

Marie looked up at her and replied, joking, "And there's so much of you to feed, see, how tall you are!"

"You're a real beast and not my best friend at all!" Céline answered, grinning broadly. "I think this is the last time I shall come to rescue you. You insult me instead of falling on your knees, thanking me for my kindness!"

Marie just laughed and embraced her, and arm in arm they entered the main hall of the lodge.

Jean had been very efficient. The altar had disappeared and the table, miraculously grown in size, was laid for three persons now, candles burning merrily. They saw that he had prepared a second table with simple plates for the groom, John and himself, discreetly positioned in the corner. All looked as if they had arrived just for a merry hunting weekend and the last hours had been nothing but an illusion, a terrible but unreal nightmare.

Charles entered the room and, rubbing his freezing hands, he examined the table loaded with delicious food with a look of keen satisfaction.

"I don't know about you, but I'm so hungry, I could eat a horse," he said good-humouredly.

Céline and Marie started to laugh and Céline replied, winking towards Marie, "Charles, if you're in the habit of eating a complete horse it does rather explain your size! Marie, who I thought of as being my best friend, just told me that at my size, I should consider eating a complete pig!"

Charles laughed and just said complacently, "Yes, I am a bit solid, I admit!" and looking at Céline he said simply, "I also prefer my wife to be tall. It's a bit tiring to bend down all the time if you want to kiss someone."

Now Céline turned crimson red and Marie, completely forgetting her past ordeal danced around them. "Oh, Charles, you have to propose to her, you two make such a perfect couple!"

"Marie, your manners are barbaric," Charles replied, then after a pause, "But you're quite right. Well..." Charles cleared his throat and paused awkwardly before he found the courage to continue. "Céline, my dear, I know it's the wrong time and wrong place for romantic declarations. But I must ask you now, please understand and excuse me. You are the bravest woman I have ever seen. Since the first day I met you, I felt that you're the one I have been waiting for, for so many years. It seems to me that every day I love you more, I want to share my life with you, I cannot imagine letting you return to France. Will you agree to become my wife?"

Charles had gone down on one knee and taken her elegant hand in his huge palm.

Céline cleared her throat and gently she answered, "Charles, I love you too. But I have no penny, no dowry to offer, even our good name in France has been tarnished by my father's debts before he died. You have just lost the Duchy of Hertford to Pierre, you must not throw yourself away on a penniless spinster of advanced age. Forget me, marry a rich and young lady, this is all I can say and the best service I can do for the man that I also truly love."

Tears had started to run down her cheeks. She had intended to remain composed, cool and calm, a true lady. But how to remain composed if the man of your life is proposing and honour demands that you decline?

Charles stood up and, towering above her, answered, "Well, let's forget my proposal then."

Céline couldn't gather the strength to look into his eyes. She kept kneading a piece of her green scarf, shedding glass beads as she worked relentlessly on the embroidered fabric.

Charles continued, his voice stern now. "I simply regret to inform you, my lady, that you're here under my absolute power. So I apologize if the elegant way of courting doesn't work. I'll use the old English way."

And before she had realized what was going on or digested the meaning of this statement she was lifted up and, holding her in his strong arms, he kissed her.

Céline struggled to break free but she didn't seem to be doing so very convincingly, as he held her even closer.

"You're a silly little goose," Charles told her. "I have enough money for the two of us and if God grant us of plenty of children, don't worry, I can feed them."

Now Marie intervened. "Don't be stupid, Céline, he's the right one for you. And Pierre told me, Charles can buy half of England, Hertford is just a pittance against his investments in the new colonies." Charles grinned but didn't comment. He had placed Céline back on the floor, but still held her tight. Céline didn't mind any longer; she was happy beyond all imagination.

"To Céline and Charles!" Marie shouted and, taking a glass of red wine, she toasted the new fiancés. Although they were exhausted from their long and trying day, they went to bed late. Marie confessed her story of hiding the fake letter and, blushing deeply, she narrated her story, halting from time to time when the memories became too painful. Charles clenched his fist when Marie told them of Henri's behaviour inside the coach, and only when he heard that she had managed to vomit right into his face did his grim look change to one of sheer satisfaction.

Marie decided to keep secret the last episode when Henri had mentioned a *ménage à trois* and his intention to make her share her bed with Jean. Sometimes it was better to keep one's mouth shut.

Later she would try to convince Pierre to engage Jean as his personal valet. Jean could help to protect Pierre; he knew Henri well enough to understand how dangerous he was and Marie was sure that he still wanted his personal revenge.

After a last round of toasts to the fiancés, this time joined by the servants, the ladies went to bed and the men settled down to camp in the main hall, sharing between them the watch outside to make sure none of the bandits could return and steal their horses or set fire to the building.

The next morning when they woke, they were greeted by a thick fog that covered everything like a milky veil. Clouds of mist floated above the ground, obscuring all shapes and swallowing all sounds, therefore their departure had to be delayed as they had no option but to wait until the rays of the pale sun could clear the worst of the fog and they could find their way out of the forest. Time seemed to stand still, and anxiously they peered out of the lodge again and again, looking full of despair into the clouds of mist that were floating around the clearing, like a shroud of mourning for the dead bodies that John and the groom had buried hastily only the day before.

All the same, Charles and John had decided to explore the path leading into the forest to see if they could finally dare to leave the lodge when they heard a faint nickering sound very close to them. John answered with some clucking sounds and two huge silhouettes materialized; faint shades at first, but gaining shape and substance quickly and to their great joy, two of the horses that had been freed by John yesterday had found their way back to the lodge. This would solve the headache of transporting Marie and Jean, especially the latter, as he was muscular and heavy.

John caressed the horses, which seemed to be happy to have found their way back to human care and companionship, nudging him in the hope that he'd produce a tasty surprise for them. John laughed; he loved horses and softly he started to speak to them.

Charles and John decided that they should risk leaving. The fog was still heavy but soon it would be noon, and as the sun set early in November they'd need to leave now or stay another day and leave Pierre and Marie's relatives in the grip of fear.

The group thus obediently set off, but Marie would never forget this day, riding, sometimes walking, through a strange and menacing forest, wrapped in white mist, mysterious and frightening.

They moved as if in a hazy dream through an eerie silence, noises distorted beyond recognition, all shapes blurred by the fog that enshrouded the naked trees. John and the groom were leading them, searching for clues as they moved forward, everybody in constant fear of losing their way and straying far into the deep forest. Marie thought that she had never seen a forest as cold and foreboding, probably the home to wolves and other wild and dangerous animals. She heard a bird cawing, loud and displeasing, far too close for comfort. Her thoughts wandered on; if there were crows, would there be witches? She shivered, feeling cold and miserable; even her new bright velvet gown and coat couldn't keep her warm in this white, peculiar and silent version of hell.

The hours seemed to stretch endlessly; the party kept walking and walking in silence, riding whenever possible and praying secretly they would find their way back to the main road and not encounter any of those scoundrels who might have succeeded in escaping, and were probably roaming the forest, searching for them. When Marie had almost given up hope of leaving the forest during daylight, Charles suddenly cried out in triumph when he recognized the red ribbon with the arrows that John had left in place; their prayers had been answered, they had found the road, they were safe!

Outside the dense and wet forest the fog had started to dissipate under the warmth of the pale afternoon sun and they gained speed and confidence as they rode towards Sevens. When they passed the small chapel where everything had started, Marie first wanted to stop but then decided to move on. The memories were still too painful. Later she would thank Sainte Marie, but now she simply couldn't.

They reached Sevens and miraculously all of the servants seemed to appear immediately on the scene – word of their arrival had spread instantly.

Arthur and his mother rushed out to greet them, Arthur laughing, Marie's aunt shedding copious tears of relief, hugging Marie and Céline and scolding them at the same time.

"How on Earth could you do this to me, never, ever, could I have dared to meet your mother again if something had happened to you, you're such a naughty girl," she chided Marie but embraced her at the same time so tightly that Marie had difficulty breathing, clinging to her as if she would never let her go.

243

Giving Marie a second look she gasped when she noticed the colourful details of her velvet gown. Looking at her doubtfully with a long glance, she ushered them inside. They were made to drink and eat from a sumptuous buffet that had been waiting for their arrival, servants scurrying around, laughing, everybody relieved that this nightmare had ended well. When Charles announced his betrothal to Céline, everyone cheered – but nobody was really surprised.

Only Marie was secretly sad and disappointed; in all this exuberance she had longed so much to see and embrace Pierre, but he hadn't turned up, although Arthur confirmed that he had sent servants to urge him to come to Sevens immediately.

Darkness had fallen and they all suddenly felt how terribly tired they really were and, yawning profusely, Céline and Marie went to bed, happy to be back at Sevens in their comfortable and cosy rooms. Marie had thought that she wouldn't possibly manage to sleep after so much adventure and excitement but the tedious journey and her ordeal had worn her out beyond her imagination, and as soon as her head touched the wonderfully soft pillows she was deeply asleep. No nightmare disturbed her sleep this night and when she woke it was nearly noon. Stretching and yawning she rang her maid, hoping for a delicious cup of steaming hot chocolate from her aunt's secret reserve.

But it was Céline, already dressed and still radiating happiness, who entered the room instead. She carried a tray with the deliciously smelling beverage and she carried news that was even better. "Guess who's been waiting for you downstairs since early this morning?" said Céline as she deposited the tray next to Marie's bed.

"Pierre?" Marie asked with wide eyes.

Céline grinned. "You're very bright this morning, my dear, yes, it's him. And he is very anxious to meet a lady who has been sleeping like a log for nearly sixteen hours."

"Oh, *bon Dieu*, why didn't you wake me up?" Marie screamed, and jumped out of her bed, making the cup dance dangerously on the saucer.

"Oh, stop jumping around like a child! Because you needed your sleep after this adventure! Your aunt forbade us from waking you up, she was guarding you like a Cerberus, and I think that she was right. You looked like a ghost when you arrived here. And not a very pretty one, let me tell you!"

Marie rushed to the mirror but the sleep had restored her usual beauty and she merely grimaced at Céline. Soon the two ladies arrived downstairs where Pierre and Arthur were pestering Charles with questions about his adventure. Pierre was so excited that he kept walking up and down the sitting room, like a caged lion. Armand had joined them, still stunned by the fact that Pierre and he had missed the biggest adventure of the past weeks.

244

Marie was the first to enter the room and Pierre, forgetting his dignity and all convention, rushed towards her, drew her into his arms and holding Marie tight, he whispered, "Marie, my darling! I only heard yesterday night what happened, I was retained by the fog and only reached Hertford late yesterday evening. I think I would have died if anything had happened to you, my love!"

Marie could see that unmanly tears were glistening in his eyes and she felt touched. She sighed happily, how much she had missed him!

They all strolled into the garden, further down the forlorn lanes towards the pond, now a dark green hole strewn with leaves and the last dying flowers of autumn. Marie and Charles told the story of their adventure, sometimes interrupted by Céline. Marie tried to sound cheerful but fought back the tears once she remembered the scene where Henri had trapped her in front of the chapel, the memories bringing back a terrible feeling of total despair.

Charles held Céline's arm tightly during their short walk and Pierre and Armand were not really surprised when he announced that he had proposed to her the day before.

Pierre congratulated them enthusiastically. "That's wonderful! You two do belong together!" Looking sheepishly at Marie he added, "I'd love to do the same!"

But Armand brought him back to earth immediately. "You can't, not yet, my dear friend. We're not yet masters of our own destiny, you and Marie will need the consent of her father and incidentally, that is the proper way to do it, especially if you call yourself a Marquis or a Duke!"

Charles cleared his throat. "There's another obstacle!" he remarked cautiously.

Pierre looked curiously at him. "What do you mean? Isn't this complicated enough already?"

"I'm afraid not," continued Charles. "As a duke of England you may only marry with the consent of your sovereign. Marriage without royal agreement can be interpreted as treason. It's normally a mere formality, but don't forget that many people of great influence want your head on a platter – and any mistake you might make will be a nice opportunity for them to get it!"

Pierre looked shocked. "That means I'm in an utter mess here. I wish I could get rid of all of this pomp and just become Pierre again!" he shouted, visibly becoming more and more upset.

To Charles's surprise, it was Marie who took the initiative to cool him down. "Oh Pierre, don't talk rubbish!. Do you really want to go back to that horrid monastery with those beastly teachers? Of course not! We're still very young, we can wait a bit!" Marie gave a dazzling smile to Pierre and looked so lovely that he had no option but to surrender.

Charles was amazed. He secretly admired this ability of women to be so emotional on the one hand and transform to cool-headed masters of the purse strings whenever it came to business. Marie loved Pierre, no doubt about that, but she clearly appreciated his accession to the highest aristocracy and wouldn't put this in peril.

A very sensible head on extremely pretty shoulders, Charles concluded in silence.

*****

Later they were all sitting around the dinner table, which was loaded with delicacies. Arthur and his mother had joined them, and wine flowed freely while they discussed their plans for the coming weeks. Cheeks were flushed from the wine and, with a hot fire burning behind them all, the discussion was in full swing.

Armand was pushing hard to leave immediately for London. "Any further day we stay here could bring a new disaster. My father insisted that we go to London and see some influential friends of his there!" His eyes were flashing, his usual good looks heightened by his flushed cheeks, his black hair shining in the candlelight. Marie's aunt looked at him, fascinated, regretting not being twenty years younger. She sighed deeply and took another sip of her red wine.

Pierre had noticed of course that Armand had omitted to mention the Templars in his speech; apparently he was keen to keep their true destination secret.

Armand continued, "My father's fears have been proved right, only yesterday Richelieu tried to use Henri to destroy Pierre's future and what a diabolic plan it was, to use a helpless woman like Marie as a weapon! But next time the danger could come from a total stranger. I have the feeling that we haven't see the last of Henri, he's bound to trouble us again as long as we can't finish him off. As long as Pierre has not taken possession of his heritage in France, it's available and clearly, next to Henri, the Cardinal Richelieu is stretching out his greedy claws to get it!"

"But as I understand it, this would mean going back to France," Arthur interjected. "I don't see how you can solve this problem by staying in London."

"He needs to make sure first that his Hertford title and succession are safe – that is an absolute priority!" Charles reminded them. "Once he is back in France he'll need to bribe plenty of people at court in order to gain access to King Louis, as Richelieu will try to prevent any such contact. In fact, Pierre will need a great deal of money or Richelieu will feed him alive to his cronies!"

Marie exclaimed, "If it's so dangerous, why don't we just stay here? If going to France will put Pierre into jeopardy, we just stay in Hertford!"

The room suddenly and very embarrassingly fell silent and, feeling increasingly ill at ease, she realized that she must have committed a major blunder as four gentlemen looked at her full of contempt.

"Give up my French heritage, knowing that my parents sacrificed their lives for me? Never!" Pierre said with emphasis, and that was it, Marie understood that she wouldn't be able to change his mind; this was part of his code of honour and would not be discussed.

Armand continued, ignoring this interjection. "Charles, do you have any idea how much time it will need to obtain an audience and meet King Charles in London? And will he need to get the consent of Parliament?"

"The King should be enough, but he has to address Pierre in public as his beloved cousin, the Duke of Hertford and kiss his cheeks. Until this is official, King Charles will be under pressure from his courtiers to deny this heritage as being legal. The King always needs money as he's as broke as a beggar. His courtiers will try to find ways to acquire Pierre's estates for a pittance once they fall back to the Crown. Don't have any illusions, being at court is like being among a pack of hungry wolves. Pierre has to meet King Charles and appeal to his royal sense of justice. But we'll need to buy some influential courtiers. I'll join you in London and I'll try to use my influence." *And my money*, Charles added silently. He knew that this would become an expensive enterprise with a very uncertain end. He loved Pierre now as a brother and would spend whatever it took to put forward his case, but times were changing and the Roundheads were gaining influence daily; the King's supporters were melting away like snow in the sun.

Aloud he added, "We'll have to neutralize the influence of my cousin, you know, the one nicknamed 'the frog'. From the rumours that my London friends are passing on to me, I know that he's busily working against Pierre already, insinuating that granting the heritage to a French-born Catholic is against British interests and I imagine that we may soon see a petition from some pious men in Parliament requesting the exemption of foreign Catholic offspring from accession to the British peerage."

Pierre digested this new threat and after a short deliberation he answered, "If our King Henri IV converted from being a Protestant to a Catholic to become King of France, I can convert as well, if Hertford can only be inherited by a Protestant. Having spent most of my life in a Catholic monastery, I must confess, I lost my illusions about religion early enough!"

Armand, Céline and Marie looked at him in shock. Armand recovered first and, slamming his hand down hard on the table, he shouted ,"Pierre, you're my man. If you don't even fear eternal damnation, why should we fear Richelieu or your lovely cousin?"

247

Céline decided to abstain from this discussion; she had realized earlier that this question might arise once she married Charles, but she had decided secretly that she preferred happiness on earth to the vague promises of life in paradise.

But Marie's aunt, a devout Catholic herself, was utterly shocked. "Pierre, how can you even imagine giving up the true Faith? Your soul will be damned for eternity!"

Pierre took her hand and looked at her with his charming smile, "Not if you'll be in heaven, ready to speak for me!" The Principessa had intended to be very stern and aloof, but looking into his charming blue eyes, she melted. Impossible to resist or be angry with him!

Marie's thoughts though were in turmoil. Could she ever envisage converting? What would her parents say; would she need to confess to them? They'd probably never give their consent to marry Pierre if he became a heretic Protestant. But Marie was a spirited fighter – she definitely wouldn't go back to France and die as an old spinster, as she was certain that she would never love anybody else. Time would tell, why worry today?

The women decided that it was time to retire to their rooms and leave the gentlemen, who had decided to open a bottle of brandy.

Once the brandy had been sampled, they broadened their original topics and were discussing more than matters of religion and the religious wars that were destroying Europe as a consequence of blind hatred. Somehow they had reached the works of a French philosopher named Descartes, who had dared to make the human mind and rational thinking the focus of his work. This was scorned by the Church – but it soon appeared that Armand was a staunch supporter of this revolutionary way of thinking.

The discussion went on until the candles had burned down and everybody was tired.

Pierre, feeling a bit tipsy by now, said, "Let me make a short summary of our discussion. In essence I need to go to London in order to be kissed by the English King. Otherwise my Duchy is lost. On the way there I must be careful not to be murdered by my cousin, or alternatively, to be disinherited by the Roundheads in Parliament. I might need to sell my soul to keep my title. Then I'll need to leave for France, spend a fortune to bribe half of the court there, receive another kiss from another king and be careful that Richelieu, his agents or my beloved cousin Henri don't kidnap and kill me during this exercise. If ever I survive all of this, I'll be a Duke in England and a Marquis in France, and let me tell you one thing – then I *really* will have merited my two titles!"

The others had listened in silence and when Pierre finished, broke into hilarious laughter.

"A very pithy summing-up!" Armand quipped. "Good job! And let me tell you one thing. I admit that I was a little jealous, I mean to say, inheriting one title is fine, but two seems rather excessive. But do I want to be in your shoes? You have just opened my eyes – you can have your two titles, I still wouldn't want to have them with Richelieu and your precious cousin snapping at your heels!"

They cheered once more and emptied the second bottle of brandy, a decision they profoundly regretted the next morning when they woke up with splitting headaches.

LONDON

Pierre had been naïve enough to assume that travelling to London meant packing some clean shirts and riding together with Armand and Charles; altogether it was an exercise that should take a good day and be a pleasant change to their daily routines.

Charles merely laughed when he explained his vision. "Oh Pierre, these days are gone. You're the Duke now and as so many people will be trying to cast doubt on your eligibility you need to show them that you are the real thing, and so you will have to travel accordingly. Let me arrange this."

And Charles had been true to his word. It took a good week until everything was arranged and they were ready to go. Messengers had been sent to London to prepare his residence in the city for the great day. Finally at dawn one morning they were ready to leave Hertford.

Pierre stepped outside and nearly fell over in surprise. Before him was an immense coach he had never seen before, decorated with feathers and gilded framework glinting in the early morning sunshine. The Hertford coat of arms with its proud stags had been freshly painted; Pierre doubted that a king could own a more pompous and magnificent vehicle.

Behind his coach waited an armada of other coaches, all painted with his coat of arms, loaded to the roof with footmen, luggage, furniture and anything else that his butler had deemed necessary for their stay and comfort in London.

An army of grooms and footmen was assembled with their horses, all dressed in the Hertford livery, golden embroidery glistening in the sunlight. Pierre noticed that many of them were armed; Charles wasn't taking any chances. Looking at this convoy, Pierre decided that even Richelieu would have to give up, unless he arrived with the entire French army.

Pierre stepped into his coach and sank into the soft cushions. How he would have preferred to ride and enjoy the fresh air, to move freely. Now here he sat, in a gilded and swaying cage, with nothing to do but to wait until they arrived at his new home in London. Luckily, Armand and Charles decided after some time to join him so they could talk and play cards!

Slowly but steadily they made progress, with only short breaks to refresh themselves, and thus they approached the gates of the City of London in the early afternoon.

Here their convoy stopped, as Charles had asked his agents to find out what was waiting for them in London, and indeed his agents brought bad news. Some people had spread rumours that the new Duke was a villainous foreigner, a

Catholic agent in disguise, a distant relative of the treacherous Queen Mary of Scots who had tried to murder their beloved Queen Elizabeth.

These rumours had incited the mob and the infamous apprentices of London, known to be dangerous militants and even feared by the King. A crowd was waiting for them and nobody could judge what they were about to do, but it would be prudent to make a deviation and approach London secretly via a different road.

Charles looked worried and he was about to leave the coach to give orders to change the route when Pierre interrupted him.

"What are you doing, Charles?" he asked, visibly upset.

"You've heard that a dangerous crowd is waiting for us, ready to eat you alive. I cannot take the risk of entering the city and causing a brawl in which you might be hurt. This is exactly what the people who spread the rumours intend to happen. Luckily I placed my agents in London and we shall avoid this trap!" Charles answered.

"You can," Pierre answered evenly. "I won't. I'm Pierre de Beauvoir and I'm not going to flee from some London scoundrels. I'll do it my way."

And before Armand or Charles could argue any further, he left the coach and mounted his favourite horse, a proud black stallion. He gave some orders to his valet who hurried to one of the heavily guarded coaches and reappeared with a heavy bag, his face showing clearly how scandalized he was.

Soon they entered London where a hostile crowd was indeed waiting for them as expected, lining the narrow street behind the city gate, ready to pounce on them at any minute. It only needed one spark and the crowd would explode in a rage of hate and violence. Some soldiers were posted for their protection. Understandably they looked ill at ease, knowing that they would never be able to take on this mob once it got out of control. Charles could see that some peddlers' wives held buckets with putrid vegetables in their hands; one word and they'd start to shower them with filthy debris of all kinds. Charles felt extremely uncomfortable and cursed Pierre for being so pig-headed. He held his arms close to him, sure he would need them at any minute to defend their lives.

The crowd watched the convoy of liveried footman approaching, then the huge gilded coach and finally – totally unexpected – the young and handsome duke riding on his horse accompanied by two other men who followed him closely with grim faces. He was not hiding in his coach; he sat slender and proud on his black stallion, visible to all. The young duke was dressed in midnight-blue velvet, diamonds sparkling on his collar, a black ribbon showing that he was still in mourning for his grandfather.

Had rumour not said he was a dark villain? This young prince's natural grace and his warm smile immediately charmed the hearts of the female bystanders who

251

dropped their buckets of garbage and unconsciously fumbled at their clothes and bonnets to look their best.

His blonde hair was shining in the sun, and slowly his hand dug into a bag – and then the young duke threw something into the waiting crowd, their mouths gaping open, unsure what to do when faced with this fairy tale appearance, a vision so unlike anything they had expected.

Only seconds later the first cries emerged from the crowd where the first coins had fallen down: "Gold, he's throwing real gold, God save His Grace! Gold, he's throwing gold!"

The cries became louder and louder and like wildfire the news spread through the crowd. Like wild animals, young boys, elderly men and stately bourgeois women forgot their hostility and fell to the ground, madly scrabbling around for coins. The first brawls sprang up among them, loud cries turning hysterical and the formerly hostile crowd dissipated into tumultuous groups praising Pierre whilst cursing their neighbours whenever the clinking sound of coins falling on the ground could be heard.

They reached Hertford House unscathed. Pierre had kept his relaxed pose, with only a satisfied smile showing his state of mind. Armand needed to break the tension; he burst into cries of joy as soon as the gates had closed behind them and they had entered the courtyard that gave way to the imposing entrance.

They dismounted from their horses and Charles embraced Pierre. "Pierre, I am truly proud of you. I could have cursed you when we entered the city and saw this ragtag mob ready to tear us into pieces any minute. But you showed me today that you're ready and worthy to take your place among the peers of Britain."

Armand also embraced his friend, whispering, "You're a damned gambler, my friend, but Charles is right, you showed us today that you have the courage of a lion whereas we were behaving like mice."

Pierre laughed. "I thought I had nothing to lose, I could only win. They wouldn't dare to kill us. If we had avoided the mob my reputation would have been tarnished anyhow. Now London knows a duke has arrived and our beloved cousin from London will have a much more difficult hand to play. But let me thank you as well. You were indeed true friends in following me, I saw Charles's face and for some minutes I was persuaded that my only real danger of being killed came from him!"

Charles laughed and together they entered Hertford House.

*****

The title of 'house' was of course a typical British understatement. Hertford House was, in fact, a sprawling palatial building erected alongside the Thames, a palace with sumptuous gardens fit for a duke. To Pierre's French tastes it looked most outdated with its dark oak panels and small leaded window panes, lacking the splendour of the new palaces he had seen in Reims and Calais with their gleaming white stonework and impressive façades. The shingled roof with its turrets gave Hertford House an almost medieval look although the major part had been constructed under the Tudor reign. Charles explained that its location close to the river had several advantages. Traffic in London was terrible, as the city had been growing fast during the past decades; it was a sprawling monster, now beyond control.

The Thames allowed easy access to other noble and royal palaces. Charles grinned when he pointed out a second advantage. A duke was never safe from the whims of his sovereign or enemies in Parliament and Pierre's ancestors had sometimes used the Thames to escape at the last minute from unwanted excursions to the Tower of London, a royal guesthouse of dubious reputation due to the quality of its dwellings and its effect on the health of its guests.

Pierre continued his visit through his new home in London, losing count of the many rooms and galleries, dark paintings and ancient suits of armour and he couldn't hide his satisfaction and relief when he finally arrived in his new pompous bedroom overlooking the river.

Jean, who had now taken his place as Pierre's personal valet, as proposed by Marie, helped him to undress and with a sigh of satisfaction Pierre thanked Jean and stretched out in the soft cushions, pleased that his plan had worked out so well.

Jean couldn't believe his luck; he had immediately taken to Pierre and served him with real pleasure. How could people look so similar and be so different, he wondered? As much as Henri had been abusive, Pierre was kind and Jean swore to himself that he would protect his new master, as he was sure that Henri would already be planning his revenge. Only his death could end the menace.

Charles had been actively preparing their arrival, already writing to his large circle of friends and acquaintances from Hertford, making sure that Pierre would be received by the right people of influence at court. As they were still in a period of mourning, there would be no question of throwing a lavish party but Pierre was allowed to attend private invitations and Charles had made sure that there were plenty of those. Some people had reacted immediately, writing to him that they had been looking forward to meeting Pierre and Charles with pleasure, and those were their real friends, he had concluded.

Many had been more cautious. The rumours circulating in London about Pierre's ancestry and his chances of being received by the King had had their effect. Those people preferred to remain cautious and keep all options open. Charles had been in politics long enough to know how to deal with them. A second letter arrived regretting that – unless a meeting could be arranged shortly – certain monetary or political favours would not materialize or would go to their worst enemies. His letters were very subtle, of course, mentioning no names, merely hinting at opportunities that they would miss.

Charles's strategy seemed to work. New letters had arrived at Hertford, mostly carrying invitations. The last of these arrived in London as news of Pierre's triumphant entrance into London had spread like wildfire and produced an immediate effect. Pierre was most definitely a new star on the London horizon and the people who mattered in London wanted to meet him now.

Charles grinned as the last invitations arrived, lying shamelessly about the reasons as to why they had come late and assuring him of their deepest affection and devotion. The English aristocracy had been beaten; now they needed to convince the King's counsellors and obtain a swift decision from the King. This proved to be a different and more complicated story. The King of England was under heavy attack from his new and decidedly bloodthirsty Parliament. They were claiming nothing less than the head of his de facto prime minister, the Earl of Strafford. The helpless and perplexed King, desperate for money, was trying to manoeuvre out of this and save himself, but in fact his position worsened daily, as the more he gave away, the more Parliament demanded.

Consequently the King kept himself more and more isolated, inaccessible to outsiders and even Charles didn't know how quickly he would be able to arrange a royal audience. Even if Pierre had now been accepted by his peers, the King's official recognition remained a necessity.

*****

A middle-aged man sat on a chair in his sumptuous bedroom, bent and tired, a costly lace collar dangling carelessly from his long fingers. Two small dogs had settled at his feet, his famous spaniels; he would never be without them. The man had a longish face, his moustache and beard trimmed to the latest fashion, his dark, intelligent but tired eyes fixed deep and hollow in their sockets. A scene of grandiose pomp surrounded him: gold chandeliers and gilded furniture, blue velvet and purple brocades wherever he looked, precious stones gleaming in the candlelight – it was truly a bedroom made for a great king.

He felt so tired. Today had been one of the days he hated, spent in endless, even worse, fruitless council with his ministers, trying desperately to find and raise additional revenues. But all these useless and worthless imbeciles could discover was that even more money needed to be spent! Probably their own pockets were bursting from the bribes that they had amassed during his reign.

His personal army was restless and weakening, his enemies growing stronger and more brazen day by day. After this frustrating council he had dined in state, changed and dressed for a ball. Court etiquette demanded that the King and his Queen attended the ball, greeting their subjects, applauding the musicians. A King had to be at the centre of his court, the shining sun around which everything should revolve.

The Queen had been her usual self, merry, wearing a new brocade gown lavishly decorated with pearls. He could only guess the money she must have spent on it – most likely it had been outrageously expensive. King Charles sighed. The Queen had been in debt ever since her immense dowry had been squandered soon after her arrival in Britain. Whenever he admonished her, she would repent, promise in tears to stop spending, only to buy something else the next day. Born a royal princess, a daughter of France, she had never learnt the value of money, and the King sometimes doubted that she could even count.

His thoughts went back to the ball. The herald had announced his titles, starting with his royal titles of the Kingdom of Great Britain, an endless litany designed to impress and inspire awe. As usual the trumpets had sounded triumphantly as he had entered the room, leading the Queen. The ladies had curtsied, the men bowed, so low they nearly touched the marble floor. And yet, he could feel and almost see it: things had changed.

How much had he looked forward to these evening festivities when he was younger. The music, the wine, the company – how much he had enjoyed all of this. The young and beautiful ladies of the court had given him subtle signs, ready to be seduced, fighting for his attention. Hardly any evening would he have spent his nights alone as he did now. And there had been Buckingham, dashing Buckingham, his close friend. How much he had loved and trusted him. Everything had seemed possible in those days: reigning over Britain and conquering the world had seemed so easy.

Now he was sitting here, alone, buried under an avalanche of problems that never seemed to end. Even during the evening festivities they wouldn't leave him in peace. One of his courtiers had approached him, pressing him to make a decision and officially spurn this young French heir of the Duke of Hertford, a man everybody seemed to be talking about, and bestow the title on the second cousin. His courtier had lowered his voice like a conspirator and whispered in his ear, "Sire, the Crown will gain a lot of money and greatly improve relations with Parliament if the title goes to a staunch Protestant. It's a unique chance, not to be missed!"

The amount he had mentioned was huge indeed. He had calculated quickly in his mind, careful not to show how eager and desperate he really was. This money would pay for his army at least for one month. For one month he could then wield a strong hand over Parliament, one precious month in which he could avoid sacrificing Strafford. These bloodhounds were after his prime minster, as they couldn't get the King, yet. He had learned to become an actor as well; if he dragged the decision further, the price Hertford's cousin would be willing to pay would probably go up. Consequently he had just shown polite interest, a readiness to continue this discussion at a later stage, but at least he knew that there was some money he could lay his hands on fast if his situation became desperate – who cared about this unknown youngster Pierre de whatever-his-name – it was up to the King to appoint a duke!

His Majesty patted his dogs, who had been nudging him to gain his attention. Then he looked down; his expensive lace collar had become a wet, chewed rag, a third spaniel profiting from the King's absent-mindedness to crawl to his chair and chew happily on the tempting object. But the King only laughed; his dogs were his only loyal subjects. He yawned and rang for his valet. Enough of thinking, he needed to go to bed and sleep.

*****

In Hertford House, cousin Charles was still pondering over possible schemes for obtaining an audience for Pierre as he entered the library, where he bumped into Pierre and Armand sitting in comfortable chairs, legs stretched towards a gentle warming fire. Hertford House in December was glacial. It was impossible to heat the numerous rooms, therefore the library had become their favourite spot. It was a relatively small room and the ever present cold and damp draughts were kept outside with the help of heavy velvet curtains. The fact that the butler kept a good supply of claret and whisky ready on the side table only added to its attractions.

"You look like two fellows hatching secret plans," he joked, but Pierre's face flushed. Apparently he had hit the nail on the head and interrupted them in the middle of an animated but secret discussion. They looked at each other and after a short pause it was Armand who decided to speak up.

"Charles, we'd like to ask for your opinion, but please promise that you'll keep this discussion confidential," Armand asked, and his face became very serious.

Charles didn't know if he should be amused or insulted. "If you don't know by now whom to trust or not, I had better leave this room," he answered roughly.

"His lordship is offended," Armand remarked to Pierre conversationally and turning to Charles he said, "Don't make a show of it. The reason I had to ask this silly question is that my father sent me a secret message, only for Pierre and me. Thus I'm asking more on behalf of my father, the august Marquis de Saint Paul and not for my humble self."

Charles's irritation melted away and he had to laugh. Armand had disarmed him – this man truly was a charmer!

"All right, I swear, my lips are sealed, let me know what your secret is."

Armand took his crystal glass of wine, which reflected shards of red onto his otherwise spotless white shirt. Taking a sip of the delicious claret he started to talk.

"We told you that my father sent a secret message to warn us. This message urged us to meet the Order of the Templars in London as they should be able to help Pierre to gain access to the King and have his position in Britain secured before we leave for France and try to confront the odious Cardinal, who seems to

256

be the man keeping all the puppets dancing on their strings. As we know by now, my father proved right in warning us of the threat to Pierre, so I have no doubt that his advice to ask for help from the Templars will be the best course of action, but how do I achieve this? I cannot walk around London and say, 'By the way, where can I find the shortest route to the secret Templars' assembly place?' We were discussing how to proceed and were just about to take the decision to write to him to give us more details unless you, with your magnificent brain, could enlighten us!"

Charles looked at them, apparently upset at their stupidity and said, "You didn't really listen when we discussed this matter at Hertford! I'll repeat it once more, but we are all bound to keep this secret. I can tell you that Pierre's grandfather was one of the leading members of the organization that succeeded the order of the Templars here in Britain. In fact it's a family tradition stemming back to medieval times when the first Neuvilles accompanied our King Richard the Lionheart to conquer Jerusalem. Later, when the Order was stamped out and persecuted in France, all the kings in Europe gladly followed the example of the French king and disowned the Order on their territory. The enormous wealth the Templars had acquired made them an ideal target. You cannot even imagine how much wealth was diverted to the bottomless pockets of their beloved sovereigns. Thus the English Order was dissolved like the rest of the organization but luckily its members were never persecuted and tortured as they were in France. Having seen the fate of their brothers in France, the English Order officially relented, handed over the visible parts of the Order's wealth and estates to the Crown and hid the rest. The Order then became a secret and secular organization."

Charles took a sip of wine; the long speech had dried his throat.

"Needless to say, the enormous fortune of the Templars was squandered away in less than a year by our sovereigns. I really don't understand why, but it seems to be a law of nature that most kings are incapable of understanding the basics of sound household accounting." Charles paused before he continued. "But I'm straying from our subject. Tradition now commands that the head of the Neuville family, soon to be represented by Pierre, should join the Templars in London. The Templars are still the most influential secret group in Europe and here in England they include the most important members of the old aristocracy. Armand's father is right; meeting the Templars is our answer, their influence is still so great that they can quickly obtain an audience, and probably more, for you. I happen to know that King Charles's cabinet ministers are all indebted to the Templars, which basically means they have to dance to their tune. I really wonder how your father in France knows about these things; I thought those were well-guarded secrets?"

He looked at Armand, his eyebrows raised, prompting him to become more explicit.

Armand grinned and simply answered, "Because the same applies to France; the de Saint Paul family and the de Beauvoir family have been members of the Order and later the newly founded secret French organization for centuries now.

This is how my father and Pierre's father became best friends. Cardinal Richelieu has tried to break into our network but until now we have outwitted him. My father will use his influence to stop Richelieu but we have learned to be subtle; I have no clue as to how he'll proceed on his side. For us the course of action seems clear – we'll have to meet the Templars in London with Pierre as soon as you can arrange it for us!"

The next day, Charles visited one of his friends who he knew was an active member of the secret brotherhood. But he returned downcast as the bearer of bad news: a quorum was needed and only by mid December would enough members be present – if weather permitted travelling at all. The only good news was that his friend had promised to use his influence to stop the petition in Parliament that endangered Pierre's heritage. At least they would gain some time.

The days passed, December arrived and the only positive news was that Céline and Marie had finally arrived in London, staying with Marie's aunt and uncle in the Savoy Embassy. Since Marie's abduction at Sevens, her aunt didn't allow her any visits unless she was surrounded by a guard of armed servants, making any planning of visits as complicated and tedious as a royal visit.

Marie hated this fuss but she understood her aunt's concerns. The Principessa had proposed to accompany Marie and attend the balls at court, but Marie had flatly refused to be presented at court until Pierre had been officially acknowledged. Life therefore was unusually quiet and with the exception of Céline and Charles, who were planning their marriage as soon as possible, everyone else was waiting, very much aware that precious time was being lost, time they could have used to return to France and tackle the burning issue of Pierre's heritage there.

A MESSAGE FOR THE CARDINAL

The smell of hot chocolate filled the library, delicious and heavy, mingling with the pungent smells of the fire and the slightly musty smell of books and vellum. Cardinal Richelieu held the golden cup in his hands, clasping both hands around it, eager to soak up the heat emanating from the hot beverage for his ever so cold hands and inhaling deeply the wonderful aroma.

Chocolate was, in his opinion, the only positive thing that Anne d'Autriche had brought with her when she had left her Spanish home country to marry the young King of France, two children thrown into a marriage by the compelling logic of their royal destiny. For decades this Habsburg Queen had only created trouble, he thought contemptuously, although now he had to admit that she had changed since, finally, she had given birth to the Dauphin two years ago. After twenty-two years of childless marriage she had miraculously done her duty in securing the succession to the throne and it seemed that she had finally arrived in her role as Queen of France. Richelieu carefully sampled a first mouthful of the thick brown liquid. He sighed with satisfaction; his cook had remembered that he liked it sweet and had added plenty of honey in addition to some exotic spices. He inhaled the steam coming from the cup and closed his eyes.

Yes, he thought, *there's a hint of cinnamon with the honey*, and with joyful anticipation he took the next sip. Being ill and in almost constant pain, he cherished these rare moments of peace and pure delight.

Suddenly Richelieu heard a soft knocking at the door. Irritated by this interruption he put down his cup and answered, "Come in, if it's important!" hoping to deter the person requesting entry. Unfortunately his visitor seemed to understand this as an invitation to enter the room and the door swung open. Brother Joseph appeared, panting hard; apparently he had run all the way to see him. Richelieu looked at him expectantly, automatically extending his hand with his ring of office. Brother Joseph kneeled and kissed the ring before he followed the gesture that allowed him to sit down in front of the impressive desk, covered as usual with papers and files.

"Your Eminence, please excuse me if I disturb you without asking for an audience in the proper way through your secretary, but I have just received a report from London and I thought that you would wish to be informed immediately."

Richelieu took another sip of his precious chocolate and looked curiously at Brother Joseph. The friar must be the bearer of bad news – it was obvious that he was very upset and beads of perspiration had collected on his forehead, rolling down and leaving dark stains on his cowl. Brother Joseph inhaled deeply and produced an envelope, whose seal had been broken as he had already read the contents.

Richelieu took the document and slowly and painstakingly unfolded the letter that was the apparent cause of Brother Joseph's turmoil. It took only a few minutes to read through the document and Brother Joseph's hands started to tremble, wet with perspiration and fear, as he expected a violent outburst at any minute. Having read the letter himself he knew that the mission in London had been nothing else but a total failure. The Cardinal would be furious.

The Cardinal finished reading the document and to Brother Joseph's great surprise a faint smile was playing on his thin lips. Richelieu looked at him and with a soft voice he said, "How do you interpret this letter, Brother?"

Brother Joseph answered nervously. "There is not a lot to interpret, Your Eminence, this mission has been a complete failure, there's no other way to put it. Pierre de Beauvoir has arrived safely in London, still presenting himself as the Duke of Hertford, Henri de Beauvoir is missing and the abduction of Pierre's future bride has failed, none of our objectives has been reached. It's a total triumph for our enemies!" His voice broke as he uttered the last words.

Strangely enough the Cardinal did not only remain relaxed, but suddenly his shoulders began to move and to Brother Joseph's total surprise, convinced that he couldn't trust his own eyes, the mighty Cardinal started to laugh, uttering a dry asthmatic sound and clasping his belly.

If he were not facing the Cardinal, for Brother Joseph the situation would have been clear enough – his counterpart must have been drinking too much – but such a thought in connection with the venerated Cardinal Richelieu was sheer blasphemy. His face must have betrayed only too clearly his consternation as Richelieu stopped his strange behaviour abruptly. He looked at him and then he condescended to give him the rare honour of an explanation.

"You look surprised and somewhat shocked, my dearest Brother, but if you examine the situation closely, We, the Church, can only win. Please recall that we made a deal with Henri's father as I insisted; I always do keep my contracts, written or not. Henri de Beauvoir thus received the address of his cousin Pierre and we helped him once more to have a second chance to, let's say, solve the problem of his succession in England."

The Cardinal paused briefly, and in his thoughts added, *I also needed to get Henri away from the King of France as soon as possible; regrettably our King is far too quick to take a fancy to handsome and charming young men.*

Aloud he continued, "You may remember that we received an amount of 50,000 livres and, as Henri's father's assets were not liquid, he had to mortgage his estates to the only person in Paris who was ready to loan him money for this questionable enterprise, and by chance – let's say – the loan was granted by a Jew with whom we happen to entertain excellent relations. Of course these estates have a value far beyond the 50,000 livres and now that Henri has failed in his mission, they will be auctioned off. I made an agreement with the Jew that half of the exceeding amount will come back to us; I estimate conservatively that we will receive another 50,000 livres. The Jew has never betrayed me, he knows his business. This leaves the issue of the heritage of the Marquis de Beauvoir, Pierre's father. My brilliant Mazarin had the excellent idea of unearthing some old laws and procedures that will deal with this question in our favour. A legal procedure has been started that will bring the estates of the late Marquis under the sole mandate and ownership of the French Crown and I'm sure that our thankful Sovereign will know how to show his gratitude towards his servants and the Church for this truly regal gift we shall bring to him."

The Cardinal mechanically folded the document and put it carefully back into its envelope before he continued. "In fact – to be perfectly open with you – Henri's mission had become a nuisance for me, now his failure is the best solution for us and in due course will become our profit. I won't ever deal with this fool again." Richelieu's voice had suddenly become hard, his words cutting like steel. "He had his chance twice and he lost. I'm not interested in working with failures; the glory of this Kingdom and this Church commands that we fight and be victorious. Heaven is for those who succeed."

He gave a nod towards Brother Joseph who listened in awe, and knew that he had just been dismissed. Richelieu took another sip of his chocolate; it was lukewarm by now, but thankfully still drinkable, despite this disturbance by what had turned out in fact to be good news.

*****

In the South of France, winter fortunately tended to be less cold and rainy than in Paris. But once the sun had set, nights became chilly and fires were lit. The Grand Inquisitor of France had settled comfortably at his dinner table, which was laden with the most expensive dishes and the best wines France had to offer. He had loosened his fur-lined cleric's robes, his grey-haired chest showing fresh stains of gravy and fat. Opposite him, his young mistress was sitting, her bodice cut invitingly low, displaying her impressive bosom to its best advantage. She sat there like a purring cat with a chicken leg in her greasy hand while she looked at him invitingly, her pink tongue licking slowly and seductively the bone she held in her hand.

From time to time her perfect white teeth dug into the juicy meat. Her blonde hair had been adorned with a light blue silk bow, matching perfectly her large innocent-looking blue eyes. Of course he knew that she was anything but innocent, but he adored this contrast of childish looks and sluttish behaviour and even after six months he still hadn't grown tired of her. Now a large drip of the gravy was falling on her bosom and she made him a sign, prompting him to come over and lick it off with his tongue. He felt his manhood stirring; he would need to add some more Spanish fly to his wine for tonight, even if his physician had warned him that he had been overdoing things lately. This girl was worth dying for, especially if it meant dying in pleasure.

261

He was just about to lean over her, swallowing hard in order not to dribble with excitement, when a servant knocked, first softly, then more strongly and insistently.

The Grand Inquisitor was furious. He had given orders not to be disturbed unless something really urgent was at hand. Then he sighed as he realized that this must be the case and he went back to his chair, trying to rearrange quickly his robes and breeches to look dignified. If they disturbed him, something annoying must have happened, probably a fire somewhere close by in the parish.

A footman he had never seen before in a livery bearing his coat of arms entered and brought a letter, falling to his knees in front of the irate prince of the Church. The Grand Inquisitor frowned, but before he could start to admonish his servant, the latter stammered, "Your Eminence, please excuse this disturbance but this message seems to be a matter of life and death!"

The Grand Inquisitor looked at him, more astonished than worried, and tore the envelope open, and immediately several documents and a letter fell onto the table. His eyes had become weak lately and he had difficulty reading the message. The writer had covered the paper in hasty and irregular handwriting, and only the signature looked strangely familiar. When the contents of the letter started to make sense and the truth dawned on him, he gasped and the collar he had just fastened before the servant had entered, suddenly seemed to suffocate him. Holding the letter tightly and trying desperately to apply some order to his panicked thoughts, he read the letter once more, holding it as far away as possible, as the words kept swimming blurrily in front of his eyes:

Beloved Father,

I have been abducted and I am a prisoner of brutal villains. My abductors demand that you stop all proceedings against Pierre de Beauvoir. You are to sign the two documents that are enclosed. One is a judgment that will acquit Pierre de Beauvoir's mother of heresy and witchcraft and formally reinstate him as sole and lawful heir. You will receive 20,000 livres in gold once you sign the second document in which you confirm that you, as representative of the Holy Church, will also in future relinquish the pursuit of any further claims against him or his family – either in France, or in Rome. Father, you must sign the agreements tonight and deposit the letter outside the drawbridge under the oak tree in the adjacent field. If any of your soldiers are detected, I am a dead man, or worse, my abductors will start cutting off my fingers and my ears, one for each day you delay or wait. Father, I implore you, sign the documents, have pity on your eldest son.

In eternal filial love,

Jean Baptiste d'Abbeville

PS: My abductors tell me that as a proof of their power and commitment to pursue their cause, tonight, as soon as you have read this message, something terrible will happen to someone close to you. This is also bound to happen to yourself, if you do not act quickly.

The letter was covered with watery stains – this coward of a son had apparently been crying whilst he had written the letter. The Great Inquisitor was disgusted – what a weakling! Then he cursed, as he now remembered that the oak tree was located on the top of a barren hill, close to a river. It would be impossible to hide his men and follow the messenger if he came by boat. Whoever had arranged this knew the surroundings perfectly well.

Nervously the Grand Inquisitor looked at the clock ticking away on the sideboard. The letter said that something terrible would happen right here? He would deal with this! He was not to be intimidated like this weakling of a son, and taking fate into his own hands, he bellowed out orders to his servants to send for the guards.

Six members of his armed guards arrived quickly and noisily, some still wrestling with their uniforms, trying to look presentable, totally surprised at being disturbed at this unusual time of the evening without any prior warning.

The Grand Inquisitor felt reassured, seeing his men appear in the dining room, weapons gleaming, ready to defend him. His rattled nerves started to calm and he sank back into his chair, closing his eyes for some minutes. He needed to concentrate and find a suitable answer that might save his son but especially secure his future career.

If he signed the documents as requested, he might save the life of his son and gain 20,000 livres. But there wasn't the slightest doubt; he would make terrible enemies! Both Richelieu and Mazarin – now also a cardinal – would never forgive him. His career would be finished! It would just be a matter of months – if he was lucky, a year – until a letter from the Holy Father in Rome would arrive, urging him to purify his soul and give up his office for the benefit of living like a poor monk in a monastery, the usual punishment for any member of the clergy who had strayed away from the declared path of the Church. There would be no more future for his sons, at best they'd become insignificant priests, and the d'Abbeville family would be erased from the social map.

He had two more sons; hadn't God also requested once of Abraham to sacrifice his own son? Twenty thousand livres was a mere pittance compared to what he and his family would lose.

His thoughts were still in turmoil but the Grand Inquisitor felt more and more inclined to reject the demands of this letter. This was a matter of great consequence for himself and his family, didn't he have an obligation to protect their interests?

His thoughts were all of a sudden interrupted by a choking sound. He opened his eyes and noticed with horror how the lovely face of his mistress had

263

transformed into a horrible grimace, eyes bulging out of their sockets. She still held her glass with the Burgundy wine that she had been drinking to wash down the chicken, but as her hands started to clench, taking a life of their own, the fragile glass broke and it cut deeply into her fingers, spilling a horrible dark red mix of wine and blood onto her silk robe.

She moaned, fighting for breath, then slid to the ground where she lay helpless like a beetle on its back, choking, crying for help, and writhing in pain.

Shocked and alarmed, the Grand Inquisitor called the guards to search for his personal physician. He didn't dare touch her, he was too scared. Watching from a frightened distance he saw his young and once beautiful mistress lying there, looking so strange now. She was dying a terrible and painful death right before his eyes. Before the physician could arrive she was already dead, lying there, strangely rigid, her once beautiful face blue and repulsive.

The Grand Inquisitor looked around dazed, as if he was expecting some guidance on what to do next from his guards, but they were of no help. Shocked and paralysed themselves, they gaped at him and waited to receive his orders. He decided to question the footman who had delivered the letter, but the latter had vanished. When enquiries were made later on, nobody ever recalled having met him before and nobody understood how he could have entered the Episcopal castle unnoticed.

The Grand Inquisitor suddenly realized that there was a terrible smell of excrement spreading through the room and worse, it was emanating not only from his dead mistress but also from himself. In his panic and fear he must have lost control of his bowels. He grabbed the documents and rushed to his library as if the devil in person was chasing him. There he grabbed a quill, signed and sealed the documents. His valet followed him, his face a frozen mask of bewilderment, abhorrence and fear.

The Grand Inquisitor gave orders to have the documents delivered immediately and stored at the indicated place under the oak tree. He didn't even bother to have the spot supervised. The people he was dealing with meant business and having seen the terrible death of his mistress, all he wanted was to survive. Then he limped to his bedroom, his soiled breeches clinging to his legs. He needed to clean himself and later he would drink heavily until he sank into oblivion, trying to forget that this evening had ever happened.

At the end of the week, Jean-Baptiste reappeared, pale and thin. Father and son greeted each other with more affection than usual, his son full of gratitude, painfully aware of the dire consequences of his rescue for the family.

The Grand Inquisitor had made sure that all witnesses of the scene in his dining room were dispatched the next morning to some forlorn outpost, minimizing the spread of rumours. To make sure that they'd keep their mouths shut he bought their silence with coins of genuine gold. But he added the threat that he would

264

make them disappear in the deep and damp dungeons of the Episcopal castle if one word of the unusual end of his mistress and the arrival of the letter spread. He was known not to be squeamish when it came to dealing with his enemies and as the Grand Inquisitor still held an impressive array of medieval torture instruments at his disposal, they preferred to keep silent.

Father and son sat in the library in rare harmony. The father had tended to avoid the dining room lately. Their mood was dark, and Jean Baptiste listened as his father explained the dire consequences of his agreement to acquit Pierre de Beauvoir and his mother.

A leaden silence had settled in the room. "Do you have any idea who is behind this game?" his father asked coarsely. His son just nodded but instead of talking he took a sheet of paper and under the watchful eyes of his father he drew first a cross and then a horse with two men riding on its back. His father's eyes nearly glazed over as he whispered, "May God save us, it's the Templars. You couldn't expect any clemency from them. How much they must hate the very institution of the Church that helped to annihilate and torture them."

Jean Baptiste just nodded before he spoke up. "They gave me a message for you. They're aware that any judgment must be signed by the court and later by Parliament in order to be valid. They're ready to keep your documents secret as they are keen to keep Richelieu and Mazarin under the illusion that their plan is working. They told me that you're known as the master of diplomacy and Church intrigue, therefore their message is: delay, delay, and delay, write several versions of judgments with serious legal flaws so that in the end the committee in Parliament will be able to reject it. Playing for time will be in the interest of both of us. As they have your signed document in hand – and you know that they can strike again at any minute – they know that Pierre de Beauvoir is safe from you now."

The Grand Inquisitor looked at his son thoughtfully. Jean Baptiste was small and bony, and had inherited his father's thick crop of black hair and his dark eyes. Whereas his father had thick lips, a square fleshy chin, and a face that showed his lust and inclinations for the sins of the flesh, his son had thin lips and a receding chin, and always looked unsure of himself. Until today he had always believed that Jean Baptiste was not a son to be proud of, but now an upsetting question had taken possession of him: Could his son be proud of him?

I nearly sacrificed him for my own comfort, the father thought, ashamed. He would need to repent tonight in prayer.

A new chapter in their life would start now, deceiving the great Cardinal in Paris and the man who most probably would become his successor. Aloud he said, "We have no choice, they are right. I'll delay the procedures and deceive them. But you'll have to play an important part as well, our family has to start hiding treasures outside France; only God knows how long this game will last. Time is of the essence! My son, you'll discover next week that you have misread God's will and that your future path will be outside the Church. You'll leave for Venice and open a small trading house. This venture will become the place to invest most of our money. I shall sell estates and transfer our gold through our Italian bankers. The moment the d'Abbeville family risks falling into disgrace with Paris, we must be strong enough to build our future outside France, I am counting on you!"

Jean-Baptiste flushed and his face became crimson red. He looked, if possible, even more unbecoming than usual, but he seemed to have grown a little. This was the first time in his life that his dominating and choleric father had confided in him. Sending him to Venice was like a dream come true, no more boring church services, no more musty bibles to plough through. Adventure was looming, and didn't they say that the women in Italy were the most beautiful in Europe? What had been a nightmare was turning into a wonderful adventure. Life was beautiful!

Pierre had become extremely restless; waiting patiently was definitely not his strong point. Even when he visited Marie he paced up and down in her salon like a caged animal, although Marie did her best to divert him and to calm him down.

Christmas was approaching fast but they were still stuck in a cold and damp London, waiting and waiting. No invitation from the royal court had arrived yet, and excuse after excuse was forwarded for this offensive delay, but of course all of London knew that the King was bargaining hard for a final deal, trying to fill his empty pockets.

Pierre's cousin Charles had decided that it was time to intervene and approach the King. He offered a substantial amount if he would recognize Pierre, thus the King was in the comfortable position of bargaining with two interested parties and, like a gambler, he increased the stakes every week with devious pleasure.

Pierre's nerves had practically worn threadbare and when all of a sudden Charles announced triumphantly that a meeting with the Templars had been set up for the same evening, he thought it a bad joke. But it was true enough and both of them were to go, Armand as well as Pierre, with Charles offering to guide them.

After a hasty dinner they dressed with elaborate care. Pierre knew from Charles that the Brotherhood represented a good part of the old aristocracy and Pierre was aware that he needed their support if ever he wanted to follow in the footsteps of his grandfather. Charles had hired a barge from Hertford House to take them to an unknown destination.

Once they were sitting back in the cushions of the luxurious barge, Charles painstakingly blindfolded their eyes with a black cloth and both friends sat there, next to each other, in the middle of the swaying boat, listening to the gurgling sounds of the water and the rhythm of the moving oars.

They could discern the cries of crows while the distant sounds of the city faded away as they seemed to be moving out of the boundaries of London. Pierre was amazed how he suddenly became aware of the intense, sometimes putrid smells of the Thames, noxious odours and fumes floating in the air. As Pierre couldn't see anything, all his senses were concentrated on noises, scents and the eerie sensation of floating above the water in a fragile shell; he wondered why he had never before really paid attention to all of these sensations.

He had lost track of time in this dark world but to his annoyance he started to feel the cold as the damp of the river was permeating his boots and breeches, enhancing the effect of the biting December cold. A light drizzling rain had set in and added to their discomfort.

"It's time we got out of this rowing bathtub," he heard Armand say. "I'm freezing to death."

Charles laughed. "You heroes, a bit of cold and darkness and you whinge like sissies! But don't worry, we'll be there soon."

And indeed it only took a few more minutes and they could hear and feel that the rhythm of the oars was slowing down. Finally the barge bumped against a pole and they heard a scratching sound, their barge apparently hitting the jetty. They were led out onto firm ground, a strange feeling, as even the ground seemed to continue swaying and to Pierre's dismay, they were not allowed to take their blindfolds off.

Charles led them into a building, then further on into a room – fortunately well heated – where helpful hands took care of their coats and hats. They were made to sit down on chairs with carved backrests, at least Pierre could feel the bulge of wooden ornaments sticking uncomfortably into his spine. Both of them were terribly nervous and excited. They hadn't heard Charles's voice for some time, but they guessed that he'd be close, ready to help if needed, as he had promised. The hushed noise of several voices talking animatedly was audible, but Pierre couldn't really catch the sense of the conversation around them.

After what seemed like an eternity but probably amounted to only five minutes, a bell tolled and the voices fell silent. The blindfolds were removed at last and, rubbing their eyes, Pierre and Armand caught sight of their mysterious hosts for the first time. Pierre gasped – he had to restrain himself in order to keep a straight face and not to show his consternation.

Thirty or more men were standing around them, dressed in the white cloak of the Templars with its imposing red cross, holding heavy swords in their hands. Pierre had expected some sort of medieval stage set, as the Brotherhood was known to date back hundreds of years, however, he hadn't been prepared to encounter a group of knights wearing the black masks of the plague with their frightening long beaks. The effect was unnerving; like a crowd of white and red crows descended from a nightmare into reality they seemed ready to attack their victims at any given moment. Pierre looked behind him, hoping to detect the reassuring presence of his cousin Charles, but Charles had apparently left...

*****

Henri woke up; it was still early and only the first rays of daylight could be seen, but he had to pee – urgently. He had drunk far too much yesterday. He got up from his bed into the corner where the chamber pot had been placed. It was dirty, like everything else in this rotten guesthouse. The stinking latrines, nothing but dirty pits dug in the ground, were located outside close to the stables, but nobody in his right mind would leave his bedroom and walk into the freezing cold just to relieve himself.

He finished and returned to the bed. The young sailor lying there was groaning in his sleep. The blanket had moved and Henri could see his naked chest with its light blonde hair. He had met the sailor yesterday in the tavern of this sleazy guesthouse, and he knew immediately that he wanted to have him. Until recently it had been easy enough to get young men or women into his bed; he himself was a young gentleman, handsome and rich, and the thought of being rejected would never have occurred to him. But here in this shabby inn, he was a nobody, a fugitive like so many on his escape back to France. He knew that he needed to be more cunning and more careful if he wanted to conquer the lad. It was a new experience.

Bizarrely this had seemed like an exciting challenge to him, only increasing his desire to get this fellow into his bed. He had approached the young sailor, and they had shared the cheap red liquid they called wine here until the sailor was tipsy enough to move to the next step. Henri then had asked one of the younger and nicer sluts serving in the tavern to join them upstairs. She had accepted readily; it was rare to have two handsome customers who wanted to pay, usually they were disgusting, totally drunk or stupid enough to ask for love for free.

When they made love, Henri watched with mounting excitement the young sailor and the girl, both noisy and unrestrained, longing to touch them and participate. They were a beautiful pair, the young sailor with his muscular frame, long shapely legs and blonde curly hair, chest and legs covered with short blonde hairs that glistened in the light of the tallow candle, the girl dark with a sensuous mouth, firm breasts, and slim hips. Henri would have fancied her if his desires hadn't been transfixed on the young sailor.

After they had finished it had been his turn to make love to her and he had seen the lust in the eyes of the sailor while he was watching them. He made sure that the young sailor would get a good show. Afterwards he had paid the girl handsomely and sent her away, continuing to fill the sailor with cheap booze, until the fellow had dropped into the bed next to him, totally drunk. Then Henri had made love to him, slowly, silently, touching his body as he had longed to do so much already before.

The young sailor was moving now and apparently was about to awaken.

If he remembers what happened last night and raises a scandal, I'll have to kill him, Henri thought dispassionately. He couldn't take any chances. Sodomy was a capital offence in England and France, punishable by death. A de Beauvoir would not end his days on the gallows.

Henri stopped and watched the sailor, who now had opened his eyes, evidently trying to understand where he was and what had happened. He rubbed his eyes and saw Henri stark naked standing in front of the bed. He paused and apparently started to remember, staring at him.

269

To Henri's relief he didn't shout or object. He hesitated, then grinned, full of mischief, and slowly and invitingly he moved his blanket back, showing Henri that he was ready for another round of lovemaking. Henri grinned in return and gladly obliged.

They needed to wait a full week in the tavern before they could find a job on a sailing ship bound for France, more a wreck than a boat, but the owner wouldn't ask any awkward questions about their identity.

Henri took pains to stay away from the young sailor during the daytime; he had to be careful, but each night they would share their bed, inviting from time to time the maid to join them. Henri was insatiable. He was painfully aware that once he touched ground in France a new life was waiting for him. He would need to fight for his survival, no longer able to afford to follow his whims.

Henri had been reviewing his situation; there had been ample time for serious thinking during the past few weeks. He hated to admit it, but he had fouled up his mission, there was no doubt about it.

This spider Richelieu would drop him like a hot coal and the damned Jew would sell off his estates – he had probably expected this outcome anyhow. Henri realized that he was now a man without any money and no fortune or resources left. All that remained were his good looks, his title and his hate, his burning desire and thirst for revenge. He would never give up, he would fight his cousin down to his last drop of blood.

Sitting with a tankard of ale at the dirty table of the guesthouse, Henri had felt oddly detached when he had analysed his own situation – at least the ale was drinkable.

What was left was his brain and body, but no title. No potential father-in-law of sound mind would accept him as a husband for his daughter, so the obvious solution employed by impoverished nobles of proposing a rich marriage to a provincial heiress of ambitious parents who might be blinded by a title wouldn't work.

He had considered returning to his former mistress, the rich duchess in Paris, but he was pretty sure that she must already have filled the position of pet lover with somebody else. She never remained alone for very long. He had also had the experience that when it came to money, she was not the silly woman she pretended to be – she was actually quite shrewd.

The Duchess de Limoges would never be foolish enough to bestow enough money on him so as to grant him any real independence. The only solution he could find, and he flinched when he thought about him, was an old admirer, the Comte de Roquemoulin.

This elderly beau had been smitten with Henri, but the latter had spurned and ridiculed the count's timid efforts to approach him. Needless to say, circumstances had now radically changed. Roquemoulin offered all he needed; he held one of the biggest fortunes in France and would probably be besotted enough to make him his heir. Henri hesitated. Straight murder might be too blunt; there should be a more elegant solution. Lost in his thoughts he took another deep sip of the ale.

His mind was now fully active, and he felt that he was on the trail to finding the right solution. Accidents did happen. Of course, *tout Paris* would whisper behind his back and some friends would shun him openly, but there was no alternative. If he had to prostitute himself to get his revenge later, he was ready to do so.

Then a brilliant idea dawned on him, in fact the solution seemed so simple. Henri smiled with satisfaction and his eyes glittered dangerously; this was exactly the kind of devious and daring plan he loved. Even the dirty tavern suddenly looked more inviting to him.

*****

Pierre looked around, still stupefied by this strange masquerade – at least he detected the same bewildered look of total surprise in Armand's eyes. What was going on here?

The men around them bowed slowly and ceremoniously, first towards their guests and then to a man who stood right in front of Pierre, slightly crooked with age, leaning heavily yet proudly on his huge sword. The sword was decorated all over with the cross of the Templars set in precious stones. Pierre and Armand decided to stand up and bow in reply to the formal greeting they had received and to pay special homage to the man with the ceremonial sword. It seemed certain that he was in fact the Grand Master of the Brotherhood.

A huge man detached himself from the rear ranks and moved forward. He towered above all the others and when he started to speak his deep voice easily penetrated the vast assembly hall. His voice was partially muffled by the strange birdlike mask he was wearing but like lightning it dawned on Pierre that he had heard this voice before and, baffled, he became more and more certain that it was nobody else but his dear cousin Charles who was speaking to them on behalf of the Templars.

Pierre's first reaction was anger – why hadn't Charles told them that he was a member of the secret Brotherhood, instead of making this show of not knowing how and when they'd be invited!

But almost immediately Pierre chided himself for being unfair. If Charles was a Templar, he must obviously have sworn a vow of absolute secrecy and it would be undue criticism to disapprove of his observance of a holy oath.

271

All these thoughts flashed through his mind in a matter of seconds but then he forced himself to concentrate on Charles's speech. This meeting could be a deciding influence on his future and he wouldn't receive a second chance to ask for help from such an illustrious assembly.

Charles had finished greeting the assembly and now turned towards the two friends who were listening attentively. "We greet and welcome you, Pierre de Beauvoir and Armand de Saint Paul. This will be the last time that we will address you with your full name as in our Brotherhood we only use our Christian names. We are all aware here that Pierre has requested the favour of meeting our Brotherhood in order to ask our patronage and assistance to gain his heritage and to ask for our assistance in convincing His gracious Majesty, the King, to recognize him as Duke of Hertford."

Charles paused; the hall had fallen silent.

Now comes the snag, let's see what they really want from us, thought Armand, who had started to recover from the impact of the impressive masquerade.

Charles continued. "Before the venerable Brothers here make their decision we have to pose an important question: are you, Pierre, and you, Armand, willing to enter the Brotherhood yourself and swear, after the requisite period of initiation, the holy oath of obedience and secrecy? Will you be willing to sacrifice in need your life for the Brothers of the ancient and secret Order of the Templars?"

Pierre felt elated by this unexpected invitation to become part of this old and venerated Brotherhood. He was still deep in his thoughts when he heard his friend answering already in his pleasant and deep voice, "Yes, I accept, and I will."

Pierre hastened to catch up with his friend and repeated aloud, "Yes, I accept, and I will."

Charles continued in this strange muffled voice, "We welcome you soon to join our circle of Brothers and Friends."

Charles paused, and although there was hushed silence, Pierre felt that suddenly the tension was rising in the hall. He started to feel nervous; what had been decided and what would the Brotherhood expect from him, apart from to become one of them?

Charles continued to speak. "The Brothers have decided to grant you their assistance and will ascertain that you are recognized soon by the King. It is a tradition, though, that ascending to our ranks will be subject to a test of your sincerity and your total commitment. Are you willing to listen and decide?"

Pierre and Armand were taut with curiosity by now. They agreed formally to be prepared and Charles started to explain.

272

"I must go back far into history when our order was great and powerful. During the reign of our King Richard, called the Lionheart, the King personally led a holy crusade to Jerusalem. He had vowed to rescue the Holy Land from the assault of the famous Sultan Saladin. As is common knowledge, King Richard succeeded in winning back the Kingdom of Jerusalem and a truce was signed and the city and territories around Jerusalem reverted to Christian rule. Saladin and Richard had learned to respect each other greatly at the end of their battles. As a token of their mutual appreciation they exchanged precious gifts. King Richard received three rings from the Sultan: the first, with a pure diamond representing purity of faith, the second, a large ruby, representing the power of love and passion, and the third ring was adorned by a huge sapphire, representing the clarity and power of Heaven.

"Saladin gave the rings to the King and told him to guard them well, but our King was always generous and gave them away as a gift to his three dearest friends. Until today we do not know if he was extremely foolish or extremely wise, as on his way back to England King Richard was to be captured by the treacherous German Emperor and it took Richard's courageous mother Queen Eleanor a fortune and years of bargaining to buy him free.

"Richard's three friends became the guardians of the great treasure that had originally belonged to the Kingdom of Jerusalem but had passed into the safe-keeping of our Brotherhood during the last chaotic years of the Kingdom of Jerusalem. The three friends hid the treasure before Jerusalem was reconquered by the Muslims and they decided to engrave the key to finding the treasure onto those rings. As far as we know, they found such a way that only the three rings united can guide the way to the hidden treasure."

Charles paused, it had been a long speech. Pierre was wondering what this story was about. King Richard, if he remembered correctly, had been first a good friend and then the hated enemy of the French King, Philippe II, but had died a good two hundred years ago. How could they chase a treasure that had been buried and lost for such a long time? This sounded unreal.

Charles continued to speak, now assuming a very formal pose. "The Brotherhood is asking you, Pierre and Armand, if you vow to engage yourself in the quest of these rings. They must be returned to the rightful possession of the Order of the Templars, as those treasures rightfully belong to us."

Pierre swallowed hard. Up to this moment he hadn't been able to guess what kind of commitment the Brotherhood would request from him, but he certainly hadn't expected to be sent on a medieval treasure hunt with a strong smell of the fairy tale to it.

Charles had stopped and was looking at Pierre, his eyes glittering behind his black mask. Pierre didn't really know how to reply. He was aware that he was trapped. His position – in England as well as in France – was fragile at best, but hunting for three rings seemed such a bizarre task. Were these men really serious?

273

Before he had made his mind up, he heard Armand speak. "May I ask, as a future Brother who has committed with all of his soul to the cause, where these rings can be found and what is expected from us, in order that we may retrieve them for the Brotherhood?"

Well spoken, thought Pierre. *It's a polite form of giving a conditional yes – and now it's up to them to come out of hiding and disclose more details.*

Charles answered almost immediately and the lips behind the mask seemed to smile.

"Finding the ruby ring should be easy enough: it has been part of the treasury of the Duchy of Hertford for more than a century. With the help of the Brotherhood, Pierre will gain access to the Hertford treasure vaults soon enough. The diamond ring used to be in the possession of Pierre's father. One of the three friends of King Richard was his ancestor. Now, as for the third ring, the sapphire, we know that the ring is in the possession of a noble family in Italy, now the highest members of the Signoria of Venice. We're confident that the third ring can be acquired – but we count on your imagination and diplomacy as to how this can be achieved! The Brothers are convinced that you have the unique opportunity to reunite the three rings after two centuries. They have full confidence in your integrity; this is why we have invited you to join us! Therefore I ask you a last time, Pierre and Armand, will you accept our request?"

Pierre and Armand looked at each other. Pierre was surprised to find Armand's eyes full of mischief; he had expected to find him impressed by this colourful ceremony, full of awe – not amused.

Later at Hertford House Armand would tell Pierre that he had heard of Venice and immediately knew that he had to go there! Everybody in France knew that the most beautiful women of Europe lived there, although well guarded by jealous fathers and husbands. Who cared about rings if beautiful women were waiting to be conquered?

Armand smiled and nodded enthusiastically and – with the confidence that his best friend would accompany him on this new adventure – Pierre answered, "Esteemed Brothers, we gladly and with deepest reverence for the Brotherhood accept this mission. Armand and I, we accept your proposal! We are truly honoured by your trust and we shall not fail you."

Everything had been said, the meeting had ended. Charles and the other members who had remained silent throughout the meeting bowed once more slowly and ceremoniously, leaving the assembly hall in a solemn procession, led by their Grand Master who had not uttered a single word and whose identity remained a mystery.

Once more they were blindfolded and led back onto the barge. Pierre was deep in thought; he didn't even realize or feel that the night had become much colder.

274

The light drizzle of rain had turned into snow, tiny crystals that first tickled then melted on the skin of his face.

His mind was racing. Hunting for these rings meant travelling to France and then on to Venice, the famous powerful and mysterious city called the Serenissima, a city that held itself in such high esteem that it had given itself the royal title of a 'highness'.

Marie would need to stay in France – how would she react to this news? And there was still his cousin Henri and Richelieu to be reckoned with. He doubted that a Brotherhood as remote as London could have any sway in Paris. His mind went back to Venice; they had made it sound so simple to acquire the third ring. He'd bet a fortune that there was a hidden snag; why hadn't they simply acquired the sapphire ring through some middle-man?

Am I totally crazy? he thought. *I'll be putting my hand right into a hornets' nest.* His thoughts continued in this vein but secretly he had to confess that he felt elated all the same. Not only had he received tonight the support he needed so badly to swing the scales in England in his favour, he also had the perspective of new adventures looming with Armand at his side, which simply thrilled him!

This time Charles removed the cloth that had been blinding them on the river journey. They could thus watch their slow approach to the private jetty where Pierre's footmen were waiting for them, torches in their hands. It was a captivating picture: the flames made their golden liveries glow in the dark, the stags on his coat of arms seemed to dance and bow to him in the flickering light. Pierre glanced up from the bank of the river towards Hertford House and the sky and he gasped with excited pleasure. He had never really seen Hertford House from this perspective, nor at night. The building stretched along the bank of the Thames – lit by an abundance of torches, it seemed to have come straight out of a fairytale.

His eyes lingered on the majestic façade. Touching the dark sky with its turrets, Hertford House looked like a true palace fit not only for a Duke, but for a King.

Pierre suddenly felt unbelievably proud to be the owner of this beautiful place and something else happened to him. Until tonight – subconsciously – he had kept a guarded distance between the 'true' Pierre and the 'other' Pierre, the one who was supposed to be the heir to the Duchy of Hertford. He had always felt French; Pierre de Beauvoir had been his real identity. But tonight something strange had happened, he had arrived home – to his mother's home.

Pierre, Armand and Charles walked to the library. Subconsciously all of them had felt the need to meet up and discuss matters after that night's impressive experience.

As soon as the butler had closed the doors, Pierre exclaimed, "Charles, what the hell is this extraordinary story about? Do you really think we can pull it off?"

Charles looked at him, bewildered, with an expression as if Pierre had gone mad.

"I'm sorry, but I don't have the faintest idea what you're talking about!" he answered calmly.

Hotly, Pierre answered, "Of course you have, you've been talking for them all the time, I recognized your voice and someone of your size can't hide his figure!"

Charles looked at him and repeated, "Pierre, I really have no idea what you're talking about, so I'm sorry, but I can't answer this question and that's final!"

Before Pierre could say anything else, Armand interjected, "Pierre, don't be so damned stupid. This mountain of a man has the advantage of having a brain as well and he's trying kindly to tell you to shut up – if ever you wish to become member of this exclusive club, which I won't mention. *Tu comprends?*"

Pierre looked downcast and felt utterly dim. Armand was right, he must be more careful.

Armand continued, "These people have learnt their lesson once, they were tortured and killed because they were unguarded and they vowed that this would never happen again, so we have to learn and respect this rule if we want to join."

"Let's change the subject," Charles said calmly and took a glass of claret. Looking absentmindedly at the reflections in his glass he remarked casually, "Rumour has it that you might leave for France soon?"

Pierre was stunned. This was indeed a strange way to discuss the issues that were burning in his mind.

Charles continued in the same casual way, "I really don't quite understand why you intend to leave Britain at this time of the year. But I have a foreboding that by the end of December his Majesty will suddenly have changed his mind and will be pleased to welcome his new beloved cousin, the Duke of Hertford. This would allow you to leave by January, of course the worst time to cross the Channel. But some people do love adventure, I've heard. Rumour also has it that you long for some sun in Italy. I was therefore wondering if I could convince my future wife to spend our honeymoon on the Continent instead of visiting one of our cold and draughty castles in Scotland; you know women are always a bit choosy in these matters. She might even want to drag Marie with her to France."

With an exclamation of joy, Pierre bolted out of his chair and embraced Charles, who was rather taken aback by this uninhibited display of Gallic emotion.

"Charles, you are the best!" he said and Armand added, "I told you, this mountain does have some brains, he could even be French!"

Charles grinned. He knew that this was probably the highest praise he might ever hear from Armand.

*****

The spaniel approached his master cautiously; he sensed that his master was in a foul mood. No real hope that his master would take a biscuit from the bowl of finest Chinese porcelain and share it with him. All the same, he tried to gain his master's attention and first nudged him cautiously, then his pink tongue started to lick the hand that was dangling carelessly from the chair. His master's reaction was brutal and unexpected. Not only did King Charles slap his favourite pet, but he roared at him and sent him with the help of a booted leg right into the remote corner where the royal dogs had their home.

The spaniel got the message and retreated quickly, whereas under normal circumstances he would have simply ignored the royal command. He tried to look dignified and settled on his red silken cushion with the royal coat of arms. There he lay down, burying half of his muzzle under his paws. First he turned his head away to show his master that he was truly offended, but when no reaction came, he turned his head slowly, opening his huge brown eyes with a doleful look towards his master. Usually this trick worked and his master would call him and they'd reconcile – and he would get his biscuit.

But today, King Charles didn't even look up. He sat in his chair, a glass of whisky in his hand, lost in deep and bitter thought. Sometimes, Charles thought, the only real benefit that he enjoyed as a crowned king of Scotland was the virtually unlimited supply of first class whisky; for the rest, these Presbyterian zealots were nothing but trouble, just a matter of time, he concluded, before they would rule alcohol to be the work of the devil and would try to stop his supply as well.

It had been a terrible day. His Chancellor of the Exchequer had approached him during the Privy Council to inform him that it was about time to accredit the new Duke of Hertford. Charles had replied impatiently that his last suggestions regarding the sums to be paid to the royal treasury for this favour had remained without any satisfactory answer. His minister had paused, then visibly embarrassed, he had cleared his throat and answered, "I'm afraid, Sire, that there is no further choice. The second contestant has unexpectedly withdrawn his bid and has left London in a hurry."

A bomb exploding close to him would have probably had the same effect. Charles was stunned. Whereas he had comfortably expected to increase the stakes even more, he suddenly was sitting there, facing a minister – who had to remain standing according to tradition – who was telling him straight to his face that he'd remain a pauper, a king without means, his last source of raising money for his private army evaporated.

277

"What do you mean, he left London?" Charles asked in a hoarse voice, unsuccessfully trying to mask his embarrassment.

"It appears that the competing Neuville cousin was informed yesterday morning that his castle in the North of England was destroyed by a fire – we suspect that this did not happen by accident..." and the minister cleared his throat to mark this point before continuing. "He left for the North immediately to see what could be saved but it seems that the damage was extremely serious and not only his castle but also the complete harvest of last summer has been destroyed. In fact he's has no means left to come up with any substantial payment at present."

The King and his minister looked at each other, reading in their minds the same suspicion. "How extremely lucky and convenient for Pierre de Beauvoir," the King remarked dryly and his minister nodded in agreement.

"Neuville could have paid us from his income from the duchy once he gets the title?" the King suggested lamely, but his minister only replied, "I agree, Sire, but unfortunately he has informed us in writing that not only does he withdraw his own candidature, to our entire surprise, he now fully accepts and supports the validity of his cousin's claim."

His minister then produced a document that he had kept in his leather briefcase, an object made from dark red leather and showing the proud coat of arms of the Kings of Great Britain.

Charles viewed the documents with disgust. He needed to digest this information – whoever it was behind this change of mind who had put the fear of God into this coward Neuville, it seemed that Pierre de Beauvoir had unexpectedly gained some very powerful allies in England.

Hope flickered through his mind a last time. "What about Parliament?" he asked. "You told me that Parliament would oppose his nomination violently as he'd be seen as a Catholic intruder? I could override this objection, against a certain contribution of course."

His minister looked studiously at a painting across the room showing the King victorious in his coronation regalia whilst he answered the last question, trying to keep his voice even. "Sire, I had the privilege of discussing this with some leading members of Parliament. It seems that Pierre de Beauvoir has agreed to take lessons and later convert to the Protestant faith and therefore their objection has been withdrawn. We will not be able to play this card."

The King understood that he had lost this battle. Whoever stood behind Pierre de Beauvoir had played his cards masterfully. He had no other choice but to grant an official audience now to his new 'beloved' cousin. The King closed the Privy Council and retreated into his private salon, where he sat now, drinking whisky and trying in vain to find ways to save his army and build a position of strength, an impossible mission if there was no money.

They would now demand the head of his prime minister and if matters became worse, his own life might be in peril. Charles's gaze went to the pictures of his ancestors. Their lives had been continuous struggle and fighting. If they had given up, he wouldn't be sitting here. He owed it to them and to his son to fight for his cause! He became a bit more cheerful; Parliament would need to confront a true king, and he was ready to fight!

*****

"Oh, come on Pierre, don't be such an oaf!" Marie cried. "Tell us all the details of your investiture."

"Yes, we want to hear it all, until the last detail, people, gowns, all of it – and don't dare to tell us that any woman at court could outshine us!" Céline added laughingly.

Pierre found several pairs of expectant eyes fixed on his face. He smiled and answered, "I'll try to do my best, but believe me, I'm still trying to convince myself that this has been a reality and no dream." Then remembering his manners, he added, "But I can assure you that your beauty will easily surpass that of any lady at court that I have seen!"

Immediately he was rewarded by a radiant Marie you blew him a kiss from her fingertips. Céline just smiled, her eyes teasing him, not believing a single word.

The long awaited ceremony had been scheduled for the early afternoon, only days before Christmas. Leading up to the great event Pierre had started to rehearse again and again with his cousin all the steps, movements, his speech and questions of social etiquette: whom to greet, how low to bow in expressing high esteem or just to give a passing nod to. Needless to say, he was a nervous wreck when the hour finally arrived.

As soon as his cousin left him in peace and he had the opportunity to reflect on his situation, he still couldn't believe that he, the former orphan boy from a provincial monastery in France, was going to ascend to the highest ranks the British aristocracy had to offer.

He had been dressed by Jean to look his best, in elegant dark velvet, with white lace collar, high boots shining to perfection in the light. When he came down the sweeping staircase to the great hall to meet Armand and Charles, they too were in their finest, ready to accompany him for his great day at Whitehall Palace.

Armand was nervous too. During the last tedious negotiations Pierre had insisted that they should be knighted together and, following his own investiture, the King was to proclaim Armand an Earl of the Kingdom of Great Britain.

Together they stepped out of the great door that led towards the jetty. As soon as the King had signalled his readiness to receive and acknowledge Pierre, Cousin Charles had changed his tactic and suggested offering a substantial amount of

279

money to soothe the irate sovereign. Cunningly he had used this occasion to request the King's approval for Pierre's betrothal with Marie and simultaneously to endorse Pierre's decision to transfer the estates and title of the Earl of Worthing to his friend.

Under normal circumstances King Charles might have hesitated to allow the marriage of a peer of Britain to a French lady of mere provincial background and to accept access of the son of a French Marquis to his nobles, but King Charles had bargained once too much and now he snapped up the amount that was offered by Cousin Charles greedily and was ready to sign whatever was presented to him, as long as it allowed him to buy weapons for the royal army that he was starting to assemble outside London, as an armed conflict with Parliament now seemed unavoidable.

As a token of his appreciation for the money that had arrived like a gift sent from heaven, King Charles had offered to dispatch his own royal barge to Hertford House in order to fetch Pierre and his friends. The golden barge was thus berthed outside, the royal flags waving joyfully in the frosty wind. The oarsmen in their magnificent red and golden royal liveries formed a guard of honour with their oars presented upright in honour of the three friends as they stepped onto the luxurious barge. They settled in the purple velvet cushions and as they listened to the commands that were bellowed by the mate the barge was set in motion, and the oarsmen started rowing with the precision and routine of a perfectly tuned clockwork mechanism.

Whitehall Palace was reached fairly quickly and Pierre was amazed to discover such a huge and sprawling complex of buildings. With the exception of the newly constructed Covent Garden, all of London was mostly old and narrow. It was therefore a total surprise to discover Whitehall, sprawling from the banks of the Thames into the city, a huge and impressive palace spreading and twisting into London like a city of its own – some said that it was the biggest palace in Europe.

They had been led into the hall that was used for official audiences, a vast room with coffered ceilings, proudly displaying carved Tudor roses as decoration. Pierre and Armand took their places among the other nobles, the room humming with voices until the piercing sound of trumpets announced the arrival of the King.

King Charles arrived, leading his Queen, and graciously he walked towards the two thrones that were positioned at the opposite side of the room, placed on a podium and covered by a canopy showing his coat of arms.

The herald announced the endless litany of his royal titles and Pierre saw in fascination how every noble bowed low while the King and Queen walked slowly and graciously through the crowd of noble men and women who parted and bowed before the royal couple, as Moses must have walked through the parting waters of the sea.

The King and the Queen were dressed in full splendour, the Queen's tiara glittering in the light of the torches and candles, competing with the vivid reflections emanating from the strands of her impressive diamond necklace.

Once they had settled down, the ceremony he had so much longed for – but dreaded at the same time – began. But as hard as Pierre tried later to remember all of the details, his memory from now on was just a blur.

He could remember that he had kneeled in front of the throne, he remembered the feel of the cool blade of the King's sword when he was elevated to his new position and he remembered the herald calling him 'The Most High, Noble and Potent Prince, His Grace, Pierre, Duke of Hertford' in public – and he recalled a feeling of total elation that had filled his heart and soul when the trumpets had sounded again. Then the King kissed him dutifully and called him 'my beloved cousin' as century-old protocol demanded.

Afterwards it was Armand's turn to be dubbed and proclaimed Earl of Worthing and Pierre had felt as proud as when his own proclamation was made.

The two young men made an impressive picture indeed. The newly appointed Duke was extremely handsome, his pale and blonde complexion in stark contrast to his dark velvet attire, sparkling with the diamonds of his decorations.

By contrast, his friend, the new Earl of Worthing, cut a dashing figure. Dressed in a fancy burgundy waistcoat he left many hearts beating faster and he had won immediately the approving glances of numerous court ladies who were present and who interpreted correctly the shamelessly adoring gleam in his eyes when he looked back. Later heated discussions in the female quarters took place: some took a fancy to Pierre's elegant looks, while many preferred Armand, but one thing was clear: Two new stars had appeared in the firmament of the royal court!

Somehow Pierre and Armand had found their way back from the throne to their peers who were congratulating and heaping praise in exaggerated abundance on them. Charles had warned him in advance that courtiers had their own language and code of conduct. Pierre smiled and returned the same hollow compliments to everybody who wanted to listen. His answers were polished and fluent, and he noticed that his cousin was watching him with satisfaction.

The royal audience was followed by a sumptuous dinner. Of course Pierre had guessed that dinner at court must be an impressive experience but nothing had prepared him for the splendour and extravagance that was awaiting him. The gigantic tables were decorated with statues crafted from solid gold, in fact gold and silver were shimmering everywhere on the table covers of rich purple cloth.

Golden plates, bowls and cornucopia filled with all imaginable kinds of sweets and fruit competed with exotic receptacles, like the gigantic shell of an ostrich egg on a silver tripod or bowls made from the finest Chinese porcelain, a material so thin that it looked almost transparent, painted with dragons that seemed to come to life in the candlelight.

The table was loaded with the most exotic dishes that could be imagined, almost too many for Pierre's taste: partridge, a whole pig, strongly spiced venison, stuffed peacock decorated with its colourful feathers, pies of all kinds, fish from the river and from the sea. Some dishes had even been covered with thin layers of gold, all decorated to create a stunningly colourful tableau. Disappointingly, most of the taste of the food did not live up to its perfect image; it was already cold and tasted excessively spiced or even stale.

The dining hall was heated by several huge fireplaces, but with the effect that those sitting close to the fire nearly died from the heat, and those sitting close to the doors were frozen to death by the December draughts. Pierre unfortunately had taken his place of honour close to the royal couple and therefore was sitting very close to the fire. Soon he felt almost suffocated by the heat and the strong smell of the food and even more by the odour of the people around him.

Many ladies and gentlemen at court were using musk and other strong scents to cover their lack of personal hygiene. Pierre found this malodorous mix of sweat, food, smoke from the fire and heavy perfume nauseating. His head was starting to throb; he needed to leave the room or he would find himself either fainting or vomiting – and he couldn't decide which option would be worse, especially on his first day at court. Extracting himself with some difficulty from his conversation with a heavily made-up dowager countess who had decided that a young and handsome duke fitted perfectly with her ideas of a new husband, he hurried out of the doors and into a small adjacent court where he breathed greedily the cold air of the December night.

Armand had noticed Pierre's malaise and joined him quickly. He seemed to be of a more robust nature and was thoroughly enjoying his evening. Armand put his arm around his friend's shoulders and Pierre was glad that his friend was there, close to him, and he started already to feel better.

"Too much booze, Your Grace? Or did your neighbour, the charming but not so fragrant ladyship, get a bit too close?" Armand joked, while skilfully avoiding a kick from Pierre, which was to be the only answer given by 'His Grace'.

They went back into the dining hall. The wine that had been flowing freely had taken effect, the formerly strict etiquette had loosened and they managed to find some space closer to the door where the air was better. The trumpets announced that the royal couple had decided to leave the banquet and once again their Majesties moved through this sea of bowing heads and curtsying women towards the exit, the King's longish face looking tired and bored; he had apparently seen it all far too often.

Cousin Charles came to search for Pierre and Armand, accompanied by a band of noble friends. Most of them were laughing and joking about a fat lady on the opposite side of the table who had just lost part of her artificial headdress. Solemnly but not very soberly she looked at her ruined wig that had dropped right onto her plate, trying to work out what had happened to her.

Pierre knew many of the lords who were greeting him, but many were new faces to him. He tried to memorize all the faces and names, smiling politely and feeling at ease as he seemed to be genuinely welcomed by Charles's circle of friends.

When their small group moved toward the exit, Pierre heard someone muttering in the background, "Look at that pansy, what a decrepit and evil kingdom it is that chooses a duke from the stranded bastards of heretic foreigners."

Pierre turned around, as if he had been stung by a wasp. His face was flushed and he wanted to lunge at the person who had uttered this unbearable insult. Several men stood together in a small group, all clad in sober black clothes. Pierre was almost certain that the insult had come from a middle-aged man with a red face, flushed from the heat, dressed like his friends in the sober colours of the Puritans, his unbecoming short haircut a declaration of his dedication to his faith.

But Charles reacted faster. His arm had gripped Pierre's and held him as if in an iron vice; Pierre could feel how strong he must be.

"Don't let him provoke you!" Charles whispered. "A fool shows his annoyance at once, but a prudent man overlooks an insult, the bible says. You're a duke now, a person far above the crowd and he's just one of the many country squires who recently came to power, set out to save our country from supposed evil by joining Parliament, or to ruin it, if you ask me. Let's deal with these people later, but pretend that you don't care, don't ruin your first appearance at court! Duels are strictly forbidden!"

Aloud Charles made an ironic jest about the elegance of Puritan dresses and Pierre, seeing many expectant eyes on his face, decided to play the game as suggested. He made a rude remark about people who had apparently had lost their brain along with their sense of style and continued towards the exit, ignoring the furious expressions on the faces of the Puritans.

Once they were sitting in the barge, returning home, Charles congratulated him once more on his accession to his position and continued, "I'm truly proud of you, Pierre, you'll make an excellent duke and head of our family. I'm also happy that you followed my advice and ignored the provocation by that stupid Roundhead. I'm sure he had been sent there by a gang that still supports our dear frog cousin. Please be careful, many people would like to see you dead or exiled, never forget! You're now a cog in the machinery of British politics, whether you like it or not!"

Pierre tried to digest this. He had felt so elated but now Charles's comment had brought him smartly back to reality. He tried to remember an idiom that he had learnt recently — 'you can't have your cake and eat it' — well, he was a duke now, he'd have to live with the inconveniences, and the number of his enemies seemed to have multiplied, but didn't he also have more friends than ever before? He smiled back at Charles, thankful for all that he had done for him.

"Charles, let me thank you from the bottom of my heart. We all know that I wouldn't be sitting here, in the King's own boat, if you hadn't helped and supported me from the first day we met, I'll never forget this!"

He looked at Charles who looked back and smiled, but Charles's eyes were blinking and seemed a little watery – could it be possible that this cool British cousin had become a victim of Gallic-style emotions?

*****

"Pierre come on, what are you thinking of? We're waiting!" Marie's impatient voice penetrated his thoughts. He couldn't really tell her everything, he decided quickly. But it would have been unfair not to oblige the ladies' pleas and carefully Pierre circumvented any topics that might arouse their suspicion. Hence he omitted mentioning the mature but still attractive lady at court who had been sitting next to him at dinner or topics that would raise their anxiety, like the aggressively offensive comments by the Roundhead.

Knowing that Marie was longing to visit the royal court herself and that she was craving to attend her first ball there, he painted a detailed picture to his grateful and attentive audience of the pompous rooms, the beautiful clothing of the courtiers and their ladies, the music, the entrance of the King and the Queen.

"Is the Queen beautiful?" Marie asked breathlessly, eyes wide open.

Pierre was tempted to reply flatly 'not really', but he didn't want to disappoint Marie. Carefully he chose a diplomatic answer. "I would rather say that she's very impressive and regal!" thus skilfully navigating around a straightforward answer. Luckily his answer was well received and Marie proceeded to the next question but a look at Armand told Pierre that the former was fighting to suppress his laughter. Armand had told him during the evening that the Queen looked like a stuffed lifesize puppet and regrettably wasn't any more handsome or charming than her awkward stick of a brother in France, King Louis XIII.

A dinner party had been arranged by the Principessa in their honour and they passed a very agreeable evening. The dinner table was loaded with delicacies, which was no surprise as she was known to be a generous hostess, but tonight the Principessa had surpassed herself and surprised them with the finest specialties imported from France and Italy. It must have cost her a fortune to have them brought to London!

Pierre and Armand and all of their friends revelled in long-missed delicacies such as foie gras, the finest ham from Italy, marinated olives, nuts, delicious red

284

and sweet white wines and all kinds of sweet or salted tarts – a true feast for all the senses!

Charles announced with a toast to his bride that their wedding date had been fixed soon after Christmas. He let the first storm of congratulations pass before he delivered the best news of all: after the wedding all of them were bound for France together!

"Maybe it's a strange idea for a honeymoon but I thought that you might like it," he said apologetically to Céline.

Marie and Céline jumped up from their chairs simultaneously, cheering and laughing and raced over to Charles who found himself embraced and kissed – very strange indeed, these French people!

Marie's aunt was so intrigued by the news that she decided on the spot to join their party to Paris. She hadn't been there for years and it was most definitely time to spend spring in France and Italy. Nobody of sound mind could bear this British winter weather! "It's an excellent idea," she cried happily. "I was really afraid of becoming rheumatic or depressed in this terrible city, I've had a mind to leave for the Continent for weeks, you've saved me!"

*****

Christmas was approaching fast; the nights had become freezing cold and although the streets of London were as wet, muddy and dirty as usual, a fine layer of snow had covered the gardens of Hertford House adjacent to the river banks, adding to its fairy-tale charm. Charles and Céline had decided to marry in a private ceremony after the festive season. But to Pierre and Armand, who were experiencing their first Christmas in England, the festivities seemed to stretch endlessly – a string of merry parties and balls alternating with sumptuous dinners, until they thought they'd either drop from fatigue or burst from too much food and drink.

Now that Pierre had been installed in his offices, regular attendance at court was expected from him. A new style of living had commenced and rapidly he started to find his way in the intricate labyrinth of the palace. He followed Charles's advice, though, never to be alone and most times he was accompanied by Armand. Soon they were nicknamed the 'French twins', as it was rare to see one without the other.

Marie's uncle had used his excellent connections and had managed to receive invitations for his family, Marie and Céline to attend one of the famous Christmas balls at Whitehall Palace. Marie was looking forward to this occasion greatly. She spent hours with Céline choosing a gown and rehearsing her dancing skills and when the great evening came, she drove everybody mad as she wouldn't stop talking, kept running around the house and changed her mind so often about her hairstyle that her aunt had to threaten her that she would have to stay behind if she

285

didn't calm down and leave them in peace. Marie pouted for a wonderful five minutes of silence but then she discovered that she hadn't yet chosen her jewellery and to the exasperation of her maid she opened her large jewellery case and covered her bed with different necklaces, rings, bracelets and brooches until her room looked like the caves of Ali Baba, as her father had always been very generous.

When the ladies arrived at Whitehall Palace where they were met by Pierre, Armand and Charles, to their satisfaction, all of the efforts they had invested in dressing up proved to be worthwhile. Marie looked stunning. She wore a simple robe made from creamy white silk, the matching collar embroidered with pearls. Her auburn hair looked splendid, her shimmering long locks held back by a simple but elegant tiara, studded with pearls and diamonds in the shape of small blossoms. Her amber eyes were shining and Pierre felt unbelievably proud to be accompanying her.

Céline stood next to her, and as usual she looked extremely elegant. She had flatly rejected all proposals by Charles to buy her a gown for this occasion. Only she and the Principessa knew that the elegant blue and grey silk dress had been worn already and had been freshened up recently.

The Principessa looked most glamorous; she had opted to add some exotic feathers to her gown and the attire of the three ladies was much admired and commented upon as they entered the ballroom.

They were presented to the Royal couple sitting on their golden chairs at the back of the ballroom. The ballroom was lit by hundreds of candles, the warm light of the candles reflected by a myriad of mirrors. Reflections of gold were everywhere, from the chandeliers to the furniture and finally in the jewellery worn in abundance by the ladies and even the gentlemen. Marie sank to a deep curtsey in front of the King. She could see, even feel, his keen glance appraising her figure. His Majesty apparently liked what he saw and jovially he started a flirting conversation with her, proving his excellent command of the French language. When Marie was finally released and able to greet the Queen, she was greeted with a glacial look and not even the fact that Marie greeted her in French, her native language, could make the Queen smile. *What a sour face she has*, thought Marie, *poor King Charles*.

Marie's aunt introduced them to a circle of young ladies of the court and quickly Marie and Céline were seen in animated conversation with several ladies of their age until the dancing started. Arthur had asked for the first dance and Marie found herself swirling around to the sound of the music. After the first nervous steps she found that her feet seemed to follow the tunes automatically and she relaxed, relishing every minute of it. Pierre was allowed to lead her in a dance called the volta. Her dance teacher had told her that this dance had been the preferred dance of Queen Elizabeth and since then, volta tunes were played at each royal ball. Marie loved it, especially when Pierre had to lift her up and she felt a like bird flying in the sky.

Marie went back to join her group of young ladies, who had of course seen her dancing with the young Duke. The young ladies of the court were sitting on chairs like colourful birds of paradise, constantly moving their precious fans to fight the heat and attract attention, chatting animatedly. They were supervised by some matrons who kept a benevolent eye on them. One of the matrons sat on her chair, her chin sagging as she slept peacefully amidst the noise of the music and the crowd.

Marie was terribly thirsty. The heat emanating from the countless candles and hundreds of people, the restless dancing, all of this made her feel sick – she'd need to drink something immediately or she'd die. She spotted a footman with glasses of white wine standing close and moved towards him. Hastily she grabbed a glass of the cool wine and drank it greedily. Marie was just starting to feel better when she overheard a conversation right behind her.

"Have you seen Hertford dancing with this foreign nobody? She seemed so much in love with him, how sweet, how naïve!" Startled, Marie froze. She had started to turn round but now she stood still, eager to hear more.

"He's definitely rather attractive, it's so rare to have them handsome and rich at the same time, I think I'll have a try, unless of course he prefers boys." The voice had taken on a conspiratorial note.

"My brother told me that he's always hanging around with this new earl with the dark hair, you know the other Frenchman, he's also a handsome one, and that's always suspicious. And have you seen the coloured servant he's always dragging around with him, what a dream!"

Marie heard the first girl giggle. "Prefers boys? Forget it! The dark one danced with me several times tonight and if he could have dragged me to bed there and then he'd have done it. He nearly devoured me on the dancing floor. Actually I might consider giving him a chance, they always say, the French really know how to do it!"

"Not like those English hogs," Marie heard the other voice say, "they only get drunk and then get it finished within two minutes!"

"You should certainly have enough experience to know about these things," the giggling voice interjected.

Both of them burst into knowing laughter and then the first voice continued, "I think I'll have a go at the young duke, look at him, he's really stunning!"

"Forget it, my dearest Anne," Marie heard the second patronizing voice saying. "He's far too high above you. A duke can only marry with royal permission, don't forget. But I might consider him for me, father has been pushing me hard to pick a suitable husband. But I don't know, actually our family is even a cut above him, the Neuvilles are newcomers after all." The voice now had become very arrogant.

287

"Maybe he's for you," said the other girl, adding maliciously after a small pause, "if he likes long noses."

The arrogant voice didn't seem to be perturbed at all. "It's the Percy nose, my dear, and it's quite noble, if you have any idea what this word means. Our family was governing most of England when the Stuarts were still peasants sitting in their stinking castle in Scotland. My father always says it's a pity they didn't remain there."

Marie had heard enough and suddenly she felt really sick. The hot air seemed to be suffocating her. She dropped her glass and hastened out of the ballroom. The words 'naïve nobody' and 'royal permission' were hammering in her brain, repeating themselves relentlessly. Had she been living in a dream? It sounded so true, the girl had been so self-assured. Yes, she had been very naïve. She had a large dowry but her parents were of provincial French aristocracy, and Pierre was now a duke, a peer of Britain! She was a foreigner, a provincial nobody to these courtiers!

Marie had been hastening down unknown alleys and corridors until she started to calm down and came back to her senses. She now found herself lost in this huge labyrinth of a palace with no idea where she was or how to get back. Tentatively she approached a door that stood slightly ajar and entered the sparsely lit room. As soon as she had set foot in the room, she already regretted her decision.

Heavy breathing greeted her from a corner and she detected the shadows of two persons who were obviously coupling there, oblivious of their environment. Marie heard the woman starting to pant and in panic and confusion she fled the room. She reached the corridor and to her great relief she saw an elderly gentleman in elegant court attire walking towards another door.

"I'm sorry, my lord, I have lost my way. Would you be kind enough to guide me back to the ballroom?" Marie pleaded, tears in her eyes. The gentleman looked at her and Marie had difficulty interpreting his look, but he seemed to care for her plight. He ogled her once more and then offered his arm ceremoniously. They moved towards a different door and Marie sensed that despite the fact that he was trying to move in a straight line, he was apparently very drunk. They entered a dark room and before Marie had time to ask or react, he had closed the door and was starting to fumble at his breeches.

"What are you doing?" Marie exclaimed, close to hysterics.

"You asked me for a service, so I ask you for one as well, my beautiful little bird," he answered, his speech thick and slow from too much alcohol.

Marie was shocked but then a wave of fury engulfed her. What kind of people were living here at court? She approached him, and he started grinning in gleeful anticipation, looking both impatient and like an imbecile, now that his breeches were round his ankles.

But his gleeful anticipation was short lived, as Marie grabbed the decorative ceramic pot that was standing on the mantelpiece and before her victim understood what was happening to him the pot came down on his head, smashed into a thousand pieces whilst her victim slowly fell to his knees, blood oozing slowly from his wound. Marie heard him fall to the floor, a muffled noise as he fell on a carpet, then there was total silence, and he moved no more.

Marie looked at him without remorse. "Your reward, you swine," she exclaimed with satisfaction, feeling much better now and left the room. He would survive, she guessed. Perhaps she should have hit him harder.

She went down the next corridor and bumped into a footman wearing the livery of the King. Marie decided that it was time to show authority, no more pleading this time.

"Take me to the ballroom at once!" she ordered. Her resolute manner did the job, as the astonished footman bowed and obeyed. He led her across an inner courtyard and then through a short gallery straight to the entrance to the ballroom where Céline was waiting for her, evidently worried.

"Marie, where have you been?" she cried and ran towards her. Marie wanted to move forward, but Céline stopped her.

"You cannot possibly enter the ballroom like this, you look utterly distraught. My father always used to say that courtiers are the most dangerous species of all animals that God has ever created, and I think he was right. They'll eat you alive if you enter the room like this; I don't even want to imagine what kind of rumours will be running around. Tell me what has happened and let me help you compose yourself."

Marie swallowed hard. Céline was right, as always. She told her about the snippets of conversation that she had overheard and that she had run away and become lost, but she decided to omit the last adventure, as the rest seemed embarrassing enough. Céline took out some refreshing lotion and cooled her forehead, then she quickly arranged her locks and tiara, then finally she straightened the precious collar that sat askew.

"That's better," she concluded, apparently happy with her work.

"Better let me do the talking first. I have stayed out of their sight to make sure that I can cover your absence. So we'll pretend that were together most of the time. You are a silly goose, you must never ever run away on your own in this palace, God alone knows what could have happened to you!" she exclaimed.

I know exactly what could have happened, Marie thought, grimly.

Céline continued quickly, "As to the question that Pierre may not be allowed to marry you, I happen to know that Charles and Pierre proposed a lucrative bargain to the King and he has already accepted this marriage. The reason why Pierre

289

didn't tell you is simple and you should have guessed. He has to ask your father first for his permission. Anything else would be a total breach of good manners. In my case I was lucky and it's different. I'm not in the first flush of youth anymore and my parents are dead, so I was allowed to decide for myself."

Marie could have kissed her, she really had been a silly goose. Arm in arm they entered the ballroom and found themselves quickly surrounded by a circle of curious ladies of the court asking why they had been absent for so long.

Marie heard Céline chatting merrily. "We've been marvelling at some of the rooms and when Marie showed me the coat of arms of our present Queen we completely forgot the time. We were discussing if it would be desirable to be born a Royal princess or not. Just imagine, you've grown up in a country and one day your father tells you to go and marry some man you've never seen in a country far away?"

Immediately her remark launched an animated discussion and Marie's absence was forgotten. Surprisingly, most of the court ladies would be willing to share their bed with even the ugliest of princes if only a royal title were thrown into the deal.

Marie looked once more around her, saw the pompous decoration but suddenly she saw behind the façade. It was truly beautiful, the ball had been splendid and the dancing fun, but if she wanted to become a duchess worthy of the name, she needed to learn a lot. The court was a jungle full of dangerous animals and traps. Until now she had dreamt about her marriage and then imagined living happily ever after somewhere in a remote castle. This evening she understood that a marriage to Pierre meant becoming a member of this court – or the court of France – but in any case her life would be linked to politics and the need to keep up appearances. She'd need to grow up, face reality and also help Pierre if she really wanted to share his life. Pierre was no fairy-tale prince and she would have to bury her naïve notions of becoming a princess. It seemed that tough times were waiting for her.

Armand, however, was having a great time. He loved to dance and had quickly learnt the steps of the English court dances. Secretly he thought that this volta was a bit mad, but as it allowed him to touch the ladies and lift them up, he loved it! What a great opportunity to come close to beautiful ladies of the court who were normally very well guarded. He had taken care to change his partners regularly as dancing several times with the same lady would set the tongues wagging. Armand had just taken two glasses of wine from the tablet that had been offered to him, as he was thirsty, when a pleasant voice behind him said, "How kind of you to offer me a glass, I love men who anticipate the needs of the ladies!"

Surprised he turned around and his expression changed to one of purest adoration when he discovered who had been talking to him. This young lady had the most beautiful laughing eyes that he had ever seen. Her face was perfect, a small nose and full red lips that were sending him an urgent message: 'Kiss me'. She was of medium height and looked foreign, and her English betrayed a charming foreign accent. Armand felt as if he had been struck by a lightning bolt, and for the first time ever in his life, he fell in love. The lady seemed to be able to read his expression and in her pleasant voice she teased him, "It would be nice though, if you could hand me the glass. It's a bit unfair to keep it for yourself!"

Armand felt like an idiot and immediately presented the glass to her, but did so too fast and several drops of the wine spilled on his hand. She gave a soft sound of suppressed laughter and produced a clean kerchief, dabbing his hand softly and cautiously. She knew of course what she was doing to Armand; he felt as if the earth had opened up and swallowed him, catapulting him into a new dimension.

He cleared his throat and managed to say, "I'm sorry, I'm behaving like an idiot, may I introduce myself? I am Armand de Saint Paul, Earl of Worthing at your *eternal* service! With whom do I have the pleasure of conversing?" He had lingered on the word 'eternal' rather longer than necessary and gave her a look so intense that the young lady now showed a flush of colour in her beautiful face.

"I am Julia, the eldest daughter of his Excellency, Giovanni Contarini, Ambassador of the Republic of Venice, at your service as well."

No mention of eternal devotion here, he thought, *but at least it's a start.* She had changed to French now and she spoke it fluently, with a charming Italian accent. Armand was totally incapable later of telling what they had been talking about, but it seemed that they must have been discussing it for some time as Julia's mother appeared with a disapproving frown on her face. Armand knew how to deal with elderly ladies and soon she started to melt. Armand had recognized that Julia's mother was wearing a priceless necklace and astutely he praised the unique quality of her emeralds. Proudly she condescended to inform him that some of her forefathers had brought it to Venice after they had invaded Constantinople.

Armand didn't fail to look suitably impressed and then took his leave, not without having convinced the mother to grant him the next dance with her daughter. Julia's mother realized only too late that this dance was to be a scandalous volta, but the young couple had already disappeared, dancing in high spirits amidst the crowd.

Good manners demanded that he brought Julia back immediately after the dance and they said goodbye, but Armand knew at the bottom of his heart that he'd move heaven and earth to ensure another meeting soon. When he turned back once more, he saw that Julia's eyes had been following him and his spirits soared. This was indeed a promising start.

His Eminence, the most noble Cardinal Mazarin, freshly appointed by the Holy See, and the celebrated rising star of the French court, was waiting – meekly – in the antechamber of Richelieu's study. He'd been sitting there like a schoolboy for half an hour and he was extremely displeased.

Mazarin was not used to this kind of treatment anymore! Usually he was the one to decide to keep his visitors waiting; it was a useful strategy to make sure that they understood his position of power, but he didn't appreciate at all that Richelieu was playing this game with him today. The clock on the mantelpiece was ticking while its hands seemed to be stuck in the same position, but Mazarin suppressed an angry groan. Richelieu was probably just waiting for any hint of impatience or displeasure but Mazarin would not grant him the satisfaction.

Mazarin thus sat on the chair, outwardly cool and composed, the picture of an obedient servant of the Church. It took another quarter of an hour until Richelieu's secretary appeared, uttering a short formal excuse for the delay. But now Mazarin wasn't so much concerned about the length of time he had been waiting. If Richelieu had kept him waiting a good hour, it meant that his mentor was extremely upset and displeased about something that he must have done. Mazarin had spent the last ten minutes in vain trying to work out the source of his sudden fall from grace. Yet he still needed Richelieu's support, for his position at court was not yet strong enough that he could survive on his own. Richelieu still had the power to make careers – or break them.

The freshly appointed cardinal entered Richelieu's study with his nerves in turmoil, but Mazarin had faced so many difficult situations in his life and mastered so many diplomatic crises that he didn't lose his countenance but neared the mighty Cardinal Richelieu composed and apparently unshaken. Richelieu pretended not to have heard him approaching his desk, and only looked up when Mazarin had already started to bend his knee in order to greet him and kiss his ring of office as a sign that he still held Richelieu to be his senior.

Richelieu gave him a sign to sit down and without further introduction he handed him a document. Mazarin took his seat and studied the document carefully. He had immediately detected that the seal at the bottom bore the insignia of the Grand Inquisitor and curiously he started to read the lengthy letter.

Clearly this letter must be the source of the old man's displeasure, he thought, *but why haven't I heard anything? Last time I talked with him everything seemed set to succeed...*

He ploughed through the letter, studded with legal phrases and endless Latin citations. It was indeed difficult to read and even more difficult to understand for one unaccustomed to the style of language. Cardinal Richelieu had of course immediately understood its significance and it was no surprise that he was furious.

Richelieu gave him only five minutes to digest the document, then he started to speak, more an irate whisper than genuine speech.

"My dear Mazarin, you – who are so clever – what do you make of this document?" he asked sarcastically.

Mazarin gave a last glance over some of the lengthy phrases and answered smoothly, "Our Brother in Christ, the Grand Inquisitor, is telling us – of course to his greatest regret – that owing to some technical and legal mistakes during the interrogation procedure of our witnesses, of course beyond his influence, he has come to the conclusion that parts of their testimonials are questionable and the present judgment of his special court might be too easily opposable by the legal department of our Parliament. He therefore has ordered a new session of the court, necessitating regrettably once more the presence of all witnesses..."

Here he was suddenly interrupted by a totally infuriated Richelieu, who hissed, "a session that might, and I stress the word 'might', take place in May or later this year!"

Without any warning, Richelieu's hand banged on the desk. During his speech his face had become an angry grimace but now it changed to an expression of pain. His furious outbreak had caused one of his many ailments to rise up and torture him.

Mazarin had decided the best strategy for him would be not to be intimidated and faced him openly. "Do you think he's been bought by the enemy?" he asked Richelieu.

"Either he's been bought or it's political. Maybe someone told him that I'm soon to join the angels in heaven and he's trying to keep his head out of any risk. He's always been a damned liar. I'll soon know the truth; I'm putting my spies in his household already. The sober fact, though, is that we'll lose between half a year to a year at least and that *your strategy* hasn't worked," Richelieu answered.

Mazarin looked respectfully at the irate cardinal but said with a firm voice, "Does Your Eminence want me to deal with this? I could ride to the south and talk business with him. I'm sure that my strategy was right, but I was convinced that we had offered enough to have him on our side."

Richelieu looked at him with grudging respect and answered, "Soon you'll convince me that it was my fault because I didn't keep him under tight supervision or that my spies failed. Let me deal with him first; you and I know that we're treading on difficult ground. If the great families of this country find out too early what we're about to do, there'll be an unprecedented uproar in France and I'm not sure how His Majesty will react. Sometimes he tends to be... let's say, inflexible.

Kings by definition cannot be called stubborn, they are far above the criticism of us common mortals." Richelieu showed a faint smile; apparently he liked his last ironic statement. He then concluded, "Maybe our friend is just cautious because he knows that we might put our fingers straight into a hornets' nest."

Mazarin started to relax, the old man was calming down after all.

Richelieu started to speak once more. "Luckily my own little plan has worked out beautifully," he said gleefully. Mazarin lifted his head. He had been reading the document again and was coming more and more to the conclusion that it rang false, it gave too many explanations – he'd wager that money from another party was involved.

The question was how their enemies could have come to know about these proceedings and who could have raised such a big amount, as buying the Grand Inquisitor would have cost a lot of money. He was truly puzzled and would have loved to investigate further. He would have bullied the truth out of the Grand Inquisitor. But Richelieu had insisted on dealing with this issue himself so he had better relent and leave this to the old man. Watching closer, Mazarin saw that Richelieu looked transformed. He must have kept a surprise ace up his sleeve.

"You might remember our little deal with the late de Beauvoir and his son?" Richelieu interrogated.

"Yes, I do," answered Mazarin. "Did he happen to solve his little family problem in Britain in the end? I haven't heard anything recently, but I assume that means that Pierre de Beauvoir is still among us?"

"Yes, you're right, Henri did not succeed in getting rid of his cousin!" answered Richelieu, and added smugly, "Henri has been missing since his last venture attempting to deal with Pierre ended in disaster, but never mind. He'll turn up sooner or later. What I don't like is that the friar I sent to supervise Henri is still missing. That is most strange."

Richelieu hesitated for a minute, now looking truly puzzled, but then the triumphant look came back to his face.

"But let's come back to the point! As his cousin is still alive and kicking, Henri has no money and will certainly fail to pay back his mortgage that will be due on New Year to the moneylender. As it happened that the only person in this city willing to lend him money was a Jew whom I recommended, half of the value of his estates will come back into my, um, I mean of course, the treasury of my parish. And there might be the additional opportunity to snap up some of those estates soon at very interesting prices! Only if you're interested, of course. You see, this old brain of mine is still working, working well! But we still need to succeed with this court case as fast as possible, the heritage is still there, suspended, ripe for the picking, but only God knows for how long!"

With this last statement, Mazarin was dismissed. Mazarin wasn't really displeased about the outcome of their meeting, he had feared much worse. He had been admonished, true, but mildly, considering that Richelieu could be choleric and was known to raise people to the heights of power as fast as he crushed them. Richelieu had even offered him indirectly to profit from the foreclosures of Henri's estates. He might consider the offer. Actually the most interesting information he had received today, was the fact that Henri was missing. This meant that nobody was in charge to guard the famous de Beauvoir diamond ring. He would need to find a way to add this beauty to his collection before the question of this heritage was settled and whoever won the jackpot of the de Beauvoir title and lands noticed that something was missing. Mazarin was deep in thought when he walked down the hallway. It was the opportunity of a lifetime and he needed to get this ring, he *must* have it!

*****

Heavy fog had settled on the small port on the French coast but the captain did not seem to mind. Thick layers of milky white mist had shrouded the coastline and Henri marvelled how the sailing ship had found its way to the shore without being wrecked. The captain seemed to know this part of the coast inside out and Henri was sure that the bags and barrels they had been unloading after their arrival would never find their way into the records of the customs officers. The ship had been unloaded swiftly, with the speed and precision of a well-oiled machine. When the mist started to clear, all that would remain was an innocent vessel waiting for some cargo to sail back to England.

He had stayed a last night in the only available inn in the small harbour, sharing his room once more with the young sailor. But it was about time that he left! Henri had started to grow fond of the young lad, longing to touch him and have him close to him. This was a strange feeling for a man who had never been attached to anybody – and Henri didn't like it. He preferred to let his hate grow; he wanted to stay master of his own emotions.

The next day he left on a miserable horse that he had bought for a bargain, hoping that the horse would survive until he reached Paris. Henri didn't look back; maybe the young lad had watched him leaving, maybe not. Henri's lips were pressed together tightly; this was the only emotion he allowed himself to show.

Henri reached Paris swiftly, and to his own surprise the horse had shown more resilience than expected and he had been able to progress fast. The weather had stayed cold but he had been spared the heavy winter rains that often turned the roads in Northern France into slippery mudslides. He had grown a beard and looked like a peasant or peddler coming from the provinces, eager to visit the capital.

Arriving in Paris, he had considered a quick stop at the Palais de Beauvoir to bathe and shave, but after a short deliberation he had come to the conclusion that it would be more beneficial if Henri de Beauvoir remained missing from public view

– and from Richelieu's agents. Thus he had decided to rest and sleep in a well kept tavern located on the outskirts of Paris, buy some simple but clean clothes to become more presentable and go straight to the elegant house of the Comte de Roquemoulin to check his whereabouts – and check whether the Count was alone.

Henri rang the doorbell and the doorman opened up. One look at Henri and he automatically denied him entrance, suggesting arrogantly, "Folks like you are to ring at the servants' entrance!" and moved to close the heavy door. But Henri had expected that, it was the normal reaction of a well-trained doorman, and he was well aware that he now looked like a provincial commoner.

Swiftly he inserted his foot into the doorway and looked arrogantly at the doorman as if he had observed a cockroach in front of him. Speaking the polished French of the upper classes he made the doorman understand that he had better call the butler or he would regret his decision not to let him enter the house.

The doorman started to feel uneasy. This language and the self-assured appearance did not match with the humble clothes and he was relieved that Henri had presented an easy solution; the butler was an authority universally respected and feared in the household – yes, he would know how to deal with this strange person.

The doorman, eager to rid himself of his responsibility, led Henri into the impressive entrance hall. The house was decorated in the latest fashion, showing off the immense wealth of its owner. Henri was kept waiting without being offered a chair for at least fifteen minutes before the butler condescended to meet him. No wonder that he was in a furious mood by now. Henri knew the butler from the past, a slimy creature, if ever he had seen one. He doubted though that the butler would recognize him and obviously Henri didn't really want to reveal his true personality. He'd need to extract the information out of him by a different method, but Henri was pretty sure that he knew a way to do this.

At last Henri heard the scurrying sound of approaching steps, followed by the glamorous entrance of the butler in a colourful livery, a vivid creation most probably of his own design. Henri's expression twitched – the butler looked like a tall, overfed parrot.

The butler looked at him as if some species of unsavoury rodent had entered the august household of the count. In a piercing voice he said, "May I know who has the impertinence to disturb us?"

It was a stage-like appearance and might have been impressive if its main actor hadn't been verging on the ridiculous. Henri decided that it would serve his plans best if he pretended to be suitably impressed and quickly looked down as if he felt intimidated by the majestic entrance and speech of the butler. He lifted his cap from his head, wringing it in his hands. He then slowly approached the butler who stood there, erect and every inch the incarnation of the trusted guardian of the stately home.

The butler mellowed a bit when he saw that the young visitor was obviously impressed by his personality and with a slight hint of sympathy now in his voice he continued, "What do you want, why didn't you use the proper entrance?"

Henri had slowly moved very close in the meantime and as he now looked up, the butler could see his radiant blue eyes.

How beautiful! he thought, but stopped quickly as the shy young man suddenly assailed him, grabbed his private parts and squeezed them with terrible force, without mercy. Tears of pain shot into the eyes of butler, but his visitor's second hand, with a grip of iron, had already closed his mouth and his scream of pain was brutally silenced.

"You coloured toad, tell me immediately where I can find the Comte de Roquemoulin or I'll squeeze your balls until you'll never ever be able to shag your parlour maids or stable boys again in your life. Nod if you understand what I say!" Henri whispered into the ear of the butler who was nearly mad with pain, as Henri had increased the pressure.

The butler nodded immediately and the grip was loosened a little, but Henri now grabbed his arm and the poor butler found himself in a vice-like grip, unable to escape.

The butler tried to speak but failed miserably on his first attempt. When the grip fastened once more he desperately made a second attempt and with a whining sound he uttered, "He's not in Paris!"

Henri kept up the pressure. "Where is he?"

"He's visiting his Loire estates," the feeble voice answered.

"Is he alone?"

The butler looked puzzled with tears in his eyes, he didn't seem to understand the question. "Of course not, he always travels with his servants," he managed to answer.

"I mean, is one of his lover boys accompanying him?"

It dawned on the butler that his visitor must have intimate knowledge about the habits of this household. He desperately tried to search in the depths of his memory as to who the hell this secret visitor could be. But this villain of a visitor apparently didn't want him to think, as the grip was tightened once more and the pain became almost unbearable. The butler was close to passing out. Quickly he croaked, "No, he left alone," and seeing that his visitor wanted to hear more, he added, "My lord ended his relationship with his last protégé just before Christmas."

Henri rejoiced inwardly. This meant that the precious Count had retreated to his estates in order to lick his wounds from the last relationship, and not for the first time. Presumably he had been dumped again; his young lovers never stayed long and he'd not be worthy of the name of Henri de Beauvoir if he couldn't make the best out of a heartbroken and lovesick elderly aristocrat.

Henri whispered softly, "Now you sit down here and wait like a good boy until I leave this house – and you had better forget that I was ever here, or next time you'll be a dead man – but your exit will be slow and painful. Have you understood?"

The butler nodded and found himself gagged and bound to the chair with the very coloured silken scarves that he had added this morning to his toilet to give his outfit a special cachet, a liberty he had taken in view of the absence of his employer – and a folly he now regretted profoundly.

It took a good hour until the butler was found by the curious doorman who had come to chat with him about this peculiar visitor. He found a bluish butler, almost suffocated, breeches wet. Although the complete household was in turmoil when the news had spread, the butler adamantly refused to speak, he just greedily drank the water the attentive parlourmaid had offered him and then limped to his room, not to be seen again by anybody for the next two days.

His sudden disappearance afterwards came as no real surprise, and tongues were wagging, a curious story indeed. There must have been a dirty secret in the butler's past linked to this peculiar visitor, everybody was sure of this by now.

*****

The winter was biting cold; even Paris was covered by a layer of snow. The pristine blanket of white had soon turned into a dirty grey patchwork. Black smoke rose day and night out of every chimney – as long as their lucky owners still had enough wood or charcoal to burn and fight the cold. But daily the pile of the poor who had frozen to death during the night was increasing. They were dumped carelessly in front of the sad paupers' cemeteries where they were buried in haste in the name of mercy by some labourers, doing their duty listlessly, as no money could be made out of a funeral for those lost souls who had died without the blessings of the Holy Church.

The country was bracing itself for a wave of starvation, and the churches were full with repenting sinners praying to God to spare them from having to face the Last Judgement too soon, promising fervently whatever donations came to their minds. No wonder the bellies and pockets of the clergy were well filled during these hard times.

Henri crossed the city muffled in a thick coat, still riding this strange horse that looked almost dead and yet moved forward steadily in this terrible cold where nobody would leave his dwelling unless he had no choice.

298

The streets were slippery as the snow had turned into a treacherous *mélange* of mud, dirt and excrement, often hiding patches of black ice. Luckily the cold dampened the smell of this unsavoury mix and Henri's horse seemed unperturbed by the slippery roads.

He left Paris and turned south, but the cold weather had spread further, covering all of France and even the people in the countryside had started to suffer. Henri was relieved when they reached the small village of Roquemoulin in the vicinity of Tours, dominated by the grandiose moated castle that the proud grandfather of the present Count had built.

Nobody had been courageous enough to travel during these cold days – unless in case of emergency – therefore his arrival in the small inn was considered something of a sensation. The curious owner was more than willing to rent him the small guest room and glued himself to Henri, hoping to receive the latest news and rumours from the capital. He was a stout man, his belly spilling out over his breeches, a distinct recommendation of the gastronomic offerings of this establishment.

"Is it true that the Cardinal Richelieu, God bless him of course, is about to die?"

When Henri didn't react, the voice took on a conspiratorial tone and he whispered, "Will the next one of these corrupt clergymen suck us dry, it seems that this Italian fellow is just waiting to take over? Is it true the second son of the Queen was not fathered by the King? Are the people dying like flies in the streets of Paris?"

Henri had no intention of gossiping and gruffly reminded the innkeeper that his stupid questions could land him in the prison of the very Cardinal he had supposed to be dying.

The innkeeper seemed sobered by his reply and relented. Visibly offended and disappointed he removed himself from Henri's room. The staircase squeaked in protest as the massive body of the innkeeper waddled downstairs. Henri could smell delicious food being prepared downstairs; this village, or at least this inn, clearly was not suffering from starvation. He closed the door and looked around. His room was clean, quite small but boasted the luxury of a fireplace where the innkeeper had lighted a fire when they had entered the room. Henri walked up and down in the front of the fire, deep in thought – he needed to find a way to meet with the count. Upon further reflection he started to regret that he had turned down the opportunity of exchanging gossip with the talkative innkeeper. This fat man was probably in on all the secrets of the village and thus would know the whereabouts of the Comte de Roquemoulin.

He'd need to make the innkeeper talk and consequently Henri decided to make up for his initial brash reaction during dinner. The innkeeper had served the first course in an offended silence but when Henri dropped a casual remark that one couldn't be careful enough these days with Richelieu's spies all over France, the innkeeper got the message and soon Henri found himself back in favour and enjoying the confidence of the chatterbox that was his host.

He learnt that the Count had arrived about two weeks ago, oh yes, he was on his own *this time*. The innkeeper had dragged out the last words long enough to permit Henri to look at him expectantly and gladly the innkeeper spilled the beans about the scandalous customs and the orgies of some decadent nobles, although he had to admit grudgingly that the Count had proved to be an excellent master of the village as he'd leave his folk enough to eat and live decently, even in such a hard winter as this.

Soon Henri knew that the count's head groom was a regular wine drinker here in the tavern, in fact every Friday he'd come and drink only red wine – a nice sort, maybe rather talkative for a groom. Henri loved this last statement, as this was all he had been waiting for; of course the groom would know about the habits of his lord and master. Henri was eager to meet the count, apparently by surprise, outside his castle. He planned a sudden confrontation to make sure that the Comte de Roquemoulin would react instinctively, guided solely by his emotions and not governed by reason.

Henri invited the innkeeper to share a bottle of the most expensive wine of his cellar and the innkeeper immediately revised his first impression. This man with the piercing blue eyes was a nice sort after all, a bit wary of talking at first, certainly arrogant – in essence, a typical Parisian, he concluded.

The next day the groom of the Comte de Roquemoulin made his usual excursion to the village inn and found himself invited by a sympathetic stranger who spoke warmly about horses and his passion for hunting. Soon he sat next to him on the bench, accepting with pleasure to share the wine that had been brought with a large smile by the innkeeper. In no time a second earthenware jug of the cheap but strong house wine was nearly empty and the tongue of the groom loosened and he talked freely, albeit with some difficulty. He relished this rare occasion of feeling important and being listened to.

Henri skilfully extracted all the information he needed, a clear plan of action forming in his mind. He doubted that the groom would ever be able to recognize him later as he had taken the precaution of dyeing his hair and had arranged a strand of hair and a cap to cover his scar.

Henri had even taken the pains to change his accent to blend in with the commoners. But now he was starting to get bored as the groom had reached the stage of becoming emotional and tearful and Henri decided to order something stronger to finish this episode fast. His ruse worked, and after the groom had gulped down the second glass of burning liquid his body slumped and he banged his head down on the table, mumbling incomprehensibly.

Henri pushed the drunken groom from the bench and ordered a sumptuous meal, to be served in the only private room of the inn. He felt that he had earned himself a treat. After the delicious meal he sat in a comfortable armchair with a glass of excellent Bordeaux wine, smiling to himself. It was probably just as well that nobody could witness this smile because it was the satisfied and conceited smile of a devil.

*****

His lordship, the honourable Comte de Roquemoulin, sat lethargically in his splendid dining room and surveyed the table that was loaded with all kinds of mouthwatering and expensive dishes. His cook normally excelled in his skills of awakening his lordship's appetite, but these days the count was depressed, and the seductive smell and tasteful arrangement of the food left him indifferent.

Reluctantly he sampled a spoonful of the truffle seasoned pheasant soup, but more to show that he appreciated the efforts of his cook than for any real motivation to eat.

Why was I so stupid as to come down here to this deserted place? he kept asking himself. In Paris he could have visited his friends, attended the magnificent and opulent Christmas festivities, or just had some fun. But he knew the answer, of course.

He had fled Paris as couldn't stand the thought of bumping into his latest friend and lover – and as they were sharing the same circle of friends, this outcome would have been inevitable.

He abandoned me for the pretty face of a young girl, the count thought miserably, and tears started rolling once more down his face, so vivid were his memories of this young and beautiful musketeer, lying in his arms, his dark eyes locked onto his own. The young lad had encountered so many hardships, he had been in terrible debt when they had met for the first time. How thankful he had been when he had helped him, what a night they had shared!

But soon after his debts had been paid off, the young lad had dumped him. The girl was young and beautiful, no more need to offer his body to an ageing man. This truth really hurt and the count sat there – oblivious of the glances of his servants – not moving. He was not even sobbing, but his silent tears kept falling,

At last he dabbed the tears away with a napkin, but the damage had been done, stains of red, white and black showed that his make-up had been ruined by his silly tears. He probably looked like one of those travelling Italian comic actors, it occurred to him. This reflection made him even more depressed. If only something would happen, he thought, something to change his mind, something to make life gay and worth living once again.

His lordship had been the only surviving child of doting parents; his despairing mother had stopped counting the number of her miscarriages. In fact she had given up hope altogether of ever holding a living child in her arms. When her son was born and had survived miraculously the first most dangerous months and years, his parents not only had a new church built in the village but heaped all their love and hopes on their small and fragile child.

He was protected from physical exercise, harmful fresh air, bled regularly, in short all blessings of modern medicine were used to make him healthy and strong and yet again – miraculously – he had managed to survive this excess of parental love and care.

Jean Baptiste was a friendly child and the only real disappointment came when he became a man but rigorously refused to choose a bride and carry on the duty of procreation. His parents closed their eyes to the blatant truth that their son was attracted to the young grooms in the stables and neglected even the prettiest maids in the household and used his fragile health as the apparent reason for his refusal to get married.

It then happened that his father unexpectedly succumbed to a stroke and passed away in a matter of only a few days. The household was in shock and the mourning young count had to cope with the details of his sudden and unexpected heritage. It was at this moment that he had discovered how rich his family really was. A suddenly joyful Jean Baptiste felt as if he had unexpectedly dug up a secret treasure!

Immediately and against the tearful protest of his widowed mother he decided to move to Paris and settled there in great style, leaving behind the provincial village and castle of his forefathers. Paris proved to be a revelation, a life that he had never been able to imagine whilst living in the deep provinces. There were festivities, hunts, masked balls; secret meetings in dark and shady alleys and the thrill of *chambres separées*. Life suddenly had become entertaining and exciting, no fantasy seemed strange or too exotic – Paris could make it come true. Soon it was known that his purse strings were loose and the number of his friends grew quickly, but it took him several years to understand that the number of friends was directly linked to the freshly minted gold livres that he was prepared to shower on them.

He had been a moderately handsome man, but now the years, his lifestyle of indulgence and the constant lack of sleep had turned him into a tired looking middle-aged man with sagging features. The count was of course trying to freshen up his looks with the help of rouge and make up, hide his growing belly under well-cut clothes, but he had in fact become a laughing stock for his former friends – only he didn't realize the truth, or he didn't want to.

As his parents had vigorously denied him any physical activity, the count had discovered the pleasures of horse riding only very late but then he had become addicted to regular riding excursions. He used to ride out regularly even in Paris –

but when he was staying in the countryside riding along the Loire was his greatest pleasure. Even during the coldest weather he would insist on leaving the castle after breakfast and exercising his thoroughbreds, each of them having cost a fortune. The horses were his pride and joy; he doubted that even the King of France could boast of such an impressive collection of noble horses. Lately he had started to breed them and – to his pleasant surprise – discovered how much money could be made from their offspring.

Henri had heard this account from the groom and had made a mental note of their usual route starting from the castle down the valley to the Loire. The count loved this route as it yielded splendid views and only terrible weather or illness could deter him from this exercise.

On the day that Henri had fixed to carry out his plan, very unusual early morning activities could be witnessed in his room. Carefully he washed the dye out of his hair, shaved himself, and then he started to tear holes into his clothes and rubbed his arms and face with dirt. He looked into the small polished silver plate that served him as a mirror, quite satisfied already with the dramatic impression he made. As a next step he deliberately cut himself several times with his crude shaving knife, making sure that blood was slowly oozing from his brow and arms. He rubbed some of the blood until smears of dirt and blood covered his arms and partially his cheeks. Henri made sure though not to overdo the effect, he needed to be an appealing victim and arouse feelings of compassion – but Roquemoulin must still be attracted and not be repelled by his looks. He was conceited enough to be fully convinced that he would score on this front. Once more he looked into the polished mirror and, satisfied with his dramatic appearance, he silently walked down the staircase, crossed the cobbled yard and entered the stable. He knew that the innkeeper would still be deeply asleep at this early hour and therefore didn't really expect to be discovered. Then Henri dragged his skeletal horse out of the dark stable. It whinnied in protest, of course, having no desire to leave the comfortable stable and venture into the freezing morning cold.

Henri knew that he was leaving far too early but he wouldn't take the risk of leaving the inn in his new disguise once everybody was up. Earlier, when he had investigated the surroundings, he had detected a lonely barn located near the route they were about to embark on; it would serve as a shelter whilst he waited.

The sun had risen but the paltry winter sunshine yielded almost no warmth, and the Loire was still covered by dense patches of fog. Clouds of steamy white mist were slowly rising into the winter sun. Yet the scenery was of breathtaking beauty, the freezing mist having covered the barren branches of trees and reeds with ice crystals that shimmered in the sun like diamonds.

But Henri had no eyes for the beauty that surrounded him. He had spent about two terrible and seemingly endless hours in the freezing barn. By the time he embarked on the path that the groom had mentioned, not only did he look pitiful, he felt as if he was about to die. The cold was paralysing him, the freezing humidity had crept into his bones, he could barely feel his hands or move his feet.

His horse was apparently in no better state. It was staggering underneath him, moving forward only with the greatest difficulty. When Henri heard the long awaited noise of galloping hooves approaching from the top of the hill, he had reached a state of mind and body where he didn't care anymore, a strange apathy had taken possession of him, as if his soul was about to leave his body. *Dying must feel like this*, he thought dispassionately.

It was a young groom who had accompanied the Comte de Roquemoulin this morning on his usual excursion who detected the miserable horse and rider. His first instinct was to ignore them and ride on but his lord and master was a hopeless case, he had much too kind a heart. Therefore they sped on to see what kind of poor soul was travelling in this cold weather, far away from major roads and civilization.

The groom took his flintlock pistol from his saddlebag and nervously fiddled with his powder flask, just in case this poor soul shouldn't prove to be so innocent after all. They approached the horse that stood still, but the stranger didn't greet them – he seemed to be swaying on his horse. As soon as the groom had ascertained for himself that the stranger wasn't armed, he dismounted from his horse and approached the strange-looking man. He arrived just in time as Henri collapsed right into his arms and lost consciousness.

Henri had planned to surprise the count with a dramatic scene; as it turned out, he had succeeded much better than he had anticipated!

It was already late in the evening when Henri opened his eyes. In his exhaustion he must have been unconscious or sleeping for hours. He found himself lying in a comfortable bed, soft blankets on top of him and his searching glance met the anxious eyes of the Comte de Roquemoulin.

Henri smiled at him and whispered, "You're my saviour, I owe my life to you. It's yours now!"

The count started to weep; he had been sitting at Henri's bed for hours, tense with anxiety and praying to all the saints that he could remember in his agitation.

"Save the life of Henri de Beauvoir," he whispered again and again.

The count had immediately recognized the stranger as soon as he had approached the unconscious young man leaning on his surprised groom. How often had he looked at this handsome face in Paris, with the distinctive scar that only seemed to add to his attraction.

It was immediately obvious to him that Henri must have been the victim of bandits who were roaming the streets in winter. They were often poor tenants from neighbouring farms who had despaired when they saw their families starving to death. If they had to die anyhow, why not choose the gallows? The Comte de Roquemoulin secretly found it scandalous that his peers and the high clergy would spend fortunes on their luxurious lifestyles, but left their tenants to rot away in dilapidated villages that screamed of need and poverty. They sucked those poor souls empty of the last harvest of grain, fruit or wine and seized the little livestock that their tenants had managed to raise and feed once the dreaded time for tax collection had come.

No wonder the roads were unsafe in this winter, many would die, he mused. The count shuddered and thought, *But please, Mon Dieu, spare my beautiful Henri.*

His eyes fixed on Henri's gaze; he was overcome with emotion and couldn't speak. He just grasped Henri's hand, squeezed it gently and then took the bowl of hot soup that had been prepared upon his personal orders and started feeding Henri like a beloved child. A strange satisfaction swept over him. Suddenly he felt hungry himself, and his depression had gone; he had found a reason to live!

The next weeks were to pass like a dream: they went out riding together, hunting, playing chess and having animated discussions – why would he ever want to go back to Paris? Life had become wonderful.

One night Henri knocked at the count's bedroom door. When Henri took his nightshirt off and approached the bed stark naked, like a Greek god, the count's wildest dreams suddenly came true. Jean Baptiste de Roquemoulin had fallen into the trap of love and passion, a crazy, hopeless love he had no chance of escaping.

Jean Baptiste was blinded by his infatuation. In his eyes Henri could do nothing wrong, wasn't he so kind and caring? Whoever had told him that Henri de Beauvoir was a bad lot, dangerous and best avoided, must be qualified as an evil rumourmonger. When he had asked Henri to tell him about the hold-up, Henri said he couldn't remember, the last weeks had simply been erased from his memory. All that Henri could remember was the kind face of his wonderful saviour and the count had shed tears again; were these words not a token of true love being reciprocated?

On their way to the stables Henri mentioned out of the blue that sooner rather than later he would need to go back to Paris – his memory had apparently returned. The same evening they sat in the library, sharing a glass of the famous wine of the region. Jean Baptiste was touched as Henri opened his heart and in confidence he explained that he was broke. It was the evil Cardinal Richelieu who had devised a scheme to ruin the de Beauvoir family. Henri continued in a faltering voice to explain that his father sadly had died unexpectedly and that he had detected only afterwards that all of their estates had been mortgaged to pay the treacherous Cardinal, and that apparently his father had been blackmailed by Richelieu. Not a sou would be left for him. Henri had sat there, his handsome face a mask of grief and the count had suffered with him – how could this monstrous Richelieu dare to do this to his precious Henri?

Roquemoulin's heart had been deeply moved and without hesitation he had proposed Henri should move into his house in Paris. Henri had suddenly kneeled before him, kissed his hands and with a tear-stricken voice had answered, "I know that you're the kindest man on this earth. But it is impossible. I could not walk through Paris and hear people whispering behind my back that this is Henri de Beauvoir, the impoverished lord who has lost everything and is now living like a mistress with his lover. I'm too proud for this. I prefer to be poor but to lead a life of honour!"

The count looked scandalized, but immediately recognized that Henri's words were true, all the tongues in Paris would be wagging, what a scandal this would be! The old count and his new pet lover, how many gold livres must he have dished out to get Henri? Yes, Paris would talk and some of the noble families would scorn Henri, he'd no longer be a member of that exclusive club which ruled the kingdom.

But living without Henri? The count contemplated his bleak future: soon sitting once again in his palatial homes, lonely and bored to death. After having shared his life with Henri, who could compare with Henri, how could he ever contemplate taking on a new lover and friend?

"If I were your son," Henri dropped into the conversation, "our relationship would be above approach, but fate meant that we should be lovers, not father and son," he added sadly.

They skipped the subject, talking about the latest news that had arrived by letter from the count's friends at the royal court. Life at court was a subject that Jean Baptiste found fascinating and he loved to share the latest news with Henri who had lived for years in the intimate circles of court life and could vividly picture the characters. But Henri's remark remained in the back of his mind, and some days later, an idea dawned upon him that seemed like a stroke of genius. His mind raced on: *I could adopt Henri! Of course, only if he's not too proud to give up his old family name. I must be very careful how to approach the subject, but it would solve all our problems at once! Nobody could possibly object, Henri would live with me and our bond would last forever!*

A wave of joy overcame the count, he was sure that he had found a miraculous solution; not for him a bleak future, but a future of love, joy and sharing was waiting for him!

Jean Baptiste waited impatiently to tell Henri of his great idea, but he wanted to find the perfect moment to present it. Two days later when Henri sat close to him, once more brooding, he cleared his throat and said, "Henri, *mon cheri*, I have a proposal to make, I think I have an idea as to how we could continue to stay together forever, and yet solve all the problems that are haunting you." His great brown eyes were fixed anxiously on Henri's face.

You idiot, Henri thought. *If you don't stop calling me cheri-darling soon, I might kill you anyhow, I simply can't stand it! Hopefully you have finally swallowed my bait!*

Yet he skilfully managed to produce a sad smile as if he had given up hope already and answered, "Oh, Jean-Baptiste, you are quite marvellous, but please don't bother yourself with my small problems. You saved my life, isn't that enough?"

The count was moved by this modesty; Henri was truly courageous! Nervously and losing himself in complicated sentences he started to explain his adoption plan to Henri, who watched him with bright eyes, his handsome face full of admiration for this ingenious plan, modest yet fully attentive.

When the count had finished his proposal, Henri took some time to answer but he refused to follow this suggestion, surprisingly enough, not because he was too proud to give up his old name. No, Henri proclaimed that he deemed himself not worthy enough to accept such a great honour. The Comte de Roquemoulin was moved and spent the next days pleading with Henri, trying to convince him, and finally, after a whole week, Henri started to sway and change his mind. The night he came to the count's bedroom and signalled his consent, Jean Baptiste was in heaven, Henri would be his forever!

Once he had received Henri's blessing, the count hurried to tie the knot and the old family notary from Angers was called in to draw up the documents making Henri the adopted son and sole heir of the Comte de Roquemoulin. The notary met Henri and it didn't take him long to appraise Henri. He did his best to try and deter the count from such a rash course of action, but to no avail. The count could be extremely obstinate and once he had taken a decision he would stick to it.

On a sunny winter's day the count rode with Henri across his estates to show him what would become his estate as well in the near future, as soon as the notary finished with the paperwork. The scenery was truly beautiful. The ground was still frozen but the sun was stronger today and the frosty wind had ceased to blow. They rode towards the bank of the river and Jean Baptiste pointed towards the steep slope below and said, "Here we need to be cautious, Henri darling, the horses could easily trip in one of the fox holes and you'd break your neck! Nobody could help you!"

Henri looked closer, scrutinizing the path carefully. *This sounds excellent*, he thought. *It looks like the right place for a nice accident.*

He looked around and answered, "Thank you for warning me, Jean Baptiste, I'll definitely remember this spot, don't worry!"

His radiant smile met the glance of the eager count who smiled back, love and adoration shining in his eyes.

A TREASURE HUNT

The bell was ringing, and as if the loud piercing noise of clanging metal wasn't enough, the energetic sound of several fists hammering on the door woke up the sleepy household of the Palais de Beauvoir in Paris. The doorman rushed to slide open the small viewing hole in the heavy door. A pistol was shoved against the mesh guard pointing at his eyes, and a deep voice bellowed: "Open the door on the order of His Eminence, the most noble and mighty Cardinal Mazarin, counsellor of Their Gracious Majesties, the King and Queen of France!"

The doorman's heart nearly stopped when he heard what kind of illustrious visitor was waiting outside, so he hastened nervously to follow the order. As soon as the heavy wings of the door had opened, a small army of armed musketeers pushed forward, their uniforms bearing the coat of arms of the freshly appointed Cardinal Mazarin.

Among his men the famous Cardinal himself, the rising star of French politics, entered the courtyard on the back of an impressive stallion, his riding gear immaculate and elegant as usual. Only the Cardinal's skull cap, a huge golden cross dangling on his chest and his ring of office gave evidence of his high rank in the Church. The Cardinal dismounted elegantly from his horse and demanded to see the major-domo of the household. The group was guided into the impressive reception hall of the palais, but the attentive Cardinal could see signs of neglect everywhere, the rooms were cold and smelled musty, clearly no fire had been lit here for ages, the windows and mirrors needed dusting. This was a house without a master, a shadow of its former glory.

It took only a few minutes and the alarmed major-domo stumbled into the room. He was dressed carelessly, his livery stained and some buttons of his breeches were loose. The Cardinal looked disdainfully on the major-domo who cringed under this majestic stare that took in the room and then focused finally on his own person. He became only too aware of his shabby appearance and suddenly started to realize how run down he and this palace must look to this elegant visitor.

"I understand that you are in charge of the Palais de Beauvoir during the absence of his lordship?" the Cardinal said in a bored voice, "Even if I have to admit that it surprises me to find you and this household in such a state of neglect. You can be happy not to be in my service, I usually have my servants whipped when I find them neglectful of their duties."

The major-domo's face reddened, and starting to perspire he wailed, "Please show mercy, Your Eminence, you find a house without a master, it has been months now that we haven't received any salary or money to keep this place up, we're living solely on the proceeds and the food that the estates of the Marquis send randomly from time to time to Paris, nobody knows where Henri de Beauvoir has gone and if he is to be our future master or not. Some say that there is a young nobleman in England who claims to be the son of the late Marquis and our future lord, but we don't know and nobody seems to care about us."

The speech didn't seem to impress the Cardinal. He still looked at the major-domo as if he were examining a cockroach.

"You shouldn't pass your time listening to rumours, when this house is falling apart!" the Cardinal answered, clearly showing his displeasure. "In any case, as the situation of succession is unclear, as you just mentioned, it therefore pleases his Majesty to take possession of the treasures of this household until the lawful heir has been identified and acknowledged!"

He made a sign to one of his musketeers who displayed an impressive document, studded with heavy seals. The major-domo stared at the document, which resembled a royal charter, and continued to speak in his whining voice. "I beg your pardon, Your Eminence, but I can only read some French words, I couldn't read or understand such a document."

Mazarin had built his surprise visit on the ignorance of the staff and secretly congratulated himself for his idea and his bold action. He managed to keep a straight face and answered, "Let me explain it to you then. This document is giving you official orders to remit the treasures for my safekeeping; any resistance to this order will be punishable and you'll have to answer to the justice of his Majesty, the King. Please lead us to the family vault now, an inventory will be made in the presence of my officials and a copy will be remitted to you to remit it later to the rightful heir."

The major-domo seemed to be shrinking even more. "I'm sorry, Your Eminence, but there is no vault in this palace!"

Mazarin looked surprised but he had anticipated such an answer. He made a sign to his musketeers and the major-domo found himself seized by two strong young men and pressed against the wall. A razor-sharp rapier was pointing at his throat. First he could feel the blade scratching his skin, then he felt some warm liquid slowly dripping down his throat – his own blood...

His knees felt like jelly, and he could hardly think or speak.

"Maybe this can restore your memory?" the bored voice challenged him.

The major-domo tried to speak, but failed miserably. Finally he managed to utter some words. "Your Eminence, I swear by the Holy Virgin, no treasure is kept here. The late marquis had it all removed and stored in the vaults and safekeeping of his bankers, they have been trusted by the family for generations."

Seeing that the Cardinal was hesitating he added eagerly, "I can give you the name and the address. The principal of the bank was a close friend of the late Marquis. They will immediately remit the treasures to your safekeeping, they'll not dare to ignore the order of his Majesty, the King!"

You idiot! thought the irate Cardinal, who had recognized the name immediately. *They're smart, they'll immediately understand that this document is not even worth the vellum it has been written on.*

He looked at the major-domo who by now had turned crimson red, beads of perspiration rolling down his forehead and the trickle of blood adding another ugly stain on the livery.

I'm wasting my time here, the furious Cardinal thought and commanded his men to let the major-domo go. They dropped him like a bag of sand and he collapsed on the ground. But his agony wasn't finished; as soon as they saw the large wet stain on his breeches the young musketeers jeered and spat at him, as he had wet himself in terror.

The Cardinal left the palais, furious and brooding. Once he had reached his own palace he immediately ordered his private secretary into his office. "Find out everything you can about the bank Piccolin & Cie, background, financial situation, can we find a way to cancel their banking license, I need to find a way of exerting pressure on them, do you understand?"

The secretary just nodded, but secretly he wondered what had happened. Mazarin was not an easy master but generally he tended to be balanced, not like the choleric Cardinal Richelieu who was feared by his servants for his sudden bouts of temper. If Mazarin was in such a foul mood, a very important issue was at stake, but how could a small Italian bank interfere with important matters of state?

Mazarin dismissed his secretary, adding, "Make sure that nobody disturbs me for the next hour!"

Once his bewildered secretary had left and he was on his own, he started to pace up and down in his study. *I must get hold of this damned diamond ring, I simply must!* he muttered again and again, as if repetition of the words could work like a magic charm. He would find a way to intimidate the Italians; if the ring was still in France, he vowed solemnly that he would get it.

Then he carefully bolted the door of his study to make sure that he would not be disturbed and he turned towards the richly carved shelving of his study where he opened his secret cabinet. With the help of the small key he always wore on a golden chain around his neck, he unlocked the metal box that had been fitted into the wall.

Tenderly he removed the velvet cushions and placed them on his desk. Carefully uncovering the top layer, he stood there, amazed how each time the fascination of the beauty of his diamonds could touch his soul, a charm that worked its magic without fail.

His famous diamonds lay there – only for him! They were different shapes and sizes but all of them unique in their splendour. They seemed to reach out to him in

310

the light of the candles, reflecting vivid shards of colour, longing to be touched and to be possessed. Mazarin's hands stretched out, caressing slowly each stone, polishing them with the soft velvet cloth, and a soothing calm came over him.

Yes, soon he would add the Beauvoir diamond, he vowed. God had made him, the unknown Italian diplomat of low-born parents, a famous cardinal of France, counsellor and intimate friend of the Queen of France and probably soon enough he'd become prime minister of this Kingdom. God loved him, protected him, he would surely grant his obedient servant the favour of adding one more treasure to his beloved collection.

With loving hands Mazarin covered the precious stones and returned them to their hiding place. With a long sigh he sat down and started reading the files his secretary had prepared for him, but it was so difficult to get the diamond ring out of his mind!

It took the well-oiled machine of Mazarin's office only two weeks to produce a detailed report on the bank of Piccolin & Cie. Of Italian origin, the family had been established in France for generations and whilst Mazarin was ploughing through the figures and facts mentioned in the pile of documents that had been assembled by his assiduous staff, he realized that his task would be much more difficult than he had foreseen. The bank was extremely well connected. Monsieur, the King's brother, was one of their most prominent customers, but to his ultimate surprise he discovered that even the Cardinal Richelieu was using their services when he was dealing with delicate Italian issues that needed discretion. He was becoming aware that he was walking on thin ice and warning signs were flashing in his mind. But lately he had encountered difficulty sleeping, his mind and his thoughts were obsessed with the famous de Beauvoir diamond, how could he stop now? He simply must possess it!

After some more deliberation, he decided to use surprise tactics. Without any preliminary warning, Mazarin ordered his coach and visited the present head of the bank, a middle-aged elegant-looking gentleman who couldn't deny his Italian origins. He was clearly surprised to receive such a prominent visitor without the usual formalities and protocol. Mazarin explained the situation, that the treasures of the de Beauvoir family must be handed over as the line of succession was unclear and imminent danger was at hand. An Englishman had suddenly pretended to be the sole heir and wanted to claim the heritage of one of the leading noble families of France – a claim unacceptable without further proof for the counsel of the government of His Majesty. Changing into his native Italian language now, he gave the banker an ultimatum, either to hand over the de Beauvoir treasures or risk losing their banking license in France.

The banker became pale; he had not anticipated such a bold threat from his famous visitor. He requested to grant him a week of deliberation and they parted, Mazarin content with his progress, the banker obviously intimidated and very worried.

311

Three days later the secretary announced that a certain Monsieur Piccolin was requesting the exceptional honour of an immediate audience with His Eminence. Mazarin accepted but made sure to let his visitor wait a good hour in the antechamber before he was led into the Cardinal's sanctum. He hadn't forgotten how Richelieu had made him simmer the last time they had met.

To his great surprise his visitor was not the person he had been expecting at all. The gentleman who bowed deeply was well above sixty years old; obviously the family had decided to dispatch the patriarch himself. The dignified man settled in the armchair that the Cardinal had indicated, after obediently kissing the Cardinal's ring of office as protocol and the high rank of Cardinal demanded.

Then something strange happened. Mazarin had expected to meet a nervous man, a man desperate to fight for the survival of his family business. But his visitor calmly appraised him with extremely shrewd eyes and Mazarin experienced the uncomfortable feeling that this man was looking straight through him, analysing and assessing immediately the strengths and weaknesses of his opponent. He did not like that feeling at all; usually Mazarin prided himself on being on top of his opponents.

The old banker started to talk, a soft voice that still held the hint of a faint Italian accent.

"Please let me thank you, Your Eminence, that you grant me the honour of an audience. We know of course, that you are very busy and much in demand. My son has informed me immediately about your, let us call it, unusual request."

The old man paused and Mazarin had the unpleasant feeling that this conversation would not be taking the course he had intended.

The banker continued. "Your Eminence, the business of a small bank like ours is simple, all we sell is trust, our whole business is built on mutual trust. If we betray the trust that our customers have bestowed upon us, our bank has to close. We understand, of course, that the council of his Majesty is concerned and will of course deliver the de Beauvoir treasures to the safekeeping of His Majesty but you surely understand that we'll need an instrument of transfer signed by his Majesty and validated by Parliament, as one of the most noble houses of France is concerned and any irregularity could spark not only the ruin of my bank but a true political crisis."

Mazarin's pulse was racing but he managed to keep his face straight. This old fox had immediately found the weakness of his approach. He had nothing in hand – and not even for a fortune would Richelieu cover such a bold move.

The smooth voice continued calmly. "If you therefore deem it necessary to have our bank closed, we'll have to accept and assume the consequences. I was wondering though if there might not be another way to find a suitable compromise?"

Mazarin looked at him curiously. This sounded like an offer in the making!

"Our family is aware, of course, that your Eminence is most likely to become the next prime minister and, in fact, likely to govern France for the years to come as his Majesty, and let me add, especially the Queen, have full confidence in your political skills."

Mazarin started to protest wildly. It was no good if his deepest wishes and convictions were traded too early in the market place, Richelieu was still the true ruler of France and he wouldn't tolerate a second one.

The visitor chuckled and made a sign to Mazarin to calm down and suddenly continued in Italian, Mazarin's native language. "This conversation is to remain between you and me, don't worry, discretion is the second pillar of our business. We both know that this is going to happen, but we also know that speaking about it publicly now would kill your chances. All the same, my bank would like to entertain a privileged relationship with the French Government. I have here a gift that could be of interest to you. In fact the late Marquis de Beauvoir needed money, actually a lot of money twenty years ago, and at that time he pledged us this ring as security. It is ours now as the credit has never been repaid."

The banker delved in his pocket and took out a velvet pouch. He placed it carefully on the low marble table that stood between the two armchairs. He opened the pouch and the light of the chandelier set the diamond ablaze, a stone the size of a hazelnut sparkling under the candlelight with all the colours of the rainbow. The stone was mounted in an old fashioned setting, the ring with a thick frame of gold, slightly worn by age, with some ornamental wording engraved on it, a unique piece of oriental origin.

Mazarin held his breath. He couldn't believe his luck. Greedily he stretched his hand to touch the ring and hold it close to the flames of the candles, indeed all he had heard about the de Beauvoir ring seemed true, a unique piece, a breathtaking beauty, the crowning piece of his collection!

It took him some minutes to become aware that the shrewd glance of the old banker was still on him. Mazarin placed the ring carefully back on the pouch. No use pretending that he didn't want a bargain desperately, so in a rough voice he said, "Name your conditions, and unless they're totally unreasonable, I'll accept. I want the ring."

The old banker smiled and answered, "As I said, Your Eminence, it is a gift! This ring is yours now. But if ever you could find the time to drop a favourable word with the Cardinal Richelieu to grant us the trading monopoly for timber and cotton with our new colonies in North America, we'd be obliged, but I repeat, it is a gift, whatever you do or decide has no influence! Treat it well, but I can see, you are an expert and a true lover where diamonds are concerned."

313

His visitor had risen from his armchair during his speech. He had not even waited for Mazarin to end the audience. He bowed once again, kissed the cardinal's ring of office and left the room, leaving behind him a truly speechless Mazarin – a rare occurrence. His dreams had come true, but he still couldn't believe his luck. Of course the old fox knew that sooner or later he'd be obliged to return the favour to his bank, but this ring was worth a small kingdom. Gift or no gift, he was indebted now to the bank of Piccolin & Cie.

With trembling fingers he opened once more his safe where his famous collection of diamonds was kept and lovingly he stored the ring among his other treasures. Even here, in the dark shadow the diamond still seemed to live, to speak to him. Mazarin closed the hiding place and returned to his desk. He looked at the pile of documents waiting to be read and replied to. Suddenly he caught sight of his own image in the mirror hanging close to the fireplace. He saw a handsome man of middle age. Mazarin smiled at his image and said aloud, "It's time for celebration today, no files, no papers, no urgent documents. I'm still young!"

That night his mistress would not only be stunned by a beautiful necklace Mazarin had brought her as a surprise gift; she had rarely seen her lover in such high spirits. Something really good must have happened to him today, but to her dismay he refused to tell. She could only guess – maybe Richelieu was terminally ill? She knew of course that her ambitious lover was burning to inherit his position.

If every time he brings me another precious gift when Richelieu is ailing, she thought, *let him die slowly*, and lovingly she caressed her delicate new necklace.

314

VOYAGE BY SEA

The Christmas season in London had passed at an incredible pace. Pierre could no longer remember the number of balls, receptions and other festivities he had attended. Once he had been installed officially as Duke of Hertford a shower of invitations had rained upon them, and everybody wanted the new Duke and his handsome friend, the Earl of Worthing, to be present – they were the new stars of London society.

Luckily Marie was often invited to attend the same festivities, while Armand was less fortunate. He was still head over heels in love with Julia, the daughter of the Venetian ambassador, but she was a rare bird at the official balls and even when she did appear, she was always accompanied by a fierce looking chaperon or – even worse – her jealous father, who was definitely no improvement.

Armand was suffering badly, a totally new experience for him. He managed from time to time to dance with Julia and each time she cast a new spell on Armand until he was deeply and hopelessly in love. He had thought that he was the undisputable master of the game of flirting but she played skilfully with his emotions, encouraging him one evening and sending him into deepest despair on the next occasion where she seemed to have difficulties even remembering his name, pronouncing it slowly with her charming Italian accent and hiding her laughing eyes behind the precious ivory fan she used to carry, playing the game to maddening perfection.

Céline and Charles had married in a private ceremony shortly after Christmas. Pierre was becoming increasingly impatient to leave for France, visit Marie's parents and take up the challenge of the Templars. He had found the ancient ruby ring, as predicted by Charles, in the impressive Hertford treasure vaults, which were brimming over with precious jewellery that his forefathers had amassed over the centuries. Compared to him, the King of England was most certainly a pauper.

Pierre had studied the engravings on the heavy golden ring again and again with the help of a magnifying glass he had found in the study, but he simply couldn't make any sense of them. Armand had just cast one lengthy look and remarked, "No hope, I couldn't even say which language this is! Anyhow, you're the intellectual one, I leave this to you."

Time kept slipping away. Armand's father had sent yet another urgent letter insisting they come back to France as soon as possible. Richelieu was apparently occupied in trying to tame the new favourite of King Louis, the young and handsome Cinq-Mars, a genie he himself had released from the bottle and who was now proving to be more and more difficult to control. Furthermore Armand's father had made cryptic remarks that Richelieu was battling with his fragile health and was thus frequently absent from court. A change of power was in the air. A year, maybe two, and the era of the Great Cardinal would surely be at an end. By

February 1641 all were finally set to leave for France. A big party had assembled for their journey. Marie and Céline wanted to visit Marie's parents in Reims before Pierre arrived, and the Principessa had decided to join them to visit Marie's mother and then continue her journey to the south. She was keen to see her family in Italy after so many years of staying abroad. Arthur had decided that some weeks in Paris could be good fun and had joined the party at the last minute.

Charles had suggested using Pierre's private yacht, the *Beatrice*, named after his great grandmother. When they reached Dover, this time in the style and grandeur befitting a duke, surrounded by a small army of footmen and servants, Pierre set eyes on his private yacht for the first time and was amazed to find a fully fledged sailing ship, not at all the small yacht he had expected.

Charles grinned."Your grandfather loved to travel in style," he remarked, seeing Pierre's wide eyes. This statement proved to be true enough. The cabins were fitted with precious polished wood from the colonies, and gilded armchairs and velvet covered sofas with soft cushions created an atmosphere of luxury so unlike the last Channel crossing they had experienced.

"That is indeed most impressive, Your Grace," Armand said mockingly. He looked appraisingly at the main cabin. "But I imagine that you need these luxurious surroundings to compensate for your inherent lack of personality, as not all people can be as handsome and intelligent as I am," Armand continued complacently.

Pierre took the first velvet cushion he could grab hold of and threw it at Armand. He didn't think that this kind of remark was worth the effort of a verbal response.

They left the cabin and were met by their captain on the main deck. He was a lean, tall man towering over his sailors. Well into his forties, his weather-beaten freckled face bore witness to many years spent at sea, an old sea dog with a long career in the royal navy. Like many of his kind he was a man of few words and whilst he showed them around the ship he kept his explanations to the strict minimum. He was not a very optimistic person either. When Pierre mentioned in good spirits how lucky they were to have relatively calm weather for a winter month, he merely looked sceptically at the sky and muttered, "We'll know once we've arrived. Could change any minute. The sea is always a treacherous bride," hastily adding, "Your Grace," as he seemed to have realized suddenly that his answer might be somewhat incomplete.

Soon a bell rang and a sumptuous dinner was served on board. It was washed down with several bottles of first class Bordeaux wine, followed by Scotch whisky, a drink Pierre had discovered in London. By midnight Pierre and Armand retreated to their cabin. Pierre shared his cabin with the lovesick and slightly tipsy Armand and had to endure seemingly endless descriptions of Julia's various accomplishments until he feigned deep sleep in order to get some respite. He

316

decided secretly that he preferred the old Armand with a mistress in every town to the more virtuous but tiresome and love-stricken one.

The next morning Pierre woke up to find he was lying in his narrow bunk bed, still drowsy and sleepy, yet he had a peculiar feeling that something was decidedly wrong. Was it the fact that he was still suffering from an overdose of Scotch whisky? He had shared a good drink with his friends after dinner whilst the ladies had already retreated to their cabins and his brain was indeed working very slowly. His was still trying to work out what was wrong when it dawned on him that their ship wasn't moving anymore; there was almost total silence!

Pierre jumped out of bed, forgetting that his bed had been fitted into the small cabin with low beams just waiting for hapless passengers to bump into. He howled with pain when his forehead collided with the wooden structure and thus Armand was also brutally woken up. Muttering under his breath that Pierre should shut up and suffer in silence, Armand wanted to turn over in his bed and continue sleeping, but Pierre exclaimed, "Let's go see what's going on, the *Beatrice* isn't moving any more, something's wrong!"

Armand's curiosity finally triumphed over his lethargy and under protest he heaved himself out of his warm bed, shivering in the cold air of the unheated cabin. They dressed quickly, skipping the complicated and tiresome ritual of being dressed by their valets and stepped out onto the deck. It was still dark, and dawn was just breaking, but they could immediately see why the ship wasn't moving – in fact they couldn't see anything!

The *Beatrice* was surrounded by thick clouds of fog. They mounted the bridge of the ship in order to find the captain standing beside the impressive steering-wheel. He greeted them with his usual gloomy attitude.

"I did tell you, Sir, weather can change at any time. We will have to wait until it clears up a little." Looking thoughtfully at Pierre he seemed to remember that the young lad standing there was his superior and a duke, and added lamely, "Your Grace."

Pierre had to grin. He understood perfectly that he must remind his captain of one of the many young and hopeful cadets he was used to commanding.

"Any idea how long it will take until we can continue our journey? Where are we now?" asked Armand, still yawning.

"We're close to Calais, Sir, just some miles off the coast, but we can only wait until it clears up a little, it's too dangerous to continue sailing in this fog in the shallow waters, it could be today or tomorrow, nobody knows!"

With this sobering statement the two friends could do nothing but retreat to the main cabin where they were comforted by a good breakfast that was already waiting for them.

It was around noon when the fog started to lift and the ship could cautiously resume its journey to Calais. The captain had decided to dispatch one of his young sailors into the crow's nest to make sure that they wouldn't miss the coastline or any approaching vessel. Being in the vicinity of a major port, it didn't surprise anybody when the young sailor announced an approaching sailing ship in the early afternoon. It was still quite foggy but visibility had improved and they had made good progress.

Pierre and Armand had joined the captain once more; in actual fact they had fled from the Principessa who had installed her majestic figure in the main cabin and started a long and boring monologue explaining in detail her Italian family tree.

"How she can remember all the names of her hundreds of cousins, that's what I don't understand!" Pierre said to Armand full of awe. "And they all have nearly identical names, always a Maria or some Saint in it, it's incredible! She even remembers how and when they married into the family."

"Sounds like my family," Armand answered, "and on top of this, all of them are the most boring company you could imagine!"

In the meantime the anonymous ship approached them at full speed. The captain was trying to identify the boat whilst watching its approach. He seemed to have excellent eyesight as he muttered, "Seems to be French built, but how strange that they haven't hoisted any flags to identify themselves. I don't like this!"

This seemed a rather long statement for him but its significance was immediately underlined when the approaching ship started opening fire from two cannon that were mounted at the ship's bow, targeting the unprotected larboard side of the *Beatrice*.

Pierre and Armand were dumbstruck; they didn't even have time to be frightened or worried. Amazed, they witnessed how the captain's personality underwent a complete change.

"You want trouble?" he shouted in the direction of the approaching ship. "You'll get it!" and his freckled face now gleamed with delight.

"Nothing like a bit of a fight," he remarked calmly. "They're bloody idiots and amateurs, they started firing far too early! It'll be easy enough for us now!" And without any further explanations he bellowed a series of commands.

Hectic activity broke out everywhere. Pierre heard the running of feet, the thundering noise of heavy metal being moved, the rasping sound of moving wood. The *Beatrice* turned swiftly and elegantly, and now her bow was facing the enemy ship. To Pierre it seemed that the captain had decided to chase the French boat, and the roles were about to be reversed.

Charles had hurried from the main cabin to join them on the bridge once he had heard the noise of the cannon. He was looking very worried, probably thinking about Céline and Marie. They needed to be protected above all.

The captain however didn't seem at all unsettled by their presence, and unperturbed he continued bellowing his orders as the ship responded with the precision of a well-oiled machine. The enemy was firing once more, the cannon balls luckily dropping into the sea, but this time dangerously close, missing their ship by only a few yards. The *Beatrice* made another elegant manoeuvre and then Pierre suddenly heard a deafening noise and a series of several explosions.

At first he thought that they had finally been hit, but as there was no sound of splintering wood, he discovered to his great delight that it was his own ship, the *Beatrice*, who had returned fire.

It appeared that the *Beatrice* was in fact armed with several cannon and was now firing a fusillade of cannon balls in the direction of the French ship, which – unwisely – had continued its pursuit. The firing by the *Beatrice* had been well calculated and several cannon balls ripped into the fragile wooden hull of the French ship. Pierre saw and heard the splintering wood, saw the mast swaying and finally going down, another fusillade from the *Beatrice* followed and in no time the French ship was starting to sink. They were quite close now and could hear the frantic shouts of the wounded, desperate cries of "*au secours!*" – help us – from panicking sailors clinging to wooden planks in the hope of rescue.

Pierre looked helplessly at the captain for a hint or guidance; he really didn't know how to react or what to do. The captain watched the scene unmoved. He had seen far worse in his life.

"Nothing much we can do, Your Grace, the water is too cold. Better let them go down and be over with it quickly! They asked for this, better them than us."

Pierre could only underline the truth of the last statement. He continued watching the scene with a morbid fascination. He could discern some frightened men in the uniform of French musketeers clinging to the broken mast, but he couldn't make out any coat of arms; apparently their secret enemy had taken care to remain incognito.

Later on neither Pierre nor Armand could tell how much time this short fight had taken in reality – was it seconds, minutes or almost an hour? For now it seemed the fight was over incredibly fast, the last forlorn cries quickly being swallowed and muted by the fog and the sea and the increasing distance as the *Beatrice* headed onwards at full speed towards Calais where they entered the port the same evening, but decided to stay on board.

The mood on board was strangely hilarious, the crew and even the passengers were in high spirits. Pierre heard boastful voices when he crossed the bridge. What a nice surprise and entertaining pastime this fight had been, just the right thing to talk about once they were back in England, sitting in an inn, drinking with friends and sharing the story. The captain had distributed an extra portion of rum to celebrate the victory, hence spirits were running high.

Charles and Armand had done a great job cheering up the ladies, who had spent a terrible and nerve-wracking time locked in the main cabin during the fight, fearing the worst. But now they were joking and praised their captain who had joined them for a dinner in his honour. But Pierre had problems joining the festive mood. He could still hear the cries of the victims in his ears, becoming weaker and weaker. Should he have tried to rescue them? Had he committed an eternal sin? he kept asking and torturing himself.

Charles sensed that Pierre was feeling ill at ease and approached him with a glass filled to the brim with some potent liquid. He passed it to Pierre and said casually, "First time ever you witnessed something like a small battle? You didn't like it and it only confirms that you are of good character. But listen, these men wanted to kill you, actually, all of us. These cowards opened fire without any prior warning, so much for their sense of chivalry. Sometimes it's time to be lenient, but once we're facing a fight, my personal preference goes straight back to the Old Testament: an eye for an eye, there is no other choice!"

Pierre took a big gulp of the amber liquid. The whisky burned in his throat but the warmth soon spread through his body making him feel better. He smiled cautiously and answered, "I'm afraid you're right. I still pity the poor souls, though. Any idea who's behind all of this?"

Armand had approached them and overheard the last question. "There is no question about that, Pierre! This is definitely Richelieu's style. Nobody else would dare to fire so close to the French coastline. He'll pay for this, I swear!" Watching Pierre's pale face he added, "And stop wasting your sympathy on these stupid devils that drowned. They sold their souls for some cheap copper coins to the damned Cardinal, now they can explain their choice to Saint Peter as they're knocking on the doors of heaven."

He chuckled and continued. "They'll have a lot of explaining to do though to gain entrance." Then his mood changed and he added angrily, "Real bastards they were, opening fire without any warning!"

Pierre had to smile on seeing his friend so upset and actually this made him feel much better.

Marie had joined them and she took his hand, squeezing it gently. "I was terribly afraid, I must confess," she said. "Sitting inside this dark cabin and just hearing all of these cries, noises and explosions was frightening. I thought this would be our end."

Pierre looked at her, shocked. "Did you really think that? What else passed through your mind? We were so much involved in the action, we didn't really have

320

any time to be afraid, we just listened and watched, it seemed to happen so fast, and I must say, the captain was marvellous!"

Marie looked at Pierre and gave him one of her lovely smiles. "I just regretted that I might die before we should have had the chance to truly get to know each other and marry. I know, a true lady should never confess openly to something like this, but it's the truth!"

Pierre kissed her hand; it was the most honest declaration of love that he could ever have imagined.

Céline had overheard Marie's statement and steering the conversation to a lighter tone, she said, "Well, you're right, you'd have missed something. It may sound shocking, but I have to confess, being married is most pleasant. To think that everybody tried to deter me before I vowed eternal love and devotion to Charles! The Principessa even went so far as to warn me that with a man of Charles's size it would be impossible for me to find enough space in our bed – I must say, I don't regret it, that is, until now at least he's been quite a darling!"

Everybody was laughing, especially as Charles had blushed like a young maiden. They would of course now be mocking him for days to come about her comments.

Yet Pierre didn't sleep well that night, and the cries of the drowning men followed him well into his dreams. Waking up the next morning still worn out and tired, he came to the conclusion that a life of fighting in the military would definitely not have suited him.

They were having breakfast in the main cabin, almost ready to leave the *Beatrice* and move on to Paris. All or a sudden they heard a commotion outside. Soon one of the servants knocked, and, visibly intimidated, announced the visit of a French officer.

A young man strode into the cabin, arrogant and self-assured. He had not deemed it necessary to wait for the servant to finish a proper announcement. Simultaneously they could hear outside the tramping feet of several soldiers. Pierre's eyebrows rose and he gave a thoughtful look to Armand, who had been about to leave the cabin.

The young officer wore his best attire, immaculate, apparently willing to impress, with alert-looking eyes. Céline thought that he looked arrogant but attractive, probably quite smart; an opponent to be reckoned with, she decided silently.

Let's see what he's up to, she thought, *and let's see how Armand deals with him, he seems to be taking up the challenge.*

The officer greeted them curtly, not wasting his time on politeness.

321

"Let me introduce myself. I am Jean François de Martigny, officer of his Majesty Louis XIII, King of France. Can I please see your personal documents? It has been brought to our attention that a certain Pierre de Beauvoir is travelling on this ship and I have an arrest warrant in my possession as he is requested to present himself to the services of His Majesty. Furthermore it has been brought to our attention that the firing of cannon was heard before this vessel entered our port and I must insist on searching the ship as you seem to have entered French waters with harmful intent."

He had uttered his speech in the elegant accent of the French aristocracy. Clearly he was of good descent and used to dealing with people of his own class. His arrogant glance swept around the cabin, expecting the passengers to fall into a state of agitated trepidation.

To his unpleasant surprise, Armand detached himself calmly from the wall of the cabin and placed himself in front of the officer. Armand was well built and, even if he did not dwarf the officer as Charles would have done, he still looked down on the officer who kept his aggressive stance but started to feel that his mission might turn out be less smooth than anticipated.

"Monsieur de Martigny, may I introduce myself? I am Armand de Saint Paul, son of the Marquis de Saint Paul, and in my own right, Earl of Worthing. As I happen to be a gentleman, I will take pleasure in greeting you first and welcoming you, even if you have intruded without invitation or proper introduction, as might be expected from any royal officer wishing to visit our ship."

The officer made as if to protest, but Armand interrupted him with an arrogant gesture and continued, unperturbed.

"And behind me, you have the pleasure of meeting His Grace, or should I use his official title, The Most High, Noble and Potent Prince, His Grace, Pierre, Duke of Hertford, Marquis de Beauvoir, ambassador of their Majesties, Marie-Henriette, Queen of Great Britain and Charles, King of Great Britain, on a special mission to His Majesty, Louis XIII, King of France. As you might remember – if ever you bothered to pay attention – the Queen of England happens to be the sister of our gracious King Louis XIII and we are on our way to bring a personal message from the Queen to her brother. I cannot judge if it is incredible foolishness or pure insolence on your part to disturb a diplomatic mission of the highest level, and as for your accusation that we entered French territory by firing with cannon, that will make a great story when we meet your King."

The officer stood there, dumbstruck, his lips pressed together. Small beads of perspiration were forming on his forehead. This conversation was taking a turn he hadn't imagined even in his wildest dreams.

Armand's polite and slightly amused voice continued. "May I recommend now that you apologize and greet His Grace properly and then leave the ship as fast as possible? I imagine that there must be some huge misunderstanding somewhere,

322

indeed, His Grace's name is Pierre de Beauvoir, but I cannot imagine why a special ambassador and English duke should end up in French custody, unless France should want to provoke a war between the two countries?"

The officer had avoided looking at Armand during his speech, but when he raised his eyes, Armand saw that he was not yet willing to give up. *He's a fighter*, Armand thought, *not bad, but I'll get him!*

The officer cleared his throat and said sourly, "As I'm an officer on duty, I'm afraid that you have to accept that I'm here on an official mission as well. Please present the papers that will give me the proof of your identity and your *special mission*." He managed to lend a note of incredulity to the last two words.

His eyes strayed to Marie's aunt who sat there, fanning herself angrily, visibly upset by this interruption. Looking at her he said, "I do apologize for my insistence, but I am just doing my duty, my lady."

Armand smiled and said in his sweetest voice, "You have it wrong again. This lady should be addressed as Her Highness; you are in the presence of Her Highness, the Princess de Colombare."

The Principessa closed her fan angrily as if she wanted to confirm Armand's statement and the snapping sound echoed through the silent cabin as she gave a long disdainful look towards the hapless officer.

Armand gave a nod to Charles who fumbled inside his waistcoat and took out a document. Slowly he opened the envelope that contained an official-looking paper bearing the seals of the King and Queen of England. The officer watched Armand unfolding the document and pressed his lips together. Only his twitching eyebrow showed how nervous he apparently was.

Martigny's mind went back to yesterday evening when his commander had called him into his office. It had seemed like a nice surprise and a chance to make a few livres. The assignment had seemed simple enough: Thirty gold livres to arrest Pierre de Beauvoir and another one hundred if his prisoner met with a fatal accident on his way into custody, the emphasis being on 'fatal'. They had agreed that drowning would be their preferred option to get rid of their prisoner. Instructions for the demise of their prisoner had come from the highest level in Paris. How glad he had been then, it had seemed this offer had been sent from heaven! Jean François de Martigny loved gambling and women and consequently he was heavily in debt, as neither hobby could be supported by his meagre income. This small fortune would mean freedom from the most pressing debts (of course he wouldn't pay all of them) and he'd keep enough money to spend a delightful night or two in the charming new brothel that had recently opened and boasted the exotic services of women from different colonies.

Coming back to reality he tried to focus his eyes on the text of the document that Armand was now presenting to him. Although he had been taught to read and

323

write, he was no master of these complicated skills. But he could understand enough though to see that he was beaten, the seals and style of the documents were clear enough, with the words 'special ambassador' as well. He studied the seal of the Queen but it seemed genuine; it combined the coat of arms of Great Britain and the familiar lilies of the royal Bourbon family. As she was a daughter of France, she had the right to keep them in her own coat of arms.

The officer understood that it was time to retreat before his career was totally ruined and hastily he started to apologize for his intrusion, bowing profusely in all directions.

Pierre played his role to perfection. He had been sitting in his gilded armchair since the entrance of the officer, first unmoved, then visibly bored by the superfluous intervention of a low born creature. Now he just waved his hand – a weary gesture, similar to chasing away an unwanted insect.

Assuming the airs of a nobleman, he said in a bored voice, "I can only congratulate my cousin, the King of France, on having such a dutiful officer. I would recommend, though, that your sense of duty should be more balanced with your sense of propriety."

He rose from his armchair and offered his arm to Marie's aunt. "Your Highness, please allow me to lead you outside to get some fresh air. I do not know what happened but the air in this cabin went decidedly stale some minutes ago. I am afraid it is too crowded in here."

Without wasting any further attention on the officer who stood there, completely crushed by Pierre's careless attitude and his acerbic statement, the Principessa and Pierre walked outside. Not even the royal couple itself could have made a more majestic exit than those two.

Armand looked at the officer who seemed to have shrunk and had lost the last trace of his former buoyant arrogance and said in a low voice, "I'm afraid that you have upset His Grace greatly! May I ask you to leave the ship and make sure that we are not bothered again. I would also recommend that you give a hint to your commander about the special circumstances of our mission and recommend that he does not try to meddle any more. The person who gave you instructions to arrest his Grace has made you play with fire. It should be easy enough to understand that you risk being the first to be burnt once the King gets involved!"

The officer just nodded, trying to hide his shock that this soft-spoken gentleman was apparently aware of the background to this warrant. He now understood he had been just a pawn in this power game and he vowed to himself to get out of this as fast and as unscathed as possible. The warrant would be filed and forgotten.

I'm not going to put my head on the platter for some silly games in Paris, he vowed to himself, and bowing curtly once more to Armand, Charles and the ladies he bolted out of the door.

The sound of marching feet receded and soon enough Pierre and Marie's aunt came back into the main cabin where the others were still waiting and having an animated discussion.

Pierre strode forward, embraced his friend and exclaimed, "You were absolutely brilliant! You beat this man by a mile!"

Armand grinned and retorted, "You did an excellent job as well! I've never seen such regal bearing in all my life. You looked down on him like he was a cockroach and your last sentence was first class." He imitated Pierre's bored voice: "My cousin, the King – it made him cringe."

"What about me?" inserted the Principessa curiously, eager to receive her share of the praise.

"Absolutely brilliant as well!" confirmed Armand gallantly, "How you handled this vicious little fan of yours was really amazing, you nearly hit the poor officer!"

The Principessa smiled, pleased with herself and once more the fan went into action.

Pierre watched her with a broad grin and then he turned to Charles. "This document looked convincingly authentic, where on earth did you get it? It must have cost you a fortune!"

Charles cleared his throat and mockingly, he said, "Your Grace, I have a confession to make!"

Pierre looked suspiciously first at Charles, then at Armand who tried to look his most harmless, but Pierre could have sworn that he was quite well informed too.

"All right, tell me," Pierre said and waited for the answer.

Charles answered with a question. "Do you remember the evening gown the Queen was wearing for the official Christmas supper?"

"Of course I do!" Pierre exclaimed "It was a stunning dark red velvet gown encrusted from top to bottom with diamonds and pearls, it must have cost a fortune!"

Dryly Charles answered, "It did, indeed!" and named the amount.

Pierre whistled. "That's incredible – this amounts to the price of a complete village, maybe even more!"

"Even more," Charles answered evenly, and then he added after a short pause, "and you paid for it."

Pierre's eyes widened in amazement. "I paid for it? How come? I'm a rich man now – but this is frivolous! Are you crazy?"

Charles stood there, saying nothing, just a light smile playing on his lips.

"Come on, Charles, don't be such an oaf," Céline cried impatiently. "Tell us the full story now!" Charles bowed in her direction and relented.

"I had heard that the Queen had ordered this splendid gown, thinking she could coax King Charles into paying for it. When the King heard the price – and being a true woman she didn't even tell him the truth, as you can imagine – he went into a state of agitation she had never seen before. He shouted at her that he could recruit and run two regiments for the price of this silly gown and that she could send it right back to her seamstress – and if not he'd send her into exile to Scotland. The Queen then went into one of her usual tantrums, but this time the King didn't relent. Well, we all know that he's completely broke and doesn't have the money anyhow. So the Queen was stuck, she had a glamorous dress – but no money to pay for it. She had already milked her rich brother several times, therefore she was starting to panic." Charles could see that all eyes were glued on him. *Nothing like a bit of royal gossip to entertain people*, he thought amusedly and continued.

"As I happen to have good connections at court, I heard about her problems and humbly requested the favour of granting me a private audience. Her Majesty was at her most gracious, especially as I indicated that the newly appointed Duke of Hertford would be absolutely honoured to help her out of this small problem."

You bet, thought Pierre, *it's the Templars' connection again and most probably she bit his hand off, so desperate must she have been to get out of this mess.*

Charles grinned at Pierre; most probably he could read his thoughts.

"As I said, Her Majesty was very gracious and soon we agreed that she should have this small document drafted to appoint Armand and you as special ambassadors for a royal mission to visit her brother, thus granting you diplomatic immunity. In essence I spent the money to buy you a small life-insurance as I was sure that Richelieu would try to have another go at you as soon as you set foot on French territory."

"Expensive!" Pierre mumbled, but he was impressed.

"Then," Charles continued, "I asked Her Majesty if she wouldn't fancy a diamond necklace to match her beautiful gown to underline her natural beauty."

Pierre groaned. "You hypocrite, just tell me quickly, another village gone?"

326

"Sort of," Charles replied. "Of course she was very interested. Consequently we made another small deal, one of the many necklaces of your grandmother is now in her treasure chest and I got this," he said slowly, careful to keep the tension rising, and took out another document from his pocket. He handed it to Pierre who scanned through it quickly.

"What does it say, Pierre? Don't look like this, tell us, quickly!" Marie exclaimed.

Pierre took the document and read it carefully, his eyes becoming wider and wider, then cleared his throat. "Charles, you're simply a genius! This letter is worth several necklaces, it's the best weapon we could have to regain my heritage in France!" Looking into the inquiring faces of his audience he continued, "It states that I am the lawful Duke of Hertford and consequently the son and lawful heir of my father, the late Marquis de Beauvoir. The Queen writes to her beloved brother that she appeals to his royal sense of justice to stop," Pierre had to laugh out loud at this point, "his scheming subalterns who do not act in the interest of their country but only of themselves, and acknowledge me officially. She writes that she is only a woman and his sister but that she still cares about her beloved France and has full trust in him."

The room was completely silent, then Armand spoke. "Good Lord, you really made her write that? If ever King Charles sees this letter he'll have a fit. How can she do this? Meddling with French affairs as a Queen of England without his consent amounts to high treason!"

"She never really settled in England in her heart and soul," Charles answered. "She still sees England as a strange country to which fate has sent her for a certain period of time. In her mind she's a French princess first – and she hates Richelieu. I loved that part where she mentions him indirectly as a mere subaltern. She thinks that he's manipulating King Louis like a puppet on a string." Charles continued, "I promised, though, to hand the document over to the King directly. I gave her my word of honour that the letter will not pass through the hands of Richelieu."

The Principessa was still shocked. "This is unbelievable, this woman must be mad!" she exclaimed. "But the Bourbon blood was never really any good, not very noble if you ask me, if *my* family had acceded to the throne..."

Armand hastened to change her mind, as once Marie's aunt started explaining the many complications of her family tree and enumerating the occasions where one of her numerous family members might have acceded to the throne of France, they would be sitting there for hours.

"I'm sure you would have made an excellent Queen of France, but now we have to deal with the next steps," Armand interjected quickly when she paused briefly. "We have to go to Paris and obtain a private audience with King Louis as fast as possible and I believe I know the person who can arrange this for us."

327

"Not very difficult to guess," Pierre answered. "We'll need the help of your father. Will he help us?"

"Of course he will," Armand said, "as we now know he was your father's best friend, and will move heaven and earth to get you installed officially as Marquis de Beauvoir, and let me tell you, if my father wants something, he usually gets it, Richelieu or not!"

Armand grabbed a glass that was close to him and held it high. "Let me toast Pierre de Beauvoir, Duke of Hertford and soon to be Marquis de Beauvoir."

FRUSTRATION

Henri was restless and frustrated. He had already spent several weeks on the Roquemoulin estate, a boring and endless eternity, to his mind. He had been doted on by the love-stricken count until he felt close to suffocation. Playing the thankful guest and lover made him grind his teeth and although he skilfully limited any amorous contact to the strict minimum, he knew that he had to keep his host in good spirits, as until now the document for his adoption had not been returned signed and sealed by the notary, hence the need to remain extremely careful.

Luckily the count had caught a slight cold and Henri had been able to convince him that this could end in a deadly pneumonia if he didn't take extreme care of himself. Thus Jean Baptiste de Roquemoulin had been installed in his big bed, surrounded by different sorts of herbal teas and foul-smelling medicines and had received strict orders from his doting son-to-be not to move out of bed for the next few days.

The count had cherished this display of loving care and after weak protest he had happily relented. Henri had thus gained some time for himself and immediately he had extended his excursions on his horse to long periods of absence stretching over several hours. He insisted on riding alone without any groom – he was in dire need of some freedom.

The harsh winter had softened to the first harbinger of what might turn into an early spring. He rode restlessly, pushing his horse to the limit, trying to get rid of the tension that had built up in him during the past weeks. Henri was afraid of exploding sooner or later, and showing his true face far too early.

During one of these excursions he had happened to meet Marina. He had taken a break close to the Loire and all of a sudden she had materialized next to him. He didn't know from where she had come and how she could have known that he'd be there. She had approached him, free from any timidity and had sat next to him, silently taking his wine flask out of his hand, drinking from it without even asking for his permission. Small beads of red wine had remained like pearls on her full lips.

Henri was immediately fascinated. She radiated sensuality from head to toe, had a small boyish frame, but wonderful breasts, fascinating eyes and an enchanting dark voice. She must have had gypsy blood in her, for her long hair was of the darkest and most brilliant black he had ever seen.

They had made love, there in the open; it had seemed so natural, unavoidable. She had been like a tiger, scratching him and moaning, taking the initiative, making him her slave to fulfil her desires. Afterwards she had drunk once more from his flask and simply said, "I'll meet you tomorrow, here, at the same time."

329

Riding back he had felt wonderful and energetic, the tension had gone, but how difficult it had been to go back to Jean Baptiste's room and endure his whining voice, the smells of the sick room and an ageing man, after he had just made love to the very incarnation of youth and beauty.

Henri's mind had wandered off several times and he must have been day-dreaming when he heard the kind reproach of his host. "What's happening, my darling, you seem to be so absent-minded today?"

With the greatest of difficulty Henri restrained himself from seizing the chess board that lay on the bed between them and slamming it against the head of the hapless count who was watching him with doleful eyes.

Henri just clenched his fist and managed to sigh and say in a distressed voice, "I was only wondering if we will ever be able to go back to Paris. The notary seems to be taking an eternity to return the documents. How much I'd love to call myself your son officially in public!"

The count quickly diverted the conversation to a different subject. The signed and sealed documents lay hidden in his study but he dreaded the moment of their return to Paris. He might be a fool but he was aware that here in Roquemoulin, Henri was fully his. Once they lived in Paris it would be just a question of time until Henri would meet younger and more attractive companions. Jean Baptiste had been torturing himself on how to cope with this, his heart eaten away by a jealous canker. The only short term solution he had found was to drag out their stay here in the countryside at least until spring. These were his months and the count was cherishing every minute he could enjoy Henri's company exclusively for himself.

The next morning Henri had decided not to show up at the river. He would definitely not meet with the gypsy girl again; she was highly dangerous, too demanding and he had to be careful. If ever Jean Baptiste found out, he'd be dead in the water.

But somehow he ended up all the same searching for her and indeed there she was, this time seated on a black horse, but without a saddle. She sat regally atop her horse, self-assured, like a man. Together they galloped to the same barn where Henri had sought shelter before.

They dismounted from their horses and Marina led Henri to the blankets she had hidden in the straw. This time both of them took their clothes off, slowly, to let the tension rise. Under the warm shelter of the blankets they made love, passionately, but once again the gypsy girl led him, insatiable and demanding. Afterwards Henri lay next to her, completely exhausted but strangely exhilarated. He had never met a girl or man before who could arouse him so much.

The girl took his hand and with her index finger she followed the fine lines of his palm. "You are steered by greed, passion and hatred," she said in her dark

330

voice, "I can read this in your hand. You have never encountered love, you don't even know the meaning of the word."

Henri looked at her. He was even more fascinated. Every word she had said was true enough, but any ordinary girl would have been shocked. All the girls he had met before had either been whores or innocents, the latter crying for vows and tokens of eternal love. This gypsy girl spoke only of facts, as if she had seen only what she had been expecting.

"True, I've never been in love and it's the feeling of hate that's my biggest motivation!" he answered calmly. "Doesn't this shock you? Weren't you expecting me to tell you that I love you, madly, forever?"

The girl gave him a long and thoughtful glance and answered, "After I was born, my mother had my horoscope drawn by the wisest woman of our clan and later she cried the whole night. I seem to be born under the sign of evil; I also have never truly loved a man in my life. You'll be no exception. But I recognized immediately that you and I are from the same mould. We share the same destiny."

Once more she kissed him passionately. They made love, the fact that they were playing with fire just adding to their excitement. Lying there, panting and reaching his climax, Henri realized that he needed to get rid of Jean Baptiste fast now, how could he ever go back to this boring life, to the count's bed after he had experienced this passion?

She must have read his thoughts as she whispered, "You're thinking about your freedom? I consulted the cards, I saw an accident soon, a fatal one..." and then she cried out loud in pleasure.

*****

His Eminence, the august Cardinal Richelieu, was in a foul mood. He was sitting in the small antechamber of the royal château in Versailles. He had never understood why King Louis XIII loved this small castle. It was old, uncomfortable and could boast none of the luxurious style that could be found in Paris nowadays in the numerous palaces that had been built recently. Versailles was surrounded by a thick forest, therefore it was ideal of course for the King's favourite pastime, hunting. But communication with Paris was difficult and it took several hours of driving on bumpy roads to reach this forlorn castle. Richelieu sighed. He had been sitting here, waiting for the King for several hours already but until now he hadn't yet heard the sound of the horns or the pack of hounds and the galloping hooves that would herald the return of his Majesty.

He looked around him. By now he knew by heart all of the painted hunting scenes that adorned the room, painted by an unknown artist of definitely mediocre ability, he reflected. Not for the first time he stated that his sovereign had no taste or appreciation for art. But this was not why he had come here – Richelieu had

331

come to judge personally how close the King had grown attached to the young Cinq-Mars.

He had launched the young lord himself at court, in the expectation that the good-looking young gentleman would win the favour of Louis XIII. His plan had succeeded, but perhaps too well. Richelieu had started to feel uneasy about the rapid progress of his protégé, as Cinq-Mars had been promoted almost immediately to the position of Grand Master of the Royal Wardrobe, which gave him intimate access to the King. Since then, royal favours had been showered on the young man, and Cinq-Mars was today the undisputed royal favourite at court. But what had been intended as a clever move to keep the King happy and occupied was turning into a political issue – even a potential threat to his own power.

Cinq-Mars cherished his new position of influence – probably he thought himself to be unassailable – and, to Richelieu's great annoyance, his spies had intercepted letters that proved his meddling with the external affairs of France, supporting the dangerous Spanish faction at court. Richelieu was used to keeping his cards hidden and had not yet decided if he would use the letters now or later to get rid of the young favourite. He knew he was treading on thin ice and he wanted to see for himself to what extent the King was smitten with the quarrelsome lord. He had therefore invented the excuse of discussing some urgent questions relating to the religious wars that were still ravaging the German Empire to come to Versailles and see if Cinq-Mars presented a real danger to his power or not.

He must have been nodding off, sitting close to the only fire in the room in his armchair as suddenly he was startled and realized that the commotion of the royal hunting party was close to him. He heard dogs barking, feet tramping on the wooden floor, loud voices and laughter floating in the air. The door sprang open, and the King entered first, his boots still covered with mud, his face hot and flushed from the pleasure of hunting and the fresh air.

Richelieu rose as fast as he could, bowing deeply to greet his sovereign, but the King held him as if to spare him the effort and greeted him warmly. "Your Eminence, what a pleasure to see you here. I hope that you bring good news?"

A boyish voice from behind interjected, "He doesn't look it, Sire, I think I've never seen him smile in my life! He's certainly the most diligent prime minister one could imagine, but don't let him play cards with us tonight, he'll spoil the party!"

The King laughed and sent an indulgent glance to his favourite, then he turned back towards Richelieu and said, "Yes, no king could wish for a better prime minister, you're right!"

Richelieu bowed to thank him for the royal compliment and answered, "Monsieur de Cinq-Mars is worried that I would win at cards against him, Sire, some people know how to drink, some to think – and how to count their points."

He paused significantly and continued, "But don't worry, Sire, I have excellent news from Germany and need to discuss in private with your Majesty how we continue to strengthen our position there."

Cinq-Mars looked on sulkily but as the King had just laughed and then entered into an animated discussion with Richelieu his courtier's instincts told him that it would be unwise to show his annoyance openly and he decided that he'd prove soon enough to this old crab that he had a brilliant brain – and knew how to use it to his own advantage.

The King was absolutely delighted at the news and insisted Richelieu join him for dinner as his guest of honour. As the King was deeply religious, he demanded a mass to be held by his Cardinal first to thank God and request celestial blessings for the kingdom and the royal family.

Thus the cardinal found himself first celebrating a church service and later in the evening sitting close to the King, who was presiding over the large table. He had to endure the endless chatter of an animated group of courtiers who could qualify as his sons or grandsons. The young men were boasting about the numerous women that they had seduced recently in Paris, hordes of game they had apparently hunted down and while they were talking and chewing simultaneously, grease kept dripping from their lips. They devoured food in unbelievable quantities, only interrupted by gulping down red wine from goblets of enormous size. Those goblets were of exquisite workmanship, made from purest gold, fittingly decorated with scenes featuring Diana, the semi-naked goddess of hunting.

The King beamed with delight and seemed to cherish every minute of this companionship with his hunting party. He loved to spend most of his time with his fellow huntsmen, as he called them, once the wine had taken effect. Louis had also taken the habit of eating and drinking far too much, to the despair of his doctors who no longer knew how to cope with the bilious attacks that consequently followed.

Richelieu was suffering. The food was far too heavy for his delicate stomach, as it consisted of all sorts of venison seasoned with the most exotic and expensive spices, sweet pastries with almonds and eggs, all kinds of rich dishes, each dripping with fat or butter. The King toasted his health and Richelieu had to raise his glass and drink the heavy wine. The wine proved to be excellent and he permitted himself to empty his goblet, a move he was to regret once he found himself wincing with pain in his bed later that night.

The midnight hour had long passed and the first drinking companions lay snoring and drunk on the table when Richelieu was finally able to take his leave without offending Louis. The King just waved graciously and mumbled something, but his eyes remained glued on the handsome Cinq-Mars who was in full swing, telling some obscene jokes while grabbing exuberantly at his private

333

parts, interrupted by roaring laughter from those who were still clear-headed enough to grasp the meaning of the risqué story he was recounting.

Richelieu was disgusted; he had heard and seen enough. The King was obviously smitten by his new favourite and he would need to be extremely careful and have to present hard facts to eliminate this new star at the royal court. Part of his annoyance was due to the very fact that this threat was of his own making.

The night proved to be difficult and extremely painful. The room was ice-cold, the meagre fire couldn't produce enough warmth to give any comfort. The bed curtains were closed but Richelieu lay in the huge bed, freezing all the same and tormented by an awful combination of a splitting headache combined with intense stomach pain, vomiting, and profuse sweating, as he spent the endless hours shivering and feeling miserable.

As soon as daylight came, Richelieu was in his coach, speeding back to Paris. The bumpy roads didn't help at all to alleviate his suffering and by the time he had reached his palace, he was a thoroughly sick and tortured man.

The coach ground to a halt and the Cardinal alighted with the assistance of two of his strongest footmen, as he could barely walk. His arrival had drawn the usual crowds, beggars and petitioners fighting with shrill voices for his attention, waving empty hands or furled documents at him. And of course there were his own people who had been streaming into the courtyard of the Grand Palace, servants, secretaries, musketeers and monks reverently greeting the mighty Cardinal, the prime minister of the most powerful kingdom on earth.

Richelieu had difficulty seeing them clearly and identifying them individually; he made out only blurred outlines of people, pushing aggressively towards him. It took all his resilience not to cry out in pain and order his guards to send them to hell, all of them.

Slowly he managed to focus his gaze on one of the friars who was standing close to him, but something was amiss. He was trying to work out what was so peculiar. He had already stepped forward, followed by the throng of his retinue, still being safely held by the strong hands of his footmen, when it dawned on him – there should have been two friars! The one he had recognized was the new assistant of Brother Joseph. How unusual for Brother Joseph not to turn up and greet him!

He ordered his footmen to stop, then he turned slowly and made a sign for the friar to step forward. "I trust you are well, my Brother," whispered the Cardinal. "Please give my warmest greeting to my beloved Brother Joseph and ask him to come and see me today after I have rested, as I am sure that he'll have good news for me!"

The friar cleared his throat and to his great dismay, Richelieu noticed tears had started rolling down the cheeks of the monk, who seemed to be tongue-tied. "Speak up!" he ordered impatiently. "Is Brother Joseph not well?"

The brother started to speak, but his voice was breaking under the effort, and sobbing and speaking at the same time he uttered, "Your Eminence, I have sad tidings for you, the forces of evil have triumphed. We followed your instructions, hired a ship and we intercepted the ship of the enemy. We fired our cannon in the deep waters well outside the harbour to sink the enemy and make sure that he couldn't reach land. Brother Joseph insisted on leading this mission himself. He stayed onboard, encouraged the musketeers and prayed for our victory."

The brother paused, overcome by emotions, and then sobbing, rather than speaking, he continued, "I must inform you, though, Your Eminence, that our beloved Brother Joseph never returned. Only later did we hear that the enemy's ship was fitted with cannon, a true battleship in disguise. Nobody from our ship survived. We lost them all."

The Cardinal listened, dumbstruck. His face had become utterly pallid as if the blood had been drained from him. He looked frightened as he clung to his footmen, his hands clawing at the arms of his servants. The noise of the many voices and cries around him suddenly died, and an unnatural silence settled in the courtyard as if a bomb had just exploded.

With an extreme effort the Cardinal managed to answer, "May our Lord be merciful to his soul, Brother Joseph was my best friend and most diligent servant. Give me comfort and tell how we managed to crush our enemies after they had landed to avenge our dead?"

The monk hesitated again; everybody could see that he was scared to death. He knew that recounting this in public was not the right place but the eyes of the Cardinal were burning like coals and compelling him to speak. Therefore he lowered his voice to make sure that only Richelieu could hear his answer.

"Your Eminence, we tried, but the suspect Pierre de Beauvoir presented a letter signed by the Queen of England, granting him immunity and protection as her private ambassador to His Majesty, King Louis. The commander of the musketeers in Calais refused to arrest him once he saw this letter unless I could produce a warrant signed by His Majesty in person, which of course I couldn't. I'm afraid that Pierre de Beauvoir and his friends will soon arrive in Paris and seek audience with the King."

This was in fact a highly embellished and polished version of the truth. In fact, the commander of the musketeers in Calais had gone into a tantrum, the like of which the monk had never before witnessed, raging at him, "You damned black crows in your monks' robes think that you can meddle in the affairs of the State? Promise me money to arrest some young culprit? Then you take a ship without my permission, fire your cannon, drown twenty of my best men, all of them probably

335

bribed to assist you!" The voice had grown louder and louder. "And all of this happening in the waters and the territory that are under my sole authority! To crown it all, I find out that you incite me to arrest one of the most noble lords of England, a duke no less, and thus put my head on a platter for your own stupid games of power?"

In the end he had roared at him, his face crimson red, moving closer and closer, threatening to strike him at any moment. The irate commander had taken the arrest warrant that had been signed by Richelieu's secretary and torn it into pieces.

"Stuff this paper wherever you fancy, in this stupid face of yours or up your arse, but get out of here before I have you flogged by my men, monk or no monk. You won't know who you are once my whip has been dancing on your foolish back."

The commander had uttered these last words in a frenzy, spittle coming out of his mouth, when the monk decided that it was time to bolt and run for the shelter of the nearest church. Never, ever, would he go back to Calais – better to leave Richelieu's service and become a priest in a forlorn, but peaceful village in the provinces!

The Cardinal tried to digest this news but his brain, numbed and handicapped by his terrible headache, needed time to absorb and understand the full significance of this message. Once he had grasped the contents of the news, the great Cardinal Richelieu uttered a peculiar moan and after a final spasm, his body became limp and he fainted.

He would have fallen right to the ground if his footmen hadn't been so close, instinctively reaching out and catching the unconscious Cardinal before he could even touch the cobbled courtyard and holding him firm in their grip. Immediately his devoted valet reacted, and shielding the Cardinal from curious onlookers he had Richelieu carried upstairs into his bed chambers.

Of course many people had witnessed the scene and rumour spread swiftly all over Paris that the great Cardinal was ill. Later it was reported by well-informed sources that he had been assassinated, was definitely dead and some eye-witnesses swore – depending on their attitude towards the Cardinal – that they had smelled sulphur (obviously the Cardinal-haters), or seen celestial brightness around his limp body (most probably reported by those belonging to the perpetual miracle-seekers).

Physicians were called to the emergency and arrived, looking like doleful black crows in their official robes and caps. Even the King's personal doctor had been dispatched in a hurry from the Louvre palace. They examined the Cardinal who still lay on his bed, deathly pale, with only the lightest of breaths showing that he remained amongst the living.

The famous doctors of the science of medicine started a lengthy discussion in Latin and soon agreed: the case seemed straightforward enough. The bad juices of the body needed to be purged and they needed to bleed the Cardinal. Carefully, almost lovingly, they chose from the collection of sharp knives they had brought along.

The selected blade was still covered with congealed blood from the last patient; diligently it was wiped clean on a black robe. The black had been chosen to cover the stains and was most practical, avoiding the need for frequent cleaning. Afterwards the unhealthy fresh air was cleansed by burning exotic incense – an exercise which never failed to impress the patients and which had the additional benefit of later increasing their hefty bills.

When the last doctor had left the room, Richelieu's valet cleared the mess that they had left behind, and making sure that nobody was watching, he carefully took away their dressings, washed his master and affixed a fresh bandage. He threw away the vials and powders of their useless but outrageously expensive medicine. Then he started to revive his master with the tricks he had learned during the long time he had spent first in the army and later in the service of the Cardinal.

"They'll kill him one day if they continue bleeding him like a pig," he muttered under his breath. "Filthy, incompetent and greedy money bags they are, nothing else!"

*****

Pierre was marvelling at the lavish setting of the Hôtel de Saint Paul. They had arrived yesterday from Calais and Armand's father had invited all of them to stay as his guests, a gesture they had greatly appreciated. He had also suggested accompanying Pierre tomorrow to visit and explore for the first time his family home, the Palais de Beauvoir. This was the house where his father had been born and where his parents had lived for what could only be called a much too short period of time.

Their reception in Paris had been remarkable. Pierre had never seen his friend so nervous. Undoubtedly he had a lot of respect for his father and meeting him for the first time a good year after they had escaped from the monastery school had apparently made his stomach turn. The usually very talkative Armand had become more and more quiet, the closer they came to the outskirts of Paris.

The Hôtel de Saint Paul was an impressive building, though quite old and traditional by today's Parisian standards. Most noble families had lately tried to catch up with the new fashion set by the magnificent buildings of Cardinal Richelieu and the King and brand new palaces had been mushrooming all over the elegant quarters – yet the Hôtel de Saint Paul breathed an atmosphere of true wealth, tradition and power. Armand's father had stood there, immaculately clad in black velvet, dominating with his sheer personality the reception hall. Pierre had to catch his breath – there could be no mistake as to their relationship, here stood

Armand's mirror image, only a good twenty years or more older, his full head of hair an attractive shade of pepper and salt.

The Marquis de Saint Paul had been waiting for them at the end of the hall. When Armand and Pierre reached him, he had ignored his own son and to Pierre's great surprise he had been embraced like a son and bade welcome. Only then did the Marquis turn to his own son who kneeled in front of his father and nervously started to speak.

"My dearest Father, please let your unworthy son explain and please accept my deepest apologies…" It was fairly obvious that Armand must have rehearsed this speech again and again in his head during their journey to Paris.

The Marquis made a sign to shut up and dutifully, but very confused, Armand stopped, his face flushed with agitation. Armand's father suddenly dropped the inscrutable mask of courteous detachment he had worn before. He smiled and all of his personality seemed to be transformed. Stepping forward he approached his son, raised him up and embraced him. His deep voice easily filled the great reception hall. "My son, I love you with all my heart, but let me tell you one thing." The Marquis paused, and smiling even more broadly he continued, "You are a complete idiot. By now you should have understood that you did exactly the right thing, in fact you accomplished what I always wanted you to do: protect and save the son of my best friend Jean-Pierre de Beauvoir whose last wish was that I should look after his son, Pierre."

Now his strong voice quavered a little. "You cannot imagine how much I have been looking forward to this day. Why do you think I sent you to this stuffy monastery school away from Paris? Your mother and I knew perfectly well that you would never make an acceptable bishop, I've never ever seen you even look at a bible unless we forced you to." He laughed. "Even then, my son, you always found an excuse to escape to the stables."

His gaze went to Pierre and he continued, "I had hoped so much that you two would form a bond as strong as I had done with Pierre's father. I came to the conclusion it was better not to tell Armand anything in advance, better for him and a much stronger protection for you, Pierre, as the secret of your origin had to be kept for as long as possible. The past events have probably shown that my precaution was correct."

The Marquis smiled at his son and continued, "I'm reluctant to say it openly – and knowing Armand he'll become extremely conceited and big-headed, but I am extremely proud of both of you. I suppose I don't even know a small part of the adventures that you have gone through, but escaping the claws of the dangerous Cardinal Richelieu is proof of its own! Welcome to all of you and please use this humble house as if it were your own!"

Pierre looked around the reception hall of the 'humble' house, fitted in abundance with precious paintings, furniture and ancient suits of armour, at least he tried to, as his eyes had filled with tears. He had never expected such a warm welcome and couldn't believe his luck. He felt a single tear rolling down his cheek and cursed himself; how could he become so emotional, the Marquis de Saint Paul must think he had invited a weakling into his house! Cautiously he glanced at his friend and was relieved, in fact delighted to see that even the eyes of his friend had a curiously moist appearance. At least he wasn't the only weakling in the room, he concluded with satisfaction.

Pierre had noticed and was worried about the absence of Armand's mother. When he enquired after her, he was informed that she was feeling unwell.

"I'm terribly sorry to hear this," Pierre said, "I hope it's nothing serious!"

Armand chuckled. "Nothing more serious than the fact that she hates it when my father dominates the proceedings. We'll meet her later today and you'll see, she always knows how to put herself on the stage. But when my father received us, she knew that she'd have to play the humble hostess and wife, and she simply hates it!"

Pierre was rather shocked at this careless explanation; what if she really was feeling unwell?

Once they had rested and changed into their formal evening attire, Armand and Pierre knocked at the door of the private apartments of the Marquise de Saint Paul. A frail voice answered and bade them enter. The doors were opened by a pleasant-looking young maid who passed an appraising glance over the two handsome gentlemen who were presenting themselves. It was not difficult to guess what she was thinking and when she dived into a deep curtsey she ensured they had a good view of her very presentable breasts.

Rather distracted, they entered the dark room where Armand's mother presided on a huge armchair, her feet supported by a velvet-covered footstool, colourful shawls protecting her from any vicious attack by potential draughts. Several candelabras in the room had been arranged so as to cast their warm – and very becoming – candlelight on the charming Marquise who rested in her armchair, extending her arm feebly to welcome the young men.

Armand approached her first and, kneeling down, he took her hand and kissed it reverently.

"*Ma mère*, let me greet you. I'm always surprised to find my adorable mother younger and more attractive whenever I come to see her. Let me assure you that there are few sons on this planet who are lucky enough to have such a beautiful mother. Soon people will say that it's witchcraft and you should be my sister!"

The Marquise dropped her elegant pose and with surprising agility, at least for someone who had apparently been suffering from a terrible migraine, she jumped out of her armchair and embraced her son.

339

"Oh Armand, *chéri*, I really did miss you! You are indeed the most amusing and charming of my sons! Do I really still look so beautiful?" she asked anxiously.

"Of course you do!" said Armand. "I don't know how you do it, but you're still by far the most beautiful woman in France!"

The Marquise laughed, a deep, sparkling sound. "It is wonderful to hear that, but we all know it's nonsense. I'd love it if my other sons were as entertaining," she added. "They're always so..." She was searching for a suitable word.

"Dull?" Armand suggested.

The Marquise looked at him reproachfully. "A de Saint Paul can never be 'dull'!" she said with emphasis.

"Boring?" Armand suggested with a broad smile.

In answer she slapped his hand lightly and after brief hesitation she said, "Formal. They're a little too formal, but at least they respect my position as their mother, whereas you've been teasing me from the minute you entered my room."

Armand kissed her hand once more and presented Pierre, whom she greeted warmly with an appraising look.

He's still very young, but how handsome he is! she thought. *Of course my Armand is also very good looking. All the ladies of the court will be chasing Pierre though, young, handsome, a Duke and soon a Marquis, that's irresistible!*

She had started to unwind herself from her multiple shawls and carelessly she let them slide to the ground where they were collected dutifully by the young maid. When the maid got up she managed to brush against Pierre's hand. Armand had noticed this of course and grinned at Pierre; his mother's maid obviously wasn't wasting any time.

It now became apparent that the Marquise had already dressed in an elegant evening gown and was ready to join them for dinner, so graciously and in best spirits she allowed herself to be led downstairs by her son.

Dinner was served in the great dining room. Pierre had become accustomed to spectacular invitations and fancy presentations of food, seemingly endless menus, golden plates and all the trimmings that came with a formal dinner. Tonight, however, he really savoured the food; it was so good to taste some genuine French cuisine after so many months of having had to endure heavy English food!

As a guest of honour and out of respect for his high rank, he was placed next to his hostess and he could not talk with Marie, who was sitting on the other side of the table. It would have been extremely bad manners to speak to her across the table.

Pierre therefore feared the worst, expecting a long and boring evening spent conversing politely with his hostess. But not only was the food excellent and an agreeable surprise, Armand's mother proved to be a shrewd lady, well acquainted with the world of politics and the subtleties of court life. Soon he found himself involved in an animated discussion about the latest developments at the French court.

"It's an excellent opportunity to seek an audience with King Louis now. The old watchdog is still ill and is not expected to show up at court for at least another two months," the Marquise said while nibbling at a chicken bone.

"How do you know this?" Pierre asked curiously.

She looked at Pierre as if he were retarded. "We bribe his doctors, of course, to share this kind of information. In Paris everybody can be bought — and don't tell me that London is any different," she added matter-of-factly when she saw his scandalized expression.

"It's important that you make a good impression with the King, and the letter from his sister that Armand mentioned is a great introduction, but I would recommend later to seek a private audience with the Queen," she suggested.

"Why the Queen?" Pierre demanded, "I heard that Richelieu has completely isolated her and that she has no influence at court!"

The Marquise smiled and looked full of admiration in the direction of her husband.

"I must confess that my husband has an almost unfailing instinct for politics. When the heir to the throne was born three years ago, we went to the Louvre to pay our respects to the Queen, as soon as the Queen was allowed to leave her confinement. After we came home, the Marquis said, the Queen has changed. It's unlikely that the King will live long enough for his son to succeed him, I'm sure the Queen will become the future sovereign of this country; beyond any doubt she now has the resolve to become a real Queen."

She met Pierre's interrogating glance and explained. "Until she had given birth to the Dauphin, in her mind she remained a Spanish princess, always supporting the Spanish Habsburg faction. But now she's totally transformed. Thus we decided I should cultivate the relationship with the Queen. I started seeing her more often and regularly brought gifts for the Dauphin, later for prince Philippe, and my husband was right — now that I know her better, the Queen is ready to fight to keep this kingdom for her sons, she's become a true Queen of France."

"But I thought that Richelieu had ruined her reputation after her unfortunate affair with Buckingham?" Pierre replied.

"You cannot ignore forever a Queen who has borne the heir to the throne, and she's been clever enough to add the new rising star at court, Mazarin, to her

341

advisors. We're sure that Mazarin soon enough will become our new prime minister!"

"Who's Mazarin? I have heard of him, of course," Pierre asked.

"A nobody from Italy, a former diplomat. He's greedy, ruthless but can be a charmer – if he wants to and if it serves his objectives. Richelieu discovered him years ago and advanced his career. He's just been nominated Cardinal and this means he'll have the backing of the court and the Church to climb further."

The Marquise had spoken openly although the footmen in the de Saint Paul livery stood in a row behind the chairs, serving the guests.

"Aren't you afraid that Richelieu will know tomorrow what we've been discussing tonight?" Pierre asked nervously, gesturing towards the servants.

Again he heard her amused laughter. "Of course he bribes them to spy on us, but we pay double if they report in the way we suggest. The Cardinal knows – or should I say he thinks he knows – that this is a house of Richelieu-haters and that we are just waiting for his passing in order to suggest that Frédéric de Saint Paul should become the new prime minister."

Armand had been listening but at this he very nearly spat out his wine.

"Uncle Frédéric? But father hates him!"

His mother smiled and answered, "Oh Armand, my dear, you've been away from Paris and politics far too long. Of course your father hates him, this is exactly why he pretends to support him. Poor Frédéric, since Richelieu has been convinced that we advocate his nomination, all kinds of terrible things have happened to him; recently a wheel of his coach suddenly came loose and he was nearly killed in an accident."

"How devious!" Armand exclaimed. "One should never underrate my father!" He took his glass and proposed, "A special toast to my father, the Marquis de Saint Paul, may he live long and lead our family!"

*****

Pierre was so excited the next morning that he woke up very early, even before his valet had come to bring his cup of hot chocolate. This would be the day that he'd see the home of his ancestors for the first time and secretly he hoped to find paintings of his parents, to see for the first time how they must have looked. Of course everybody had been telling him that he was the spitting image of his father, but he was most curious to see his picture. In Hertford he had seen a picture of his mother, but this had been painted when she was a child. Apart from the fact that she had been blonde and beautiful he had had difficulties imagining her adult face.

He jumped out of bed and rang the bell. A minute later Jean appeared. He had become Pierre's private valet and Jean had been overjoyed to hear that they would be returning to France.

Pierre washed and dressed rapidly, savouring his cup of hot chocolate in his room. It was still early but he simply couldn't wait any more and decided to go downstairs to the library in the hope of meeting Marie, Céline or Charles. He knew that his chances of meeting Armand were close to zero, as Armand never got up early.

Once the servant opened the door of the library to him, he was disappointed; the big room lay empty and deserted. Pierre picked up some of the books that were lying invitingly on the small tables, and leafed through the pages, but he couldn't concentrate on reading any of them – especially those books dealing with the latest developments in philosophy and definitely not to be digested in the early morning.

He waited some more minutes, pacing up and down the library. Finally he decided to wake up Armand – what use was it to have a best friend if you couldn't even talk with him?

He hurried up the staircase to Armand's bedroom and without bothering to knock on the door he rushed inside. The room was still quite dark, the pale light of the morning seeping into the room but only the silhouettes of the furniture and the imposing bedstead were discernible. Pierre moved to the bed and in a loud and artificially joyful voice he announced, "Time to get up, it's already late morning!"

A shrieking sound answered, too high to have originated from his friend. Meanwhile Pierre's eyes had grown accustomed to the half light and he could now distinguish not one but two bodies in Armand's bed. The shrieking body jumped out of the bed, trying to cover herself with a sheet. As soon as she turned towards him, Pierre recognized the face of the maid they had met yesterday in the rooms of Armand's mother.

"Oh Lord!" the maid screamed, "I overslept, your mother will have me whipped and dismissed when she hears of this!"

Pierre could see that his friend was yawning and stretching like a satisfied tomcat.

Armand looked at the maid and said, "Wasn't I worth it?"

Despite her panic the girl had to giggle. "You men are all the same!" and grabbing her clothes she hastened out of the room.

"I can see that you had an excellent night!" Pierre said acidly.

"Indeed," answered Armand, unmoved by the irony of his friend. "I can't complain." In a dreamy voice he continued, "She even suggested that I should call you to have fun together, but I told her that your bride-to-be is sleeping under the same roof and that that might be somewhat improper."

Armand had closed his eyes, still revelling in his memories of the previous night and continued, "Anyhow, now that she has experienced what genuine quality is like with a *real* man, *you'll* have no chance whatsoever, we don't want to disappoint her, do we?" he added smugly.

Pierre had moved closer to the small bedside table where a basket with fruit and a big carafe of water had been placed. With a voice like honey he answered, "It's so good to have a friend like you, of course, how could I ever dream of competing with your skills and expertise regarding the art of seduction!"

Armand still had his eyes closed and answered in his dreamy voice, "Just what I said, my friend…" but whatever else he might have added was drowned in his loud screams as Pierre had taken the carafe and with a devious smile emptied it over his friend.

Armand jumped out of bed, stark naked and dripping with water while Pierre burst out laughing.

"What a fantastic hero you are, a drop of water and you scream like a girl!"

Jean, Pierre's valet, had witnessed the scene and with a broad grin he quickly brought some towels and helped Armand to dry himself. Armand started to complain loudly but at last he stopped and broke into laughter himself. "Alright, I must have looked ridiculous, I admit," he conceded, "But yet, my goodness, we had a truly wonderful night, you have missed something!" There he was once more, good old conceited Armand.

They spent the morning together waiting for the Marquis de Saint Paul, playing cards with Charles. The Marquis had asked them to wait for his return as he wanted to accompany Pierre to his father's home. Pierre had been happy to oblige, as secretly he had been rather nervous of visiting his family home on his own. Maybe he was a fool, but he felt like an imposter, although the palace had belonged to his family for generations.

Lunchtime came but there was no sign of the Marquis and Pierre became more and more nervous. Charles admonished him, "If you don't even look at your cards, why are we playing? You have again missed some of Armand's latest moves!"

Fortunately Pierre was spared having to answer as all of a sudden – and to his great relief – he heard the noise of approaching footsteps and like an eager child he hurried towards the door, hoping to meet the Marquis.

Armand's father entered the room and only once they had finished their mutual polite and formal greetings – Armand's father was always most demanding in matters of protocol – Pierre dared to ask, "Will we be able go to my home today, Sir? It's already lunchtime!"

The Marquis smiled but he shook his head. "I have excellent news, but unfortunately our visit to the Palais de Beauvoir will have to wait."

He was just about to finish his statement and Pierre was bursting with curiosity to hear more but suddenly the ladies entered the room and once more all formal greetings had to be executed and once more, Pierre had to wait.

It was only once they had settled for lunch that the Marquis continued to explain. "I've been at the Louvre Palace this morning and I have been able to arrange a royal audience for Pierre for tomorrow!"

Triumphantly he looked at the stunned faces around him.

"You truly are a genius, Father!" Armand exclaimed. "How could you achieve this so quickly?"

"That's my dirty little secret," he answered smiling, looking deeply into the eyes of his wife who smiled back. Of course she could guess exactly how he had succeeded in obtaining this audience.

The Marquis de Saint Paul had sought an audience with Cinq-Mars, the King's favourite. The young gentleman was the new and unrivalled star shining brightly at court – at least during the prolonged absence of Richelieu. The timing of the meeting had been requested unfashionably early, thus the dashing Cinq-Mars had made him wait, an act of sheer impertinence in view of Cinq-Mars's young age, and knowing that the house of de Saint Paul was far more venerable than the house of Coëffier de Ruzé, the family from which Cinq-Mars originated.

The Marquis had remained patient. Life had taught him that undue arrogance rarely went unpunished and he had waited serenely. If Cinq-Mars had hoped to find an irate or at least irritated visitor, he was disappointed. The Marquis de Saint Paul was politeness and understanding in person, of course he knew that such an important person as Monsieur de Cinq-Mars would be easily overwhelmed by the number of obligations at court, not to forget his Majesty, who might request his attention at any moment!

Cinq-Mars was flattered and his initial suspicion was quickly overcome by the smooth flow of praise that his affable visitor heaped on him in abundance. Later Cinq-Mars couldn't really remember exactly how they had arrived at the subject of arranging an audience with the King for the Marquis de Beauvoir. The young Cinq-Mars was no political genius but he had been involved long enough in the inner circles of power to understand immediately that they were entering extremely dangerous territory.

"Monsieur le Marquis!" he exclaimed, "I'd be truly honoured to render you a service, but you know yourself that the Cardinal Richelieu himself has expressed

345

his objections as to the legitimacy of Pierre de Beauvoir. The title of the Marquis de Beauvoir is one of the most prominent in France and meddling with the line of succession would be very dangerous and an enormous political risk. Involving the King at this stage would be very risky and he'd never forgive us if later it appeared that we made him meet the wrong successor!"

The Marquis de Saint Paul made a soothing gesture and answered, "I really appreciate your frank way of speaking, Monsieur de Cinq-Mars. It's so refreshing to find an intelligent, experienced and straightforward person at court! Of course I am aware of the situation and it is no secret that Cardinal Richelieu is trying at present to obstruct the course of justice, to speak also very openly to you. I just wish to explain that the legitimacy of Monsieur de Beauvoir has been acknowledged beyond any doubt by the King of England. Monsieur de Beauvoir is now de facto and de jure the rightful Duke of Hertford. Furthermore the Queen of England, who happens to be the sister of His Majesty King Louis, is recommending Monsieur de Beauvoir to her brother, wanting him to meet and acknowledge the Marquis de Beauvoir."

The Marquis took from his waistcoat the letter of recommendation bearing the royal seals of England and Great Britain, and acting like a conjuror he simultaneously produced a velvet bag, filled to the brim with freshly minted gold livres. When he placed the bag on the small table between Cinq-Mars and himself the string loosened and not only could Cinq-Mars hear the enticing sound of clinking coins but he could even catch a glimpse of the shimmering gold. The Marquis could hear how Cinq-Mars inhaled deeply, greed shining in his eyes.

Cinq-Mars led the life of a leading member of the royal court, which meant in practical terms that he was always broke, perpetually hunting for new revenues, as keeping up with the lifestyle of a King was a costly, almost impossible task.

"If you could convince his Majesty to do a favour for his sister – not for you or for me – and let justice prevail, ten more of those small bags will find their way to you. Please accept the first one as a token of my friendship, nothing else. I fully understand that this a difficult mission, but if I'm not mistaken, only one person at court has the personality and the importance to accomplish it! It will take intelligence and resolve to counter the wishes of the Cardinal, but who is the past and who is the future of this country?" the Marquis concluded softly.

Cinq-Mars was deeply moved by the speech of the Marquis. He realized of course that he had plunged into a court conspiracy, a bold play of power, but he also felt a rush of excitement: this mix of danger combined with the palatable, ultimately addictive taste of power made his head spin. Sitting in front of him was a member of one of the most exclusive families of the realm, acknowledging that *he*, Cinq-Mars, was the key to the King. He was also presented him with a wonderful opportunity to show Richelieu that his former protégé had a brain of his own – and this was a subtle and safe way, as all he had to do was to convince the King that he couldn't possibly ignore the wishes of his beloved sister. When Louis had been a boy, suffering under the iron rule and repression of his scheming

346

Medici mother and her favourites, Louis had been very close to his sister and still loved her dearly. Cinq-Mars looked once more at the document, scrutinizing it carefully. It looked and felt genuine, it must have cost a fortune to obtain, he concluded secretly. Well, it was common knowledge that the Queen of England was living far above her means and her poor husband, who wore several crowns but had no income, never had a penny in his pocket. The Queen of England probably had been only too happy to put her signature on this document if it came with a sufficient amount of money. Now he had to make the most of it, Cinq-Mars concluded.

"You do realize of course that this is a risky mission for me?" Cinq-Mars said. "I'll be happy to speak in favour of the Queen of England to King Louis, but what else could there be in it for me?"

The Marquis de Saint Paul smiled, but his smile held a slightly offended notion and answered, "Oh, Monsieur, please don't bother yourself too much. It's not *that* urgent. I can definitely approach the King myself, as you may know; my father was one of his godfathers. In no way did I want to upset you! Please forgive me, but as we're not discussing my own money I am not entitled to increase or change the amount that I can offer."

Cinq-Mars realized that the mellow and charming appearance of the Marquis hid a core of unrelenting steel and he gave in. "Dearest Marquis, I do understand fully your concerns, please forget what I just said, we are gentlemen, not merchants. I'll make sure that his Majesty will receive Pierre de Beauvoir tomorrow afternoon, that's agreed," he said hastily.

He needed the money, and badly.

*****

The following afternoon Pierre and Armand were drilled by the Marquis, together with his wife, to make sure that their appearance at court would be irreproachable. They had to rehearse how to greet the King, when to turn, where to bow. Pierre was reminded of Charles's lessons before he met the King of England, but his protest that he had been through all of this already was to no avail.

"With all respect to England, the court of Whitehall has never reached the sophistication and refinement of the French court," the Marquis said deprecatingly. "You are about to be introduced to the most powerful King in the world, even if I have to admit that most of his power has been of Richelieu's making. One generation ago, Europe was in the hands of the Habsburg clan, this century is the century of France and I cannot see how this will ever change! The Spanish royal family is degenerate, the German empire is shattered after one generation of religious wars and England is on the brink of civil war if my information is correct. France is the future!"

347

The official invitation had arrived as predicted and thus the following day they went to the Louvre palace, dressed in their finest clothes. The Marquis had insisted that Pierre should wear a sober outfit in dark colours. He should not look too glamorous. It was made from the finest of fabrics but looked deceivingly simple, a perfect complement to his shining blonde hair. Pierre wore a single decoration, a diamond studded medal he had received from King Charles when he had been installed as Duke of Hertford and – he had insisted on this – the ancient ruby ring of his grandfather, the precious key to the secret treasury he had promised to find and bring back to the Templars.

The King was installed in the great hall that was used for official audiences. He sat on a podium with a throne-like armchair under a velvet canopy in blue and gold, the proud coat of arms of France with the Bourbon lilies displayed at his back.

Gold, silver, precious stones, crystal and marble glinted everywhere, creating a splendour that Pierre had never seen before in his life; even the cathedral in Reims could not compete with this display of pomp.

He could now understand the statement made by Armand's father that the royal court of France was in a class of its own. Compared to Whitehall there were no ancient oak ceilings or century-old paintings with miserable looking royal ancestors – the royal palace was a demonstration of refinement, taste, power and wealth.

The audience hall was very crowded today. Whoever had been able to find an excuse or an invitation to come to court was present, as rumour had spread like wildfire that King Louis would receive and might even acknowledge officially the hitherto unknown and unseen heir of the late Marquis de Beauvoir. Rumour also had it that there was an unsavoury taste of scandal linked to his person – apparently he was a foreign heretical bastard, some even said he had been hidden during his youth in a monastery – but those rumours were generally dismissed as being too fanciful.

The King, who was sitting in the centre of this splendour and excitement, was in a bad mood. In retrospect he had the uneasy feeling that his favourite, Cinq-Mars, had manipulated him into this rushed meeting and he wasn't sure at all if he wasn't about to commit a big error. Secretly he had to admit that he missed Richelieu. Of course Cinq-Mars was so much more fun, never criticizing, never admonishing him – but Louis had relied these past twenty years on Richelieu's advice and had to acknowledge that he was not used to ruling without his counsel. The simple truth was that the King felt anxious, even scared to take any decision and he was totally overwhelmed by the sheer workload he had to cope with since Richelieu had been indisposed.

It had all started yesterday with a very pleasant surprise; Cinq-Mars had offered him in the morning a puppy as an addition to his pack of hunting dogs he was so proud of. Louis had been very much moved by this gesture and what fun it

348

had been, when the puppy had peed on Cinq-Mars's breeches! He had been so amused; he still laughed when he remembered the disgusted face of his favourite, who was most fastidious when it came to his looks.

Afterwards Cinq-Mars had talked about some visitors of high rank coming from England with a special mission and a letter from his sister. He had always loved his sister dearly, how sad that it was the fate of royal princesses to leave their home country and never come back! He could of course not refuse to receive those special ambassadors and it was only when he had already given his consent that Cinq-Mars had mentioned whom he had to receive!

Immediately Louis had wanted to backtrack, but Cinq-Mars had hinted at the inconveniences: not only would he offend his sister, who had named Pierre de Beauvoir her ambassador, he also seemed to have the explicit backing of the de Saint Paul family – and that Richelieu's previous efforts to meddle with this issue would soon end in an open conflict with his most prominent noblemen. The old families saw with great unease that Richelieu wanted to tamper with their sacrosanct right of succession. Of course Cinq-Mars had wrapped his message in the requisite layers of courteous speech, but Louis had understood all the same that trouble would be brewing once he refused openly to meet this claimant to the title and now here he sat, hoping desperately that his decision had been right and cursing Cinq-Mars.

Louis XIII was a slow thinker. Usually it took him weeks to take a decision, unless Richelieu gave him one of his brilliant analyses – when Richelieu talked, everything seemed so easy and clear. Louis sighed; the life of a king was truly complicated.

The trumpets sounded to announce the entrance of the special ambassadors of the Queen of England and all the members of the court stared at the huge door, the atmosphere fraught with tension and curiosity. Of course everybody hoped for an unsavoury scandal; and if he were a bastard, most probably he wouldn't know how to behave at court and would probably be outrageously ugly!

Led by the Marquis de Saint Paul and his charming wife there entered two young gentlemen and a suppressed sigh went through the rows of the female courtiers. Both of the young gentlemen looked so different, but each of them handsome enough to outshine any other of the young men who were present and who until today had paraded their good looks so arrogantly at court.

The reaction on the male side was as expected, more hostile, with the exception of a few gentlemen with moist eyes who would later send billets-doux to Pierre and Armand.

Cinq-Mars's jaw dropped as he hadn't given a single thought to the idea that the new Marquis or his friend might actually become a potential competitor for the royal favours that had been showered on him so abundantly. He was cursing himself, as he should have considered this option. Pierre was the spitting image of his cousin Henri de Beauvoir who had nearly outshone Cinq-Mars at court before he had fortunately disappeared without trace. Rumour had it that the omnipresent Cardinal Richelieu – once more – would have had his hand in this pie.

Pierre and Armand moved with grace and self-assurance. Thanks to the many rehearsals that they had performed yesterday under the critical eyes of the Marquis they knew how far to step forward, how to greet, when to stop, bend the knee and how to address the King correctly.

The King saw the two handsome young gentlemen approaching and his mood changed like the weather. It was generally known that he had a penchant for handsome young men. He now remembered that he had met and admired Pierre's father when he was still a young King – and suddenly the image of the late Marquis came to his mind; there could be no mistake that Pierre was a true member of the de Beauvoir family. Richelieu had probably never met him to have believed those stories about an illegitimate imposter.

Having Pierre right here in front of him, it seemed that his sister was right – depriving such a charming young gentleman of his heritage would not only be unreasonable, it would be totally unjust.

Originally the King had decided to remain at a regal distance and keep his political options open. But once Pierre bowed and kissed his ring, then rose to greet him with his dazzling smile, the King suddenly – and to his own surprise – rose from his throne and made a sign to Pierre to move forward. He kissed Pierre's cheeks, welcoming him loudly as his beloved cousin – court protocol on greeting the highest nobles of the realm. A commotion went through the assembled courtiers: the King had acknowledged Pierre in public! He had even kissed him! They had witnessed that a new star at court had been born, and a scandal had occurred – but so different from the one everybody had imagined!

Cinq-Mars watched this scene with unbelieving eyes. He clenched his fist in his pocket, a frozen smile glued to his face. He was only too aware that hundreds of eyes were watching him, most of them full of malicious spite. He did not have too many friends at court; you couldn't, if you were the royal favourite.

I'll have to get rid of him, he thought, *Pierre de Beauvoir will not steal my place!*

Being aware that many curious eyes were still staring at him, Cinq-Mars bowed towards the new Marquis de Beauvoir, and then he clapped his hands delicately as to applaud the King's gracious gesture. The King thanked him with a warm smile and Cinq-Mars felt reassured; he still had the love of the King and had won some time to get rid of this new rival. He had just started to relax, when he noticed how the king now turned his head and looked appraisingly at Armand de Saint Paul who had stepped forward to greet His Majesty. To his great dismay Cinq-Mars had to face the truth that he'd need to deal with the task of removing two dangerous rivals from the competition for royal favours.

He looked around and now his eyes met those of the Marquis de Saint Paul. The latter had a faint smile on his face and bowed slightly in his direction. Only the vivid image of ten more velvet bags filled to the brim with freshly minted golden coins stopped Cinq-Mars from committing a first murder, here and now.

*****

A jubilant Pierre was received in the evening in the Hôtel de Saint Paul. Everybody had decided to dress up, as the Marquis de Saint Paul had announced a lavish dinner to be served to celebrate Pierre's official recognition as the new Marquis de Beauvoir. As usual they started to gather in one of the more intimate salons, only later to take their places in the imposing dining room.

To his surprise, Pierre was the only male guest present. Usually the ladies were the last to appear. Marie, Céline and Marie's aunt were waiting already, conversing animatedly about the latest trends of fashion in Paris as both had decided to use this trip to rejuvenate the contents of their wardrobe. Decorative bows in all kinds of fabrics seemed to have become the latest trend!

As soon as Pierre stepped into the room though, Céline seemed to remember some gown that she had always wanted to show to the Principessa and rose from her chair.

"I simply have to show you this shade of green, I'm not sure that it doesn't make me look very pale!"

Marie's aunt answered absentmindedly, "Oh, this can surely wait for tomorrow, don't you think so, my dear?"

Céline was rolling her eyes in despair and dragging Marie's aunt out of her comfortable chair – placed conveniently close to the tray with the glasses of sweet wine and pastries – and said with authority in her voice, "It *is* urgent! I don't know if tomorrow we'll have the time, it's an evening gown, you should judge the effect now in the candlelight!"

Finally it dawned on the Principessa that she was being removed to leave Pierre and Marie on their own and, casting a last longing glance at the tray with the pastries, she agreed to leave the room, but not without turning backwards once more in order to send a conspiratorial smile to the two embarrassed lovers – Céline's manoeuvre had been far too transparent!

Marie and Pierre were alone now, probably for the first time in weeks. Social convention would not allow them to remain on their own – and their life had been so adventurous and hectic during the past weeks that there never seemed to be any opportunity to steal themselves away secretly.

Pierre moved closer to Marie and, checking carefully that nobody was approaching, he closed his arms around her. He didn't really know if he had expected Marie to be timid and reluctant, but immediately she lifted her head,

351

inviting him to kiss her beautiful lips. Pierre did not hesitate to answer this invitation and kissed her, forgetting time and space.

"It feels so good to be kissed by a real Marquis," she jested, when he paused briefly. "But I wonder if a Duke could kiss even better?"

Pierre read this correctly as a renewed invitation, putting all of his soul into the next kiss.

"I love you!" he murmured, his voice hoarse with excitement. "In fact I have done since I met you the first time in Reims. Do you still remember?"

"Of course I do!" exclaimed Marie. "I saw a shy blonde boy in an old and oversized monk's habit. You looked utterly ridiculous, but you didn't seem to care! But then I discovered your wonderful eyes, and I have never been able to forget you since. When Armand asked me to help you to steal the documents from the monastery's archive, I did it mainly to help you!"

Her eyes became dreamy and she continued in a low voice, "But I truly fell in love with you when I nursed you in our country house. I was scared that you'd forget me, I was so nervous when we met again in Calais."

Pierre's arms held Marie even closer now; he could feel her fragile body and smell the perfume she had put on for the evening. How beautiful she was!

Marie felt his excitement and gently drew away, chiding him. "Monsieur le Marquis, please behave properly!" Then she sighed dramatically. "Now that you have taken my innocence, I hope that you'll take the honourable course and ask my father if he will consider giving you my hand in marriage."

Pierre had to grin. "I will oblige with pleasure, but if you call stealing a kiss taking your innocence, I could show you some other ways!"

"Monsieur le Marquis, you shock me, I am a decent girl and I won't even listen to you!" but her eyes were teasing – even inviting him and arousing him even more.

Pierre was just about to answer her when he heard steps behind him and the Marquis de Saint Paul entered the room.

"Oh, I do apologize," he said, finding both of them standing there blushing. "Am I disturbing you?"

"Not at all, Sir," Pierre answered, more than happy that the fashion prescribed loose fitting breeches; anything else would have been most embarrassing!

*****

The dinner was a great success, and everybody kept toasting the future of Pierre and Armand. Consequently it was rather late, nearly noon of the next day, when two coaches left the home of the Marquis de Saint Paul. They brought the whole party to the Palais de Beauvoir, as nobody had wanted to stay behind in the Hôtel de Saint Paul when Pierre was going to visit and discover the home of his ancestors for the first time.

The Palais de Beauvoir was a fairly recently constructed building, erected by his paternal grandfather. Pierre liked the spacious cobbled courtyard, the imposing symmetrical façade with its light sandstone, so unlike Hertford House, which was a sprawling compound, changed, renovated and enlarged over centuries in different styles.

The Marquis de Saint Paul had of course sent notice to the major-domo that the new Marquis was coming and they found the palais sparkling and clean, the footmen lined up in the green and golden liveries with the coat of arms of the Marquis de Beauvoir. Pierre had to hold back his emotions when he discovered that above the entrance his two coats of arms had already been raised. Indeed, he had come a long way from the orphanage in Reims!

As they entered the great hall through the wide oak doors, he was greeted most reverently by the major-domo who was visibly very excited.

"Welcome, Monsieur le Marquis," he hesitated, his face blushing. "Oh, I beg your pardon, I mean Your Grace, Monsieur le Duc! Could your Grace, Monsieur le Duc, let me please know how we should address you?" Pierre nearly laughed, it seemed so ridiculous.

"You may call me Monsieur le Marquis, as this is the home of the family of the Marquis de Beauvoir; in England, I shall be addressed as a duke."

He could see from the face of his servants that this answer had been the right one; their heart still belonged to the family de Beauvoir.

Everybody was very excited and the group of visitors chatted animatedly, with the notable exception of Pierre's valet Jean who had entered the building full of trepidation, especially when they visited the suite of rooms that Henri de Beauvoir had occupied and where violent memories flashed back into his mind, so vivid as if everything had happened only yesterday. Pierre had watched his face but decided to pretend that he had not noticed – intuitively he understood that some memories are so painful that it is better to keep silent.

The major-domo continued to guide them through the vast building and they reached the bedroom of his late uncle.

"Here died Louis Philippe, Comte de Beauvoir, the late uncle of Monsieur le Marquis!" he said in a hushed and pious voice and everybody tried to look suitably impressed.

"Here he was killed," Jean added in a low voice.

Pierre and Armand, who had happened to hear his comment, turned around exclaiming, "Can you repeat this please?"

Jean looked at them defiantly. "Henri killed his father right here on the spot, in this bed. His father was sick, when Henri choked him to death with a cushion, I saw it all!" and he pointed to the gap in the door.

"What a monster!" Armand cried. "But you know, it doesn't really surprise me at all, it all adds up!"

Pierre was too shocked to speak. For someone who had always longed to have a father it was almost inconceivable to consider the possibility that his cousin had killed his own father in cold blood.

"Let us get out of here!" he said aloud and, turning to the major-domo, he gave his first order. "Tomorrow these rooms and those used lately by Henri de Beauvoir will be emptied and cleaned, all furniture will be given to the poor! This chapter is closed!"

The major-domo probably thought that his new master was a bit mad but he bowed dutifully. He had long ago given up trying to understand the whims of the noble classes.

They moved on and it took hours until they had visited the whole building – Pierre had spent a lot of his time studying the portraits of his ancestors. His wishes had come true – he had finally been able to see paintings of his parents. His mother looked stunning; the artist had captured her radiant smile – no wonder that his father had fallen head over heels in love with her. His father's painting was more formal and detached, yet it showed the likeness between him and Pierre and there could be no doubt that Pierre was his son.

The major-domo had arranged refreshments of cool sweet wine, the famous Sauternes from Bordeaux, and cakes to be served in the dining room. The delicious cakes and refreshing fruit tartes were served by attentive servants who seemed happy that the long period of waiting for their unknown lord and master was over.

Pierre approached the major-domo in order to know where the family treasures were kept, as the Marquis de Saint Paul had insisted that he should take the keys into his own safekeeping and even change the locks. The major-domo was happy to oblige and explained at length that for many generations the treasures had been kept in the Château de Beauvoir, the medieval castle where the family originated from.

He continued with an awed voice, "Three generations ago though, the head of the family decided that Paris would become the most important seat of the family and he transferred all jewellery and most of the valuable objects to Paris as the

Paris home had been enlarged during that period. We keep the valuable objects in a locked room and we only use them for special occasions." He blushed and continued," I must admit that there was a tacit understanding between the servants to be careful and hide them during the period of Monsieur Henri, your cousin, or Monsieur le Marquis; we were afraid that he'd sell the family silver as he was always short of money. Whenever he asked where they were hidden, we answered that they'd been transferred to the provincial estates."

"Excellent!" Pierre praised the proud major-domo, giving him one of his warm smiles of appreciation. The major-domo beamed with delight.

"What about the rest of the family treasures? Where are they kept?"

"Your father, Monsieur le Marquis, was a wise man. When he felt his end approaching, he was afraid that somebody other than his son might try to put his hand on the treasures. He had them all transferred into the safekeeping of the family bankers he could trust."

"Who is that?" Pierre asked, astonished and also touched by the way his father had cared about his heritage.

"Probably Messieurs Piccolin & Cie," the Marquis de Saint Paul interjected, as he had happened to overhear the last part of the conversation. "They have been the trusted bankers of the de Beauvoir family for generations. A very good and respectable bank, they even boast to have some noble blood running in their family."

"That doesn't really mean anything," Armand jested, "just look at the mother of our King Louis, a true Medici, she had inherited the worst of everything, cold blooded like a banker, throwing money out of the window like a true queen."

"It's strange though," the major-domo murmured but stopped immediately.

Armand's father had heard this remark all the same. He looked at the major-domo, enquiring, "What do you mean, what is strange?"

The poor major-domo seemed to shrink under the imperious glance of the Marquis de Saint Paul, his pompous airs evaporating under this merciless scrutiny.

"About two months ago the Cardinal Mazarin was here and asked exactly the same question! He told me that he was in possession of a royal order to take the treasures into his safekeeping."

"And what did you answer?" came the sharp reply from the Marquis.

The major-domo was perspiring now. "Monsieur le Marquis, please forgive me, but I told him the same: that we couldn't hand over anything as everything was already in the safekeeping of the family bankers. His Eminence was most annoyed with me, but I couldn't help it, could I?"

The Marquis, Pierre and Armand exchanged a long glance. Next to Richelieu, Mazarin was also breathing down their necks. They would need to go and meet the bankers immediately.

The same afternoon they were sitting in the office of Monsieur Piccolin, who seemed delighted to meet them. Introductions were made and Pierre decided that he liked Monsieur Piccolin and his dignified ways very much.

"I am truly happy that this nightmare of succession has ended well for Monsieur le Marquis," he smiled at them, which for a banker was a remarkable display of emotion.

"May we have access to the de Beauvoir treasures?" Armand asked bluntly, as the exchange of social niceties and polite small talk did not seem to be coming to an end.

The banker looked taken aback at him, clearly scandalized by this blunt speech.

"I do apologize, my lord, but as a bank we have to follow rules. We will be happy to grant access but I must insist that Monsieur le Marquis," and he nodded politely towards Pierre, "presents adequate papers, identifying him as the legal heir. Please understand that we have been nominated as trustees by the late Marquis and we will only remit the objects to a person that can be identified beyond any doubt."

This seemed to be final and even if Pierre looked crestfallen, he understood the logic and justification of this procedure.

The Marquis de Saint Paul cleared his throat and said, "I can only, of course, congratulate you on this correct attitude. May we, however, ask you to give us one piece of additional information?"

The banker nodded, but he was visibly on his guard.

"Did Monseigneur Mazarin show up to claim access to the treasures as well?"

The banker suddenly shut up like an oyster. "I'm afraid I am not entitled to answer this question."

"If you value your future relationship with most of the noble families in France, speak up!" The Marquis had suddenly dropped his polite mask and the man who was used to wielding enormous influence was now in evidence, his personality dominating the room.

Good heavens, Armand thought. *The old man still knows how to play his cards, I'm betting our banker is already wetting his breeches.*

The elegant Monsieur Piccolin was all of a sudden not so self-assured and composed. He guessed that de Saint Paul wasn't joking, the threat was palpable and very real.

He looked decidedly nervous. Finally he spoke, but extremely reluctantly. He kept hesitating and weighing every single word for its significance.

"I can advise you that Monseigneur Mazarin was indeed here. Your assumption that he requested delivery of the de Beauvoir treasure into his safekeeping cannot be denied. In view of the stakes involved, I decided to hand this issue over to my father, the head of our family. I regret profoundly that my father is staying on our country estate this week and cannot meet you today. I shall recommend that he come to meet you as soon as he comes back, I cannot really give you any additional information at this moment. I am truly sorry!"

The three visitors looked at each other. This answer was evasive and definitely not very satisfying. But they all felt that there wasn't anything more to be said. The Marquis de Saint Paul insisted once more that Monsieur Piccolin senior should call on him immediately on his arrival back in Paris and, exchanging the usual niceties of social protocol, they took their leave and boarded the waiting coach.

"I didn't like this at all!" Armand exclaimed, once the coach had drawn away from the entrance of the banker's stately house.

Pierre sat there, very silent, his face pale.

"Yes, in fact he only confirmed that Mazarin had been there, well, he probably couldn't really deny this. But as to what kind of decision his father has taken, we are completely in the dark!" added the Marquis. "You're quiet," the Marquis then said to Pierre, "What do you think about his story?"

"First he seemed to be genuinely pleased to meet me, I think that the Piccolins really saw themselves as guardians of the treasure that my father left to them. I'm simply at a loss as to explain the sudden change in his behaviour!" Pierre said, puzzled. "Something has happened, I don't like that, to be straightforward, I don't like that at all!"

"You are thinking about the diamond ring?" Armand asked.

"I'm afraid Pierre's sixth sense is right," interjected Armand's father. "And if you ask me, it's all about the diamond ring you mentioned yesterday evening. Mazarin's nickname is 'diamond Jules' – it's known all over Paris that he already owns an impressive collection of precious diamonds, God alone knows where the money came from, as he didn't own a single sou when he arrived from Italy and attached himself to Richelieu like a leech."

The Marquis de Saint Paul paused and frowned. "He's a dangerous opponent to have. His latest victim is the Queen, and I'm sure that he'll inherit Richelieu's

357

position as prime minister as soon as the latter passes through the gates of heaven – or hell, which in my eyes seems the more likely scenario."

Despite the gloomy news Armand laughed. "Just imagine Richelieu in his Cardinal's robes knocking at the big golden door of paradise and a huge red creature with horns opens it, smiling with big, yellow sulphurous teeth!" Armand changed his voice to a low groaning tone. "Come in, Your Eminence, there is a warm spot already waiting for you."

Armand's jest broke the tension and they agreed that nothing could be done before the return of Monsieur Piccolin.

When they returned to the Hôtel de Saint Paul, they found their home in turmoil. Céline met them at the entrance, her face grave and composed. She had apparently been waiting for their return.

"I'm afraid I am the bearer of bad news," she said. "Marie received only today a letter that should have reached her in London. Her father has had a bad accident, in fact it was more than a month ago, and they fear the worst. She has to return home immediately and I have decided to accompany her. Her aunt and Charles will also join us. She's upstairs packing, you won't have a lot of time to say goodbye, we'll be leaving right away!"

She saw Pierre's face change from surprise to disbelief and then to utter misery, and squeezed his hand in sympathy.

Finally he managed to say, "I'll go up to her room and try to comfort her!" and he hurried upstairs.

"*Merde alors!*" was Armand's only but pointed comment which drew immediately an acid comment from his father that apparently his stay in England had done nothing to improve his manners, which were already lamentable before he had left. Before his father could venture into further details of his past failings, Armand quickly excused himself and disappeared.

Pierre found Marie bathed in tears. She was supervising her maid – or at least trying to – who was packing the huge wooden trunks that were to be strapped on top of the waiting coaches. The maid apparently shared in the misery of her mistress. Sniffing and dabbing her face regularly with her wet apron she was folding and stowing away the garments.

Marie rushed into Pierre's arms as soon as he entered the room. She sobbed on his shoulder and gently he caressed her, trying to calm her. There wasn't really anything comforting he could say or do, he knew that she had to leave, whereas he was compelled to stay in Paris until all the documents for his heritage were signed and filed.

Her father's accident meant months of separation for both of them at best, for sooner rather than later Armand and he would have to leave as promised and find the missing rings for the Templars, a quest with a risk of becoming even more complicated and dangerous if Mazarin really had managed to get hold of the diamond ring, the second key to the treasure.

The maid left the room and Pierre kissed Marie gently, holding her face in his hands. "I love you!" he said, "and whatever happens, I'll come to Reims to marry you. Will you wait for me?"

Marie nodded and answered through her tears, "I'll wait for you. My poor father, he was so reluctant to let me go to London. I suddenly feel so guilty that I left him!" and again the tears streamed down her face.

Pierre kissed them gently away. "What difference would it have made if you had stayed in Reims? We wouldn't have met again and how could you have prevented his accident? Be reasonable, all you can do is pray, but don't blame yourself or fall into a state of self-pity."

Still in tears, Marie smiled at him. "I'll be a brave girl now! You're right, my stay in Reims wouldn't have changed anything, I was just in a state of shock."

Pierre smiled back. He could see that Marie was coming back to her normal assured self.

But suddenly time was racing, the house was in full commotion, and before Pierre could realize what was happening, the coaches were already waiting, the horses snorting impatiently, eager to get going. Last embraces were given, wishes exchanged and finally three sobbing ladies waved from the window of the coach until they lost sight of each other.

Pierre suddenly felt Armand's arm around his shoulder and with a hoarse voice his friend said, "Let's go inside and have a drink in the library!"

Looking at Pierre's miserable face he added, "I have an even better idea, let's get completely drunk!"

Pierre nodded and tried to smile, cursing himself that tears were in his eyes. He simply answered, "That sounds like a deal, sometimes even you can have brilliant ideas!"

*****

Pierre woke up in his huge bed. The red velvet curtains had been carefully closed by Jean, to keep out the cold night air. Slowly and almost blindly he opened a chink in the curtains and his hurting eyes could discern the first pale signs of the early morning light seeping into the room.

359

Something was wrong! Had somebody installed over night a blacksmith's shop in his head, complete with hammers that kept banging to the rhythm of his heartbeat?

How had he arrived in his bed? He had no idea. He tried to open his eyes a little more, cursing, as consequently the pain in his head intensified. The golden arabesque decorations of the velvet bed curtains were barely visible in the poor light but their shadows seemed to be floating above the cloth, moving backward and forward. Pierre moved sideways, but he regretted this move as a wave of nausea swept over him. Quickly he scrambled out of his bed and saw to his great relief that his provident valet had placed a large porcelain bowl on the side table. Pierre grabbed it, and not a second too late, as he suddenly vomited.

The hammers in his head had intensified their heavy work and the pain was nearly driving him mad. He discovered that Jean had placed a jug with water and a glass with some mystifying liquid on the table. Pierre grabbed the glass and sniffed at the content – it smelled horrid. But he didn't care if it were poison or not, his head was about to explode and an early death would be preferable to this almost unbearable torture.

He gulped down the bitter liquid, immediately followed by a cup of water as the pungent taste made him gasp. He also felt completely parched; his tongue must have turned into a piece of shrivelled shoe leather over night. Then he dropped back into his bed, ready to die.

But apparently the toxic liquid hadn't been placed on his bedside table in order to dispatch him to paradise. Some – seemingly endless – minutes later he felt that the dreadful hammers in his head were slowing and the revolution in his stomach was calming down. But he was not to receive any real respite as now his brain decided to haunt him and pictures of a sobbing Marie started to appear in front of him.

Exasperated he asked himself, "How and when am I going to see her again?"

His mind continued in this vein, lingering on and exposing as if with a magnifying glass all the problems and challenges that were lying ahead of him, waiting to be solved: How would he find and finally get rid of his cousin Henri? Pierre had been feeling quite safe and confident the past weeks, somehow even the interlude when Richelieu had tried to kill them and sink the proud *Beatrice* had not really unsettled his natural optimism, it had felt more like an adventure than like a real threat. But now he felt in his bones that his cousin wasn't dead, and every minute lying there, Pierre grew even more concerned that Henri was preparing to strike once more. With Marie now far away, they were extremely vulnerable. Pierre started to sweat, he remembered the narrow escape Marie had had last time, when thanks only to Charles and Céline's swift action had they avoided disaster.

Where can I find him, how can I eliminate him? This question seemed to spin round his head and the hammers started to do their painful work once more.

360

How to get hold of the diamond ring and how to find the sapphire one? The next difficult questions popped into his mind, and of course he couldn't find an answer.

He suddenly became aware of the revolting stench of his own vomit filling the room. He rang the bell and Jean appeared immediately, already completely dressed. Either he had got up very early or hadn't even gone to bed.

"Jean," he croaked, "can you please take this bowl away and open the windows, I need fresh air. By the way how did I get here?"

Jean smiled and grabbed the bowl that was removed in no time, and then he opened the windows, letting in the fresh air – if ever the air in Paris could be called fresh. Paris during the cold months was mostly enshrouded in clouds of smoke from the thousands of charcoal fires burning in the city.

"I carried you upstairs, Monsieur le Marquis," he answered. "I'm afraid you weren't able to walk!"

"Was it *that* bad?" Pierre interrogated cautiously.

Jean cleared his throat, hesitating whether he should continue but then he grinned broadly and said, "It was actually very touching, Monsieur le Marquis, especially when you embraced me and assured me that I was your best friend. I allowed myself to take this as a great compliment!"

Pierre only moaned. "Oh Lord, it definitely was meant like this, but I guessed Armand would become jealous."

Jean only laughed.

Pierre changed the subject. "What the hell did I drink? I've never been so sick in my life!"

"I assume it was the Calvados," Jean answered. "But it could also be the red wine and the whisky that you had before that."

"I had all of this?" Pierre said, disbelief in his eyes.

Jean nodded. "You did, Monsieur le Marquis, and I think I forgot to mention the white wine before the meal!"

Pierre hung his head. "Never again, I swear! This headache was killing me; thanks for the potion, it smelled horrid, but worked wonders. What is it?"

"A family secret, Monsieur le Marquis. Disgusting, but it helps!"

"Could I have some more?" Pierre asked hopefully as the hammers hadn't quite stopped yet.

"I'm afraid not, sir," Jean retorted. "If I give you a second dose like this, you'll have no more pain but will be chased by terrifying hallucinations, not something I would recommend."

Pierre closed his eyes and sank back into his bed, thankful for Jean's administrations. Jean was now rubbing his head and chest with a damp cloth and then he changed the drenched bed sheets.

Pierre was trying to catch some more sleep but a relentless carousel was turning in his head, endlessly mulling over the same questions he'd been pondering on before without any result. *Madness must start like this*, Pierre thought, before he finally dropped into an uneasy slumber. He felt miserable, distressed over Marie's departure but he also felt a new sensation, a threat hovering somewhere in the dark.

He was suddenly sure, his cousin would be back, and soon.

ACCIDENTS DO HAPPEN, BUT SO DO SURPRISES

"Henri, darling, can you bring me some blotting paper?" The plaintive voice of the Comte de Roquemoulin penetrated the study into which Henri had retreated, trying in vain to escape the erratic whims and the ever present whining voice of his tiresome host. Henri's strategy to insinuate that a simple cold should be taken seriously had worked wonderfully in the beginning, until his host had started to view himself as suffering from a serious onslaught of pneumonia and had started to demand Henri's almost constant presence, acting like a spoilt child.

Henri clenched his fist and bit his tongue to prevent himself from uttering a fitting and straightforward answer. He counted to ten in order to regain control until he answered loudly and with artificial cheerfulness, "Of course, Jean Baptiste, anything else I can do?"

"You are ever so kind," the wailing voice responded. "How did I ever merit meeting such a kind, darling sweetheart!"

You didn't and you haven't! Henri answered silently in his mind. He let his eyes sweep around the study, a depressingly dark room with richly carved ebony furniture and dark panelling, the height of fashion one generation ago.

A slightly musty smell hung in the air, as most of the books on the shelves must have dated back several generations already. The present count was no avid reader and only entered the study when the steward of his estate succeeded on nailing him down to go through the books with him.

Jean Baptiste de Roquemoulin much preferred the spending aspect of his immense fortune; anything linked to administration and digesting figures seemed to be immensely boring and tiring for him.

"Any idea where I can find the paper?" Henri cried, as he couldn't spot it at first glance.

"I think I left it in my desk, in the top drawer," the voice from the adjacent room answered.

Henri stepped behind the desk and he opened the drawer. Indeed, several sheets of blotting paper had been neatly stacked there. Henri tore a sheet of paper out of the stack when he heard a slight metallic ring, as if a piece of metal had touched the wood. He put his right hand into the drawer and explored its contents until he suddenly felt the coldish sensation of a piece of metal hidden at the bottom of the drawer. He knew instinctively that it had to be a key and, checking quickly to see that nobody was watching him, he took the key out of the drawer. Then he checked quickly to find out which drawers might have been locked, but to his disappointment, none was locked, and all opened smoothly.

His eyes scanned the room and then he discovered, inserted into the dark wooden panels, a small door, most probably part of a built-in cupboard. Henri moved silently to the cupboard and inserted the key. To his great joy the key moved smoothly and the door of the cupboard opened silently; the hinges had been well greased. Inside the cupboard he detected several piles of documents, but his eyes were immediately attracted by a brown envelope, seemingly of newer origin. He glanced once more around him and hastily opened the envelope.

He started reading: *In the year of our Lord MDCXLI, under the reign of his most catholic Majesty Louis XIII, we the notary public...*

He couldn't believe his eyes. In his hands he held his adoption papers, signed and properly certified. His first sensation of jubilation turned to cold rage. His host, this whining coward, had been playing around with him. The documents had been hidden here already for weeks! He would make him pay for this.

"Henri, darling, did you find the blotting paper? Can you bring it to me?"

The whining voice broke through his thoughts. If his first reaction had been to stop this comedy here and now, Henri's brain brought him back to reason. He breathed deeply and, carefully closing the cupboard, he cried, "Yes, Jean Baptiste, I had spotted an interesting book, just let me put it back, I'll be with you in a minute!"

His mind was racing. Liberty and a fortune were his now! He now was Henri de Roquemoulin, heir to an immense fortune as soon as his adopted father closed his eyes forever! But how to use this discovery to his best advantage? Should he confront the count with his discovery and force a public acknowledgment? Pretend to be overjoyed, out of his mind, finding out about this wonderful surprise from his wonderful father?

But then a devious plan formed in his mind, so much more suited to his means.

Yes, he concluded to himself, *I'll keep this secret. If Jean Baptiste can play a comedy, I can do so even better!*

A radiant Henri brought the blotting paper to the count and, sitting at his side, Henri let his hands rest on his shoulder, massaging his back slightly.

The count purred like a cat, simply adoring this kind of attention.

"You're right," Henri opened the conversation. "I've been thinking about what we should be doing during the next few weeks but going to Paris at this time of year would not be the right thing to do!"

Jean-Baptiste looked surprised. Until now Henri had been pressing him impatiently to come forward with a date for their departure. He couldn't believe his ears. "What did you say, my darling? I thought you wanted to leave for Paris and visit your friends?"

364

"I might have been a bit selfish, I must admit," Henri answered, "But what could Paris offer us right now? I think it would be better to stay some more weeks here in the beautiful countryside, I have really started to feel at home in our castle and this beautiful region."

The count looked at Henri. He still couldn't really believe this sudden change of mind to be true.

"There's only one thing that I really do miss," Henri continued, his face downcast and sad.

"Oh, tell me, my darling, you know that above everything, I want to see you happy!" the count answered quickly, patting Henri's hand. Henri felt the soft, slightly damp touch and cringed. He forced himself to take the hand and place a soft kiss on it.

The count closed his eyes in blissful joy.

"You know, I enjoyed so much our excursions together, if only you felt well again, we could take our horses and ride together in the spring sunshine, as the weather is starting to be quite lovely!" He let his hand linger on Jean-Baptiste's neck. He could feel the count shivering with delight. "There's a lonely farm with a barn on this beautiful path that you showed me alongside the Loire, wouldn't it be wonderful to have a picnic there, just the two of us?" Henri said, his fingers massaging the count's neck.

Jean Baptiste cleared his throat and managed to answer, "That would be lovely, indeed. A pity that I haven't been feeling well lately!"

During the next few days the count – to the surprise of his servants – showed a remarkable improvement. Hence three days after Henri's casual remark he felt strong enough to venture out for the first time on horseback.

Despite his pretended ailments he had continued to shovel huge quantities of food into himself and his belly had grown visibly, wobbling above his belt. Two strong grooms managed to heave him onto the back of a strong mare and proudly he followed Henri and his grooms for a short first stroll around the park on horseback.

He had to admit that the fresh air was indeed fortifying and a fortnight later he had regained his old love for riding, his only regret being that his belly stubbornly refused to recede and continued to bulge and wobble embarrassingly as they galloped along their favourite paths.

Soon came the day when Henri had everything prepared for a companionable picnic, riding *à deux*, as Henri had convinced him to forgo the presence of the grooms.

"We'll have a lovely day, just the two of us," Henri said and gave a long and meaningful glance to the count who blissfully smiled back. He had intended his smile to be seductive, but to Henri it appeared simply repulsive.

They rode at a leisurely pace across the fields bordering the famous Loire vineyards, the first curious flowers greeting the rays of the spring sun. Jean Baptiste inhaled deeply the crisp air; how stupid he had been to stay inside for so long, playing the sick invalid! This excursion was really lovely and he was looking forward so much to the promised picnic. Remembering Henri's hand slowly caressing his neck, he felt a shiver of pleasurable anticipation running down his spine.

Riding further they discovered the first fresh green shoots of the vineyards and the Loire stretching like a silver band at their feet. When they approached the river, Henri pointed with his hand towards the path that wound down to the river bank and further on to a picturesque farm that nestled between a slope and a loop of the shimmering river. The sky was blue, and the spring promised to become even lovelier.

"Let's have some fun and gallop down there!" Henri cried, smiling broadly at his new father. "Isn't it lovely to feel the wind stroking your cheeks?"

The count looked sceptically at the narrow and steep path and hesitated.

"Come on, don't be a kill-joy!" Henri now challenged him openly.

Jean Baptiste sighed but put on a brave face. If he wanted to keep his much younger friend happy, he'd need to oblige, and act like any other young man would.

Faking an enthusiastic smile he cried, "You're right, let's have some fun!" and he started to ride at full speed down the path. Jean Baptiste had to concentrate fully on the treacherous path, overgrown with slippery patches of damp grass and roots. Hence he could only guess that Henri was following closely, hearing the thudding of hooves and the hard breathing of Henri's horse close behind. Henri must be right behind him now, he reckoned, fully concentrating his attention on the way ahead.

Jean Baptiste couldn't see the whip that Henri was wielding, a whip he had secretly studded with a sharp nail at the end. With an ugly hissing sound the whip suddenly came down on the croup of Jean Baptiste's horse.

The horse panicked at the sudden sensation of sharp pain and reared up in protest, eyes white and wide in panic, uttering almost human shrieks of terror and pain. The count was taken unawares and immediately lost his balance. He was catapulted from his horse, plunging and rolling down the steep slope like a boulder.

Eventually his fall was stopped by the thick vegetation, and there he lay on his back, motionless like a huge beetle.

Henri immediately slowed down and reined in his horse that had started to rear in panic. He had to use all of his force, brutally imposing his will. It was a narrow escape as his horse nearly slipped on the narrow path and he almost followed the count's fate.

Managing to calm his horse, he was able to stop and ride back to the site of the accident. There he dismounted without any sign of undue difficulty, and slowly and cautiously he climbed down the overgrown slope until he reached Jean Baptiste, who lay sprawled on a narrow plateau amidst some scrub which had stopped him from falling further down the steep slope of the river bank, to the Loire flowing directly below them – Henri could hear the ripple of the river's currents.

The count was still breathing. Henri watched the count's face, bloodied and bruised from the painful fall, with contempt. Suddenly Jean Baptiste de Roquemoulin opened his eyes and started to moan in pain. He tried to speak, apparently recognizing Henri, and joy filled his face to find his friend and lover so close at hand to rescue him.

Henri looked dispassionately at the bloated and bruised face, and came to a conclusion. He cleared some plants at the edge of the plateau and then he rolled the moaning and shrieking count like a stone pillar to its edge until the body gained momentum, started to roll and finally plunged down the embankment into the Loire.

"Goodbye, my silly, fat Jean Baptiste." Henri saluted the disappearing body, instantly devoured by the river. Satisfied with his work he turned back to return to his horse. He felt jubilant, ready to embrace the world – a huge fortune, his return to Paris and the royal court were just a matter of weeks now!

In high spirits Henri lifted his face to climb back towards his waiting horse, but his steps suddenly froze and the world seemed to stop.

Right above him, waiting on the narrow path next to his horse, he saw three strangers silently sitting on their horses, watching him intently, and waiting for him…

Travelling by coach – even if drawn by four horses – at full speed to Reims in normal circumstances took about three to four full days. Marie had hoped to beat this timeline, insisting on travelling even by night under the full moon. But although Marie had been pushing to drive as fast as possible – fervently supported by Céline who was anxious to arrive quickly in Reims as well – Marie had forgotten how much her aunt's ideas on speed and comfort of travel differed from hers.

To their dismay they stopped regularly in order to have lunch, dinner and refreshments as soon as the Principessa felt that she needed fortification – which happened frequently enough. And of course there could be no idea of travelling at night.

"*Far* too dangerous, my dear!" she only said and there was no way to change her mind.

Marie started to despair, but her urgent pleas to move faster only fell on deaf ears.

"There's no use arriving in Reims starved like a skeleton," her aunt reprimanded her. "It won't help your father in the least if you look as thin as a ghost. And just imagine, what would your parents think? That I neglected you?"

It took therefore nearly five full days until the coaches finally arrived in front of Marie's home. Marie was almost hysterical with anxiety; having had no further news, she had spent her time imagining all sorts of further terrible accidents, sufferings and complications.

Despite Céline's attempts to calm her down, now that their journey was about to end, she was fully convinced she would find her father either dead or maimed for life.

As soon as her coach ground to a halt Marie rushed out and hastened towards her mother, who was standing at the top of the majestic staircase, alerted by the servants who had seen the coaches approaching the house.

She was out of her mind with joy to see her daughter, her arms thrown wide open to welcome Marie.

"Mother, oh Mother, tell me the truth! How's Father?" Marie cried, burying her face in her mother's bosom.

He mother stroked her lovingly. "Calm down, Marie, he's already feeling better, didn't you receive our last message?"

Marie raised her face, wet from her tears. Slowly she shook her head, choked by her emotions, and unable to speak.

In the meantime her mother had spotted the other visitors. She stepped forward and, shedding tears of joy, she hugged Céline and Marie's aunt, not without giving an appraising glance at the huge figure of Charles who had also arrived and who was waiting in the background. Looking at Céline she exclaimed, "You look marvellous, my dear!"

It took a considerable time for the turmoil and level of noise to die down and for everybody to be comfortably installed in the drawing room.

Turning towards Marie and holding her hand, her mother now resumed her story. "I'll bring you to your father as soon as you have freshened up a bit, but if he's going to see you in this state he'll have a relapse. He's now already feeling much better and I'm sure in another month or so he'll be up and walking. I'll try to make it a short story: Your father had a really terrible accident! During his journey to our estate in Epernay the wheel of his carriage broke and the coach turned upside down, straight into a ditch! His grooms brought him back home immediately, but several bones were broken and he was bleeding all over. I was shocked when I saw him, I thought that the end was near. Immediately I called the best physicians of the city, but they couldn't help. His wounds started to fester and all they were doing was bleeding him again and again. I was out of my mind, it only seemed a matter of days until I would be a widow!"

She paused dramatically, evidently cherishing the drama and the full attention of the audience. Marie held her hand clasped to her mouth, her eyes wide open.

"Then I remembered Brother Infirmarius from the monastery, the physician Marie had brought to me when I was nearly dying last summer. He had saved my life and I decided to fetch him for your father. And what can I say? Once more he worked miracles. It took him a good week but then the fever started to recede and your father regained consciousness. Maybe it's just because in the monastery they're closer to powers of heaven – or he knows secrets that our physicians don't know of – but he definitely saved my husband!"

She was wiping away a tear that had started rolling down her cheek, but then she resolutely resumed the ways of a good hostess and busy housewife and she started to call on the servants not to stand around idle but to look after the visitors and install them comfortably in their rooms.

At last Marie was allowed to enter the room where her father was resting. He looked thin and frail in the huge bed with the velvet canopy. The black wood-panelled walls were swallowing most of the light and provided a sombre frame for the dark red velvet with its golden trimmings. Marie found the room depressing; she had never liked it. Then she forced herself to fix her glance resolutely on her father, afraid she would find him much changed. Her worst fears came true: his

369

hair had turned almost white. Marie was shocked: her father had aged terribly; he now looked more like her grandfather.

She rushed to his bedside where she kneeled down and took his frail, blue-veined hand into hers, the skin almost transparent.

He turned his head and smiled full of love at her. "I must look terrible, my dear," he said in a low voice. "They all tell me that I look fine, but I know that I had a narrow escape from death. And even if your mother keeps telling me lies, the mirror tells me the truth."

Marie couldn't help it, tears welled up in her eyes.

"Don't cry, my love, it's all right now. Soon I'll be strong enough to walk, look – I'm practising already!"

Marie saw that he had moved his foot out from under the heavy bed-sheets and made it wave at her vigorously. She had to laugh and suddenly the strain seemed to be gone – yes, her father would be much better soon, she was sure now.

Her mother, who had been standing silently behind her, now raised her voice, and smiling at Marie she said, "Father and I have excellent news for you, my love!"

Marie looked at her expectantly.

"You may remember the beautiful Saint Remy estate that is neighbouring ours in the Champagne region?"

Marie nodded. "Oh, yes, I remember the castle. We used to be invited there from time to time when I was a girl. The family was always very nice to me!"

"Yes, very nice people! Although only of the lower aristocracy," her mother added deprecatingly, then in a brisk tone, "But your father thinks that with their money and influence, the head of the family may be elevated to the rank of a count easily. King Louis and Richelieu always need money."

"Why should we care?" asked Marie.

"My love, we've agreed with Monsieur de Saint Remy that his son may propose to you. It's an ideal match, he's a very nice and handsome young man and the two estates will form one of the biggest vineyards in the Champagne!" and both parents beamed with delight.

Marie had to hold on to the bedpost, the earth seeming to sway beneath her. She managed to smile at her father and excused herself under the pretence that she was very tired from the long journey.

But her mother had of course detected that something was wrong and not long after Marie had withdrawn to her bedroom, she entered her room, where Marie sat on her bed, sad and crying.

"What's the matter?" she asked sharply, "I expected you to be full of joy and now I find you crying?"

She eyed her daughter suspiciously. "You are not in love with somebody else? Maybe even with this youngster you mentioned in your letters who was trying in vain to get hold of his heritage?"

Marie nodded but she was regaining her composure and fighting spirits and protested vigorously: "Not in vain, Maman, he's a duke in his own right now in England and last week he was received by King Louis and finally acknowledged as the rightful Marquis de Beauvoir! You always wanted me to leave Reims, be introduced to the Royal Court and to have the life that you have missed. Now I've found the husband you've always dreamed of for me!"

Marie's mother looked impressed but then she asked, "Is he poor? Does he have to marry money?" her voice steady, matter-of-fact.

"No!" Marie exclaimed eagerly. "He's rolling in money, as Father would put it!"

Her mother's eyebrows rose. "Why, in God's name, should he then marry a pretty, young goose from the provinces with no political clout or useful connections such as you?" she asked brutally. "You'll have a very comfortable dowry but if he's got two of the highest titles you can imagine and enough money of his own, he can choose whatever princess he fancies either in France or in England, he can even marry a princess of royal blood. Wake up, my dear, love is one thing, but marriage is nothing else but a matter of business between families, believe me, nothing else! He'll never marry a mere nobody like you and there's no use spilling any tears for him! Yes, I wanted to you to live in Paris and have success, but marrying into the Saint Remy estates is a unique opportunity for our family!"

To her mother's dismay, Marie remained obstinate and she cried out angrily: "I don't want to marry Saint Remy, I want my Pierre!"

Her mother hesitated for some minutes and then she sat down, next to Marie. She took her hand and said, "Listen, I think the right time has come to tell you a story!"

Her mother's tone was very stern and Marie sensed that she was about to tell her something very important. Strangely her mother seemed to be extremely reluctant to come forward with her story. She hesitated until the last minute, unsure of how to start and whether she was doing the right thing.

371

"I think that all fairy tales start with 'Once upon a time'," she said, "therefore – even if this is not really a fairy tale – let's start like this: Once upon a time, in this city there happened to live a beautiful young girl, very much spoilt by her parents and the numerous young men who besieged her home, adoring her, courting her and calling her fancy names like 'my beautiful ice princess'. The girl used to laugh at them, in fact she had a fine time, but she had decided that she'd never marry for convenience, love it had to be – or nothing! Her parents were very kind and indulgent, and all they wanted for their child was happiness."

Marie's mother paused a moment, her eyes fixed on some remote object, as if she was conjuring up this young girl in front of her right now.

"One day the charming prince of her dreams arrived. He was on his way back to Paris with a party of merry young musketeers. Soon she found out that he was the eldest son of a great lord of the highest position at the royal court. He met the beautiful girl and started to court her – he was so skilled, refined and handsome! His dark eyes were burning with desire when he looked at her and soon the girl was head over heels in love. She was sure: this was the right husband for her! First he encouraged her, then he showed her the cold shoulder until she was desperate to gain his attention. To keep my story short: he played with her like a cat plays with a mouse and finally he seduced her. The beautiful girl was in heaven, never would she forget the night when he had managed to sneak into her room secretly, he had bribed her maids to gain access. The girl was of course very naughty, but the next morning she woke up blissfully happy. She chose her most beautiful gown, sure that her lover would come back the same day and ask her parents for her hand. The whole night he had sworn his eternal love and painted wonderful pictures of their future life together."

Her mother's tone had changed now and Marie could see the strain of her emotions in her hard face.

"But he didn't appear. She was young, she was naïve, she was convinced that some accident must have happened. The same evening a servant arrived with a letter. Her lover had written that he had been called away urgently, back to his father and the royal court, but very soon he would return to Reims. The girl searched and read and reread it several times, but the letter did not contain one single word of love or marriage."

Her mother's voice had become a whisper now, and to Marie's horror she detected tears in her mother's eyes.

"Of course he never came back, and as the girl would come to know much later, he married a princess from a powerful family of royal ancestry and was made a peer of the kingdom. The beautiful girl suddenly fell sick, and her parents were extremely worried as she wouldn't eat and developed a high fever. It took her more than a month to come back to something that could be called normality, but the next shock was waiting for her. With all her distress and illness she hadn't noticed that she was with child! First it was only a suspicion, and then she was

372

sure. She was not even seventeen years old, couldn't speak with anybody about her condition and when she fully realized what she had done, she was first frozen with fear and then she started to panic. If ever her parents discovered the truth she'd be dispatched to some remote nunnery, to be imprisoned there for the rest of her life. No respectable family could bear such a scandal."

Her mother was wringing her hands now, but forced herself to go on.

"The beautiful young girl suddenly woke up and faced reality. In a matter of seconds the dreams of her childhood were forgotten, she had to think and act like an adult now. She reviewed in her mind the young men who had been courting her and decided to talk only with one of them. The young man she had in mind had been the kindest of them, visiting her every week even during her illness, although there was no real hope ever of gaining her hand. He wasn't particularly handsome or witty, had no great title and owned just a modest fortune. The girl invited him to visit her, managed to get rid of the maids and proposed a deal to the surprised young man. If he would raise the child she was expecting as his own, she would never ever look at any other man and promised to become the best wife he could imagine, and her considerable dowry would be at his disposal. Only Heaven knows how difficult it had been for her to come forward with this confession and make this proposal, forget about her pride and give herself entirely into the hands of a stranger."

Marie's mother's voice broke and she assembled all of her force to continue.

"He was shocked and hurt, the beautiful girl could see that he was deeply offended, his image of the immaculate princess shattered by the revelation of the ugly truth. Politely he asked for a day of consideration and during this day the beautiful young girl was once more in torment. If he decided to tell her parents or somebody else, she would be doomed. The next day he came back, precisely at the time that he had promised and when she looked at him, pale, scared and speechless, he solemnly opened his hand, but didn't speak a word. In his hand she saw a beautiful diamond engagement ring. His answer was yes."

Marie's mother now was crying openly and Marie joined in. She was shocked but the end came as no surprise.

"This is how I came to marry your father," her mother finished her narrative.

The room lay in total silence; Marie didn't know what to say.

"Do you hate me now?" her mother whispered.

Marie closed her arms around her mother and said in a low voice, "I love you even more. Not many women would have had the courage to do what you have done. I can imagine that you went through hell!"

Marie hesitated and then she burst out, "But why don't I have any brothers and sisters?"

"God only gave me one child. We tried, of course, to have more children but I never became pregnant again. Your father always comforted me and said that apparently it was God's will that we should have only one child, and he never ever let me or you feel that you weren't his daughter by blood, he loves you dearly! So please, don't disappoint us, don't live in your world of dreams, I don't want you to repeat my mistakes! Please receive tomorrow the young Saint Remy and if he proposes, promise me to accept, please swear to the Holy Virgin!"

Marie nodded, although her heart was breaking. She didn't have the heart to disappoint her mother after this painful confession.

Her mother embraced her, kissed her and rose to go back into her room. Turning to Marie she said, "Not one word to your father! Promise me!"

"I promise!" Marie answered. "And don't worry, he'll always remain a father to me, not that handsome rascal who made you lose your head."

*****

Céline had felt restless, Marie's behaviour at dinner had been odd, her eyes red from crying. All the same Marie had felt obliged to appear cheerful, talking too loud and a lot of nonsense, but she had failed miserably to convince anybody at the dinner table. Even Charles had sensed that something was amiss.

Céline was not a person to leave problems unresolved and thus she invented an urgent need to borrow a hairbrush in order to stroll into Marie's room at bedtime. As expected she found her crying and it didn't take a lot of encouragement to make Marie confess her troubles. She didn't betray her mother's secret but she made Céline understand that if she didn't accept tomorrow the proposal of the young Saint Remy she'd risk losing her parents forever and that probably the best solution would be to die here and now as the prospect of either losing Pierre or her parents was simply too much to bear.

Céline tried to work out why Marie's parents didn't want her to marry Pierre. Marie explained to her that her mother was convinced that Pierre would never ever marry her.

Céline frowned and exclaimed, "But that's total nonsense. He was just waiting to get his heritage arranged and this will be done soon enough."

"Mother will never believe this," Marie sobbed. "And either I do what I promised or I'll die an old spinster in a convent."

Céline had to suppress a smile; she couldn't really imagine Marie withering away in a convent.

"Then there's no other way than to do what you mother says," Céline said briskly.

374

"No!" Marie wailed, "I simply couldn't, although I promised!"

"You said that you promised to accept if he proposes tomorrow, right?" Céline said.

Marie nodded.

"Then the solution is simple: all we need to do is make sure that he won't propose. Tell me all you know about this young man. What does he hate most? Now listen carefully and stop crying, it's unnerving me and ruins your face. Where's the pretty and strong Marie I've known so long? Gather your wits; if you know what you really want, you'll get it, have confidence!"

Marie started to feel much better now that Céline was taking her problems into her capable hands – and Céline was right, she had to decide her own fate – and fight for it.

Céline explained her plan and when she left, a giggling and confident Marie remained in her bedroom. *No more talk about wanting to die in a convent,* Céline thought happily.

*****

The young baron Saint Remy felt highly uncomfortable. His breeches and large leather belt were squeezing his belly, and the collar of his shirt seemed to have shrunk since the last time he had worn it. His parents had made him dress in his best Sunday clothes and when he complained that they had become too tight his excited mother had only chided him.

"It's not the clothes, you're becoming too fat, you're still young, stop eating too much!"

He was an obedient young man and consequently he had not dared to raise any objections to his parents' plan to lock him into matrimony with their neighbour's daughter. Of course he perceived the obvious advantages of adding such vast and well kept estates to his own impressive stretches of vineyards, but he couldn't suppress a feeling of uneasiness.

His parents had told him to propose to Marie but he had only a shady memory of her. A pretty girl, certainly, but very lively she had always been, and a bit too skinny for his taste. He also remembered that she had teased him without mercy when he was too slow to understand her witty remarks. The young Saint Remy loved his comfortable lifestyle of the rural squire, he had no aspirations to change it for the benefit of some high position at court in Paris. He hadn't dared to discuss this issue with his parents but at the bottom of his heart he was scared to death of finding himself betrothed to an agile bride who would probably put everything in motion in order to turn his comfortable life upside down.

The young baron was led into the smaller salon which was usually used by Marie's mother, an intimate room decorated in lighter shades of brocade displaying the wealth and excellent taste of the owner. Impatiently he sat on the highly uncomfortable chair that was usually reserved for visitors, waiting nervously for the arrival of his bride-to-be.

Marie had insisted that she should meet her future husband chaperoned only by Céline, arguing that the presence of her parents might be intimidating for her visitor. Her mother was so happy that Marie had regained her spirits and even seemed to be eager to receive her young suitor that she had been only too happy to oblige.

The door opened and Saint Remy rose immediately to pay his courtesies to the two ladies who entered the room. Marie was dressed in a golden silk gown, adorned with brocade bows shimmering in all kinds of colours, a diamond necklace sparkling on her bosom. The gown had a very low neckline, leaving almost nothing to the imagination. She did not look at all like the future wife of a squire, more like a young lady dressed up for a ball, ready to take Paris by assault.

Saint Remy was no expert in female make-up but he did not find the chalk white paste on her face very appealing, nor did he fancy the grossly painted poppy red lips that were displaying a welcoming smile. He was taken aback to see that one of the front teeth shimmered in darkest black – apparently his young bride-to-be had a weakness for too many sweets.

He gasped when Marie approached him. She had bathed in perfume and the heavy and nauseating scent of musk filled his nostrils and the room.

The lady accompanying Marie was exceptionally tall, dressed in black all over as if she were in mourning and wore an imposing black lace mantilla. She looked dour, conveying an air of righteousness and rigorous morals.

Marie greeted him, spontaneously reaching out for his hands.

"Sit down, my dearest friend," she said, interrupting his elaborate speech that he had studied and rehearsed so carefully.

Saint Remy obeyed but he was rather shocked. He didn't remember her voice being that shrill before?

The lady in black now spoke. Seemingly embarrassed by Marie's impulsive behaviour and despite her frightening appearance she started to tweet like a bird, "Marie, my sweetheart, you should wait with your welcome until our dearest guest has finished his speech, see how red his face is already, you've upset him!" then she tapped herself playfully with the tip of her ebony fan.

"Oh, I'm so sorry, I shouldn't have mentioned this. *So embarrassing*! Of course a gentleman is entitled to have a red face, it's a sign of virility, they say!" and suddenly she started to cackle like a hen.

Saint Remy was only too painfully aware that he must look terrible: with the tight collar, and the appalling smell of musk he grew hot, and his head was throbbing. Beads of perspiration were forming on his forehead and slowly started rolling down his face.

He decided to ignore the last comments of the lady, carefully wiped his hot face and made a new effort to continue his speech, praising Marie's beauty and virtue as his mother had carefully instructed him to do.

Apparently he managed to impress her as she was now rolling her eyes at him alluringly; nevertheless, playing coy at the same time she said, "Oh, Monsieur de Saint Remy, this is too much, I'm blushing. I really do not merit this praise, do I," and she now looked at her chaperon.

The lady clad in black only uttered yet another cackling sound before she answered, "You'll make the most wonderful Marquise ever, my dear."

Saint Remy did not grasp why the tall lady mentioned that Marie should become a marquise, but it seemed important to clarify matters, so he hastened to say, "Of course Marie would be worthy of marrying a Marquis, but I'm afraid I can only expect one day to call myself a Baron, the Saint Remy family is proud to own the finest lands of the Champagne region but my father is merely a baron, not a Marquis!"

Marie looked at him soothingly. "Oh, of course, we know, my dearest friend – if I may already call you this. But my father promised me that once we are married we'll move to Paris into our own palace. He's already searching for a suitable building for us. Once we live in Paris in grand style, he'll make sure that you'll be promoted to the highest ranks – he has many influential friends at court."

Marie's eyes took on a dreamy expression. "I can already imagine you sitting in the council of his Majesty, your advice will be sought by so many people! We'll attend court daily and I'll do whatever it needs to support your career, don't worry!" and she sent him another beguiling smile.

Saint Remy started to feel extremely upset. This encounter proved to be even worse than anything he could have imagined; in fact it was turning into nothing else but a sheer nightmare. He looked at Marie in her fancy gown and shrill make-up displaying her bosom and with a shudder he imagined his future. He'd be married to this glittering girl, stuck at the royal court, his wife chased and probably even encouraged by the lusty glances of the other lords. He pictured himself sitting there, uneasy, probably still looking like the simple squire he was, his peers teasing him relentlessly. He would never belong there!

377

Marie's shrill voice brought him back to reality. "Oh darling, it will be *wonderful*. We'll have masked parties, hunting parties and maybe we could even buy a small chateau close to the Loire, it seems to be so fashionable to have summer invitations there. We'll have so much fun!" Marie looked flushed and excited. "And you'll have to live with us," she continued turning affectionately to the tall lady. "I couldn't image leaving you behind in Reims!"

The lady in black seemed to be taken by surprise and became very embarrassed by this sudden display of affection. She started to speak but she just managed to utter, "Your ladyship... so kind... so unnecessary... so caring... what an honour ..." losing herself hopelessly in the complications of her own incomplete and incoherent sentences.

Saint Remy had heard and seen enough. He was an obedient son but this was too much to bear. Marie would say later that he had looked like a frightened rabbit when he rose from his chair and bowed to the ladies in what he considered to be grand style.

"Please accept my apologies, but I must leave you now. I had in fact come to transmit sad news. I had been intending to invite you to visit us at Saint Remy, but my mother suddenly feels unwell. All the same I still wanted to see you personally and convey our heart-felt excuses, we'll not fail to send a new invitation as soon as my mother feels better!"

The ladies rose as well and started to shower him with different exclamations of sympathy and compassion until his head started to spin.

As soon as Saint Remy had left the building he heaved a deep sigh and deeply inhaled the fresh air, vowing never to come back again, regardless of what his parents might order him to do.

Only when he was in his coach, comfortably driving back to Saint Remy and feeling extremely relieved that he had managed to stage this elegant if narrow escape, did he realize that he had failed to detect any signs of disappointment on Marie's face, as if the bride-to-be hadn't really cared for his proposal?

*****

Céline made sure that the young Saint Remy had left the house before she hurried back to the living room. She found Marie in tears, but this time it was tears of laughter that were running down her cheeks, leaving deep marks in the heavy make-up she had applied.

Céline grinned, embracing her quickly but making a sign to stay silent. They opened the window to let in some fresh air and dilute the strong smell of her perfume. Then they swiftly started to remove all treacherous traces of their little comedy: the chalk white lead powder from the face and the red paint from Marie's lips were rubbed off with a damp cotton cloth that Céline had prepared already.

Céline removed the black stain from Marie's immaculate tooth while Marie quickly took off the expensive diamond necklace Céline had lent her – a gift from Charles. Off came the fancy coloured bows from her gown.

Céline tore her black lace mantilla from her head and quickly put on a shawl in gay colours to brighten up her unusually sombre appearance. They were still applying the last finishing touches when they heard the steps of Marie's mother who was approaching the salon burning with curiosity to hear about the outcome of the first encounter with Marie's future fiancé.

Marie had just enough time to get her face under control when her mother entered the room, with a prying look and radiating satisfaction. To her dismay, she found her daughter downcast in the arms of her friend whilst Céline was trying to comfort her.

"What has happened?" Marie's mother enquired sharply. "And why does it smell so strongly in here?" she sniffed. "It smells as if you shattered my precious bottle of musk!"

"He hasn't proposed!" Marie answered with a tragic tone. "Apparently he didn't find me suitable or attractive enough!"

"And even if he didn't like Marie, it seems he liked musk, apparently," Céline added dryly.

Marie's mother looked suspiciously at Céline."Can you explain to me what has happened?"

Céline cleared her throat. "We don't understand ourselves, really! He seemed very charming in the beginning. When Marie mentioned timidly that she'd like to visit Paris with him he insisted that she should remain in Saint Remy, in fact he said that he'd insist on living for the rest of his life in Saint Remy, not even Reims, can you imagine – your beautiful daughter buried deep in the provinces?"

Marie's mother looked surprised and uneasy. "What happened then?"

"Marie was very kind actually, she tried to encourage him. But when she mentioned that she had been dreaming all her life of having a social life and inviting friends and spending some months visiting Paris, he suddenly shut up like an oyster and pretended that he had to leave immediately as his mother was sick. Very offensive towards Marie, I must say!" Céline said, making clear the young Saint Remy had lost her esteem.

"It's none of my business, but are you sure that you want to marry your only daughter to a peasant who has no ambitions to leave his fields?"

Marie's mother's face was flushed now. "Of course not, Céline, we only want the best for our daughter! I'll have to see your father now," she said, turning towards Marie. "And we'll have to discuss this, maybe I can talk once more with

379

his parents! There must be a huge misunderstanding somewhere!" And she left the room, frowning, obviously deeply disturbed.

Marie looked expectantly at Céline. "We won a battle, but not yet the war. They won't give up so fast, the Saint Remy estates are too good a fit with ours."

Marie sat there, her amber eyes shining in the light. "I made up my mind. You were right yesterday, I have to fight. I want to leave for Paris. Please talk with Charles and convince him to take me with you. It will hurt my parents, but I have to choose now between my love for Pierre and them – and now my decision is clear!"

Marie stood in the room, pale and erect, looking very serious. "It's Pierre and that's final. I also have the feeling that he might need my help soon. I couldn't say why, it's like a premonition, some danger is brewing and we know that he has more than enough enemies. Am I a bad daughter?" she asked Céline, her eyes wide open.

"Maybe," Céline answered, coming to the point. "But you'll make a wonderful wife for Pierre – and that seems to me so much more important."

*****

Perhaps it was Marie's presence or just the natural course of healing, but it took only some days more and her father left his bed and another fourteen days and he started walking again. Marie's only condition for returning to Paris had been that she wanted to be sure that her father was on the mend.

The day came when Marie was preparing to leave. Tears were running down her cheeks when she secretly packed her most important belongings, but the letter she left for her parents was covered with watery blotches.

"Dearest Virgin Mary," she prayed secretly to the picture hanging in her bedroom, "send me a sign that I'm doing the right thing!"

But the Virgin only smiled as usual; no miracle occurred.

Marie sighed and closed the trunk – she'd leave anyhow. Seeing Pierre's face in her mind, she started to smile. Céline was right, there could be only one true love in her life.

She suddenly heard a cooing sound from the window. A turtle dove had settled on the window sill.

Marie smiled at the picture of the Virgin. "Thank you!" she whispered. What stronger sign was there than to send her a turtle dove, the eternal messenger of love.

380

About the Author

Born and educated on the Continent, Michael has spent most of his working life outside the UK. Although an Economics graduate, Michael's first love has always been history, and he indulges his thirst for reading at every opportunity.

It was during yet another tedious business trip and a severe lack of suitable reading matter that the characters of Pierre, Armand and Henri came to mind; once they were conceived, so to speak, it was only a matter of time before they became real and took over any free time Michael had. The rest, as they say, is history. Or historical fiction, perhaps...

Coming soon...

If you have enjoyed this book and want to know what happens next, the sequel, The Secrets of Montrésor, will be out soon.

94348096R00215

Made in the USA
Lexington, KY
27 July 2018